LIFE IN A HAUNTED HOUSE

LIFE IN A HAUNTED HOUSE

(A Budget Studios Production)

Norman Prentiss

CEMETERY DANCE PUBLICATIONS

Baltimore

❖ 2023 ❖

Life in a Haunted House

Cemetery Dance Publications
132B Industry Lane, Unit #7
Forest Hill, MD 21050
www.cemeterydance.com

Trade paperback Edition

ISBN: 978-1-58767-871-4

Other people might tell you they grew up in a haunted house. Maybe it's a metaphor: haunted by alcohol or drug addiction or abusive parents. Or secrets that eat away at the whole family, growing stronger and stronger, the longer they remain unspoken.

That's a kind of haunting, I guess.

Maybe somebody will make claims about the supernatural. A dead relative or former tenant rattles chains in the night, passes through walls, moans into the ears of people just drifting off to sleep.

But I'm not talking about metaphor, or some vague supernatural presence.

I'm talking about real ghosts and monsters.

You know: the kinds in the movies.

If you saw Budget Studios' *The Stone Stairway,* you'll understand what I mean.

I've seen that stairway. Walked on it myself. They filmed the movie in Melissa Preston's house.

They filmed all the movies in my friend Melissa Preston's house.

The Animator

Today I'm an animator. I'm in tenth grade, bored out of my mind. The teacher is droning on about a book I haven't read, something called *Green Mansions*. To keep myself amused, I've decided to animate the items on my desk. I push the pencil slightly, remove my hand from view, then imagine the quick click of a camera shutter. I push the pencil again, another imaginary click, and the frame of film advances. The teacher says something about the color green and nature, and a few other students jot down notes. They're doing something useful with their pens and pencils, and will earn a higher score on the test, so perhaps I should follow their example. But, if projected on a screen at 24 frames a second, my animated pencil would arc across the desk like a thrown javelin.

I don't know if the other kids have read *Green Mansions*, but at least they're familiar with the concepts from previous lectures. Civilization vs. nature, the exotic "other," symbolism of the color green—even the teacher seems bored with the obviousness of that last point. It's still mostly confusing to me, since I joined the class mid-book.

I've joined life already in-progress, which is a familiar feeling. I'm always having to catch up.

My animated pencil finishes its arc. There's still a half an hour remaining in class.

I start to unravel a paper clip. A spiral, then straightened into a small metal snake. My movements are meticulous. I decide that I've studied the movements of different animals, to add realism to my animated effects. If I could afford a super-8 camera with a single-frame attachment, if I had skill with constructing a ball-and-socket armature, adding latex muscles and skin over it—if only I had talent as an artist—I know I could make an interesting film. Award-winning, maybe.

My seat neighbor, Geoff, reaches across the aisle and grabs the paperclip from my desk. He doesn't really understand the game I was playing, the little mental exercise that was maybe connected to some childish filmmaker dream of mine. And it's not like he's ruined an actual film. But he knows he's taunting me.

He holds the bent clip just out of my reach, knowing I'm not likely to lunge across the desk at him. He bends the metal back and forth, back and forth. Smiles.

On the bus ride home, some of the kids start picking on Geoff. He'd missed an easy catch during gym, made a stupid joke about "blue genes" in Biology—that kind of thing—and the natural high school progression leads them to insult his crooked teeth and the pimples on his forehead.

For once it isn't me under the microscope of cruelty, and it seems like a good moment where I might join in. I plan to score a few choice digs, ingratiate myself with the pack. Besides, I'm still a bit miffed at Geoff's interference during English class, and doubly annoyed he sat behind me on the bus, after assigned desks at school had already made me weary of his company.

So I swing my knees into the aisle and twist around, checking for physical flaws his friends have neglected. Geoff is taking the jibes in stride, nodding his head and shooting back comebacks—*No I'm not. Sounds like you're describing yourself*—all so ineffective they merely stir up laughter and further taunts from nearby rows, Geoff half-laughing along with them.

Then I discover my opening shot. Can't believe I haven't noticed this particular detail before, and that his long-time friends had steered clear of it. "His eye," I say. "The right one seems glazed over and doesn't follow the left. Is he, like, drunk? Or half asleep?"

All laughter stops. I'd been poised to expect agreement—somebody else piling on about big ears, at the very least. Our section of the bus grows silent. The driver edges a little close to the curb on Dennison and the wheel goes up on one side, but everyone manages to resist making a snide comment about his steering.

Kevin, who's made probably the meanest jokes about Geoff, acts like I'm the biggest jerk on the bus. "How could you be so stupid, Brendan?"

Until now, these other kids have barely registered my presence. In the half week at my new school I'd deliberately stayed quiet, to avoid exactly the kind of attention they'd been giving Geoff earlier.

They give it to me now. Some stocky kid I didn't even know mimics my squeaky voice, and his friend says I walk funny; Greta, who until now seemed sweet-natured, points out that I've worn the same plaid shirt two days in a row, and it probably smells.

As if I'd have known the story about Geoff's accident, how the whole school responded two years ago after his eye infection took a turn for the worse, each grade making a card for him, adding signatures and jokes and well wishes to cheer him up in the hospital. How, for two years, nobody ever mentioned it, hoping to preserve an illusion that his glass eye was indistinguishable from the other one.

I know I wasn't blameless here: joining in with the taunts of a crowd isn't an admirable way to introduce yourself. But honestly I hadn't intended anything worse than what my peers were already doing. Why would I intentionally jab at some kid's forbidden sore spot, with months of agonizing history behind it? Yet all their comments were deemed innocent, while mine was mean-spirited and heartless.

Damned if I hadn't made a similar gaffe at my previous school. I'd joined there mid-year as well, and the assistant principal gave me a poorly mimeographed map, and assigned me to a "buddy" who would escort me to my classes the first day. Well, Buddy made himself scarce once we'd left the office, then kids spilled out of open classrooms, and all the halls looked the same. I turned the map 90 degrees, then 90 more, trying to figure out which way was north and what it meant that my locker was located on "Jefferson" corner, and I was nervous I'd be late to class and make a horrible first impression, all out of breath when I finally reached where my locker was supposed to be. Some lanky girl stood in front of it, her back to me, and I said Excuse Me, polite as can be, and she's a statue, I repeated myself and got the same reaction until I finally shouted, *What, are you deaf?*

And of course, she was. Turned out she didn't notice my rudeness, but everybody else in that crowded hall did, and they all stepped back, prepared to avoid me for the rest of the day, the rest of the school year.

A moment like that feels like some kind of cosmic conspiracy. Like that deaf girl was placed there by a cruel universe, at that specific moment, just to humiliate me.

Different school, same story. I'd tried to maintain perfect behavior from the start, but in one moment of weakness on the bus—not even meaning anything—I end up making the worst possible comment. A handful of people are disgusted with me, and I know they'll share the story the next day, and it will spread faster than an announcement over the morning intercom. New Kid will be branded an insensitive jerk, before anybody ever gets the chance to know me.

The Twisted Face

Today I'm the Twisted Face of Edison High. I walk through the crowded hallway, and two tenth grade girls stand in front of the trophy case and share a joke. They are both laughing, and their smiles make them beautiful. The shorter girl's attention flutters away from her friend, lands on me as I pass, and my hideous presence is enough to freeze her smile then contort it into an awful grimace.

Her friend turns as well, curious what could have produced such a visceral reaction. She soon regrets her curiosity. Her hand raises to cover her mouth, stifling a scream.

Neither of them has ever seen a face as deformed as mine.

They will never get used to it. I will always horrify them.

I'm remembering a movie I watched with my dad when I was younger—an early production by Budget Studios with the evocative title, *The Twisted Face*. It's filmed in black and white, with lots of shadows to cover flaws in the cheap production. The first half of the movie contains scenes filmed from an unusual perspective, as if through the eyes of the presumed killer. You see his hands struggle with a match then light a cigarette, and next smoke billows from the bottom of the frame. You see him open a desk drawer to pull out a large jagged knife. He lifts the knife and twists the blade, catching the light. A pair of superimposed eyes, simulating a reflection, appear in the gleaming metal.

You see him walk a night-shrouded street, heavy boots scraping along the pavement. A woman leans against a streetlamp, calls to him for a match, but the camera starts to pull back. *C'mon, promise I won't bite,* the woman says, and he steps reluctantly toward her, head down, boots entering the circle of light on the sidewalk. The camera tilts up at her, and she finally sees him. *Oh God, the Twisted Face!* she screams, and then rough hands reach from the sides of the frame to strangle her.

Daytime scenes follow a police investigation, with other night-walking scenes interspersed as the investigation drags on. In a repeating pattern, the audience sees through the walker's eyes; whenever he stumbles across other people, they react with disgust and fear, and strangling hands reach forward.

A change occurs halfway through the film, when a sequence from the killer's point of view enters the day-lit police station. A woman in the waiting area screams, while a father covers his daughter's eyes. The desk clerk grimaces and accidently knocks over a coffee cup. The camera moves into the main station area, where an officer's mouth drops open, cigarette still dangling from the corner. Nobody stops the visitor as the camera heads straight to the Police Chief's office, then a hand comes from the right side and forces the door inward.

The Chief is the only one who doesn't register surprise, though it's clear he struggles to maintain a calm exterior. "Have a seat."

"I understand you've been looking for me," the visitor says.

Finally the point-of-view breaks. First the Chief's neutral face from the side, then a pan to the guest chair.

The monster sits there. We finally see the monster with the twisted face.

The title's description is accurate. The man's head sits large on his shoulders. A growth on his lower jaw twists the orientation of his lips so that his mouth is nearly vertical. More growths balloon his cheeks, the nose is bent crooked, and one eye peers through a bruised donut of flesh. The forehead juts out on one side, forming a horn-like point.

In the bright lights of the office, the facial deformities are shockingly realistic.

They should be, since the actor isn't wearing a mask.

Bud "Budget" Preston, the producer, director and writer for most Budget Studios productions, made the controversial decision to cast Thomas Hendricks, an actor who suffered in real life from acromegaly—the same affliction made famous by The Elephant Man. Large cysts form on the skin, mutating the face, limbs and body. The growths sometimes press into the skeleton, twisting it into a grotesque posture. In fatal instances, these same growths can swell to crush internal organs.

Although Hendricks didn't appear to have skeletal deformities, his facial distortions were a perfect fit for the horror-mystery genre—and of course, saved Budget Studios the expense of creating convincing monster makeup. The film company's moniker doesn't specify high or low budget productions, but it's clear from even a cursory screening that the second adjective applies.

In some cases, however, a low budget contributes to a film's ambiance. The night scenes of *The Twisted Face* have a washed-out, shadowy effect that mimics documentary realism. In addition to the shock-value of Hendricks' appearance, the actor's untrained performance manages to earn the viewer's sympathy.

His character—spoiler alert—turns out not to be the killer. Instead, he cooperates with the investigation, and the police eventually capture a man who has been wearing a cheap fright mask that mimics Hendricks' natural deformities. At the end of the film, Hendricks has a wonderful bit of dialogue as he bids farewell to the team of police officers.

"You think it must be awful to be me. Everywhere I look, I see people recoil in horror. You'd never trade places with me."

There's no music on the soundtrack as the actor struggles to force the scripted words through his twisted mouth. His puffed eye squints in suppressed rage.

"It's actually not so bad," he says. "My world has no illusions. When people react to me, I see their real faces."

The film ends with a montage of faces from earlier in the movie, each fading into the next, all of them twisted.

The memory of this film provides a convenient escape during the school day. The other students avoid me, whisper behind my back. Perhaps the fault lies in the way they perceive me—rushing to condemn a single unthinking comment, as if it represents the inner workings of an evil mind.

I'm the New Kid, and they should be making an extra effort to welcome me. They should at least give me the benefit of the doubt.

My innocent-victim status is a little harder to sustain during English class. Geoff has his usual assigned desk beside mine, and at first I'm happy that he's leaving me alone for a change. I move stuff around my desk as much as I want, sketch pictures in the margins of my notebook, and he keeps to himself. Meanwhile, Mr. Camen draws a Venn Diagram on the board, trying to make some point about intersecting cultures in a novel few of us care about.

Then I notice Geoff's hand moves absently to his face, fingertips hovering near the eye I'd unwittingly mocked. I'm fairly certain I've not previously seen him make this kind of insecure gesture. He touches the glass eye as if worried it will fall out, or attempts a subtle movement to shift the eye's gaze to match its functioning partner. At another point, his fingers reach higher. They pinch a strand of hair, clipped too short to hang past his brow, but he pulls the strand anyway, hoping it would cover his false eye.

I did this to him. He'd learned to accept his situation, and I'd made the injury fresh.

In Art class most students are involved in group projects that began before my mid-trimester enrollment. In practice, group work usually means that one or two people finish the bulk of any project while the others talk or wander the room, occasionally joining in to paint a small section of canvas or glue some clip-out letters to a mural. Group-work students sit on stools around large tables, similar to the lab islands in science class. A few students sit at isolated desks, permitted to draw independently in their sketchbooks. That's what I've been doing.

I'm not very good. I mostly trace images from magazines, then add some half-hearted shading effects to give Mrs. Brinkton something she can pretend to praise. As teachers go, she's got a pretty good quality: when she's helping one student or group, her full attention stays focused on that specific project, oblivious to the rest of us. We can do whatever we want.

I'm near the side wall, keeping my distance from other kids as if it's my choice. I thumb through an issue of *People* magazine to find other subjects to trace, while the teacher gives a color-wheel lecture to the painting group across the room. The students who already understand these concepts listen carefully; the others ignore her.

A folded scrap of blue construction paper drops into my open magazine. I didn't see who dropped the note, but I'm pretty sure the student is nearby.

Should I turn around? Perhaps a whole gang of students stands behind me, waiting to watch me read the note. The note might tell me I'm a horrible person. It might contain a threat. *Better watch your back, New Kid.* Or, complete with grammatical error: *Meet us after school, behind the north field. Your dead.*

The teacher stands too far away. She waves her brush in the air as if conducting a delicate symphony.

My new enemies need not wait until after school. They could tear into me right now with items from the unsupervised supply cabinet: X-acto knives, clay-carving tools, taut pieces of wire.

I lift the folded paper. Flip it open with one hand.

Inside, white chalk marks form thick capital letters on the blue page.

DON'T SAY ANYTHING on one side of the fold.

DO NOT REACT on the facing page.

I feel a tap on my shoulder, and turn slightly in my chair.

A fist raises into view.

But it's a delicate fist, not aimed toward me in a punch. The ring finger and thumb are curled to enclose a round, glistening object.

It stares at me.

My first thought is: I recognize that eye.

Not how unusual it was for an eye to appear in someone's fist. Not relief that the gesture was too bizarre to be a threat. None of that. Just: *I recognize that eye.* Shortly followed by: *Where have I seen it before?*

Geoff's sitting with the mural group by the window. They're goofing around, but nobody nearby seems shocked enough to indicate one of Geoff's eye sockets is empty. Perhaps he has a spare. It's rolled out of his pocket across the floor, and some polite girl has tapped me on the shoulder.

Excuse me. Did you drop this?

Then I consider the way the girl's forefinger and thumb encircle the eye, similar to the bruised donut of flesh around Hendricks' squinting eye in *The Twisted Face.* That movie has been on my mind today, which explains why I make the connection, but that solution is hardly possible. Thomas Hendricks was a real person, probably long dead, and this girl's fist couldn't be holding a real eye.

And yet, I feel closer to the truth.

It's not a real eye, so it's something the girl must have made from art-room supplies. White clay shaped into a ball, dried then painted with pupil and iris and blood vessels, a coating of clear glaze overtop to make it shine.

Yet that explanation doesn't answer why I recognized the eye. And the paint is faded in spots, like a book cover fades if left in sunlight. Some of the varnish on the surface has flaked off over the years.

It's old.

I realize my connection to *The Twisted Face* wasn't as far off-base as I thought. A few years later. A different movie.

Different monster.

One of the eyes of *The Lake Monster.*

“Took you long enough.”

Her lips curl in a slightly lopsided smile. The girl lets her hand drop to the side, palming the eye like in a magic trick. She’s short and thin, with frizzy hair that hangs to her shoulders. Her skin is pale; her eyes are an unremarkable brown. I’ve seen her before, but never really noticed her. I don’t recall her name.

“I know I told you not to react, but it’s like you were frozen.”

“How did you…?”

I didn’t know how to finish the sentence. How did she get that item? How did she find *me,* the exact person who’d know what it was?

An actual prop from a Budget Studios monster movie.

I’ve watched this one with my dad, too. *The Lake Monster* is actually the first Budget film I saw with him, back when I was eight years old. He turned the channel after I complained I’d already seen the *Johnny Quest* episode. Dad clicked through a religious program, then local news, and settled on Channel 20’s weekend movie slot.

On the fuzzy UHF image, two hands part the branches of a tree. The hands are as green as the leaves, and covered with scales.

When the monster walks into the spotlight, it’s wearing a sports coat and trousers—a typical Budget concession, to avoid the need for a full-body costume. Mask over the head, two gloves for the webbed hands, flippers for the feet.

Other movie fans might disagree, but I find the cheaper costume more effective than the elaborate, head-to-toe rubber suit Ben Chapman wore in Universal’s *The Creature from the Black Lagoon.* Sure, the make-up guys at Universal were master craftsmen, and they created an iconic, classic monster. But the incongruity of the human clothes and the monster elements in Budget’s version strikes me as a little more unnerving. Their Lake Monster wears clothes you’d see on people in an office building or shopping mall, or on the sidewalk outside your suburban home. A hideous scale-covered head sprouting from the collar of a J C Penney workshirt creates its own brand of uncanny shiver.

The mask itself was fairly gruesome, with a stretched fish-frown mouth, and gill flaps at the neck. A string of tentacles hangs like dreadlocks from the scalp. The eyes were the most startling feature. Instead of cutouts for the actor to look through, this mask had bug-eyes attached to the deep sockets. The eyes looked human, as if they'd been plucked from a man's face to dangle glistening from the mask—a spherical, unblinking horror.

Mom walked into our rec room during one of the scare scenes. A woman sits reading in a chair, and she thinks her husband stands behind her. The camera pans up to reveal The Lake Monster. The tentacles on his head shake, and the eyes bobble as well. "Oh, turn that off, Scott. He'll have nightmares for weeks."

"Oh, he's okay. Aren't you, kiddo?"

I nod agreement, and the woman on the television screams.

My overprotective mom turned out to be right—those eyes, especially, those eyes!—but this was an important bonding moment between father and son. He sided with me, assumed I was mature enough to handle new experiences. Another kid might accompany Dad on a weekend fishing trip as a rite of passage. My dad and I watched a fish-monster on Saturday-afternoon TV.

Maybe that's why I like Budget's monster better than Universal's. I guess a sentimental reason is as good as any.

"That was kind of fun, wasn't it?" my dad said once the movie ended.

And he did a really cool thing after that day, finding a few more Budget films on Betamax video tapes and bringing them home for us. He kept tracking them down, and eventually we had a near-complete set.

Those movies are pretty much my only remaining connection to my dad.

So I ask the girl, "Can I see it again?"

There's no doubt in my mind that it's the real thing—a forgotten piece of film history.

"Not here," she says. Her cupped hand stays at her side. "Maybe later."

I glance around the room, locate the empty desk which is likely her usual spot. Another sketchbook misfit, like me. I'd never bothered to notice her.

"I'm Brendan," I said.

"I know." She doesn't lift her hand to shake, considering it has an eye in it. She doesn't volunteer her name, either, and I feel rude for not knowing it. I wish she'd signed her note. If I follow her to her desk, she might have written her name on a backpack or on the upper corner of a notebook.

"Why did you bring that…?"

"On the bus yesterday. That wasn't fair the way people turned on you."

I search my memory, but can't recall where she'd been seated.

"All that fuss over Geoff's eye," she says. "We all know about it. It's not like losing it made him into a better person." She gave me that half-smile again. "I just thought it might be funny to show you."

Yes, funny—in an odd way. I smiled back, to acknowledge the joke. Then I attempted an innocent observation: "You know what it kind of looks like, right? From a movie?"

"Of course. I saw one of your sketches. And in your lab notebook yesterday, you'd written a few of the names in the margins. Titles, I mean. Of my father's films."

I'm still the Twisted Face of Edison High, an outcast among my peers. Perhaps my infamy will eventually slip away—a repulsive mask pulled off my head, revealing a normal kid, worthy of anyone's friendship. For now the gossip is still fresh, and the other tenth graders mostly recoil from my presence.

But now I have an ally. I've learned her name is Melissa.

Can it really be Melissa Preston, daughter of the man who created Budget Studios? The idea seems impossible.

Melissa has boarded the crowded bus before me, and there's no room beside her at the back. I end up sitting near the front, among a clump of twelfth-graders. During the monotonous ride home, I nod at her reflection in the driver's giant rear-view mirror, but she does not seem to respond. I wonder which of the stops will be hers, which of us might get off the bus first.

The bus pauses at the edge of a field, and I see her reflection stand. Melissa and two other kids walk down the aisle toward the doors beside the driver. As she passes me, her hand lifts in a shy wave.

Judging from the intersection, I try to calculate how far Melissa's home is from mine.

She's invited me to visit sometime soon. I hope she means tomorrow.

The Fan

Today I am a Fan. For once, that status is enough. I don't dream of becoming a special effects artist, a potential writer or director, a child star growing into a handsome matinee idol. I am simply someone who appreciates movies. I watch them, memorize my favorite lines and images. I am hoping to visit the home of my new friend, Melissa Preston, who just happens to be the daughter of my all-time favorite filmmaker. If I'm lucky, she might be able to locate a few other movie props to show me.

I won't meet the director himself. Like me, Melissa lives in a single-parent household. Her father died a few years ago, during a location shoot for his final, unreleased film.

I can't believe how lucky I am to have ended up in this town. And after I'd been so angry with my mom, whose government job requires us to move frequently. Typically, I'd join a school community long enough to make a lousy first impression, and never have enough time to recover and make lasting friends. This latest move brought us to Graysonville, Alabama, a place I'd never heard of. I'd dreaded it, complained in advance about this small southern town in the middle of nowhere, with nothing but a large, nearby Army base to recommend it. And then it turned out to be the town where Budget Studios got its start.

Why wasn't *that* little detail listed on the "Moving Packet" my mom's Pittsburgh boss had provided with her other reassignment papers? Why wasn't there a billboard at the town entrance with the Lake Monster shaking his tentacle-dreadlocks at visitors? Alongside town square statues of Civil War heroes with unlikely names such as Bibb Graves or the Mighty Pelham, there should stand a statue of Thomas Hendricks from *The Twisted Face*—and a plaque beneath to commemorate his immortal screen words: "My world has no illusions. When people react to me, I see their real faces."

Instead, I had to find out by accident. If Melissa hadn't spoken to me, I might never have known. Her last name was common enough. I never would have suspected she'd be related to *that* Preston.

I have a momentary panic when I get home from school. The way she joked with me, the half smile and the teasing air of mystery. Perhaps Melissa was in league with the other kids. Once again, I'm the victim of some elaborate cosmic hoax.

I rush upstairs and pull the box of videos from under my bed. The Sony Betamax format was discontinued in favor of larger, more prevalent VHS tapes, and we no longer had a machine that would play them. I couldn't watch the videotapes, but I kept them anyway—fond memories of the films themselves, and of watching them with my dad while he was still around. The cardboard sleeves to the tapes were mostly in rough shape: faded, with bent corners; some of them with "Used" stickers or other tags obscuring part of an image or the synopsis on the back. I had most of the descriptions memorized, though, and let my imagination supply any missing words.

I lift the tape for *The Space Visitor,* since that was a rare one my dad had found in "new" condition. The shrinkwrap is intact, except for a cut we'd made at the bottom to allow removal of the video cassette. The picture on the front displays a silver spaceship over a field, with a wide beam spreading out from the undercarriage. At ground level, the Visitor appears in the beam's spotlight, transported to Earth. The alien figure stands in silhouette, a large yellow question mark over his vaguely humanoid torso. The lettering at the top turns the film's title into a question: **Who is...*The Space Visitor?***

I flip to the other side, with four color stills from the movie—none of them showing the Visitor, but a cool flying saucer image in one, and a car in the process of being disintegrated. Beneath appears the cast list, then the crew, ending with the usual "Produced, Written and Directed by Bud 'Budget' Preston." The release year (1962) and running time (84 min). All of these details I've pretty much memorized, and of course a familiar logo, the Budget Studios name superimposed over a dollar sign.

Beneath that logo, in small print I'd never paid any attention to: Distributed from Graysonville, AL.

I breathe a sigh of relief. Melissa Preston isn't playing a cruel trick on me. She really was telling the truth.

When Mom arrives home from work later that evening, she's immediately suspicious when I ask about her day. Guess I deserve that, since any other time I'd barely expressed an interest. And there I am, meeting her at the front door, opening the hall closet to help her hang up her jacket.

"Still getting used to things." She shrugs out of her jacket and takes the hanger I offer. "It's a big change, the way they work here."

"But you like it?"

"Oh, honey." She puts away her jacket then closes the closet door. "Do we have to start this again? You need to give this place a chance. If you're hoping I'm going to hate my job so we'll move somewhere else, that's not going to happen."

"That's not what I meant. I..."

"Let me guess: something happened at school." Her shoulders slump. She's been waiting for this conversation, dreading it. "Couldn't we get through your first week without a call from the Principal, or some teacher note I have to sign?"

"Nothing bad happened at school." Not technically a lie, since my problems began on the bus ride. "I was just thinking that my bedroom here is a little bigger, and school seems kind of easier. It's possible, maybe, that..." I smile, hoping it would serve as partial apology for all the complaining I'd piled on the past few weeks. "... that I don't hate it here as much as I thought I would."

"Well, that's a switch."

"So maybe, if your job's okay, we might stick around longer than usual."

Her expression falls, and I think she's going to get angry again. Instead, she gives me a hug. "I'm sorry we've had to move around so often, Brendan. I know it's been tough on you." She pulls back from the hug, then lays her palm gently against the side of my head. "I have to follow where we can get government contracts. That's my job. You understand, right?"

"Yeah. I know it's not your fault." I twist away from her hand, the way any teenager doesn't want his mom treating him like a baby. But I also let some bitterness slip into my voice. An undercurrent saying, *Try, won't you? This* one *time, try to keep us in the same town for a little while.*

She heads toward the kitchen to pour a glass of Diet Rite. I follow, since I've already put two Swanson dinners in the oven for us. Practically cooking for her, so another suspicious instance of good behavior.

"Something changed your mind about Graysonville," she says. "You make a new friend?"

"Uh huh."

Her soda fizzes over ice, and Mom waits for the foam to settle before she takes a drink. "What's his name?"

"Geoff." The name just comes out, before I've made any conscious decision to lie. Maybe I worried my mom would make too much fuss if I wanted to visit a girl's house—not that I thought of Melissa in any romantic way. She's nice enough, but whether she's a boy or girl honestly doesn't matter to me. There's that bigger thing, about her dad and those movies I used to watch with *my* dad.

And that movie part, I'm not ready to share yet. Budget Studios' films were never something my mom approved of. She tolerated them at best, walking into the rec room as we watched, lingering just long enough to comment how the acting was bad, or that some special effect looked fake. "We *know,*" Dad would say. If she asked, "Haven't you watched that one a hundred times already?" I'd say "more like a thousand," and me and Dad would both laugh. Mom would shake her head, mutter something like "I'll never understand what you two see in those films."

So when I tell her I might be late from school the next evening, that me and my new friend are going to study together or hang out or whatever, at a library or at the ball field or maybe at another kid's house, she can think of that kid as "Geoff" for a while. It isn't a malicious lie.

The movies are a bond between me and my dad. Mom isn't part of that world.

It's a day later and, still in my role as Fan, I talk to Melissa during Art class.

"Yeah, today might be okay," she says. "We can get off the bus at my stop."

She asks if I can get a ride home, and I tell her I'll be fine to walk. I'll agree to just about anything, because she's told me she looked through her father's old stuff, and found a few more props from the movies. "Almost a whole box full."

To mix metaphors, the eye was merely the tip of the iceberg.

As I grab my bookbag and stand to leave the bus at Melissa's stop, I get the sensation that everyone watches me. Geoff and his friends wonder why I exit early, maybe laugh behind their hands at New Kid's apparent mistake. The driver says nothing, and I step down through the accordion doors.

I risk a glance back. Nobody seems to have noticed.

A field stretches out on one side of the road, and two kids head toward a small wooden house at the far end of the open property. They're a brother and sister, and the girl is in my algebra class—last name something like Brickman or Brickson. I wave to her, then wait to follow Melissa's lead.

A dense thicket of tall trees lines the facing edge of the road and continues after the intersection. The path through the trees shifts from well-maintained blacktop to a rough packed dirt, with gravel instead of painted lines to indicate the shoulder. Melissa begins to walk in that direction, and I follow her without a word. After a bit, the gravel thins out—a cosmetic improvement begun by the county, I guess, but abandoned once the road stretched too far from the busy intersection.

The road is wide enough to keep the trees from overwhelming the path with shadows. We're here at a good time of the afternoon, since the sun's angle follows the road. I'm grateful for the light, because Melissa walks quickly. When she makes an odd jump or veers to the side, I copy her movement even if I don't perceive any obstacle in the path.

"How far is it to your house?"

"Probably fifteen minutes, at this rate." Without missing a beat, she adjusts the shoulder strap to her denim backpack. "Usually takes me ten."

"I can go faster," I say, but hope she doesn't take me up on the offer.

The sunlight catches her hair but doesn't add a glimmer. Melissa is an interesting girl, in the way she acts, but to be brutally honest, she's not someone who'd be described as pretty. She is slim, and loose-fitting clothes disguise any slight curves to her figure. I know the word "plain" is meant to be an insult, but it suits her. Perhaps that's exactly the appearance she intends—to avoid standing out, to avoid being a target of attention at school.

I study the quick motions of her feet, wondering how she keeps her tennis shoes clean despite daily walks along this sloppy road. My sneakers already show scuff marks and dustings from the path, plus a cake of mud attached to my right heel after I'd stumbled into a tire-wide trench.

No need to watch for traffic, because there isn't any. Time of day is a factor, since our school lets us out at 2:30, but I doubt any semblance of rush hour occurs later in the evening. We've passed a few side roads, but none of them have a mailbox to match some nearby home.

We eventually approach the first road sign since the bus dropped us off. It's a faded yellow rectangle, announcing DEAD END in black letters.

"Almost home," Melissa says. She stops when we get to the sign.

I don't see anything. The way my mind typically works, I imagine a horror-movie scenario. She'll pull a knife from her backpack, stab me before I've got a chance to defend myself, and my body will fit neatly into a grave she's prepared in advance. That's the initial fear, but only a starting point. Next I imagine she's opened this grave before, behind an obscuring bank of trees, and the bodies of former classmates fill the pit. She tosses me in, the blood still draining from my wound, but I haven't died. I feel the uneasy bed of bones beneath me, and I try to wriggle away. Instead of a shovel, Melissa uses her pristine white shoes to kick dirt from the sides of the pit, slowly covering me. Perhaps she will make a villain speech: "Oh, Brendan, you were the easiest one of all. I found your weakness right away, and how simple it was to lure you to this secluded spot. You never told anyone where you were going, did you? I can see by your eyes that you didn't—but those eyes will be covered soon. Scream if you want. You'll only get dirt in your mouth. I suppose you're wondering if I'm really the daughter of your favorite movie director. Well, I guess you'll never know." And she kicks more dirt, still more, then stamps it down, forcing it into my nostrils, tight against my face and my closed mouth. Then I wriggle again against the bones and rotting flesh beneath me, until I realize that I'm lying perfectly still. The bodies themselves are moving, and the scratch of a skeletal hand twists bony fingers around my neck.

Then I think of something worse: a scenario I call The Ambush of Humiliation. There's no knife. This slight girl isn't strong enough to attack me on her own. The more plausible nightmare would involve other students. They all exited the bus at the next stop, doubled back to this location from a different direction, and now they wait to jump out, point and laugh at New Kid, the pathetic movie fan: Well, wouldn't you know it, this girl's only pretending. She hates you like the rest of us do. Aw, don't cry, now. Oh look, he *is*. He *is* crying.

"This way, Brendan."

Melissa's voice pulls me out of the reverie. She motions like a crossing guard, her arm swinging to the right. The way the road ends doesn't quite qualify as an optical illusion, but it has a similar effect. A fresh bank of trees cuts across the path fifty or so feet beyond the Dead End sign, and if your eyes follow the same stretch of road there's nowhere left to go. But a grassy stretch leads away on the right, with well-worn lines to indicate the passage of cars.

A strange odor like motor oil overlays the typical wooded scents, and I hear the ripple of a distant stream. The new path curves around and opens into a clearing. It's not quite as big as the field outside the bus stop, and not nearly as well-maintained. All the effort was apparently expended years ago chopping down trees, and little had been done since—other than to keep the car path relatively clear, and to approximate a small lawn in front of an ordinary two-story house at the end of the path.

As we get closer, the house seems less ordinary. For one thing, it's larger than it looks. There's a mismatched addition to one side, and possibly an extension to the back of the house, too. The front entrance is the strangest feature. Although the main facade wouldn't be out of place along any of the country roads in this town—weather-worn brick at the base, and the top story covered with wooden siding that hasn't seen a fresh coat of paint in years, perhaps decades—the main doors and surrounding porch fit the style of another house, another era.

It's a double door entry, with paneled doors of thick, cherry wood. An elaborate mantle supported by faux marble columns forms a protective overhang that casts the front doors into shadow. The mantle's recessed triangular panel contains a carving that depicts a mythical scene: Theseus at the end of the maze, sword drawn as he encounters the Minotaur.

In the middle of each door is a lion's head knocker with a heavy brass ring beneath.

Early in *The Stone Stairway*, newlyweds Martin and Samantha Goodwin huddle under this same overhang, seeking dry shelter after their car runs out of gas on a desolate road. Thunder booms amid the heavy downpour, while Martin wonders aloud: *What's a house like this doing way out here, in the middle of nowhere?* His new wife tells him not to look a gift horse in the mouth, and nudges him to raise the brass ring and let it fall. The knock echoes heavy on the soundtrack, louder even than the thunder, and they wait. *Again, try the knocker again, Martin,* but he hesitates. A fresh flash of lightning highlights beads of nervous sweat and raindrops that fall down his face. He raises his hand to the door, then pauses at the sound of a deadbolt sliding back. With a loud, sustained creak, the door opens inward.

Dry-ice fog and a simulated night-time thunderstorm help preserve the on-screen illusion. Fifteen years later, it's clear the Minotaur bas relief is painted on the mantle, rather than being an elegant carving. The supporting pillars are painted as well, and flecks of the design have chipped off over the years.

I follow Melissa up the porch steps. The doors themselves, once stained to a rich cherry, now look cheap and faded. Like Martin in the film, I reach for the ring beneath the lion's-head knocker. It's rusted, and way too light—as hollow as the chrome-plated ring that holds a roll of toilet paper in our downstairs bathroom.

Melissa pauses to let me take it all in. As cheap and faded as it is, I'm standing in part of a movie set.

To me, it's magic. It's a doorway Melissa passes every day, and to her it's probably grown blandly familiar. I flatter myself that she sees it fresh through my eyes. That's the reason she rushed us here, and why she pauses now. She couldn't wait for me to experience it.

If I shift my position, I can block out the normal sections of the house. As if to assist the illusion, a cloud passes over the sun. The afternoon's still not dark enough, but I relax my eyes and the porch shifts out of focus—a blur that simulates the grain of 16mm film, transferred to video with all its flaws intact. Chips of paint are actually scratches on nitrate; instead of weather-worn decay, the front doors display wear and tear from countless feedings through the clumsy sprockets of a drive-in movie projector.

In my mind, the cloud over the sun is heavy with rain. It bursts into a sudden downpour that rattles loud against the overhang, plashes onto the mansion's surrounding cobblestone path, and batters like flung gravel against the bricks and window panes.

"Sorry to bother you." I do my best imitation of the actor's delivery. "Our car broke down, back the road a ways."

"Yeah, um, I guess you can use our phone to call for a tow truck." Melissa smiles, and it's cool that she was ready to play along. Her local accent is actually a decent fit for many of the voices in the film, but she's overplayed it, slipping into the accent people adopt to mock the snooty upper class.

Besides, it's not the right line to follow mine.

There isn't another line, actually. In the movie, when the deadbolt slides back from the other side and the door creaks inward, Martin delivers his explanation to a person standing in the shadowy interior. Except there isn't anyone there.

The door opened by itself. The house is dark and empty.

I wonder what it would be like to live here, to experience this sense of wonder and magic every day. To spend your life in the haunted house from *The Stone Stairway.*

"Let's go in," Melissa says. She unlocks the door and pushes it open. It moves easily, without the creak of ancient hinges.

Sunlight through half-closed curtains brightens the disappointing interior. No marble-tiled foyer and high ceiling. No massive stone stairway leading to the darker floors. Instead, there's a simple hallway entrance with a cable-rug doormat, a small coat closet, and an oval mirror mounted over a plant stand. If I stood on my tiptoes and stretched my arms, I'd almost be able to touch the ceiling. There's a den to the left, with mustard-colored shag carpeting beneath a sofa set and matching chairs.

It's nicer than the apartment my mom's rented for us, which is furnished with rejects from the landlord's garage and with paint and wallpaper choices that reflect the competing tastes of previous tenants. Still, Melissa's place seems the kind of house the Brickman/Brickson siblings would return to after school each day. I could imagine Geoff's friends visiting him in a house like this, too, spreading out on the sofa and on the floor, passing around a bowl of popcorn while watching football and insulting each other.

"My mother would apologize for the mess."

"But it's..."

"Spotless, I know." Melissa brushes the top of the oval mirror with a finger to prove no dust has accumulated. "That's how she is. Works all day, then comes home and straightens. This way."

She leads me through the den and down a brief hallway to the kitchen. Like the entryway and den, everything is in its place. The stove and refrigerator are olive green and look brand new; metal knobs shine on varnished wood cabinets, and bright white countertops are clear of clutter. No napkins with crumbs from the morning toast, like at my house, or a jam knife in the sink and a cereal bowl with residue of milk and soggy Quisp.

Melissa opens the fridge. The stuff inside is organized like stock on a grocery shelf, and I get the feeling if I opened a random cabinet I'd find items similarly arranged. Possibly alphabetized.

She offers me a soda—a generic can of Triple Cola—and we sit in padded chairs at a small Formica table with bamboo place settings. Before she pulls the soda tab, Melissa cups her hand over the top to prevent any spray from making a mess. I do the same, then take a quiet sip. *Tastes just like the expensive kind,* my dad would say, sometimes followed by a gagging face as if he was being poisoned.

"Cold," I say, for lack of a better comment. This clearly isn't a house where you can wander from room to room with an open soda can, setting it down on a book or balancing it on the arm of a chair. I'm not here for the soda, but I don't want to be rude by gulping it down.

Melissa laughs, and I think maybe she feels as awkward as I do. Either that, or she's making fun of me.

I consider the usual conversation starters. Weather. School. Politics. I could compliment the house, or the shirt she's wearing. Would it be too obvious if I only want to talk about movies?

Another sip. The can feels heavy, slick at the sides as if ready to slip through my fingers and fizz carbonated stains into cracks of the linoleum floor.

The silence of the kitchen makes me nervous. Aside from my fear that I'll smudge some immaculate surface, there's another odd quality to the room. I can't quite figure out what it is.

Maybe Melissa is the problem. She watches me as if she expects something. Is this a date—where I should reach across the table to touch her hand? Or, should I bemoan how I've moved from town to town, never put down roots long enough to make real friends? I'd confess that I've always been alone, raise an eyebrow, say: *But, in you, I sense a kindred spirit.*

All ridiculous. We barely know each other.

She comes to my rescue, tilting her head to indicate the front of the house. "That prop was a little too big for me to sneak into Art class."

"I still can't believe it. I've seen *The Stone Stairway* a half-dozen times." Closer to three dozen, but that might seem excessive. I could also mention how the same doorways indicate the governor's mansion in *Night of Shadows* and the LeMott Manor in *Unmarked Grave,* among other film appearances—but I keep that trivia to myself. "The movie set. The actual movie set."

As I say it, I want to go back to the porch. I'd stood there a scant two or three minutes, and there were details I hadn't time to savor. I feel like I have to confirm the location is as special as it seemed. What if, as we sit here in a fairly normal kitchen and drink generic sodas, make meaningless conversation—what if the magic of the place somehow leaks away?

"I guess that was a good surprise," Melissa says.

"Yeah. Yeah, it really was."

It occurs to me that, in an ideal world, she'd be famous for her family connection. Other kids would want to visit this house with the strange and fascinating front porch. When the English teacher showed a movie in class, he should single her out: *Today we're watching Orson Welles in* Macbeth. *Oh, Melissa, how do you think your father would have filmed the scene with the three witches?*

"Do people at school know about your dad?"

"Not really." She takes the top napkin from a wicker holder and wipes at her mouth, then at the condensation on the soda can. "They wouldn't think it was such a big deal."

"Wow. But it kind of is, though. Right?"

She beams a little bit then—that pride kids always feel when somebody compliments their parents. That's when I realize I can stop trying so hard to make casual conversation. It's okay for me to gush about the movies her father made. She's singled me out and brought me here because I love those films. I am the one kid who can appreciate them, the way nobody else in our peer group ever could.

I'd been too shy to prompt her earlier, but I'm more confident now. "You said you had more stuff to show me..."

"Yeah."

Melissa's room is nice, although not as meticulously clean as the rest of the house. That's as it should be. A teenager's room needs to look lived in, with a bit of clutter and confusion to reflect how strange life seems during our unsettled years before adulthood. It should also serve as a sanctuary from parents: for Melissa, a place where she can spread homework papers on a desk, and needn't worry how her mom might react if she places a book or knick-knack on the wrong shelf. Where she can throw the covers over her bed without aligning the quilt pattern with the corners and smoothing the fabric over her pillows. Where she can thumb-tack posters to the wall, instead of hanging framed art prints.

Melissa has taken me here because it's the one room in the house where she can relax.

She'd initially set her school backpack in the hall closet, but now she's brought it upstairs. She drops it beside her bed, then offers me the plastic chair at her desk. When she sits on the edge of the bed to face me, she bounces slightly as if testing the springs.

Her bedroom has some of the things I'd expect in a girl's room. A few stuffed animals sit and stare from different shelves of her bookcase; the wallpaper is mostly white, with a floral pattern suggested in faint blues and yellows. The bed has a frilled ruffle hiding the frame and the space beneath. In contrast, her bulky wooden desk reminds me of one I loved in my old St. Louis room: a wide and deep surface good for drawing, and a nice hutch at the back to hold books and art supplies. She has the same set of pastels I used to like, and a plastic cup filled with different-colored markers and paint brushes.

An office file cabinet stands out-of-place in the corner beside the closet. The gray four-drawer cabinet is dented in spots, with scratches that have turned brown with rust. To help cover these flaws, Melissa has put stickers of animals and cartoon characters on the exposed side. Fuzzy white patches grow like a fungus on this side, too: an indication of previous labels or stickers, imperfectly removed.

Of the two posters on the back wall, I like the mountainscape the best: gray sky and wispy clouds above snowy caps, reminding me a bit of the Paramount movie logo. The other picture's a sunlit field of flowers and tall grass. A little too bright for my taste, but the image is so clear I can almost smell the flowers.

Then I realize it's a stand-up air freshener I'm smelling: one of those twist-up plastic cones with weird fragrant jelly inside.

"Hey, who am I?" Melissa's played the magician again, pulling out that Lake Monster eye before I realized it, and she holds it over her own. "No, wait. One more thing." She pulls a strand of her hair close to the eye, as if to cover it.

"Geoff. Now stop. I feel bad enough."

"That's how they want you to feel," Melissa says. But she moves the Monster eye away from her face.

Tosses it to me.

Usually I drop things, and I'm worried about grabbing too tightly—closing my fingers around an eggshell and popping it, yolk dripping through my fingers. I'm lucky this time, and the eye lands in the center of my upturned palm. It's heavier than I expect—shaped like a ping pong ball, but filled with sand that rattles when I give it a gentle shake. A hole's been punched in the back where it would have attached to the eye-stalk on the actor's mask.

"That's all I could salvage from the head," Melissa says. She reaches under the bed ruffle and pulls out a flat envelope with a crude image of the Lake Monster's face painted on the outside. I find a groove on her desk where the eye won't roll away, set it down and take the envelope.

The bottom of the envelope is squishy, and I can see through it. It's a clear plastic bag, actually, and what I thought was painted on the bag had melted there from the inside. The rubber mask had stuck to the plastic, stamped its image then melted or liquefied over the years, settling in a seaweed sludge at the bottom of the bag.

"Kind of like the Shroud of Turin," I say, then laugh at how silly and sacrilegious that sounds.

"The other eye's in there too." Melissa points at some broken white chips in the slosh. "A lot of this old stuff just falls apart."

The thought makes me sad. Items tossed in drawers or boxes or bags, and somebody like me years later might think of them as treasures, but decay sets in, air and mold and heat do their work. I would have given anything to own an original mask from a favorite movie—even try it on, look at myself in the mirror and test out the monster's growl. As it turns out, this baggie of slush was pretty gross. Like some foul smelling mystery-pudding the previous tenant leaves at the back of the refrigerator.

She's right. Whatever movie props had been saved, they'd have mostly disintegrated by now.

It should be consolation enough that these items are preserved on film. The Lake Monster can walk and breathe and growl on television or movie screens, two intact eyes dangling from his ghastly face.

Then Melissa reaches beneath her bed again. "Funny how some of it's still in decent shape." She slides out a faded shoebox and hands it to me.

A cardboard tube sticks out of the box, so the lid cants up on one side. As I examine the shoebox, I imagine myself as an archaeologist who's been handed a small coffin from a newly excavated tomb. The Pharaoh's linen-wrapped body lies in a large, richly ornamented sarcophagus. This modest container likely holds little of importance—trinkets, small ceramic vials, a few scraps of rolled parchment marked with hieroglyphs—but there's a slim chance it preserves the bones of a favorite pet, or the mummified remains of a stillborn child.

The Egyptologist would sweep sand off the coffin's surface with a fine-haired brush, blow at the dust of ages with a gentle breath. He would remove the lid gently, to prevent further deterioration of the contents.

"Go ahead. Open it."

From Melissa's tone, I'm not an archaeologist after all. I'm the ridiculous grandparent who won't open a present because the wrapping's too pretty.

I pull off the lid and set it behind me on the desk. I'm braced for disappointment—whatever's inside could instantly disintegrate upon exposure to light and air.

At first I think I'm staring into a tangled mess of wire and metal cables, wrapped around a discarded black wig. The cables resolve into intertwined sections of several gooseneck lamps, forming a skeleton beneath patches of short, bristled fur. The item is turtled on its back, or I would have recognized it instantly.

"Spider House," I say. With the box in my lap, I reach beneath the curved metal legs—six instead of eight, to make the puppet easier to animate—and I gently lift the central body of the model. The gooseneck legs had been bent in unnatural angles to fit inside the shoebox, so I have to wiggle the entire model a bit to remove it. The bristles of hair tickle and scratch the underside of my wrist, and the legs make faint scurrying noises against the sides of the box as I pull it free. When I flip the model upright, the features on the spider's domed torso are intact: black hair all around, and with a painted red hourglass shape on top; yellow beaded eyes stare from the front end, with pipe-cleaner mandibles beneath.

The legs aren't as well-preserved—which makes sense, since those would be the sections the animator touched the most while manipulating the model frame-by-frame. The fur hadn't been attached as effectively to the legs, either, so coils of the metal gooseneck shone through for long stretches.

"This is really cool." I bring the football-sized spider close to my face, to simulate how a close-held camera can make a small model appear gigantic. "They only used this model in one sequence. Maybe that's why it's so well preserved?"

Melissa shrugs her shoulders. She's seen the movie—she *must* have—but she doesn't seem to know it as well as I do.

"Sure," I explain. "When they're in the house, and there's spiders of different sizes attacking the actors...Well, some of the little ones are rubber like those boogers you can buy at the drugstore on Halloween. The cat spider's a marionette—you can see the strings if you look close enough, but you could just as easily say they're strands of web. The dog spider's actually a kid in a fur costume, and the huge one in the basement is a real-life tarantula filmed in slow-motion to give it the lumber of a larger animal."

Melissa seems pleased I know so much about the film, though maybe she's just surprised I've become so talkative.

"This guy's just for the end of the movie. You remember, right? I'm not spoiling it for you?"

She smiles and waves for me to continue.

"So, the heroine's the only one alive, and she's finally found the key so she can escape. She runs out onto the porch—"

Again, it's *this* porch. The porch to *this house* where I stood a scant half hour earlier.

"—and she breathes a sigh of relief, but suddenly the ground shakes and she looks around in fear, and a giant shadow falls over the moonlit sky. Because this guy"—indicating the spider model—"comes out of nowhere, scurries over the mansion, his legs like hairy tree trunks, crushing the house and crushing her while she screams."

"That's how it ends?" She sounds disappointed.

"Yeah. The monsters win, like in a bunch of your dad's pictures."

"You're right," she says. "I just didn't know which prop got used in which part."

"I've kind of studied the films, if that doesn't sound weird. Found a few behind-the-scenes articles in magazines, too, and put pieces together." I gave a careful bend to a few of the spider legs, then leaned forward and set the model on the bed next to her. The yellow eyes caught a flash from the overhead light. If I had a movie camera, and if Melissa held perfectly still, it would be cool to animate the spider crawling across the bedspread to attack her.

"There's another thing for you to look at," Melissa says.

Once I'd lifted out the spider model, the shoebox didn't feel that heavy in my lap. I'm sure she only refers to the cardboard tube, since there's nothing else in the box but wadded newspaper to protect the spider model. When I lift the tube, however, some of the paper scraps shift aside to reveal a glint of metal.

Strange. I pull away more crumpled scraps of newspaper to reveal a silvered contraption with a hand grip and finger-trigger, and a small speaker grill on the upper right.

Despite the metallic appearance, the gun is incredibly light—which is why I hadn't noticed it at the bottom of the box. On closer inspection, I realize the item was carved out of balsa wood, sanded smooth and coated with silver paint. I hold my mouth to the wire screen glued to the upper corner, speak an approximation of alien language into the microphone: *T'ch klbar. Vr'gh taous Oiduts Tteg'dub.*

I point the gun at Melissa's head. Pull the trigger.

Because that's part of the joke in *The Space Visitor.* The alien's transference pistol is shaped like a laser gun. He holds it to his mouth and records what he assumes will be a calming phrase. *Don't worry. I mean you no physical harm.* Then he aims the pistol and "fires" the translation close-range into a trembling Earthling's head.

For a second, Melissa lifts her hands in fear like a movie heroine. Please. Don't shoot.

Then she breaks character and slips back to normal.

"This transference gun's in amazing condition," I say. The silver paint has faded in a way that makes the prop appear more like actual metal. I test its weight in my hand, and I can almost believe I'm on a planet with lower gravity. If I stand too quickly I will keep going, shoot up in the air until my head bumps into Melissa's ceiling.

"There was a broken one, too," she tells me. "Must not have been packed away as carefully."

I shake my head, because I've got a different theory. "The device gets destroyed in the movie. When the audience sees the broken translator gun, that's how they figure out the first alien visitor has died." I aim the gun again. "This must be the one Troy Clement uses for most of the scenes. That other one is probably the 'broken' prop from the movie's final sequence."

Melissa nods, but she clearly doesn't have as much knowledge of the films as I do. She might have discarded other items, thinking them similarly broken or useless.

"These props should be in a museum." The words sound stupid once I've uttered them. On one level, sure, they'd recently put a model of the *U.S.S. Enterprise* in the Smithsonian. But none of the Budget Studios productions ever entered popular culture the way *Star Trek* has. Not even close. As much as I love Bud Preston's films, I have to be realistic.

"To me, they're family stuff," Melissa says. "Not much different from a photo album, or garage-sale merchandise like a wind-up music box or grandma's cameo brooch. But these aren't for sale, of course."

She added the last part quickly. Had I inadvertently reached for my wallet, ready to make an offer?

"The cardboard tube, though. That's for you. A gift."

"Really?" My mind races with ideas about what might be inside. Nothing as cool as the gun or the spider model, but still some kind of prop—from the scientist's lab, perhaps, or from the Withered Hag's shelf of occult items. I lift the tube, a postal mailer about two feet long and three inches in diameter, sealed at each end with metal caps. It's light; nothing moves inside.

I work my fingernails under one of the caps and pry it off. At first glance, the tube is empty. Maybe the tube itself is the prop—from an office scene I can't recall, or a strange delivery to LeMott Manor.

Melissa has an expectant gift-giver's look. Which is uncannily similar to a prankster's expression, waiting for the victim to realize he's been tricked.

I peer into the tube. A dark telescope, aimed at the ground.

Random designs emerge as my vision adjusts. White scratches on black, with a gloss finish that catches a flash of overhead light.

It's a rolled sheet of paper, flush with the inside of the tube. I find a top corner, curl it inward to loosen the sheet and remove it.

"A movie poster," Melissa explains. "I hope it's one you like."

In the time it takes me to unroll the poster, I squint like someone trying to solve a puzzle.

Actually, once I understood it was a poster I recognized the image immediately. The white scratches were the cast and crew names against the black background of a tree's deep roots. Midway up the trunk, a human face emerges, mouth open in a scream. Leafless branches intersect above to form the movie's title: *The Haunted Oak*.

"Oh," I say. "Oh yeah, I remember this one. Family members disappear, and you can hear their whispers when you pass the tree at midnight."

"There's a tear on the bottom, but you can fix that with Scotch tape."

"Like new." And I remember to say: "Thank you. It's really for me?"

"Yeah."

I use both arms to hold it up, miming admiration of the image, how it might look pinned to my wall.

And I *do* like it. Very thoughtful of Melissa to give it to me.

It's a cool souvenir I likely wouldn't otherwise be able to own.

But it's not a *prop,* which is what I'd been hoping for. I feel ungrateful at my disappointment, but can't help myself. A prop is a unique item that appears in the actual film—not a promotional image mass-produced after the fact and shipped to theaters around the country.

Maybe if her father signed it...but nope: I scan the front quickly, check the back as I roll it up and return it to the tube. No signature.

"Thanks again." I mean it. I'd mean it a lot more if she gave me the spider model, the space gun, even the loose eye from the Lake Monster mask. But I still mean it.

At the same time, I wonder what other treasures lie hidden in her family attic or basement. Enough to fill another box, maybe two?

I'd be the best curator, since Melissa could easily overlook an item's true value.

If we become good friends, she might let me search parts of the house with her. We'd make some amazing discoveries. Out of gratitude, she'd give me another gift—this time, an actual movie prop.

I realize this isn't the most admirable reason to befriend someone. But I'm fifteen years old. A little insensitive, a little self-centered—like a lot of teenagers.

For the rest of my visit, I shift us away from film talk. We decide which classes we hate—most of them, with Camen's English high on the list. Only Mrs. Brinkton's Art class emerges unscathed, mostly because she leaves us alone.

We tear into students, too, mocking different cliques—athletes, drama group, A/V and chess club geeks. The math nerds, the kiss-ups. Melissa's opinions are pretty fixed, since she's lived among the same kids at three different schools, nine years total. "They never change," she says. "If anything, they get worse."

That explains why she's singled me out. She can predict everybody else, but I'm new. Maybe I'll do something to surprise her.

To change the subject, we talk about music. I flip through the collection of LPs on the stand beneath her small record player, say which albums I like best—though we don't actually play any. Next I make a comment about the posters tacked to her wall. Not movie posters like the one she's given me, but outdoor landscapes. I wonder why she's chosen them. A mountain. A field. "Are you interested in photography?"

"Not really. Those are my windows."

An interesting idea, and I guess I understand her. Landscape photographs can take you out of the everyday world. A painting of a bowl of fruit doesn't quite do that. I never much cared for those impressionistic daubs, either, sidewalks cafes or cobblestone streets in the rain. Impossible to forget they're *art,* all mixed paint and brushstrokes and some fancy frame to convince you you're seeing something special. A photograph seems more matter-of-fact to me. I can stare at it, get lost in it; imagine I'm at the location, same as the photographer, the grass beneath my feet or the mountain air crisp and cold.

Movies often work the same way. Turn down the lights, stare at the screen, and you're in another world.

Then it hits me. The way Melissa tacked the posters to her wall. She's placed them at the same height on the back wall, spaced exactly apart the way two windows would be, if the room had them.

I understand now what had bothered me slightly about the downstairs kitchen. Anyplace I've lived with my mom, even the cheap apartment back in St. Louis, there was a window in our kitchen: pretty handy for when you burnt a slice of toast, since you could let in some air while you frantically waved the smoke outside. The kitchen in Melissa's home must have had some kind of vent over the stove, but there was no window or door that opened onto their back yard. The entry hallway and the den enjoyed natural light from front-facing windows, but the kitchen, like Melissa's room, needed bright overhead lights. Instead of fresh air, the Preston household settles for stand-up fragrance cones with floral scents.

Melissa announces it's time for me to go, since her mother will be home soon. She's keeping me a secret for now, I guess, the same as I'm doing with my own mom. With a reluctant parting from the spider model and alien gun prop, I take the poster with me and head downstairs. Melissa follows, and she accompanies me out the front door and onto that strange and magical porch—ushering me through without giving me time to linger. I barely have a chance to glance back, struck anew at how odd the porch looks attached to the front of an otherwise conventional house. She walks with me around the curve of the car path, towards the Dead End sign at the end of the long road from her bus stop.

"No detours," Melissa says. "You know where you're headed, right?"

"Yeah." Her bus stop is two ahead of mine, so I've got a ways to go, but it's hard to get lost in a small town.

I touch one end of the cardboard tube against my forehead as we part, an improvised salute.

Walking home, I wonder what it would be like to steal back under cover of darkness. I could stand on that porch again, wait for a rainstorm and lightning to add the proper ghostly atmosphere. In that setting, I'd gain courage, test the doorknob, search for an unlocked window. At the side of the house, the lower quadrant of a basement window pane is already cracked. I wrap my fist in my jacket to finish the job, scrape the shards away then reach through to unfasten the latch. I slide feet-first through the small opening then get stuck at my armpits, legs dangling inside until I shift my torso, work through one arm at a time then drop to a dark floor.

The unfinished dirt feels cold. Odors of mold and cardboard and pine deodorizer assault me. I stand and stretch my arms in front, feeling for a wall or the swinging chain of a light switch. As I move forward, I drag my feet to avoid leaving incriminating prints in the ground.

I stumble against a box, and its contents clatter into the dark—much louder than the broken window. Loud enough to alert the occupants of the house.

For a moment I hold my breath, waiting for the sound of a distant switch, slippered footprints on the floor above then down the basement stairs.

Nothing. I let out my breath.

The overturned box may hold the items I seek. With quiet steady motions, I put my arms around the box and restore it upright. The cardboard is cool and moist. There's nothing inside.

I pat the surrounding floor with my hands, but find no trace of the fallen items.

Then a click, and the brush of slippered footprints.

They aren't from the floor above me. The feet are small, and move with an odd synchronization. Three soft taps, one close after another. Followed by three more.

Again, I stretch my arms to the air in front. My palm presses against a breathing mass covered with bristled hair.

Another click of mandibles, the flash of multiple yellow eyes in the dark.

The Screenwriter

Today I am a screenwriter.

I've always written. The stories stay in my mind, mostly. Little vignettes or scenes to entertain myself.

I almost never share these stories. Sure, whenever a teacher assigns some creative writing project, I'll dredge up one of my classics, tone it down a bit to fit the class guidelines—and keep me from getting sent to the guidance counselor. Worst thing is when we're expected to keep a daily journal. I make stuff up, since it's easier than sharing my personal life . . . so I guess that makes me a kind of fiction writer. Currently, Mr. Camen has us write "reaction paragraphs" for the first 10 minutes of English. I've already figured out he never reads the entries, so I'm free to jot down whatever I want.

Choosing a different approach this time, I decide to draft my ideas in the shape of a movie script. I pencil the title at the top of a fresh notebook page: RETURN TO SPIDER HOUSE. Although I'm not an expert in script format, I include camera directions where they seem appropriate:

FADE IN. LONG SHOT of a DARK HOUSE surrounded by bare trees.

CUT TO image of SPIDER WEB in shadowy corner, then PULL BACK to reveal FRONT DOORS.

SOUND FX: offscreen, approaching FOOTSTEPS through fallen leaves; heavy breaths of exertion.

(Same shot as above) YOUNG GIRL, her back to us, ENTERS FRAME from bottom, reaches for the DOOR KNOCKER, misses, and collapses against the doors, slides to the PORCH.

SOUND FX: slow creak of hinge.

DOOR opens from the weight of YOUNG GIRL's body.

Before I get to my first piece of dialogue—which I anticipate will involve variations of *Hello?* and *Anybody hear me?* echoed in a dark, cavernous room—I go back to the lines I've already written and scratch out YOUNG GIRL. Above the deletions, I write the character's name: MELISSA.

The change makes sense. Melissa is the only person in this town I might be able to convince to act in the movie.

The movie I don't have a camera for, or film, or lights. Just the beginnings of a script.

For many students, lunch break is time to relax. It offers relief from the tedium of classes, from the near obsessive oversight of teachers hoping to inspire even the dullest among us—or at least direct our attention to facts or skills, laws of nature or society that, in some hypothetical, long-distant future, might acquire some vague significance.

It's only an illusion of freedom. We cannot leave the school property.

I eat quickly, my brown-sack sandwich usually devoured in the first ten minutes, and I'm supposed to occupy myself for the remaining thirty-five.

Presumably I'd interact with my peers, but their scrutiny is worse than the teachers', who at least make some attempt to hide their disinterest. Mostly, I find some out of the way spot to observe, a wall or tree to lean against, and I imagine my body crusting over with camouflage bricks and mortar, leaf and limb casting a net of shadow over me. Or, I'm a movie camera in plain sight, and the surrounding actors have learned to ignore my presence. Occasionally an amateur might turn his head with a stray acknowledgement, then realize his mistake. *Oh, that's right. I'm not supposed to look at you.*

Melissa has her own strategy. If I had paid attention before we met, I might have half registered her as the girl who walks alone. During lunch period she walks the perimeter of the school property, her feet well-accustomed to the sanctioned boundaries. She isn't exercising, though she might wave her arms as if pretending to be. The real purpose, I realize now, is to avoid interaction with other students. Like me, she never joined the cheer or chess or quiz clubs that meet indoors; she also avoids the various cliques that gather and laugh about nothing. Her head is down, no interest in the games on the field, all those active kids throwing and catching and hitting, making noise as if that's required to advertise their enjoyment.

Earlier I had considered Melissa plain, and I don't fool myself that she's become suddenly attractive. As much as I'm obsessed with her father's movies, that glow of association doesn't transform her, doesn't add a gloss of beauty to her features. I look at her more closely, though, with a generous eye. She is different. Smart, and puzzling. I haven't had a friend like her before.

Here is the thing. At fifteen, what do I know about affection? In English, we pretend to read a book about a man who's captivated by an exotic girl. She is like another species—and if that were literally true, I might enjoy the story more. If she really were part bird, as the cloying narrator suggests. If she arrived from another planet where people grew feathers and spoke in strange clicks and chirps. But in the story, she's a foreign girl who becomes the object of fascination for a stereotypical, mesmerized Victorian gentleman. Her strangeness—her "other-ness," as Camen writes on the chalkboard—supposedly makes her more fascinating.

I uproot myself from my current vantage point against the school building and begin walking across the field. A Frisbee lands across my path and I pause as Craig Some-such runs towards me. He doesn't stop short, stand his ground, say *Hey, throw that back wouldja?* Just runs up, scoops the plastic disc from the ground then runs away, tossing it towards his circle of friends.

I resume my journey to the farthest edge of the school property. A rusted waist-high fence marks the boundary, overgrown with stray twigs and leafy vines. If a softball or Frisbee ever made it over, a student was not permitted to retrieve it. But the fence is so flimsy the top rail would buckle under the slightest pressure. So easy to press down, swing one leg over to straddle it, then fling yourself to the forbidden side.

As easy as jumping off a cliff.

Into that dark world of irretrievable things.

When I reach the fence, I peer over it. Grass and stone and dirt. I wave my arm across the top as if tempting school regulations. No alarm bells ring.

In a few minutes Melissa approaches, following another counterclockwise lap around the property. Her short, thin legs keep the same rapid pace as on previous laps—not quite a run, but as if trying to outdistance an unwelcome follower. I'm camouflage again, blending into the background where I stand against the fence. Melissa's head is down, and her frizzy hair blocks her peripheral vision. She will crash into me if I don't step aside.

So I do.

"Hi, Brendan," she says, and keeps walking.

Not much has changed. We were friends last night at her house, but today we barely acknowledge each other across our shared English and Social Studies classrooms. The assigned seating keeps us apart, and there aren't any group projects this week; we aren't lab partners in Chemistry, either.

The Art elective is our only chance to interact, but we're sketchpad misfits at opposite ends of the room. On her pad, Melissa uses a ruler to draw straight lines, creating odd shapes and intersecting angles. I've traced the image of a horse grazing in a field, and add quick pastel smears of brown and gray and green.

Mrs. Brinkton stands at the back of the room and adjusts a lamp's shade to highlight an overturned vase of flowers. She's busy teaching the still-life group a detailed lesson on lighting and texture.

My horse-and-field drawing is merely a cover sheet, in case Brinkton stops by to observe what I'm doing. I've tucked pages from my English journal into my sketchpad, so I can continue working on my movie script.

CLOSE-UP of light switch. YOUNG GIRL [strike-thru] MELISSA flips the switch up and down several times, but the electricity doesn't work.

MELISSA: (to herself) That's funny.

LONG SHOT. Room not completely dark, and MELISSA squints to identify her surroundings.

PAN OVER, POV MELISSA, observing bookcase filled with stacked books and small items, all covered with dust/cobwebs. Her hand enters the frame from the right, and she sweeps aside some of the dust to reveal small framed photos.

MELISSA: (to herself) I've been here before. I'm sure of it.

MEDIUM SHOT, over MELISSA's shoulder. Her hands fall to her sides, prepared to reach behind her.

MELISSA: Someone's here. Someone's here with me.

CLOSE-UP of MELISSA's face. Frozen with fear. Her lips tremble. Sweat beads on her forehead. The CLOSE-UP lingers uncomfortably long, until…

VOICE (off-screen): Yes. I'm here.

That's as far as I get. The handwriting is a bit messy, with quite a few cross-outs, but I think I've done okay. No idea where the story is going, of course, and don't know if I'll ever finish it.

A small commotion erupts at the window group. This is Geoff and his rowdy friends, who usually spend more time talking and looking outside than attempting any artwork. Apparently Gavin absently sketched an airplane, but his companions suddenly decided it looked like something *else*, so *much* like something else, guess you've got it on the *brain,* Gavin—and Mrs. Brinkton has to abandon light and texture to calm them down, shifting into impromptu lessons on perception and how the viewer completes an artist's drawing, and also how art isn't funny if people tried their best, and what if Gavin actually planned to draw *that,* would it really be so bad, if it was art?

The distraction pretty much occupies the entire class. I rise from my place, move quickly beside Melissa's chair, and pass some folded papers to her.

The next day I'm headed back to Melissa's house again, and time is limited. I'd repeated my Geoff-lie to Mom—because God knows how much follow-up grief I'd get if I mentioned Melissa. A girl, Brendan? A *girl*? Oh, my young man's growing up quick. There are things I need to tell you about, might seem a little early, and a bit awkward coming from your ol' Mom, but better safe than sorry. Sit down. This will take a little while...

Much easier to go with the quick fabrication about visiting my pal Geoff, to buy myself another free evening after school. But Mom always cooked dinner on Wednesdays, and instead of offering to change the day, she invited Geoff to join us. Caught in my own lie, I sighed and said we'd be done studying by dinner time, and I'd just come home. "Geoff eats with his family," I said—since, obviously, I'd know my new best friend's routines and could answer for him.

Which left me about two hours at Melissa's place, before I had to rush home for Mom's spaghetti.

The front doors still look familiar and glorious and run-down, my imagination projecting an acetate gloss over the faded, chipped paintjob. As much as I want to stand and stare, Melissa ushers me inside to the spotless kitchen, for another sit down with generic soda.

The Triple Cola is her after-school reward, and I guess it feels good after our brisk walk from the bus stop, but I gulp it a little too fast. I feel a coughing fit coming on, and as I try to fight it my attention diverts and I end up knocking over the can.

Luckily I'd almost finished the drink, and there wasn't much left to spill. Melissa practically leaps out of her seat, one hand pushing the cloth placemat aside to avoid the spreading pool of soda, the other hand maneuvering a paper napkin to wipe away the mess.

I apologize, and she tells me it's no big deal. She gets a spray cleaner from the cabinet beneath the sink, then goes over the spot again with the sponge. "Good as new," she says after she dries the section of table. She probably wants to scrutinize the placemat for any faint stain, but she restrains herself to spare my feelings. "The way my mother likes it."

It's nothing, of course, and Melissa's fairly gracious about it, but I feel so clumsy. This is the kind of stupid thing that gets you uninvited, *I think*. Melissa might never ask me into her home again.

"Sorry for the nuisance," I say.

"No worries." But she takes my soda can, then carefully empties hers down the sink before throwing them both away.

"Backpacks," she says, lifting hers off the floor and pushing one of the loops over her shoulder. She wants me to follow her, I realize, so I grab my pack and head upstairs to her room.

It's just as I remember from my previous visit. Posters on the strange, windowless wall above the bed. An out-of-place file cabinet tall in one corner, cartoon stickers covering the scratches on one side.

Melissa shrugs off her pack and throws it on the bed, opening its main compartment then moving books and pocket folders aside to retrieve some loose pages. "I wanted to talk about your story," she says. "The script you started."

"Yeah. Seemed like a fun idea. A sequel, you know?"

Melissa nods, unfolding the pages to look them over again. It's time for me to be judged, which makes me a bit nervous.

She's complimentary, as any polite person must be when sharing an opinion in the artist's presence. Mrs. Brinkton is like that, too, even when glancing at the worst scribble. *I see what you've done with the perspective here. Nice sensation of movement*—because the lines aren't straight.

Melissa tells me these handwritten pages show a lot of imagination. She's impressed with my camera directions—FADE TO, MIDDLE SHOT, POINT-OF-VIEW, etc.—as if I've studied script format rather than just winging it. "Have you written any more since yesterday?"

"Not really." I'm not sure how serious I should act about these pages I'd scribbled in my spare time. Who knew if I'd ever finish writing it? It wasn't *real,* not for a *real movie.* "There's one cool part I was thinking about adding, but I need the pages back."

"Like what?"

"Oh. Um." Something clicks, and I'm at a pitch session, or I'm a director explaining the scene to an actress. "Okay, so the shot where she notices the pictures on the mantle—before the weird guy sneaks up behind her? Framed photographs, which would normally be family portraits. She reaches out for one of them." My hands stretch forward as if picking up and admiring a small frame. "She stares at it"—then, correcting myself—"*You* stare at it, and realize it's a close-up picture of a hideous spider. Then cut back to the shelf, and *all* the pictures are of spiders, and you scream. Pretty cool, huh?"

Melissa smiles. At first I think she's pleased about the creepy moment I've envisioned, but there's an odd quality to her expression. Maybe it a false smile: a *wince,* because she has to pretend something is good, when it's not.

Her eyes wrinkle, her lip curls up, and she starts to turn away in revulsion.

Then I realize her hand is in the air, holding up the story pages. She looks *through* them, like she sees something else.

Acting. Grasping one of those weird spider-family portraits, and acting horrified.

Which makes me feel pretty good about the scenario I've written. Sure, it's not Bud Preston responding here, not the actual filmmaker I've admired for so long. But it says something that his daughter's impressed. It's a kind of connection to those films—one I never expected to have.

The acting moment fades, though, and Melissa seems shy now. Expectant, as if I'm supposed to judge her performance. Burst into applause.

"I'm flattered you put me in the story," she says. "That you wrote this for me."

Oh, you have the wrong idea, *I want to tell her.* I hadn't meant it like that. I wrote it for myself, and a tribute to your father's films; I only added you as an afterthought—can't you tell from the way I scribbled your name between the lines?

Because really, not that I was planning to *film* the scene anyway—that would be impossible—but it was a kind of daydream, and to follow the fanciful logic...well, who else did I know in this town? Who else could play the role of heroine?

That's all I meant.

The room is close. Windowless, with that faint cloying scent from the floral air freshener. I try my best to keep a blank expression. She reads something there, maybe, because she hands the pages back to me. "Write more of it, if you want," Melissa says flatly. I can't tell if she's offended.

We're new friends. That's all. It's not like I have any experience with dating girls, other than what I've seen in movies or TV shows, but that's what this situation feels like. There's nothing romantic going on here, no attraction on either side, but it's still like I'm on trial. Anything I say or do. I spill a soda and I think, *She'll never invite me back.* I say the wrong thing, have the wrong facial expression, and it's over.

"Be right back," Melissa says. "I have to…" and she lets her voice trail off so she doesn't have to add, "use the bathroom."

As Melissa leaves the room, her footsteps trailing down the hall, I wonder how long I have before she comes back. My thoughts start racing.

Last time. This could be my last time in this house.

The only time I'll be alone here.

The spider model could still be in her bedroom. That space-gun-translator, and the Lake Monster's eyeball.

I kneel next to her bed and lift the ruffle to check beneath for the shoebox.

Not there.

The hutch over her desk contains only school books and supplies. I consider the vinyl accordion door of her closet, and before I can even think about it I've crossed the room to slide it open.

I tell myself it's not like my daydream after the previous visit, where I imagined returning after dark to smash a window, break into her home and steal souvenirs from my favorite films. What I'm doing now isn't as bad as that—I'm already here, and just taking a quick look. Melissa wouldn't mind. I'm sure she'd let me if I asked.

Except I'm sweating. I worry that she could catch me, I have to hurry, she could catch me, and I'm half-listening for a distant flush or running water or approaching footsteps, but more of my attention focuses on the shelf above hanging clothes—only sweaters up there, no shoeboxes—then sliding a few hangers aside to check the floor—

And if I find a movie prop, that doesn't mean I might take it. Definitely not anything priceless, something Melissa would be upset to lose, because I don't want to hurt her, I don't want to mess up our friendship just as it's getting started, especially not over something that's so small it would fit into my pocket, or even something I could hide in my backpack, or a prop so large I've just gotta grab it and run from the house, not looking back, thinking Melissa's been nice but she's unpredictable, too, so I need to make my own luck here while I can—

But my conscience is safe because there's no shoebox on the closet floor, just shoes, and a pile of dirty clothes, nothing worth the risk of sorting through, time's probably running out, better to act like a decent person, a respectable friend—

Then it occurs to me that the file cabinet is the better place to search. So large and inappropriate in a teenager's bedroom, since Melissa wouldn't have files, certainly not four large drawers full, so that's where her father's props would be if she's hiding them. I pull the closet shut, a heavy tug as the vinyl door almost pops out of its metal runner at the bottom, making a scrape that might be audible in the hallway, might mask the sound of Melissa's footsteps as she returns to the bedroom, but that can't be helped, too late for me to stop now, and I cross to the file cabinet to open the top drawer.

It's locked.

I try the other three.

Locked. Locked. And locked.

Maybe I should pull harder on a drawer, bang it on the side and break it open. Or just hit a wall or the top of her desk, slam my fist down in a frustrated panic.

Or maybe I should collect myself. Move to the center of the room and stand still, breathe evenly, innocently.

Melissa stands in the bedroom doorway.

A flush of embarrassment heats my face. *She didn't catch me,* I try to convince myself, even as a tell-tale bead of nervous sweat trickles down my forehead.

She stares at me for a moment, then steps into the room. "I've decided I can trust you," Melissa says.

"I'm not supposed to go in here. My mother will have a fit if she finds out."

She's taken me to a door near the end of the upstairs hallway. It seems an ordinary door, but the wood is unfinished: nobody has bothered to paint it to match the rest of the hallway. Instead of a door handle, it has a simple hook-and-eyelet latch.

Melissa gently lifts the hook then pushes the door inward.

A musty odor hits me: mothballs and chalk and sawdust and damp newspapers. It's not a room beyond the door, but a cramped, dark corridor.

"I have to go first." Melissa practically needs to turn sideways to fit. She pats the walls as she moves forward, and although I can't see them, I know clouds of dust form with each strike. I side-step behind her.

My eyes adjust slightly to the dark. The makeshift passage seems to run between two normal rooms, and I judge that it's about the same depth as Melissa's bedroom. We're walking up to a dead end, at the back of the house.

"Careful," she says. "Here it is."

The rustle of a chain, the click of a switch.

Ancient lands of elves and orcs and dragons never captured my imagination. And it always seemed silly to me that a world of talking animals could be entered through a bedroom wardrobe.

Quite honestly, I never cared for theme parks either. Dad took me to Safari Land when I was ten, and that place couldn't fool me with its jeep-on-rails "expedition through Africa": lion statues with recorded roars; a cheetah propelled across painted sand by a blast of compressed air; a well-timed arc of water from the fixed trunk of a fiberglass elephant. I remember getting sick from spinning rides, caramel apples, and disappointment.

Maybe I'm presenting myself as a hardened skeptic here, immune to wonders that kids typically ooo-and-ahh over. If something breaks through my cynicism, it's got to be really amazing. Authentic.

Or maybe it's simply that I needed something far away from the cheering crowd, dark and forgotten. Not necessarily better, but *mine*.

We all want magic of some kind.

And that's why I mention Middle Earth and Narnia and Wonderful-World-of-Whatever theme parks. Because the kind of magic I was supposed to associate with those places...that's what I felt when Melissa clicked that light switch in that dark hallway at the back of her house.

Because it wasn't the back of her house. There was so much more.

One more analogy. An appropriate one, as will become clear:

Consider how a movie set can trick the viewer. There's a missing fourth wall we can see through, but we're conditioned not to think about it. The room doesn't have a ceiling either, because arc lights and boom microphones need easy access to the set and cast. Again, viewers don't think about what's outside the frame, and imagine they're spying into a normal home with a roof above the characters' heads.

Melissa Preston's house had played the same kind of trick on me. Despite the unusual entryway, I saw an ordinary house with a kitchen, a den, bedrooms and bathrooms.

And as she led me down that corridor, the most I expected to find was a closet, a tiny side room, or the pull-down entrance to an attic.

Because when I'd approached the front of the house, I'd never thought to look behind it.

Click.

The end of that dark passageway opens into a large enclosed space. A tremendous, cavernous addition to the back of the house, and the reason—I finally realize—why Melissa's bedroom has no windows facing the back yard.

Her bedroom is an internal room.

And the back yard is a movie studio.

She'd gone first, telling me to be careful, because there's no protective rail on the staircase leading downward.

The staircase. Even in the dim lighting from the passageway we leave behind, and a few lights along the way flickering on, other bulbs dead or missing, I recognize those stairs instantly. It's the title edifice from Budget Studio's first film, *The Stone Stairway.*

"This is amazing," I say. I'm so happy Melissa decided to show this to me.

Unlike the illusory front doorway, the steps are a sturdy mix of stones over concrete, and retain much of their original condition. Dim lighting helps make the stairs look exactly as they did when newly-married Samantha Goodwin floats down them in a perilous sleepwalk, as ghostly whispers tempt her to stumble. And, repurposed for a later film, these same steps lead from the basement laboratory of *Spider House,* and the mad scientist screams and races up them, pursued by several of his oversized, venomous experiments.

"Stay close to the wall." The roof slants down at an angle away from the staircase wall, and it's hard for me to judge how far back the building extends from the wall. I sense, more than see a floor below.

She leads me down, and we pass beneath a wooden archway. A spiderweb stretches between the beam and the wall, and I half expect any of the steps below might be overrun with skittering shadows. I will crush a plump hairy torso, eight twig legs splayed in a fan pattern from the heel of my shoe.

I notice a damp earthy smell mixed with the oils of a handyman's garage. The roof is far above us now, and the stairs continue longer than they should. "Your house is two stories," I say.

"Father dug through to the basement and extended it back," Melissa tells me, and I realize why. A lower camera angle makes the staircase even more impressive.

As we hit ground level, it seems like a dark, mostly-empty warehouse. Instead of boxes and shelving, I can make out thin partitions that separate the floor into a maze of makeshift rooms.

"Some of these lights still work, but they get hot." Melissa steps to a beveled light panel and flips one switch, then another. They snap loudly, with no result, but the third takes, and a blinding spotlight flashes from a grid attached to the slanted roof.

That's when I fully realize the wonder I'm standing in. Not just the staircase prop, but an entire film studio attached to the back of the house.

"Everything." I'm standing with my mouth open in disbelief. I know I look like a dumbstruck kid, but can't help it. "Everything. Every *place*."

It's slightly bigger than our school's gymnasium. The ceiling stretches higher than I would have guessed, but the sets are smaller than they appear on film. The partitions I'd seen in the dark now clearly delineate different locations: an office, a bedroom, a den; a castle dining room with a long table and a fireplace mantle at one end; the interior of an antique shop; a mock storefront with a sidewalk and streetlamp, an alleyway off to the side. Everything's in horrible disrepair, but still magnificent.

The arc spotlight hangs over and illuminates the far end of the studio, and I decide we should explore that area first.

I step into the office set. Two metal desks face each other in the center of the three-walled room; the closest chair tilts to the side, one of its casters missing. Like the other partitioned areas, it's set up as a generic room, so it could be easily redecorated for use in different movies. With an obsessive fan's knowledge of film chronology, I know the last use would have been as Ferguson's accounting office in *The Haunted Oak,* but I can trace its earlier incarnation as the police station a deformed Thomas Hendricks walks through in *The Twisted Face.*

I've imagined being Hendricks, walking into this same office to confront the Police Chief. Now I'm really here. My eyes are the camera. I'm him.

I walk toward a door at the back. A frosted glass window holds a metal guide-slot for the occupant's name. It's empty, but a half-opened cardboard box sits on a lopsided table beside the door. I see broken pieces of plastic name cards inside, including GEAN and OSS and DR. I reach toward the box, ready to match pieces.

"Don't touch anything, okay?"

And I'm so grateful for what she's done, bringing me here, that I don't protest. Besides, the place feels like a museum. Closed for more than a decade, faded and falling apart, but still a museum. There should be "Don't Touch" signs posted all over.

"Sorry," she says. "It's my mother. She doesn't want me down here. I'm taking a big risk."

"I appreciate it."

The frosted glass makes it impossible to see through the door. Maybe there's another set behind it, maybe there's a wall. The door might not even open.

My hands itch near the handle. I want to try it.

Instead, I respect Melissa's warning. Hands off. Simple enough, considering how much else there is to see.

We walk from the office set into the metallic interior of a spaceship.

I'm struck by the randomness of the floor plan, each set built as needed for a current film, placed wherever space was available, partitions moved, furniture transformed and rolled from one false room to another. If there was ever a blueprint, it was soon discarded.

In one of my magazines, I'd read about a house in California—Winchester House I think it was called. The woman who owned it was rich and eccentric, and thought she was being haunted. Her solution was to build new rooms onto the house—with the theory that any ghosts would get so confused by the bizarre layout that they'd leave her alone. A corridor might twist back on itself; stairs led nowhere; a window overlooked an interior wall, rather than outside.

The same chaos applies here, but with an authentic purpose: not to frustrate ghosts, but to bring them to life on celluloid.

Or a space alien, in Budget Studios' single attempt at science fiction. Some of the props actually are metal: an auto dashboard turned upside down, an old television screen welded in place of the steering wheel; scrap levers and switches and light panels arranged next to exposed circuit boards. Other elements are plywood sprayed with silver paint, and a similar effect had been applied to the floor tiles. A shelving unit contains trophies or weapons. On closer inspection, many of the alien artifacts are simple household items wrapped with tinfoil: a piece of foil has torn off the side of a long metal tube, and I recognize the label of an overturned can of Pringles potato chips.

"Doesn't look very real, does it?" Melissa thinks I'm disappointed, which couldn't be further from the truth. I'm fascinated how this haphazard arrangement of, well, *junk,* still managed to look okay on film.

"With the lights blinking and stuff, it's better." I wave my hand over the instrument panel, as the Visitor does to navigate his ship. Nothing happens, of course, but...

"Can we turn it on?" I ask her.

She shakes her head. "It doesn't work." Melissa breaks her own "no touch" rule, reaching forward to flip a few switches, turn a few dials. "See?"

I know something she doesn't. One of my back issues of *Monster Project* has an article on *The Space Visitor,* including a behind-the-scenes photo. The actor Reuben Venn stands to one side, in full costume save for the "metallic" gloves he's removed and set beside the dash. Bud Preston kneels beneath the console, where a panel has been slid aside to reveal a network of tangled wires.

A photo I'd looked at countless times, never dreaming one day I'd visit the same set.

"Let me try something, okay?" I kneel in the same spot beneath the console and reach toward the wood panel.

My hand stays suspended for a moment, to give Melissa time to stop me. She doesn't speak.

I press my open palm against the wood. The silver paint feels rough and sticky. The panel slides easily.

The wires are all tangled. The rubber coating on a few of them is stripped in patches, fixed clumsily with black electrical tape. I realize that I'm sweating: as Melissa mentioned, the arc light above puts out a lot of heat. My armpits are damp. There's sweat on my forehead and on my hands, too.

The sweat could carry an electrical charge, if I touch an exposed wire.

So I reach in like I'm trying to defuse a bomb.

It's hard for me to see under there. Melissa moves closer as if to help, and she's actually blocking my light. The wires tighten over my arm, and I pull back carefully.

A wire is caught on the band of my wristwatch.

I turn my arm one way, then another, to break free. A bead of sweat falls down the side of my face, and I imagine another one drips off my fingertip onto the wires.

"Maybe try this later…?"

"No, I've almost got it." I reach deeper, trying to find where the wires converge. I feel for the back wall, then towards the floor. Half my arm's in there now.

There's a raised rectangle, about the size of a mousetrap. It's too dark, too many wires block my view. I trace the perimeter of the shape with my damp fingers, braced for a spring then a snap of the trap.

I find a raised bump of plastic and realize what it is. A light switch, set in the floor instead of flush with the wall.

I flip it.

"Oh!" Some of the buttons Melissa pressed earlier must have toggled to "on," waiting for the master switch to send power. The reflection of multi-colored lights flash over her face, in her glasses, in her smile.

It takes me a minute to extricate my arm from the tangle of wires, but I manage. I stand up beside her then turn to face the spaceship's navigation panel.

A simple effect, but those lights manage to transform scrap metal and silver paint into something glossy and futuristic. Or, at least a mild approximation of how they looked on film, where a lens filter spread sparkles of light into twinkling stars.

It's easy to pretend the controls might actually work. I could forget we're in a tiny three-walled cubicle with no ceiling, in a warehouse studio attached to the back of my new friend's house. I wave my hand over blinking lights in that strange zigzag motion Reuben Venn applies before take-off, and the panel seems to respond. The lights grow brighter and mimic the motion of my hand; a low hum begins to surge from the panel. An alien motor revs up; the spaceship prepares to take off.

The hum grows louder, until I feel a slight tremor beneath my feet.

We're moving. I glance overhead, expecting a rush of midnight sky to appear through the windowed dome of the spaceship.

A blinding flash explodes above me, followed by a loud pop and a shower of sparks.

The arc lamp goes out, leaving us in darkness.

"You overloaded the circuit," Melissa says. "Shouldn't have touched anything."

She sounds nervous, so I don't respond to the accusation. Better to focus on practical concerns. "Is there a fuse box down here? Maybe try one of the other overhead lights, see if it comes on."

The shadowed outline of her head moves, but I can't tell if she's nodding yes or no. "My mother's not gonna be happy. We might have blown power to the whole house."

"The stairs," I tell her. "Look toward the stairs."

In the distance, dim wall lamps along the Stone Stairway help identify the path back to the house proper, to the upstairs corridor where we'd entered the studio.

But I don't want to leave yet.

"If those lights work, the house is fine. Listen, I'm kind of handy. I've lived in a lot of different apartments with my mom, so I've learned a few tricks about quirky electrical circuits."

"Let's fix it and get out." Melissa sounds comforted that her house still has power, but she's firm about wanting to go. "I'll lead the way."

Easier said than done. The staircase lamps mostly dwindle before they reach us. I'm more *aware* of Melissa than I'm able to *see* her.

I follow the idea of her, where I think she should be.

Despite the urgency not to trip or collide into furniture or a partition wall, I can't fully concentrate on the journey. I'm thinking also about the movie sets around me, briefly glimpsed when I thought I'd have more time to explore. I need to remember them *now,* before the image fades.

I recall a game in Psychology class, where the teacher projects an intricate drawing on the screen: I'm giving you one minute to take in every detail, then I'll turn off the slide and ask you questions about it.

We pass the office set, and I'm pretty sure the next area is big enough to be the castle dining room. For all I can see, Count Verlock stands by the mantle, welcoming his wary visitor. The characters are as real to me now as Melissa—images my mind projects into the dark, more solid than ghosts.

"This way."

I follow her voice, and step past a dark Victorian alley. A prostitute attempts to catch my attention, but a stranger's hand covers her mouth and a knife blade traces red across her throat. He drags her deeper into the alley, and I keep walking.

Towards the faint lights along the stone stairway.

The podium for the arc lights stands near the bottom step. A guide-light makes it easy to see the switches, but the labels taped beneath each one are smudged and impossible to read.

One of the toggles points in a different direction. "This the one you pulled?" Before Melissa answers, I jiggle it up, down, up then back again.

Nothing.

There's a fuse box attached to the side of the podium, and I open the metal front. Again, no clear labels, and the circuit probably wouldn't pass an electrician's inspection, but it seems easy enough to figure out. I find the odd switch and flip it.

"Anything?"

"No." Then: "Wait. Over there."

The spotlight had exploded, so that wouldn't come back on. But at the other side of the studio, multi-colored lights flickered across the distant spaceship set.

I'm ready to try some of the other arc lights, to visit more set locations.

"Turn it off," Melissa says.

It hits me like the championship ballgame has been rained out. More like: I go to the museum, look at one or two paintings, then get kicked out.

"Okay," I concede. "I'll help fix it next time."

"I'm not sure we should come back down here."

"We *have* to. I could bring flashlights to use, instead of the big lamps."

"Maybe," she says. "Maybe."

I don't love the way she dangles the possibility in front of me. But "Maybe" is better than "No." It's something I can work with.

Melissa's upset now, after the scare when the lamp exploded, after our confused walk in the dark. On calmer reflection, she'll relent.

Especially since she knows how much this place means to me.

"I wish my dad could see this." I feel ready to cry, but try to hold back. "He loved watching these movies with me."

From the quaver in my voice, Melissa probably guesses that my father, like hers, has passed away.

Maybe the secrets of this house could bring him back.

No. Not through a séance.

My father's not dead. He's in Cleveland.

The Interesting Son

Today I am an interesting son.

With my mom's current job, she works late on Thursdays. That's the reason she fixes a large dinner on Wednesday, to spend time with me the night before and to leave me a pot of left-overs for the next day. I appreciate the effort she puts into fixing dinner, the attention she tries to give me. But she always seems worn out during the Wednesday meal. She'll lob a conversation starter, about school subjects or TV programs, and although I try my best to give a lively answer, it never quite wakes her up. My fault as much as hers, really—especially now, since I have a new friend and an amazing discovery about that friend's house, and I've decided not to share.

My mom wouldn't grasp what was so magical about the Preston home. She's never understood the appeal of those strangely atmo-spheric movies from Budget Studios.

I saved that secret for my weekly phone call with Dad.

We talk on Thursday nights now—because there's awkwardness with him, too, and better we speak when my mom's not around to overhear in case things get heated.

- Why can't you come visit?
- I'm working. Alabama's a long ways from here.
- We could watch movies, like we used to...

- You'll have your driver's license soon. You can drive up to see me then.

- That's two years away, at least. And Mom wouldn't let me borrow the car.

- I'll try to work something out, but I can't make any promises.

- No you can't. You *never* can.

Then I'll slam down the kitchen phone, because it's clear he doesn't want to see me. That our time together always meant more to me than it ever did to him.

I wouldn't want my mom to hear that kind of outburst. To rush from the other room to ask me what's wrong, what did my dad do *this* time?

Then there'd be the calls when I didn't get angry. When we'd talk about the past, repeat all our in-jokes, reminisce about things we did together, and I'd feel that wonderful connection with my dad again. But the call has to end. Then, instead of an angry outburst, I might start crying because things went *well.*

And right when I'd finally start to calm down, I'd wonder if things actually *did* go well. Had we actually discussed anything meaningful? I'd realize that I never ask him any details about his job. I don't know if he's seeing someone else now, instead of my mom. We don't talk about these things…I guess because I don't want to imagine he's happy without us.

By the same logic, I assume he's not really interested in my day-to-day life. I live somewhere else, and he's not responsible for me anymore. My school life isn't exciting. There's nothing special about the latest apartment we're living in. My life is as dull and inconsequential as a weather report for a distant city. I usually say everything's fine, offering no details. I never have anything interesting to tell him.

Now, I finally do.

"You're early."

"Yeah," I say. "I'm glad you were home."

I hear the rustle of a jacket, some papers being moved aside. "Brought some work with me so I could prep for a meeting tomorrow."

He mentions a presentation to Division Heads, and I respond on auto-pilot. "That sounds important."

"We need to change priorities. We focus so much on production, but marketing is just as important, right?"

"Sure." I know what products his company makes, but need to stop him before he practices a sales pitch. "Listen. I have some news."

"Your teachers are good? You're doing your homework?"

"Sure. But not about that. This girl in my class—"

"Oh." The "oh" is two syllables, an octave apart. I can't always picture my dad's face as we talk on the phone, but I can see his smirk now. "What's her name?"

"Not that, Dad. She's not the important part. Her last name is Preston."

He doesn't react.

"As in *Bud* Preston."

Still, it doesn't sink in, so I have to prompt him further. "Budget Studios. The movies we like."

"Oh." Only one syllable this time. "That's why you like this girl? It's a common last name. You shouldn't read too much into the coincidence."

"It's *not* a coincidence." He should think about what I'm saying, instead of getting sidetracked by the possibility I might have a girlfriend. "She's his daughter."

"His daughter, eh? Well, did I remember to tell you that I'm dating Raquel Welch's sister?"

The comment surprises me, since it's the first time he's mentioned himself dating—even in the context of a joke. "I'm serious, Dad."

"You are, huh?"

I want to say, *Why would I lie?*, but I caught the sympathy in his voice. He's thinking about how unhappy I often seem when we talk. He's heard me repeat "Nothing" whenever he asks what's new or exciting in my life. So now his pathetic son has invented a girlfriend, to make him seem interesting to his dad. But that's not enough: she has to be the daughter of the movie director we both admire. *My son's got quite an imagination,* he's thinking. *When you tell a story, you go all out. You've always had trouble facing reality, Brendan. Remember how you acted when your mom and I split up?*

I don't give him time to say such things. Instead I explain how I met Melissa, how she showed me the eyeball prop from *The Lake Monster.* I speak quickly, offering specific details that reinforce the truth of my story. I talk about visiting her home, the mansion archway over their front porch, the props she showed me of the spider and the alien pistol. *There's so much more,* I tell him. *Yesterday, after school, she showed me the rest of her house. It's larger than it looks from the outside. The whole back of it is a movie studio as big as a warehouse. They made all our favorite movies there, in my friend Melissa Preston's house. You should come see it, Dad. It's really cool.*

He doesn't interrupt. When I finish, he's silent for a moment, and I wonder if we've been disconnected.

"Dad? You still there?"

A sigh. "Brendan, I told you I can't visit right now. They can't spare me at work. That's a cute idea, though. Maybe you should turn it into a short story."

In retrospect, it seems obvious he wouldn't believe me. The idea's so ridiculous—crazier than the most outlandish movie plot. *Of course* my dad would think I invented the story to convince him to visit. Easier to believe in a pathetic, delusional son, than to accept the fanciful coincidence I'd described.

But I took the risk because he was my dad. If I insisted that I spoke the truth, he'd have to believe.

It really happened, Dad. I'm not making this up. Repeat this mantra, and eventually it sinks in. That's what I thought would happen.

"I've got to work on tomorrow's presentation," Dad says. "Talk to you again next week."

Then he hangs up.

In my mind, the call continues:

Yes, next week. When you might be more sensible. Otherwise, I'll have to talk with your mother. Consider sending you to someone.

A school counselor, probably, since we can't afford a psychiatrist. Maybe I made a mistake letting you watch those films, Brendan. They've obviously done something to your mind. Something horrible.

All that unspoken doubt. So frustrating, I didn't know whether to kick the wall, or start sobbing.

Parents shouldn't be like this. It's awful when someone you love doesn't believe you.

I needed to find a way to convince him.

The Crooked Frame

A bell rings as a customer enters the dimly lit store. He stumbles like a drunk as he navigates an aisle, but viewers blame his unsteady walk on the scattered merchandise: wooden chests and ceramic figurines crowding the dusty shelves; small pieces of furniture positioned like an obstacle course along the floor.

The man bumps against an end table, and a vase nearly falls off. He steadies the vase, then lifts it for a closer look. Next he rubs his coat sleeve against part of the vase, stares at the revealed design for a moment, then turns the item upside down. "No price tag," he says, replacing it carefully on the end table. "Must mean I can't afford it."

"You have to inquire." Without warning, the owner of the shop has appeared behind him. The shopkeeper's rough voice seems unlikely to encourage a purchase. "We must decide what an item is worth to you."

"Nothing's worth more than I can afford." The customer prepares a good natured smile, then turns to greet the shopkeeper—

—and the smile freezes on his face, because:

The shopkeeper wears a mask over his head. A normal face has been painted on plaster, and the flesh tones approximate those of a department-store mannequin. But the shape of the mask is wrong: small painted eyes and eyebrows, a tiny-bump nose and protruding ears, but the entire plaster head is too large and asymmetrical. It weighs heavy on one side and the head tilts so that it almost sits on the shopkeeper's left shoulder.

"Most people have a similar reaction." His hand touches the side of the mask with an absent-minded pat, similar to how someone might smooth their hair after removing a hat. "I assure you, this covering is for your benefit. Were I to remove it, you'd find my appearance even more disturbing."

A hole beneath the nose forms an opening for his mouth, and a small attached flap of cloth has been draped over it. A lopsided image of a mouth has been painted onto the cloth, and these lips ripple from the man's breath as he speaks.

"It's fine, it's fine," the customer says. "I don't mean to be impolite." Despite himself, he stares at the mask, perhaps attempting to locate the eye holes, or wondering about the shape of the actual head beneath the plaster.

"What would you like to see?"

"I need a camera. I'm a reporter, and my regular guy's not available." He slips into a nervous ramble. "Thought I'd try my hand at it, you know. How hard can it be? I mean: point and shoot, right? Like this."

The director chooses an odd angle for this last phrase. We see through the eye slits of the mask, from the shopkeeper's point of view. The slits are uneven: both tilted, and one higher than the other. As the customer says *Like this,* he mimes holding a camera and clicking his fingers, as if taking the shopkeeper's picture.

Even though the character never removes the mask, I know who he is. The shopkeeper represents an uncredited cameo appearance by Thomas Hendricks, the deformed star of *The Twisted Face.*

"I have something that will suit your needs." He raises his arm to point out a back corner of the store, then bows slightly. The weight of his head threatens to make him topple over. "Follow me."

The customer nearly knocks a lamp to the floor, but eventually manages to reach the indicated shelf. A box camera sits on the top row. Unrelated items surround it: a stack of leather-bound books, a teapot depicting a pastoral scene, a plastic model of a human heart.

If you look closely, there's an embossed pentagram design in the spine of one of the books. On the teapot, several of the painted shepherds run as if they're being chased by a wild animal. The plastic heart, however, does not beat.

"May I?" The customer lifts the camera from the shelf and brings it to his level. He examines the flash attachment, squints at the front lens; opens the film compartment then snaps it closed. "It works okay?"

"Of course."

"I was hoping for something more recent."

"That's why you've come to an...*antique* shop."

"You've got me there." The customer offers a weak laugh. "Honestly I wasn't planning on buying anything tonight. I was walking by, noticed your store, and simply felt compelled to step inside."

He tests the weight of the camera in his hand, then shrugs and returns it to the shelf.

"How much is it worth to you?" the shopkeeper enquires.

"Well, maybe I need a camera, but not necessarily *this* one. Like I said, a newer model might suit me better."

"Perhaps. But I have no other camera for sale."

"Yeah. Tell you what." The customer pats his pockets. "Wasn't planning on shopping tonight, so don't have much cash."

An extended close-up of the oversized mask fills the pause in dialogue. The shopkeeper's fixed expression is unreadable, of course, but viewers sense this exchange is some kind of test, and that the customer is failing. The mask has recovered slightly from its odd leeward tilt, and although the shopkeeper doesn't speak, his mouth-flap flutters as if from heavy agitated breaths.

"I've got a few bucks. Two."

No response. The close-up of the mask continues.

"How about three? To take that old camera off your hands?"

Silence.

"We're bartering here," the customer says. "You're supposed to come back with your own price."

"Whatever you think it's worth."

"Really? 'Cause I'd go back to the two bucks I opened with."

A repeat of the point-of-view shot, through the eye slits of the mask. The customer takes out his wallet, fumbles with it as if attempting to hide its contents, and eventually produces two dollar bills. "You said it works. Guaranteed, right? 'Cause if it doesn't work, it ain't worth nothing. I'll return it." He pays the money, then retrieves the camera from the top shelf.

"You won't return it," the shopkeeper says.

Then a medium shot of the store as the customer turns to leave, bumping against a coat rack, dodging a child's wooden toy. The bell rings as he exits the shop, and the title card appears onscreen:

The Crooked Frame

In an interview published in *Monster Project,* Bud Preston explains the origin of the movie's plot. "If you go to film school—which I didn't, I'm self-taught—you learn that anytime the image is unbalanced, it means you're at a crisis point in the story. If the angle is framed too high, or too low, that indicates a power struggle between characters. If the shot's got a crooked angle, it means the rules have changed: for a moment, the world is bizarre and out of whack.

"I decided to apply that commonplace film technique, and make it *literally* true. The haunted camera in *The Crooked Frame* can only take distorted pictures. And those pictures change the world for our main character, played by Alan Darnell. At first it's something simple: a houseplant photographed at an odd angle soon withers away. Later, the changes get more serious. For example, a photographed highway might twist, causing an accident. And what might happen, I wondered, if our hero used that camera to snap a picture of himself in the mirror?"

A still photo of the film's masked shopkeeper accompanies the article. In typical genre magazine fashion, the caption gets the facts wrong. As if the editors don't care, or they deliberately distort the truth to insult Preston and his films:

"Wearing a grotesque mask, director Bud Preston appears briefly in his own movie, a la Hitchcock. However, most would agree that

Preston has a long way to go before he can approach the accomplishments of filmdom's Master of Suspense."

The pawn shop I visit after school is nothing like the seedy, mysterious stores depicted in gangster and horror movies. It's bright and spacious. Items are neatly organized, with prices visible in large handwritten tags.

Many stores in this small town serve a dual purpose. The video rental shop is called "Sun and Show," because they have a tanning booth in a back room. Paula's Shoe Store also serves as the local newsstand. And the corner pawn shop, capitalizing on its proximity to the high school, stocks sheet music and rents musical instruments to students in band class.

I pass a wall of guitars and a shelf of flutes and clarinets and trumpets in black, velvet-lined cases. There's a middle section labeled "Appliances" at the end of the aisle, and an arrow pointing to the opposite side, "Electronics."

The electronics are mostly televisions and car radios, but I also see a laser disc player and a fairly new small-screen TV/VCR combo unit. A small selection of cameras occupies half a shelf. There are more expensive ones up front, beneath a glass countertop, but these are closer to my price range.

The cheapest one has an index card attached, with the notation: "Takes Polaroid 300 instant film cartridges." The bulky camera has an ugly sloping front and a mouth at the bottom that spits out the photo—blank at first, but you wave it in the air as it dries and the image slowly blurs then fades into view.

It's just what I need. I take it with me to the back counter, where a thin elderly woman sits at the cash register.

I hand her the camera while I get my money ready. "Guaranteed, right?"

"Ten days," she tells me. "Keep your receipt."

She takes my cash, then begins writing in a notepad. I talk while she works: "Honestly I wasn't planning on buying anything. I was walking by, noticed your store, and simply felt compelled to step inside."

She stops, probably wondering if I'm taking recreational drugs. Her head tilts to the side and her eyes squint as if she examines me through the uneven slits of an oversized plaster mask. She tears off a yellow carbon slip and hands it to me. "You want a bag?"

"No thanks." I stuff the camera into my backpack.

Then I'm off to Diamond's Pharmacy and Sporting Goods, to buy a film cartridge.

The Photographer

Today, I'm a photographer. I've combined two flashlight beams as my lighting rig, placed them carefully on a nearby shelf and aimed them at my subject. The beams illuminates only one side, which I hope will add a mysterious tone to the finished image.

"Stay perfectly still." I'm talking to my hands as much as I am to Melissa. Any slight tremor will add too much blur to the photograph.

The camera shutter clicks once, then again a second later.

A small motor whirrs, and a white square rolls out the front slot. The undeveloped photo hangs at the end of the camera until I pull it free.

"Let me have it." Melissa sets aside the movie prop she's been posing with, and takes the photo paper from me. She waves it in the air, the sound of bat wings, then pauses to look at the image. "I can't make anything out."

"Give it time."

Another flap of wings. Pause. Repeat. She holds the photo in the crossbeam of the flashlights. "I don't think it's very good. You can't even tell it's me."

"Let me check." I move closer to examine the instant photograph. Melissa is mostly in shadow, barely recognizable. The spider prop has caught more of the light, as I intended, but overall the picture's not clear enough.

Not good as evidence.

"Let's try again." I suggest she stand to the side, so her face catches more of the light. That way, she's also blocking less of the shelf behind her: part of the antique shop set from *The Crooked Frame,* transformed for a later Budget Studios production into a Tarot Reader's séance room with occult curios on the shelf.

I touch her shoulders to help her pivot to the right position, then step back and look through the viewfinder. "Lift it up a little bit," I say, putting my hands beneath hers and raising them to display the spider prop at the best angle. Her skin feels warm, and I realize it's the first time I've touched her. A photographer's touch, though, precise and workmanlike. "Good. Now hold that pose."

"Cheese," she says.

A click as the shutter opens, a pause for the camera sensor to absorb enough light, then it clicks shut.

The motor whirs, and another tongue of photo paper rolls out the camera's mouth.

A flap of bat wings in the dark cave of the abandoned movie studio.

"At least you can tell it's me this time," Melissa says after the photo develops. "The light's just not good enough in here."

"Maybe we can try the overhead lights again."

She shakes her head in the negative, and I know not to push her further. After I busted the arc light, it was hard enough to get her to agree I could visit the studio again.

"I have an idea," she says.

It's taken me almost two weeks to reach this point.

Each day at school, my backpack had been heavy with my newly purchased Kodak Instamatic, along with a high-beam flashlight I borrowed from our apartment building's maintenance closet.

All in the hopes Melissa would invite me to return to her house.

We spend a little more time together at school now, but with an unspoken distance. Since we are both sketchbook misfits in Art, basically recognized as loners, we're already a topic for teasing or snide remarks. Being linked together wouldn't make us stronger: instead, we'd be twice the target.

The biggest change was that I started walking with her at lunch as she followed the perimeter of the school grounds. We barely speak during these times. Sometimes I keep pace with her; sometimes I fall behind. Observers might assume we are two people who had the same idea of getting exercise, and occasionally crossed each other's orbit.

As the bell rings to signal the end of lunch, we might exchange a few quick phrases.

Last Friday, I hinted about the weekend. I had nothing to do. We'd have a lot more free time to talk or (bringing this in as if the idea just occurred to me) maybe explore the movie studio. What do you say?

She said no, without volunteering a reason. We went separate ways to different classes.

As the memory grew distant, I started to worry that I'd invented the whole place—in that active, sad imagination my dad attributed to me. Melissa lives in an ordinary house, with windows that open onto a regular back yard.

Perhaps Melissa simply didn't want a lengthy weekend visit. It would be much easier to meet in that limited afterschool span between 3:30 and about 5, when we've escaped the scrutiny of teachers and (worse!) our peers, and before either of our mothers have returned home from work.

When I mentioned that possibility—stressing that I couldn't stay long, needed to get home for dinner—I got a Maybe Later. My next attempt I got a Maybe Tomorrow, which near the end of the week became Maybe Today, if the weather gets better.

It had rained during lunch, and we were forced to spend our break indoors. In Social Studies at 2:00, I looked out the window to see sunlight streaming through thinning clouds.

After school, we follow the old pattern. Separate seats on the bus, and I exit at her stop. A long walk down the quiet road to her house, approaching the painted "mansion" entryway, which Melissa unlocks for us. Sodas in the kitchen ("Do *try* not to wreck the place this time, Brendan"), then some small talk in her room (the math test coming up; a production of *Our Town* neither of us wish to audition for; the odd spectacle of Ryan and Amy, a clingy couple who seem to rely on each other's limited intelligence, to the point where we've dubbed them "One-Brain").

Melissa controls the agenda. She knows I want to visit the studio, but doesn't mention the possibility. As we talk, I deliberately avoid checking my watch—even as I realize time is running short.

I start to feel like a fraud. I'm joking with Melissa like a friend, but I'm also the guy who previously searched through this very room, half-planning to steal any souvenir that wasn't nailed down. I'm a ruthless, obsessed fan of her father's films. Melissa can see right through me. She's going to throw me out of her house.

Instead, Melissa stands and goes to the file cabinet. She unlocks the top drawer with a small key, reaches inside and pulls out a red plastic flashlight.

"I brought one, too," I say, taking it from my backpack.

I push aside my doubts and self-reproach and eagerly follow Melissa to the end of the upstairs hallway, to the unfinished door with the eyelet latch. She clicks on her flashlight, and I do the same as we make our way along the musty, tight corridor.

In *The Stone Stairway,* Samantha Goodwin searches for her husband, who seems to have been swallowed up by the strange house they've visited to escape a rainstorm. A bookshelf slides aside, and she discovers a secret passageway that leads to a hidden room. The Death Room.

Previously, Melissa and I had walked through this corridor in darkness. This time, my flashlight illuminates a repeating pattern in the peeling wallpaper: small ovals, with circles in the center. Like eyes.

In the movie, if you watch carefully, two of them blink.

At the end of the corridor, Melissa pulls a thin chain that triggers the intermittent set of lights along the staircase that leads down into the studio. In the earliest film, iron wrought torches were spaced along the descent; in *Spider House* these became light fixtures, and occasional archways were added to adorn the path to Count Verlock's basement coffin.

Melissa pauses at the foot of the stairway, next to the podium that controls the overhead arc lamps. I'm hoping she's gotten over her fright from our previous visit. We'd see so much better with one of the spotlights.

She walks past the podium, toward the dark studio sets.

Melissa leads me past several partitioned areas, until we reach a set that simulates a family living room. A sofa stretches beneath a curtained pair of windows. I point my flashlight at the cushion where Marion Ferguson sits in *The Haunted Oak*. A coil spring emerges from torn fabric, and a thick layer of dust dulls the blue material into gray.

A crash of glass, and a large tree limb breaks through the curtains above the sofa, loose branches wriggling like fingers that grasp at Mrs. Ferguson's screaming face.

I tell Melissa I want to show her something, test a theory. We cross the 60s shag rug and slide between the coffee table and the sofa.

"Let me hold your flashlight a second." I concentrate both beams on the curtains behind the sofa. "Pull one of them aside."

She agrees, since I'm letting her move things around instead of charging forward myself. She reaches above the sofa.

In movies, when a hand moves slowly toward a closed curtain, a tremulous violin might play on the soundtrack, or an urgent discordant tapping of piano keys.

Wouldn't it be awful if a homeless person had broken in here? Or maybe an escaped patient from the facility in nearby Gadsden. He's been here for years, hiding behind partitions, living in a lunatic world of shadows and false rooms. He heard us visit weeks ago, and has waited ever since for these two unsuspecting teenagers to return. The man is hungry, and cruel.

Melissa grips one of the curtains, tugs it aside.

A square hole in the partition wall, with a small crawlspace behind. No glass. "Proves my theory," I say, waving the flashlights over the empty space. "When the tree limb crashes into the house, they kept the curtains closed on purpose. You *hear* glass shatter, but your dad avoided the cost of a broken window. He was smart."

Melissa nods. She leans over the couch, placing her hands on the lower ridge of the hole so she can peer inside.

I wonder about the sturdiness of the false wall. The ridge might not support her weight, and she could tumble through to the space behind. Into a storage area, with loose nails and screws and razor blades. And fragments of shattered light bulbs, to produce dramatic sound effects in that long ago film.

The vagrant huddles down there, tiny lacerations on his face and along his arms. He has wedged shards of glass deep beneath his fingernails, extending them into claws.

"Let's look at another location," I say, returning Melissa's flashlight. Other than the false window, the living room is a fairly unimaginative set. The antique store from *The Crooked Frame* has occupied my mind recently, and that elaborate interior set is adjacent.

As we step into the set with our flashlights, we are burglars breaking into a shop after hours. The floor is crowded with the end tables and vases and knickknacks that the customer nearly trips over in the film. In one area the shelving has been pushed aside to make room for two chairs and circular table draped with a purple, gold-fringed cloth. A crystal ball sits in the center of the table.

"An antique store, later used as a séance room." I move to the back wall of the set, where a top shelf still contains a set of books, a teapot, and a plastic heart. "The camera's missing. Good thing I brought my own."

I reach into my backpack and pull out the Instamatic.

"Find something," I tell Melissa. "Find something cool to hold up, and I'll take your picture."

"I have an idea," she says after my two failed attempts at photography. "There's another prop we can use. One with better lighting."

She points to the staircase, its weak intermittent lights visible against the back wall of the house. I tell her I like the idea, but we'd have the same problem. "The lights are spaced too far apart. Still won't be strong enough to give us a good exposure."

"Up the stairs, then outside."

Immediately, I realize she's right. The front entryway will be the perfect backdrop for a photograph. I would have thought of it to begin with, if I hadn't wanted so badly to visit the studio again, to see more of the sets and props I'd only glimpsed during my previous visit.

We cross the studio floor, ascend the stone stairway into the corridor of watching eyes. Through the house and out the front door.

Instead of stopping at the entryway, Melissa walks to the side of the house. I'm holding the camera and want to take a quick photo of the front doors, but she's fast-walking and I have to hustle to keep up. We turn the corner, and I get my first glimpse of how far back the property stretches. The studio warehouse is like a metal mountain that has grown out of the ground behind the house. The walls are aluminum siding reinforced with steel girders. No windows, but with ventilation slits lined around the middle section. The slant roof is metal also, with more evidence of rust and weather-fading than the support walls.

A metal mountain? No, it is more like a spaceship turned on its side, half of it buried in the earth where it crashed behind the house. Imagine the terrifying noise, the incredible shaking of the ground that would have wakened residents in the middle of the night. What would it be like to open your curtains and see the windows blocked over by the undercarriage of an alien craft?

A perfect subject for a photograph, though I'd have to step far back to get more of it in the frame. I survey the surrounding field…

And notice what Melissa has taken me to see.

"It's the one from the poster I gave you," she says.

A tree can bear its age better than most living things, certainly better than man-made objects. Melissa stands beside the massive tree I recognize from *The Haunted Oak*. Fall leaves litter the base of its trunk, with clusters of orange and red and yellow still hanging from overhead limbs. These colors soften the monstrosity I recall from the film, its bare limbs scratching at winter clouds, crosshatching the nighttime moon. But the hideous shape is still there, partly up the trunk: a knot or burl that twists humanoid features into the bark, approximating a distorted and screaming face.

In Bud Preston's film, a witch once hanged from a limb of this tree, and in her dying breaths she cursed the owners of the property and their descendants. As midnight wind whistles through bare branches, a modern-day family hears something like an ancient whisper. Family members and friends gradually disappear; instead of a dead body, broken tree limbs appear beneath the open door of teenage son's car, or fill the rocking chair where the missing grandmother usually sat. New voices join the tree's ancient whisper.

The youngest daughter misses her siblings terribly, and one night she hears tapping against her bedroom window. The dry scratch of branches against glass. Whispered voices say, *Let me in.*

Grandmother? *the girl says as she gets out of bed and wanders to the curtained windows.* Kenneth? Is there someone else with you? I think I hear someone else.

"Go ahead," Melissa says. "Take the picture."

She stands next to the tree, the face in the trunk nearly parallel with her own. I pull back, trying to get as much of the tree into the shot as I can, then snap the picture. "One more," I say, catching the photo as it whirs out of the Instamatic. Before that picture has a chance to develop, I move closer and kneel to the ground.

I'm trying the technique I learned from the *Monster Project* article, where unusual camera angles add atmosphere to the composition. The viewfinder frames Melissa and the tree from below. I tilt the camera slightly to the side, adding an additional distortion.

"Make your face match the one in the tree," I suggest.

Melissa widens her eyes, opens her mouth in a combination snarl and scream.

The camera clicks, then whirs out another square of paper.

I won't let her see either picture until they've fully developed. I flap them in the open air as the images fade into permanence.

The long shot is fine, capturing a good mix of colors. Melissa stands perfectly straight beside the tree.

"Here's a good picture of you, finally." I hand her the close-up with the distorted angles, and her face screwed up in a grimace.

"I look horrible," Melissa says, and laughs.

We don't go back inside, since it's too close to the time I'm supposed to leave. Although a chill remains after the day's earlier storm, the sun makes the temperature bearable. The ground is too damp to sit on, but Melissa takes me further from the house, to a line of trees at the outskirts of the family property. A section of rock juts from the ground, forming a rough surface that approximates a bench.

A few pockets of water sit in the natural indentations, but they are easy enough to avoid. The rock feels cool and hard where I sit, but it's mostly dry.

I put the photographs and camera in my pack to keep them safe. The haunted tree seems ordinary from this distance, but the movie studio behind the house looks even more like a crashed spaceship.

Melissa doesn't speak. It's a spot of contemplation for her, I realize, which suggests how different we are. For me, it would be better to spend spare hours in the movie studio—a much better place to daydream than an outdoor spot, no matter how scenic.

"I never really knew my father." Her voice seems loud after the extended silence, but she actually speaks softly. The tone of sharing a secret. "I wish I had more stories to tell about him, but he died when I was still a baby."

"I'm sorry. I don't want to bring up sad memories."

"I don't have any memories at all."

You have all the movies, *I want to tell her.* You should treasure them the way I do.

As curious as I've been, until now I've avoided asking personal questions about her father. I talked about his movies, certainly, but not him as a man.

He seems bigger than life to me. A filmmaker, and not some girl's father.

"Does your mom ever mention him?"

"Oh sure." A half-smile. "Not things I'd repeat in polite company."

"My mom never says anything negative about my dad. But once they separated, they were *really* separate. In different states, but they might as well be on different planets. Universes, even."

She nods, but I feel like I've said the wrong thing. My father's on another planet, metaphorically, yet I can still reach him by phone. Her father's in a grave.

No new subject occurs to me. The rock feels tough beneath me, and as I reposition myself, I accidently put my hand in one of the indentations filled with water.

The silence extends, and now a change in topic would seem forced. *Hey, have you done your math homework?*

Or, worse, to suddenly realize it's getting late. *Oops, gotta go!* Bailing out, just as the conversation gets awkward.

Despite Melissa's hesitance to talk about her family, this might be the right moment for it. There are things you won't say about your parents at school, and it's wrong to say them in the home they've made for you, too. Even when her mom's at work and can't overhear, maybe unkind words can seep into the walls, to be triggered later during a heated argument or whispered out in those weak-willed moments before sleep.

"Is it tough for you," I finally say. "Living with just your mom?"

"We're fine. I get a lot of time to myself, which I like."

"Exactly!" The agreement comes out a little strong, and I tone down the rest of my reaction. "That's how I feel, too. Gives me a lot of independence."

"My father, though..." Melissa lowers her gaze, as if avoiding the house and the studio that battens on the back of it. She avoids me also, speaking only to the ground. "I don't know what my life would be like if he was still here. I'd always assumed it would be worse."

"From what your mom says?"

She doesn't answer.

I think about the life of a temperamental genius, underappreciated by the public, his films underfunded and poorly reviewed. His wife couldn't make up for that neglect. After a while, she'd probably stop trying.

"He was my father." Melissa lifts her head and turns slightly toward me. "I've never met anyone who wanted me to *like* him."

"Oh."

She caught me off guard. Such a nice thing for her to say, with genuine appreciation in her expression. The conversation had grown so serious, almost intimate. And it occurred to me that I'd also asked to take her photograph—another moment that signals a big step forward in a friendship. A relationship.

"Your dad's movies are really special to me," I say. "Maybe you'd like to see some of the magazine articles I've collected about him? I could bring a few to school. Or here."

She nods. Says yeah. Sure.

I can't stop myself from thinking of her as this young girl with a legendary father. She has to appreciate him, because she's literally spent her life in a haunted house—haunted in the most magical, cinematic sense, the way only a movie nerd like me can honestly appreciate. At the same time I worry that, in the process of idolizing her father and his films, I'm losing sight of Melissa as a friend.

In my defense, I'm not used to long-term friends. My mom's job moved me from town to town, school to school. For me, relationships didn't last; it was only the movies that remained constant.

"You better go." Melissa seems distant now, like she wants to be alone, but maybe I'm reading too much into her words. She's simply offered a gentle reminder that I've got a long walk ahead of me.

I'm late getting home, and Mom greets me at the door like she's stood there waiting the whole time.

"You should always let me know where you are, Brendan. Give me your friend's phone number, so I can call if I have to."

I think fast. "I wasn't with Geoff. I went to the County Library after school, to get some stuff for a research project." I heft my backpack, still heavy with the camera and flashlight, knowing it will look like it's full of library books. I'm safe, as long as Mom doesn't call my bluff and check inside. "It's due tomorrow, or I would have waited."

"When did you get the assignment?" she asks.

My answer needs to be bad enough to trigger one of her automatic lectures. "Two weeks ago."

"You know better than that. I've told you, if you do a little bit each day, those big assignments are much easier. When I get an important project at work, I set small deadlines for myself along the way, and make steady progress."

Good. She's distracted, and forgot about my being late.

"I'll get it done," I tell her. "I just need time alone."

Before I head up to my room to work on my non-existent research paper, I see several white cartons on the kitchen table. Chinese takeout, which Mom knows is my favorite. Maybe she has good news to share. Maybe she's just being nice.

"Thanks, Mom." I pile generous portions of fried rice and Hunan Chicken on a paper plate. She gives me a quick hug, then tells me it's okay to eat in my room, which makes me feel even more guilty.

Instead of the non-existent research paper, I write a few more pages of my movie script.

Again, I know the film will never get made. Still, to keep the illusion alive, I confine myself to available materials.

Just as Melissa is the only person who could play the film's heroine, I have to cast myself as the male lead. The house's owner, perhaps. A creepy butler, or nephew to the mad scientist. I figure it out as I write:

VOICE (off screen): Yes. I'm here.

MELISSA jumps in fright. She drops the picture frame, and the glass shatters.

MELISSA: Oh, I'm so sorry. I'll clean it up.

MEDIUM SHOT, LOW TO THE GROUND as MELISSA kneels to gather the broken fragments. The MAN's feet and legs are visible in the shot, where he stands behind her.

MELISSA POINT OF VIEW as she lifts the picture frame. She's stacked the shards of glass over the photograph, and moves the pieces gently down to uncover the picture. It's not a portrait of a spider, as she earlier thought, but of an old man in a lab coat.

MELISSA [wondering if she'd hallucinated]: That's not what I saw...

MAN: I wish I could help you. I've been in an accident.

OVER THE MAN'S SHOULDER. He wears a robe or smoking jacket, and his hands are in the pockets. MELISSA turns her head towards him.

MELISSA POV, from the ground looking up at the MAN. He slowly removes the right hand from his pocket.

MAN: My name's BRENDAN VERLOCK. Forgive me if we don't shake hands. [His hand is wrapped in a thick bandage that goes all the way up his arm and disappears beneath the robe sleeve.]

MELISSA [standing; quickly explaining herself]: I didn't break in. The door was open. Somethi— (correcting herself) some*one* was chasing me. At least, I thought so...

BRENDAN: I'm glad my home can offer you shelter.

MELISSA: Oh, what you must think of me. [She straightens her hair, smoothes the front of her blouse.] I show up out of nowhere, and then break the first thing I touch. [She offers the broken picture frame, then realizes he can't take it from her—because his left hand is also heavily bandaged. She sets the picture on an end table.]

BRENDAN: That's my uncle in the photograph. If he were here, he'd welcome you warmly. So I try to follow his example.

SPECIAL EFFECTS SHOT: A close up of the damaged photograph, and the UNCLE's impassive face, which then DISSOLVES TO: his nephew BRENDAN's younger but similar face, which attempts a weak smile.

BRENDAN: You may stay here tonight, if you like. But there are rules to this house. There are places where you cannot go. Understood?

My castle-in-the-sky movie idea would begin with the dining room and fireplace area, and maybe the living room set as well, but the MELISSA character would be forbidden to visit the upstairs rooms or, especially, the basement.

I could use the Polaroid to take a picture of myself. Wear old-age makeup or a paint a beard onto the photo to turn me into the character's uncle.

I set the script aside for a while, finish a bit more of the fried rice remaining on my plate, then I write a brief letter to my dad: *A quick hello from your favorite and only son. Enclosed please find the evidence, since you didn't believe me.*

I put three photographs into the envelope.

A Shocking Twist

Today, I anticipate a shocking twist.

The kind of thing where the poster would announce in bold yellow letters: *Do NOT Tell Your Friends about this Film's ELECTRIFYING SECRET!*

Now we are taking a bus to the next town. Melissa has promised me a surprise. She won't tell me anything about our destination, but I know it will be good.

She is pleased with me. I shared the recent pages from my script, which she has begun to refer to as "our movie." On two more occasions, I've visited her house and movie studio—this time aided by an electronic lantern I bought at the local Music/Pawn Shop. The battery on the lantern was an enormous 6-volt cube that helped produce an impressive spread of light.

During one of the visits, I placed the lantern on the tabletop of the Séance Room, then pointed out some of the "occult" items in the shelf behind where Madame Olga sat. I assumed her thick Hungarian accent and borrowed some of the film's dialogue.

Sit, child. Do not tamper with the special ingredients in these jars. *(Here, I waved at the various dusty containers, some filled with ordinary kitchen spices, others with plastic plants that had been painted or cut into small pieces so they'd resemble exotic herbs).* Some could make you fall in love. Some could make you commit murder. One mixture might restore your youth, where another might transform you into a withered hag. Only I know the beneficial combinations, and I am not inclined to share them with you now. You seek knowledge, do you not? *(I nodded expectantly at Melissa, prompting her to speak, but she didn't have a response ready).* Oh, a shy one, are we? Well, place your fingertips against the crystal. Close your eyes, and I will attempt to discern your question. Now remember, I cannot make any promises. The spirits do not always cooperate. Either way, my fee is still the same.

The next visit, I set the lantern on a low rectangular table with manacles attached, a winding rope winch at one end: the torture rack from *The Dungeon of Count Verlock*. As the Count explains: *When people lie on this bed, they do not sleep so well, eh?*

In the corner, beneath another set of manacles bolted to the wall, lay a heap of plastic bones from a disassembled medical skeleton, scattered amidst scraps of clothing. I informed Melissa this dungeon was also the Death Room from *The Stone Stairway*, her father's first movie.

Don't you remember the ending? *I said.* Let me help you reenact it. Take the lantern and hold it ahead of you, glancing at the walls as if searching for clues. Your husband has disappeared in the house, but you saw a sleepwalking man walking away from you. The man—or is it a ghost?—opens a secret door. He leads you through a passage then down a stone stairway to this basement room.

Keep looking. But save that pile of bones for last. Bring the light closer. Reach out to one of the bones, pick it up, and recoil in horror as it crumbles in your hand. *(Melissa did a great job miming the scene, following my directions perfectly).* Now this is my cue to enter. *(I step quickly off the set, then walk in slowly, assuming a somber voice:)* I see you've found your husband. This has been a long night, hasn't it? For him...and for you. That clothing around the bones. You recognize it. The overcoat your husband wore, the night your car broke down and you sought shelter in my mansion. Try touching that other piece of cloth. Perhaps the texture will jog your memory. It's old and faded to rags, but it's familiar isn't it, Samantha Goodwin?

Your nightgown, from the night you died. Exactly thirty years ago... when I killed you and your husband both. *(My next cue, the character's maniacal laugh—which I overplayed, hamming it up until it prompted a real laugh from both of us.)*

We call her home Budget House now. These were special times for me, inhabiting the sets and props from my favorite movies—an amazing museum I never expected I'd get to enter. I'm so grateful she's allowed me to visit, and I know she appreciates how I've brought her closer to her past, closer to the father she never really knew. I've been the perfect tour guide, reenacting her family heritage for her.

A heritage that had been so close to her, yet had remained inaccessible.

She reveals nothing about her surprise during the bus ride. "Just wait," she says. "You'll like it."

"Better than the studio? Because I don't see how you can top that."

"Different."

We sit together on a hard seat-bench near the middle of the bus, opposite the side exit doors. I keep looking out the windows for clues.

"It's a movie thing, right?" Because at the back of my mind, I half worry she's simply taking me to a favorite ice cream parlor or pizza joint.

"You'll like it," she repeats, which almost satisfies me. I mean, she knows me well enough by now—pretty much everything I like is connected with the movies.

We pass a sign announcing the city limits to Gadsden. A cemetery becomes visible on the left.

Maybe she's taking me to see her father's grave. I wonder what's carved into his tombstone. It should include his full name and the "Budget" nickname. And beneath the dates: Filmmaker, Husband, Father. Instead of an angel or cross on the stone, a carved image of a film reel.

Considering the negative impressions her mother has reinforced over the years, Melissa might never have visited her father's gravesite. Now, with my encouragement, she'll pay him proper respect. She'll speak to the stone: *Father, this is my friend Brendan. He knows a lot about your movies. He's taught me to appreciate them, and you.*

The bus stops a short ways past the cemetery, and a few people exit. We remain seated.

A few turns, and some people get on at the next stop.

"A couple more blocks," Melissa says.

The bus soon makes a turn onto a cobbled road, driving past a guard booth and up a steep incline. We pass parking lots on either side, and a long low building looms at the top of the hill.

A medical facility.

As I mentioned before, in the small town of Graysonville, a lot of the stores double up: video store and tanning salon, music rental and pawn shop.

The same was true the next town over. Add another combined business to the list: Evergreen HealthCare and Senior Community. The building wasn't really a hospital, but it housed a few doctor's offices. One wing was a retirement community, and also included rehab nurses to help people of any age learn to speak again after a stroke, or walk again after a car accident.

In the wing with the doctor's offices, one section was closed off behind a mesh gate. I knew about it, because other kids made a standard joke if you said or did something stupid: *You'll end up living in the crazy side of Evergreen.*

Not a place for the criminally insane—those folks would go upstate to a heavily guarded facility. This area housed people who weren't a danger to others, but might be to themselves. Recovering alcohol or drug addicts. People with a benign mental illness or limitation, unable to function in society.

In the crazy side of Evergreen, although the residents were harmless, they weren't allowed to leave.

But they could have visitors.

We approach a circular Information Desk, and Melissa gives her name to the seated attendant.

"He's expecting us," she says.

The woman adjusts her bifocals, staring at each of us in turn, then down at a clipboard. She's a thin red-headed woman, about fifty years old and wearing a lot of makeup that does nothing to soften her expression. "He doesn't get many visitors."

"I called ahead."

"Uh-huh." She flips the clipboard around and sets it on the raised countertop. "Sign here. Both of you."

There's no name listed on the indicated row: just a room number. Melissa signs and writes the date and time, and I add my signature beneath hers.

"You'll have to leave your backpacks."

We pass them over the counter. The attendant attaches a numbered clothespin to each, then gives us a cardboard tag as a receipt.

"Now use this marker and write your name on these labels." As we fill them out, peel off the backing and stick them to our shirts, the woman recites a list of prohibited items. "No food or drink. No sharp objects, including pens or pencils. No metal. No money. No outside medications."

I hand her my wallet.

"Turn your pockets inside out, son. Let me see."

I comply, even though she doesn't make the same demands of Melissa.

"Now, remember you're speaking to a person, no matter what's wrong with him. If he asks for something, just tell him you're not allowed. If he says the doctors and nurses are mean to him, even that they're trying to poison him or smother him at night, just nod your head and change the subject. They all say things like that, to gain your sympathy. He'll also tell you he wants to go home. You can remind him that he *is* home. He should be used to that by now."

She aims the lecture mostly at me, so I gather Melissa's heard it all before. I wonder how many other times she has been here.

Melissa still hasn't revealed the identity of the resident we've come to visit. I can make only one guess, though it seems impossible.

At different schools, if teachers found out what kinds of movies I liked, they'd tell me those trashy horror stories would warp my mind. My mom sometimes offered a gentler version of the same notion, and recently my dad had followed suit. *Maybe you should spend less time with those films, Brendan, now that you're older. Make more friends, play sports, that kind of thing.*

Apparently they're worried I spend too much time in a fantasy world.

Well, what about the adult who devoted his life to *making* these kinds of movies? Wasn't it more likely that *he'd* be the one to lose touch with reality? With each creative effort, Bud Preston built a world where supernatural horrors could walk among us. Perhaps the challenges of each production chipped away at his sanity—until the films became real, and life was the illusion.

We didn't visit her father's grave, because there *is* no grave.

His death was merely a cover story, intended to save his family from embarrassment. Better to pretend to the public that this maker of monster movies has died, than to reveal that he'd driven himself insane.

He's here, living in the crazy side of Evergreen. Melissa is taking me to meet her father.

Such was the scenario that unspooled in my imagination as we stepped off the bus and went through sliding glass doors to enter the Evergreen facility.

Can you blame me? Melissa promised me a big surprise, and I imagined the biggest surprise of all. The kind of unexpected twist that makes a movie so memorable.

But instead of going to the left, past the doctor's offices and to the infamous gated wing, we go toward the nursing home section of the facility.

We are allowed to carry our backpacks. We don't need to sign in at a security desk.

Melissa leads the way down a corridor, past a small cafeteria. Opposite, a group of elderly residents congregate in a lounge area. A few of them stare glassily ahead at nothing, as still as the potted plants next to their wheelchairs. Several at a small table play a card game, and one woman angles her cards away from us as if we'd try to peek at them as we walked past.

We follow a sterile hallway lined with closed doors. Some of the doors have elaborate nametags and decorations: a needlepoint welcome sign, or pictures of grandchildren in heart-shaped frames. The door we approach is bare, but it's been left ajar.

I still grasp at the impossible hope that the resident will be Melissa's father. Even if he's older, and less sound of mind, he would retain some vague recollections of his filmmaking days. I could jog his memory, listing titles and reciting long passages of dialogue, and he'd know how much I loved his movies.

We step into the room. It's bright, and there's a standing wooden cupboard beside the entrance, and a half-size dresser with a television on top, but there are no flowers or picture frames or decorations. A floor curtain obscures most of the bed against the back wall, save for the lump of the resident's blanketed feet.

Melissa pulls part of the curtain aside. The resident lies with his back to us. "Knock, knock," Melissa says, and the man struggles to move.

An arm stretches from beneath the blanket, and the man turns his head on the pillow.

I wish Melissa had done more to prepare me.

Not her father in the bed.

A monster.

"My friend's name is Brendan. He knows a lot about you."

An arm reaches forward, but the hand at the end of the sleeve looks like a rotten eggplant, the purpled fingers bruised and swollen together into a horribly inflated lump. "My glasses," a scratchy voice says, and the arm swings to indicate an end table.

"Brendan, why don't you help him put them on?" Melissa takes the glasses from the table and offers them to me.

Imagine a normal pair of glasses that's been run over by a car and then fed through a meat grinder, and you'd come close to the bent and battered frame I now hold. It seems a miracle that the lenses are still intact. The nose bridge is bent at a right angle, so the eyeholes are strangely uneven. An extra bar extends from beside each lens, hinged to the metal arms that would attach to a person's ears. Like the rest of this device, the metal arms are uneven and misshapen.

Custom-made to fit a monstrous, misshapen head.

Melissa steps back, and I'm supposed to bring the glasses close to that terrifying face. Purple, like the hand, and with skin the texture of a deflated basketball. A swelling beneath the man's jaw twists his lips out of shape, and a devil's horn juts from his forehead. His nose is a puffy, bruised plum, and his uneven eyes are nearly buried beneath dark folds of swollen flesh.

I try to judge where the lenses should fit. I lean closer, guiding the metal arms of the frame towards the odd protrusions that I hope are ears on either side of the man's head. They glisten like large wet lumps of grape chewing gum.

I must have hesitated, because I feel a soft squishy pressure against my elbow—the eggplant hand, guiding me forward.

It's so hard to look at him. I'm close enough that I see blood vessels near the surface of his rough skin, gray and red discolorations, a few brown moles with tiny sprigs of hair. I close my eyes even as I'm pressing the glasses into his face.

When I open my eyes, I'm startled afresh. The crooked mangled frames look comically incongruous, as if I'd put glasses on a shoe or on a pumpkin.

"Thank you, young man." The voice is similarly incongruous, a mockery of a refined gentleman's diction, emerging from a jutting mouth with lips that pucker towards the ceiling. Then his voice deepens to a bitter rasp: "You think it must be awful to be me.

Everywhere I look, I see people recoil in horror. You'd never trade places with me."

I'd recognized him almost immediately, of course—although he was older now, and the disease had progressed. The distortions of acromegaly seemed even more dramatic in person and in bright light, compared to how they appear onscreen. Nonetheless, it was undoubtedly Thomas Hendricks, the actor who played the title character of *The Twisted Face.*

My nervousness, I'd attribute to the unease anyone would feel in the presence of dramatic and unfamiliar illness.

That, and being starstruck.

When he quoted those lines from the film, all my nervousness vanished.

"It's really you," I sputtered. "Oh, such an honor to meet you Mr. Hendricks. *Twisted Face* is my favorite film."

"Call me Tommy." He's dressed in a pajama top, with a blanket pulled to the middle of his chest. The shape beneath the blanket suggests two different body types: a slender man on his left half, and an obese man on the right.

I wish I'd brought the Instamatic, so I could have my picture taken with him.

Without thinking, I reach out and shake his hand. The skin is softer than I expect, and my fingers almost sink into it. If I squeeze too hard, it might burst like a giant blister.

"You," I say in mock accusation to Melissa, who is smiling wider than I've ever seen her. Back to Hendricks: "She wouldn't tell me who I was coming to visit."

My smile must mirror hers, with an added touch of goofy fanboy. I recite one of the Police Chief's lines, and Hendricks supplies his character's response.

"Tell me what it was like to make the film," I say next.

"How much is it worth to you?" He adjusts his voice slightly, to match the mask-muffled shopkeeper in *The Crooked Frame.*

I decide not to play the customer in that film—failing the shopkeeper's test of his honesty, and gaining a haunted camera as punishment. "Any price you ask," I say. "I'd *love* to hear about it."

"Well, those days are long past. A lifetime ago."

He tells me some details he can recall, mostly confirming what I'd read in movie magazines. They completed *The Twisted Face* in five days with a small cast and crew. Bud Preston handwrote script changes and distributed new pages each morning. Set construction would occur between takes, or late at night after the actors went home.

As Hendricks talks, I quickly adjust to his appearance, almost forgetting the deformities. Even though the information he conveys isn't new to me, it feels special hearing it from someone who lived through it.

Still, I long to hear a fresh detail. Something personal. "What did you *think* about the movie?"

"Well, Bud worked everybody pretty hard." He looks at Melissa now, as if seeking permission to discuss her father. "The hard work was worthwhile. I knew we were making a unique film."

"How was your visit?"

Mom is relaxing with the newspaper, but I see she also has a stack of folders on the sofa cushion next to her. Even when she's not at work, she still thinks about it.

I do my best to act cool, even though I'm still glowing after the meeting Melissa arranged with Thomas Hendricks. "It wasn't what I expected."

"How so?"

I shrug out of my jacket and start to lay it across the back of the armchair, but Mom shoots me a cold glance. I go and hang it up in the hall closet, then come back to continue the conversation.

"I was hoping we'd go to a prison or somewhere cool, but our group ended up at a nursing home." I plop down in the armchair, which came with the apartment: it's a boxy wooden frame with ugly green-brown cushions, but it's surprisingly comfortable. "I thought I'd be awkward around old people, but it was okay."

"You never used to do extra credit assignments. I'm proud of you."

"Geoff was in my group. He wanted to go."

It sounded plausible that I'd do unnecessary schoolwork to keep my mythical friend happy. I'd gotten good at these kinds of stories: mixing in some truth, changing the names. There actually was an extra credit assignment, but it was a set of algebra problems instead of a Social Studies project. Further down the line, "Geoff" and I would have a falling out, so Mom would never have to meet him.

"I still need to write the journal entry. That's how we get full credit."

Mom nods. "Best to do that while everything's still fresh in your mind." She's set the newspaper section down to talk, an illusion of giving me her full attention, but now she acts like she's just noticed the work folders beside her. "Listen, Brendan. I waited here because I wanted to be home when you got back. But I have some work I could do at the Base. Would you be all right for a couple hours? Maybe have a Swanson or a frozen pizza?"

"Sure. Like I said, I have school stuff to finish." On other occasions, I might have sulked to make Mom feel a bit guilty for working on Saturday. Such moments were like currency for a teenager, later exchanged for reluctant permissions: I can stay out late on a school night, because *you're never home anyway!* Not too logical, but it doesn't need to be.

Except I'd already stolen a break earlier today, visiting (I could barely believe it!) Thomas Hendricks in Evergreen. Since I'd lied about it, Mom actually got credit in the Guilt Bank instead of me.

"I wasn't expecting you," My dad sounds a little distracted. I imagine he's holding the phone receiver between his chin and shoulder. keeping both hands free to fix a broken shelf or replace light bulbs in a ceiling fixture.

"Mom went into work, so I thought I'd call."

"Everything okay?"

"Yeah. More than okay."

"Good."

"Did you get the pictures I sent?"

"Uh huh." I hear a metallic clatter in the background. "They're a bit blurry, aren't they?"

"Not all of them. There's two outside. Anything look familiar?"

"That girl? Never met her, but it's hard to judge, with her making a face like that."

"Not *her,* Dad. The tree. The face in the *tree.*"

"There's no face in the tree."

"Look again."

A sigh. A shuffling of papers. "I got it. Don't know what you're talking about."

"There's a face in the bark. Don't you recognize it?"

"Let me guess. Jesus? Elvis?"

"You're not even looking at it."

"I'm holding the picture right here, Brendan." Another rustle of paper near the phone. "All trees look like this."

"No, they don't. That one's from the movie, *The Haunted Oak.*"

"Hmmm." A pause to humor me. Maybe turning the picture sideways, then back. "A little similar, I guess."

"Not a 'little similar.' It's the same tree. The *exact* one they used in the movie."

"Now Brendan..."

"And the other pictures, too. I know they're blurry—"

"...don't know why you're so worked up..."

"—but she's holding the stop-motion model from *Spider House.*"

"...over a tree."

My dad talks over me, and since we're on the phone I have to guess at his expression. Probably that sympathetic downward look whenever my feelings were hurt about a broken toy or spilled cereal, but mixed with the skeptical one he'd used at Mom when they argued and he didn't figure she had a right to be angry. Since we've been apart for a while, it's hard for me to picture him accurately. That's the kind of relationship I have with my dad now, unfortunately: conversations spread out over weeks, illustrated with images that may no longer be accurate.

The story of my meeting with Thomas Hendricks might get a better reaction, but I'm afraid he'll once again decide not to believe me. I'm even worried, in the back of my mind, that he'll say he doesn't know who Thomas Hendricks is, or will deny that *The Twisted Face* is one of our favorite movies.

In the background, I hear a different voice. Radio or television, I assume, but it seemed like it asked my dad a question.

"I'll just be a minute more," he says, not to me. There's a hollow bang of wood, then a metallic chime.

"Alicia's here," my dad explains. "We're fixing dinner."

Who's Alicia?

"You haven't mentioned her before," I say.

"Just a friend." He whispers, like he doesn't want this Alicia person to hear. Obviously, she thinks of herself as more than a friend. Not enough more for his son to know about, however.

Then, in his normal voice Dad says: "Call me again on Thursday, like usual."

I say "Okay" instead of goodbye, then I hang up the phone.

That evening after dinner, I write another segment of my script. I've changed how I envision it, slightly, since the Pawn Shop recently added an old Super 8 camera to their Electronics shelf, and I'm saving up money to buy it. Instead of my impossible idea of a full length feature, maybe I could actually manage to make a short film: ten minutes or so, with title cards to represent minimal dialogue—since the Super 8 doesn't have sound capabilities.

Even better, I could write scenes that didn't require dialogue at all, like the following dream sequence:

DARK.

CLOSE UP of MELISSA lying down, head on a pillow with a blanket pulled up to her neck. Camera ZOOMS BACK into a long shot, revealing she's asleep on the COUCH in the LIVING ROOM.

Closed CURTAINS cover the WINDOWS overlooking the COUCH.

CUT TO: the face of a CLOCK, its hands set to 11:59. HOLD, until the minute hand clicks to indicate midnight.

CLOSE UP of MELISSA again. Her eyes move rapidly, indicating troubled sleep. A slant of light illuminates her face, but a SHADOW crosses over it.

MEDIUM SHOT, revealing that BRENDAN VERLOCK stands next to the COUCH, watching her as she sleeps.

POINT-OF-VIEW shot (angle of MELISSA'S EYES, if they were open). BRENDAN VERLOCK towers over her, his arms hidden beneath his smoking jacket. He leans closer, and the camera tilts to the side to unbalance the framed image.

CLOSE UP of MELISSA. Her head in shadow, but a white shape moves to her brow: BANDAGED HAND #1, as BRENDAN VERLOCK gently pushes aside a wisp of her hair.

BANDAGED HAND #2 appears from the opposite edge of the frame. Then, impossible, BANDAGED HAND #3 enters the shot.

[MAKEUP or F/X] CUT BACK to MEDIUM SHOT: BRENDAN VERLOCK stands over sleeping MELISSA. He's framed from the back, and his smoking jacket spreads open like a cape. FOUR ARMS reach out from beneath each side of the jacket.

CLOSE UP of MELISSA, as one of the bandages falls off to reveal a black and bristled appendage, with a single talon instead of fingers [MAKEUP: SPIDER HAND #1]. A syrupy ichor drips from the appendage and lands on MELISSA's cheek. Her eyes open.

MEDIUM SHOT. Melissa SCREAMS in panic then sits up on the SOFA. Her hands search around her in the dark. BRENDAN VERLOCK is not there. She rubs at her cheek, as if to remove a stain. Eventually she calms herself, shakes her head and her lips form the words, "Just a dream."

THEN: the CURTAINS part suddenly as a [prop:] GIANT SPIDER LEG crashes through the WINDOW and into the house. [STUNT and F/X:] The SPIDER LEG grabs MELISSA, and pulls her out through the shattered window.

CUT TO: CLOSE UP of MELISSA sleeping, her eyes opening. The light of morning comes through OPEN curtains.

MEDIUM SHOT: BRENDAN VERLOCK walks into the room.

DIALOGUE CARD: "Did You Sleep Well?"

The Thief

Today I am a thief. I will once again be a guest in my friend's home, and I will betray her hospitality.

But I will not be greedy. I will take something small, and of no value.

We are in the police station set, in its newspaper office incarnation, and Melissa sits behind one of the reporter's desks, with our battery-operated lantern beside a dormant gooseneck lamp. An old typewriter dominates the desk top, which is stained with rings from various coffee cups.

A piece of paper curls out of the typewriter's platen. On the sheet in all caps Courier: MYSTERIOUS DEATHS REMAIN UNEXPLAINED

I'm in the side chair reserved for the suspect or the confidential source. I wait as Melissa reads the latest pages from my movie script.

As she nears the end, I point to the bottom of the page and explain what I mean by a *Dialogue Card:* "I've revised my initial concept, and I'm thinking of it more like a silent movie."

"Why would you do that?"

She means, I'm certain, "Why worry so much about the logistics? It's not like we'll actually be able to *make* this movie, silly."

So I tell her about the Super 8 camera I'm planning to buy, hoping she'll go along with the idea. "It's for grainy home movies, so there's no sound. But I figure it could be old and atmospheric, like a creepy documentary. We couldn't really make a feature film, so why not think about a short one? A one reeler, in movie speak."

Melissa lets my script pages fall to the desk. She shakes her head back and forth.

"I know it's dumb," I tell her. "I'd have raw footage with no equipment to edit it. And no projector to show the finished film. It's all hypothetical."

She shakes her head again.

Then she reaches into her pocket and pulls out a set of keys.

She lifts the electronic lantern then stands and crosses to the door at the back of the set. The Police Chief's office, or the Newspaper Editor's—identified by whichever stenciled title would hang on the window of frosted glass.

After trying a few keys, one of them finally clicks and she turns the knob.

In the Winchester House-style haunted logic of this defunct movie studio, any room could lay beyond the door. We could step back in time to a harlot's cramped apartment in London's Whitechapel, finding the crime scene exactly as Jack left it, Mary Kelly's corpse and entrails staining the bed and a piece of her heart still warm on the end table. We could descend into the underwater cave, where the Lake Monster dragged his unconscious conquests. Or we could travel light years in an instant, stepping foot on the Space Visitor's home planet, a glimmer of diamond dust on the red, cratered ground.

The last thing I expect to see is an actual office.

Except...why is there a working lock on the door? There's no need to secure a fictional character's stack of official documents, or a cash drawer filled with Monopoly money.

As we walk into the set I immediately get an odd sensation, and realize what's different about this location: it actually has a ceiling. Movie posters for *The Stone Stairway* and *Spider House* adorn the wall to my left, and I'm convinced it's a solid wall rather than a thin partition.

Melissa lifts the lantern and lets it illuminate patches of the room. I see a file cabinet that's pair to the one in her bedroom. A huge desk faces the door, with piles of papers obscuring its surface: some look like script pages, with handwritten changes in red pencil; others depict set designs or possible creature masks or special effects ideas. A few pages are broken up into smaller squares illustrated like comic book panels, and I recognize these as storyboards a director uses to visualize a film sequence.

At the corner of the desk sits a precarious stack of more than three dozen inch-thick booklets with construction-paper covers, fastened via metal clasps through the hole-punched pages. Movie scripts.

Beside the desk, a trash pail is filled with multiple tubes of rolled paper, and I deduce this is where Melissa retrieved the poster she gave me.

I let my own flashlight beam settle on the desk, trying to read some of the pages. Upside down, I see a typewritten list of items and a "Cost" column on the right. The figures corresponding to wood and fabric are circled in red, with the word "Cheaper" written in the margin. A "gray wig" entry is crossed out, with "Reuse from DCV" offered as explanation.

Dungeon of Count Verlock, maybe? There's a gray-haired old woman who warns the tourists not to visit the Count's castle on the hill.

I take a quick look at one of the storyboard pages. One panel depicts a hand reaching for a door knob, and the next contains a crude drawing of a woman's screaming face.

My flashlight shifts to the stack of scripts. The one on top has a white label on its blue cover. Beneath the layer of dust, I can make out a title, "THE WITHERED HAG." Typed beneath, "A Budget Studios Production."

I've never heard of this film before. I reach for the bound pages, planning to peel back the cover and start reading.

"Over here, Brendan."

In a daze, I don't respond. Melissa repeats herself, more insistent. She stands before a wide stretch of metal shelving along the wall behind the desk. My hand still hovers over the movie script until I see what she indicates with the raised lantern.

Her father's office also served as a secure storage area for studio equipment. A shelf holds several movie cameras and folded tripods. At eye level sits a contraption with a small viewer and empty hand-crank reels on either side: a film editor.

On the lowest shelf, there are replacement bulbs that we could use to restore the arc lamp that exploded during my first visit.

A wheeled cart in front of the shelf contains a bulky 16 millimeter projector. A collection of metal containers, round and flat, are stacked on the lower section of the cart.

"Do you think any of this stuff will still work?" Melissa asks me.

I'm dumbstruck, but manage to nod. "Technology doesn't go out of date that quickly." In those days—our family's Betamax VCR notwithstanding—this statement was generally true.

"Probably better than that Super 8 camera you were thinking about."

"A *lot* better." The cameras look intact. Dusty and worn down, as with most things here, but probably functional. My mind races ahead: I'll need to order fresh film, and should check the model number of each camera, and I'm *sure* Melissa will let me use them or she wouldn't have shown them to me, and does this mean that we really will make a film, and should it be *my* script, or the unfilmed script by her father, the one on the desk that Melissa *apparently doesn't even know she has...*

I gravitate toward the largest camera, fairly certain it's the same one I've seen Bud Preston standing next to in a behind-the-scenes magazine photo.

"Don't lift it. It's pretty heavy." Melissa steps in front of me, and she gives the camera a slight turn on the shelf to reveal the viewfinder and the lens. She points out the metal lever for the zoom function, and the compartment in the side where the film goes. I move closer, and my fish-eye face reflects in the dark lens.

Now a rush of creativity hits me. In my imagination, I mount the camera on its tripod, then move it to the Castle set to frame the long dining table and stone fireplace. I could seat the MELISSA character at the table, while my BRENDAN VERLOCK character serves a modest dinner. Cut to the fireplace, and a large tarantula drops from inside the chimney onto cold ashes. Then a second one drops. Next I would cut back to a long shot of MELISSA enjoying her dinner, with the fireplace in the background and out of focus. She eats, and makes small talk, and all the while the fireplace fills with more and more dark black shapes, slowly catching the viewer's attention. Then cut to the floor, where the tarantula scurries beneath her feet. I'd pivot the camera to follow the rubber arachnid as it creeps up the back of her chair. And then what if, what if... What if I could manage a scene where she's set down her fork for a moment, and a spider pushes aside the scoop of meat and climbs onto the tines. MELISSA, oblivious in conversation, lifts the fork to her mouth, and her morsel of food has eight wiggling legs...

Melissa interrupts my reverie. "Time to go," she says. "My mother gets home soon."

"I wish we could try the camera."

"Later. You still have to finish the script."

As Melissa tries to usher me out, I remember my less-admirable plan for today. I'd been so distracted by the wealth of treasures in the vault of Bud Preston's office, and the idea that maybe I actually *could* make a movie...

And now there isn't time.

Unless I act fast.

Stall her.

"I need the model number for the camera."

"We can do that next time. Come *on*."

Her voice pulls at me, but I resist.

"I need to make sure I can order film stock to fit it. The number's probably on the bottom. Oh, and—"

(Here, I apply a clever bit of misdirection...)

"—I'll need a pencil and paper to write it down."

She's in a hurry, and opens the top desk drawer to check for a pen or pencil. I pretend to help. There's plenty of paper here, but I move pages aside as if looking for a blank sheet.

I slide a storyboard page from beneath a pile and (it pains me to mutilate it!) fold it quickly and stuff it into my back pocket. The rustle of other pages should have covered any sound I'd made.

"Oh wait," I say in the guise of sudden inspiration. "I've already got paper to write on." I take my flashlight and step into the other room, where Melissa has left my script pages on the reporter's desk.

"Found a pencil," Melissa says when I return to her father's office. It's a golf pencil, with bite marks on the end, but there's a dull bump of lead that should do the trick.

It takes two of us to tilt the camera back, and I aim my flashlight to help locate a metal label on the bottom. I say the serial number out loud, so Melissa can help me remember it. We set the camera down, and I scratch the number on the back of one of my script pages.

In the moment, I'd been strangely pleased with myself—at how I improvised quickly, my movements smooth and undetected.

Flawless, like a professional thief.

Walking away from Melissa's home, I worry maybe I hadn't been so smooth after all.

She'd seemed agitated as we hurried back up the stone stairway and into the main house. I could attribute her nervous manner to the fact that I'd stayed later than usual; Melissa feared her mother might arrive home to catch the unauthorized visitor.

Maybe a hint of disappointment colored her reaction. She knew I'd stolen a page of her father's notes. It burned hot in my back pocket as I left Budget House. I'd tucked it there in a rush, and an incriminating edge of paper stuck out.

Is there something you want to give me, Brendan? Tell me now, return it before you leave, and I *might* forgive you.

She could be watching as I walk away. Did I unconsciously pat my back pocket, to reassure myself the item was still hidden there?

And what was on the page? I hadn't had the opportunity to examine it. What if it's some meaningless scribble, erased or crossed out and no clear connection to Bud Preston or his movies?

If I risked my friendship over nothing...

I'd experienced such a rush of excitement stealing that souvenir from the studio. Now that the adrenaline's worn off, I feel nervous and ashamed. I'm not usually this kind of person. I don't want to be this kind of friend.

Even though I'm far enough away from her house, I wait until I turn onto the lonely access road before I allow myself to inspect the stolen page.

I tug it gently from my pocket. Part of the page catches and rips slightly.

The paper is tissue-thin. Probably "Budget" Preston ordered the cheapest stock he could find. It's brown from age as if coffee has been spilled on it.

Standing in the middle of the road, I carefully unfold the page. The boxed comic-book style panels indicate this is a storyboard sequence, as I'd hoped. Unfortunately, only the first two boxes are filled in. The first depicts a simple stick figure that any child could have drawn, and an arrow pointing to indicate that he (or the camera?) moves to the right. The second panel shows two lines converging on a point: a road heading into the distance, maybe, but it's too abstract; there's no text beneath the box to clarify the image.

There's also no header to identify which film this sequence belongs to.

The diamond thief scaled walls, cut bars from a window, disabled a state-of-the-art security system, chloroformed two guards, and slid beneath motion-detection lasers, and escaped with his treasure before police could arrive. Upon examination, his diamond is worthless plastic.

Then I turn the page to catch a slant of early evening sunlight. In the upper right header, in faint blue ink, the Budget Studios logo appears.

That's something, at least. The logo, and the document's obvious age, should be enough to convince my dad that I've been telling him the truth.

Which is the only reason I took it. I wasn't stealing for myself, but to prove a point to my dad. I'm sure I can take the page back later, no harm done.

I shift the angle of the paper again, watch the logo seem to disappear and appear.

A rustle of gravel startles me, and I see a car in the distance. It takes me a moment to orient myself—to realize that I'm standing in the middle of a road—but I recover my wits and step aside.

It's a white sedan, with green lettering stenciled on the side. I hide the storybook page behind my back as the car approaches.

There's no shoulder to the road, so it's a tight fit. The woman behind the steering wheel is about my mom's age, and I try to recognize similarities to Melissa in her harsh features. She stares at me instead of the road as she drives alongside, and I'm afraid she will stop and try to talk to me.

The green lettering on the side door reads: EVERGREEN HEALTHCARE.

I hold my breath, and she drives past.

A new letter to my dad:

Here's an ORIGINAL [underscore, underscore] document from Budget Studios. Note the blue logo in the upper corner.

I tried to copy it at the library, but the blue ink doesn't show up in the Xerox. Please don't lose it, since I borrowed it from my friend's house. Use the enclosed envelope to return it.

NOW do you BELIEVE ME?

Love,
Brendan

The Rumored Boyfriend

Today I am the subject of rumor.

It's lunchtime, and Melissa and I walk the perimeter of the schoolyard. Departing from our usual practice, however, we keep pace with each other so we can talk. At times, we slow to a stroll.

"We've got to cool it for a while." Melissa is upset that her mother saw me on the road yesterday. Where else could I be coming, except from the Preston home? "She started asking me about my new boyfriend."

"But we're not..."

"I know, but that's the way she acts. Always reading into things."

"My dad jumped to the same conclusion."

We pause for privacy at the rusted fence at the far end of the school property. The other students don't play near here, since if a ball goes astray over the fence, it's lost for good. Melissa's silent for a moment, and I know she wonders why I mentioned her to my dad. I remind her that Dad and I watched movies together growing up. "I thought he'd be excited that I knew Bud Preston's daughter."

"Was he?"

"He seemed more excited by the prospect that I'd have a girlfriend." It feels weird to say this out loud. We are friends. She is a girl. It ends there. "Actually, he thinks I'm making the whole thing up."

"I'm a figment of your imagination." She seems amused at this idea, but also annoyed.

"Parents get things wrong," I say. "They make assumptions. They want to shape our lives into predictable patterns."

She looks at the ground and rubs the back of her ear as she considers what to say next. It's a shy gesture I haven't seen her make before.

"My mother got a *good* look at you," Melissa says. "She described you perfectly. I lied and told her we've never met."

This initially doesn't seem too much of an obstacle. We can still meet after school, like we've been doing. I'll be more careful to leave early, so I won't run into her mom's car again.

Melissa won't hear of it. "If she finds out now, Brendan, it'll confirm the worst of what she's already thinking. When my mother gets suspicious, she *notices* things."

I think about the spotless kitchen and living room of her house. Maybe her mother counts the cans of soda in the refrigerator, sees the inventory dwindle faster than it should. She finds a strange shoeprint in the front drive, dusts for fingerprints along the banister.

Perhaps Mrs. Preston placed a lock of her hair in the frame of the upstairs door leading to the movie studio. She checks, and the hair has fallen to the floor.

"We could meet at your house," Melissa suggests. "Or at the mall or something."

My expression drops before I can compose myself. I should say, *You're right. Your friendship is all that matters. I'll do whatever's necessary so I can spend more time with you.* But my obsession with Budget House takes over, my fear of losing the Studio behind it, and I know Melissa can read the disappointment in my face.

Terrible arguments run through my mind. Arguments that downplay our friendship, and concentrate on my own hardships—moving from town-to-town, uprooted from schools, my dad moving away—rescued by those films, those strange wonderful film memorialized in her family home. She *knows* how important that place is to me. How could she even consider taking it away?

And I admit to myself that I'm jealous. She's the one who got to grow up in a haunted house, instead of me. I want to yell at her, say she doesn't fully realize how lucky she is, say how angry I am about the way she strings me along, never giving me enough time among the sets and props and archives. The studio is a museum, a precious museum, and she *needs* me to tell her what everything's worth.

I want to spare her feelings, and I don't want to come across as an opportunistic jerk. No matter what I say, though, I can't hold back the resentment in my voice. She's angry, too, and we're both waving our arms excitedly as we talk.

From a distance, I'm sure it looks like we're having a lovers' quarrel.

"You're spending a lot of time with the weird girl."

Geoff may have called her "weird girl," but I know he thinks of me as equally strange—the nerdy new kid with no real friends. He's cornered me in the hall. I'm holding a red bathroom pass from English, but he's left the class without one. Geoff blinks at me. Perhaps it's my imagination, but I hear a faint scrape as his lid drags over the false eye, which lacks lubricating tears. The lid gets caught on the glass and it slows the lift, throwing it out of sync with the intact eye.

"New Guy has a girlfriend."

"She's not."

"Whatever," Geoff says. "Been a while since she's had regular company."

Behind his words I envision a trail of past friends, latched onto and then discarded. They're still here at school, watching the two of us bitterly as we walk the perimeter of the school yard during lunch. They wonder how our relationship might develop.

"I don't think of her that way."

"What, as pretty?"

"No," I respond without thinking, "I don't."

"Then why do you want to—"

He says something crude. A guy comment I shouldn't dignify with a response. I hadn't expected to run into him, and I should brush past and head back to class. As much as I don't like Geoff, I don't like my

English teacher either, so I guess that's why I lingered and let him draw me in. "No I don't," I say. "Don't want to do that to anyone right now."

"There's no other reason you'd spend time with her."

He's worse than I'd been that first week on the bus. I hadn't meant anything—just a careless observation about the strangeness of his eye. Now, Geoff is being cruel on purpose.

The best way to defend Melissa might be to reveal the secrets of Budget House, but they aren't my secrets to share. Certainly not with Geoff. He's a painfully average kid—lanky build, with wavy hair that never quite looks clean. His class comments are often clueless, but he has a reputation for being good-natured. Melissa and I decided that he gets away with things because of his eye. It reminds everyone in the school of his brief, sickly past—a time when they all rooted for him to get better. They're still in the habit of rooting for him, even when he doesn't deserve it.

"We see you get off at her bus stop sometimes."

The "We" bothers me. It indicates that Geoff and his buddies talk about me and Melissa. The two of us are the subject of rumor—and in high school, rumors are never kind. The more cruel and crude they are, the better.

"I'm not her boyfriend." It's the same phrase I used with my dad on the phone. Geoff turns his good eye toward me, a smirk of disbelief on his face, and I almost want to punch him. Instead, I try to stoop to his crude level. It won't matter what I say, as long as it stops the rumor. "If I were looking for a girlfriend, don't you think I could do better?"

As soon as I say these words, I regret my awful betrayal. Melissa and I were fighting, but there's no reason I should speak of her this way.

It's just me and Geoff in the hallway, yet I feel like the whole school is watching. Teachers and students alike decide I'm the worst friend in the world.

Surprisingly, Geoff doesn't react. He's following his own thread, and doesn't want to be distracted from his next pre-rehearsed cruelty.

"Yeah, you're going to her house after school. Some quick action, right? Before her mom gets back from the loony bin."

Now I definitely want to hit him. He's only slightly taller, and my fist could easily reach his jaw. I would punch the smug grin off his face.

I should aim higher, at the false eye. If I punch hard enough, I wonder if the glass would shatter. I'd twist my fist on impact, grinding the shards into my knuckles and tearing new scars into Geoff's scabbed-over eye socket.

"Stay away from me," I say. I push past him and return to English class where, unfortunately, our assigned seats are directly across from each other.

That night, I dream of hiding in a haunted house.

I'm lying in the dark crawlspace behind the living room window. The curtains over the sofa are closed, so nobody can find me.

But I've grown unaccountably nervous. I'm certain I'm no longer alone.

The worst thing I can do is move. Even the slightest sound would reveal my location.

I shift to a standing position, having to twist my body awkwardly to fit in the tight space. My hands steady against the thin partition wall, and I feel it buckle slightly beneath my weight. My breaths come heavy from the exertion; each exhale seems as loud as a foghorn.

The breaths ripple the curtain fabric. I put my hand over my mouth.

A thin white speck glimmers where the curtains meet. The curtains aren't precisely closed, so I press an eye to the small gap, peering into the room and beyond.

In the distance, a glowing shape descends the stone stairway. The outline appears human, but the feet make no perceptible sound.

How did I know? How did I know she was searching for me?

The spirit wears a starched white uniform. When she reaches the bottom of the staircase, she calls out.

"I know you're here."

By reflex, I step away from the curtain. The area is too confining: I immediately press against the back wall, nowhere else to go.

"I got a *good* look at you," the spirit says. The voice is closer, but still I've heard no footsteps.

A sudden screech like the wail of a torture victim; the clank of chains tightened around wrists and ankles, pulling them apart.

"Got you!"

From the office far to the left, I hear a heavy desk dragged across the floor. A chair falls over.

The spirit moves closer, to a room of valuable antiques. A vase falls off a table and crashes to the floor. Books drop off shelves in a dusty heap.

Stop, *I want to cry out.* You don't realize the value of what you're destroying.

I consider surrendering. Anything to save the artifacts in the surrounding rooms.

More items fall to the ground. Glass and metal and stacks of paper.

Then silence.

"Ah ha!"

My lips tighten as I attempt to hold back a whimper. A white glow brightens and slowly begins to fill the gap between the curtains.

I hold my breath. Touching the back wall for support, I try to slide lower out of view. Four white-gloved fingers slip between the curtains. The fingers are so close that I could lean forward and bite them.

I want to sink out of view, into dark oblivion. My palms are flat against the back wall, and the partition feels flimsy, held together by a scratchy coat of peeling paint. The wall begins to buckle.

The fingers withdraw.

I watch the curtain, willing it not to open. I sense that the presence has departed.

A breath escapes my lips in an audible sigh of relief.

The wall behind me again buckles beneath my palms. The dry partition has a new texture, like starched fabric.

It breathes.

Finally the partition gives way and I fall back, landing on a pile of clothes and bones.

The bones whisper in my ear: "This house belongs to me. I'll make you regret you ever came here."

The Date

Tonight I am going on a date. Melissa has told me to bring popcorn.

Not a real date, of course, and not actually in the evening. I am meeting her at Budget House during our usual stolen time—that teenager's twilight zone, the undefined 90 minutes between the end of school and our parents' return from their jobs.

Melissa realizes, I guess, that she overreacted last week. There's no reason she should be paranoid because her mother noticed me along the seldom-travelled road to their house. Teenagers are allowed to have friends—and they don't need to gain a parent's approval in advance.

For my part, I'm glad to have things back to normal. I'd felt strange ever since my hallway interaction with Geoff, when I'd spoken out of anger, said things I didn't really mean.

On the school bus, Melissa stands up when we reach the intersection closest to her home. I wait a few beats, then gather my backpack.

A few seats behind me, Geoff snorts under his breath. I check the driver's wide rearview mirror as I hustle out. Geoff is making a rude gesture with his hands, and several of his friends are laughing.

"We have to hurry."

She rushes me to the house like we are late for an important meeting. The late-afternoon air is brisk, but I'm sweating beneath the layers of my sweater and jacket.

When we arrive at the porch, Melissa unlocks the front door. Without stopping at the kitchen for sodas, she takes me to the top floor, bypasses her room and heads immediately to the hook-latched door to the studio.

At the end of the entrance corridor, she picks up the battery-operated lantern from the ground where she's purposefully left it.

Her pace barely slows on the stone stairway. She's gotten used to these stairs, despite the lack of protective railing. I follow as quickly as I can, keeping close to the wall.

She gets about a dozen steps ahead of me, but I gain more ground as we near the bottom. I can move faster for the final stretch, since if I trip over the side I wouldn't have as far to fall.

"The living room," Melissa says.

Once on level ground, I can navigate easily, since the layout of the studio has become second nature to me. In my art sketchbook, I've drawn a floor plan of the studio, labeling each set and identifying which films were shot there. When I daydream, I think about the different locations: walking through them with Melissa in the haunted dark; sneaking there alone in my imagination, like a museum's guard who ensures each item remains undisturbed; or like the time traveler of fantasy, visiting these same sets brightened by arc lights, freshly painted, crowded with costumed actors, cameras ready and rolling. In these latter daydreams, "Budget" Preston clarifies the mood of the scene, gives orders to the crew, and as his assistant, I help ensure these orders are followed. I'm an apprentice filmmaker, and plan to follow in his footsteps.

Melissa's lantern is an easy beacon, and I soon meet her in the living room set.

She places the lantern on the coffee table, and there are two cans of soda marking our places.

A blanket covers the sofa, hiding the dusty, faded cushions.

To the side of the sofa, she's positioned the wheeled cart that holds the 35mm projector. A reel of film is loaded onto the projector, which is aimed toward the facing underside of the stone stairway.

"My father never had a screening room," she tells me. "He built this living room set in a strategic location, opposite the tallest section of the stairway."

Melissa motions for me to sit on the sofa, and she turns a knob on the projector. It rattles to life, and a countdown of numbers appears on the opposite wall, accompanied by a series of beeps from the projector's speaker grill.

Then the logo appears, larger than life and a bright sky blue: A Budget Studios Production.

The title comes next: *The Haunted Oak*.

Melissa joins me on the couch. "The tin say 73 minutes for this one. I figure we'll have time to watch it all."

Classical music plays behind the credits—public domain recordings, to avoid the expense of an original score and orchestra. The shadows of tree limbs darken random sections of each title card.

For the final card, the limbs form together in the silhouette of a crude face. The words read: Produced, Written and Directed by Bud "Budget" Preston.

I clap my hands, and Melissa joins me.

The experience is surreal. We sit on a couch in a false living room, with no ceiling or fourth wall. Instead of facing a television screen, we look across the studio floor at a giant projected image.

Although we started at 3:45 in the afternoon, the studio is as dark as a drive-in at night.

Pops or cracks occasionally obscure the dialogue from the projector speakers, but I clarify a few essential lines for Melissa. We drink our sodas, and I remember to pull the bag of store-brand popcorn from my backpack.

It really does feel like a date. It's a full size sofa, with an empty cushion between us, but the room is private and dark. I've never felt closer to her.

We're sitting in the actual location where many of the scenes were filmed. After the grandmother disappears, sinister music swells on the soundtrack. I look in her usual location: the rocking chair in the corner. Ours has a layer of dust on it; in the film, the same chair is covered with broken branches.

Melissa laughs out loud, undercutting the film's tension.

"Their Mee-maw just *died,"* I say in mock outrage.

"I'm sorry." She covers her mouth. "It's just a bunch of twigs."

The image cuts to bright white as the last stretch of the first reel threads through the projector. With the help of the electric lantern, Melissa sets up the next part of the movie. She moves the emptied reel onto the back arm of the projector, then attaches the second reel to the top arm and begins feeding the strip of film through the machine.

As she works, I decide I should redeem her father's choice of subject matter. "The tree is a smart idea for a low-budget monster: no need to build a prop, since there's a tree already in your side yard, and stray branches are easy to find. Only your dad could manage to twist an ordinary tree into something sinister."

"If you say so."

I gather this film isn't one of her favorites. Understandable, since my magazines frequently cited *The Haunted Oak* as one of Bud Preston's weakest efforts. Still, I wish she'd show more appreciation for the movie. At least respect what her father was able to accomplish within such a limited budget.

Melissa flips off the lantern as the film resumes. The teenage son argues with his mother, who begs him to stay home *(We're only safe if we stay together!)* but he ignores her and takes the car keys *(Just try to stop me!)*. He starts the car, and backs up without looking behind him. From inside the house, the mother hears a crash. She rushes outside, and the car trunk is dented as if it's hit something—a telephone pole, or a tree—but there's no such object in sight. The door is open, as if the driver fled the scene of the accident. The car seat is covered with limbs and leaves.

The next day, the entire family (what's left of it) waits in the living room for news of the missing. A storm rages outside, with flashes of lightning visible behind the closed curtains. The mother stares at the telephone—

—with a rotary dial, sitting on the coffee table next to our empty soda cans and crumpled bag of popcorn—

—anxious for it to ring. The four-year-old sits on the floor and plays with his Tonka truck, while the father smokes a cigarette and paces the floor.

Another flash of light, followed by a roar of thunder.

Storm's getting closer, *the father says.*

Sheriff Hazelbury said he'd call. The mother leans forward from the sofa and lifts the receiver. *I can't wait any longer.*

The father crosses the room, tamping out his cigarette in an ashtray, then putting a gentle hand on his wife's shoulder. *He can't call us if he doesn't know anything.*

We cut to an outside shot: the house at night, and pouring rain. A flash of light, and the shadow of a tree flickers across the closed window.

Inside the studio, there's no roof over the living room. The ceiling and dormant arc lamps are so far above they're practically invisible—as if we've no protection from the storm.

On the projected image, the mother still holds the phone receiver. She raises it slowly to her ear.

Listens. And, That's odd. *A beat. Rain patters against the window.* Edward. The line's dead. Sheriff Hazelbury couldn't call, even if he wanted to.

Let me try. The husband takes the receiver, jiggles the switchhook, then spins a few numbers on the dial. *I think I'm getting something.*

Edward, our son's out there somewhere in this storm, my mother's been missing for three days—

Quiet a second, I'm trying to listen. He holds the receiver to his ear. A crackle of static mixes with the heavy patter of rain. *A voice.*

The mother leans forward. I sit on the same couch, in the same spot, and I also lean forward.

It sounds like a woman, *her husband tells her.* She's whispering.

Dead silence, save for the storm. Medium shot: the mother on the couch, leaning forward as if she can hear the whisper; her husband stands with the phone receiver pressed to his ear.

A flash of lightning, then a pause while we wait for the rumble of thunder.

Instead, there's a loud crash of glass on the soundtrack as a huge tree limb smashes through the window and onto the sofa, finger-branches wriggling, passing where the mother's head was positioned before she leaned forward.

I've seen this movie more than a dozen times, but I jump as if the limb has crashed behind me on the sofa.

Even Melissa seems caught up in the excitement now. The experience is so much better than watching a film on television. This is the only Budget Studios Production I've ever seen in a theater setting, and the "drive-in" style setup adds the perfect touch.

On the projected image, the husband draws his wife close. His hands cradle her head, imagining how easily it could have been crushed by the limb.

Then the frame shakes as if the characters are in an earthquake, accompanied by a sputtering sound.

I jump in front of Melissa, but then can't find the shutoff switch on the projector.

"Fix it, Brendan. Hurry!"

A black dot appears on the movie-wife's face, then it expands and curls and burns. The side of the stone stairway looks like it's on fire.

The film snaps, and the broken half grinds through to the take-up reel.

Melissa pushes me aside and turns off the light to the projector, sending the studio into complete darkness.

"You should have let me do it," she says.

"It happened so fast."

"Yeah."

We wait in the darkness for a moment.

This might be the only surviving 35mm print of the movie, and I had to watch helpless as it got damaged. Maybe it's not fair, but I feel like I'm the one who should be more upset, since Melissa didn't really take the movie seriously.

As in last night's dream, I sense a presence in the studio, gliding down the stone stairway. Then I hear the thump as a destructive poltergeist begins to knock over furniture—but it's only Melissa, miscalculating where she last set the lantern.

A click, and the lantern comes on. "We shouldn't have done this." The light on the coffee table beneath casts distorting shadows over her face.

Melissa had put together a really cool event, and I definitely appreciate it. But I also realize we weren't really working together. She'd moved the projector from the locked room, chose the movie, and scheduled the date. I'm here only as long as her whim permits, and that whim seems ready to strike again, in a negative direction. If I can't improve her mood, I might lose another couple days, maybe more, my studio dreams slipping farther and farther away.

Thinking about the locked room gives me an idea. "There's the editing machine in your dad's office," I tell her. "I'm sure there's splicing tape, too."

Her disappointed face hovers in the strange shadows, dark bands under her eyes and deep furrows in her brow. "It's ruined," she says.

Even though the film is part of her family heritage, I know it doesn't mean as much to her as it does to me. I can't fathom why she's so upset.

Later it will occur to me how Melissa set everything up so perfectly to impress me. It isn't the film that was ruined, but the *date*.

But what did I know then, about dates?

When Melissa and I discussed our fellow students, we saved particular derision for the kids who identified themselves as couples. Silly displays of affection or embarrassing public spats—and all *too soon*. Playing at being adults, before their time, making themselves look even more like children. Such discussions clearly signaled a tacit understanding: any idea of us on a "date" should only be considered in ironic terms.

Most of what I learned about life came from movies—and in Bud Preston films, the plots didn't place much emphasis on romantic elements. Our relationship with the supernatural or otherworldly far outweighed our relationships with each other. Social interactions were often the root of any problem, as exemplified when the public's revulsion turned Thomas Hendricks' character into a murder suspect.

If Melissa really was a ghost or possessed by a demon, as the odd-angled flashlight suggested, I'd be better equipped to understand her. At least movie monsters follow a consistent set of rules: vampires only at night, werewolves only during a full moon.

"It's getting near time for you to leave, Brendan." She lifts the lantern and swings its beam away from her face and onto the floor in front, indicating a pathway out.

While we'd been inside and a thunderstorm raged on the projected images, an actual early-evening storm had begun to roll in. When I leave Melissa's house, the sky is heavy with black clouds, and a deep mist coats the lawn and the surrounding forest. All the day's color is muted. I step into a black-and-white film.

I walk fast through the fog, barely able to discern the path in front. I think of arctic travelers surrounded by white, with no guideposts to confirm their position. The outpost is nearby, but they can't see it. Fresh snow falls, erasing their footprints; without realizing it, they walk in circles. They freeze before they starve, which is a small blessing. Their bodies are later discovered only twenty yards from the snow-covered shelter.

Fortunately, I've visited Melissa's home often enough that I can find my way on instinct, even as the clouds finally burst open in a heavy downpour. I pull my jacket over my head and run toward the junction of the access road.

As I usually do when I reach the end of the clearing, I turn for one last look at Budget House. In the mist and driving rain, the building had completely disappeared.

I'm soaked through by the time I reach my apartment building. The jacket kept my hair mostly dry, but wind blew rain into my face and neck, and my sweater is heavy and damp with the smell of wet wool.

I pause to wipe my feet on the mat by the downstairs mailboxes, then head upstairs to the second floor. Even after wiping off the mud, I still leave damp footprints on the painted wooden stairs.

I'll have to throw my wet clothes in the dryer before Mom gets home.

As I approach our floor, I hear voices that I know can't be coming from my apartment. If Mom came home early, she'd be worried about my being outside in the storm. Possibly the heavy storm had prevented me from noticing her car in the side parking lot.

Because as I get closer, that's definitely her voice coming from inside our apartment.

Who is she talking to?

If she's home, the door's unlocked. I reach to test the knob.

Mom's voice is raised, so she doesn't hear me enter. From the living room, I finally hear the other person speak.

A familiar voice, but these days it's one I usually hear only on the phone on Thursday nights.

Connections

They are arguing about me—another familiar memory I hadn't expected to confront this evening. My mom is seated at the kitchen table, and my dad is leaning against the counter, his arms behind him.

I'm standing in the hallway, dripping water onto the hardwood floor.

"Brendan, where have you been?"

Since I hadn't expected my mom to be home so early, I don't have an alibi prepared.

"Tell the truth, son."

Although I'm happy my dad's come to visit—it's what I've been wanting for so long, after all—I don't appreciate the skepticism in his remark. He's the one I *have* been telling the truth to all along. It's not my fault he doesn't believe me.

A partial truth is the best I can summon: "I was at a friend's house."

"Geoff?" My mom has a pencil ready. "I asked you two weeks ago for his parents' phone number. Don't make me ask again." It's a bad sign that she has a legal pad in front of her, turned sideways to make room for multiple columns. Whenever I was in big trouble, Mom listed abbreviated "talking points" in the first column, to make sure she'd address each thing I'd done wrong. In the next column she'd jot key phrases for lessons she'd want to reinforce ("Respect your teachers" or "Rules exist for a reason"). Then a column to take notes on my responses ("I'll try harder" or "I've learned my lesson" or "I promise to apologize tomorrow.")

We hadn't had one of these legal pad "discussions" since Mom and I moved to Alabama. The most recent was with a Guidance Counselor in Delaware. It's been three years since my dad took part.

"Geoff and I had kind of a falling out, after I insulted him by accident. We're not friends anymore."

Mom makes a quick note in the last column, then she puts an "X" through the first few talking points. I assume these are all related to Geoff, but I'm not close enough to decipher her handwriting.

She rolls back the first sheet, and unfortunately there's another full page of topics. As she readjusts the pad on the kitchen table, some tucked-in items shift against the pad's cardboard backing. The corner of a photograph sticks out, and the edge of a time-worn scrap of paper.

"Brendan, who's Melissa? You've mentioned her to your father, but never to me."

I can't think of anything to say. My sweater smells of wet wool, and my jacket and jeans are still heavy with rain. Dad leans silent against the kitchen counter: his only contribution to this conversation has been to betray my confidence.

"She's a girl I know from school."

"Why don't *I* know about her, Brendan? Your father says you talk about her all the time. You make up stories about her."

"They're not stories." I look right at Dad, hoping he feels a little guilty for bringing Mom into this. He's been in a few fights with her, too, as I recall, so he should remember what it's like.

She lifts the notepad and pulls out the storyboard sheet that's been tucked in the back. "How about your art project? Stained with coffee or tea to make it look old." She holds the page close to her nose.

"I didn't make that. I borrowed it from Melissa's house."

Borrowed is a trigger word, and she probably has notes in a second column entry: "Stealing = wrong." "Taking something from a friend or family member is just as bad as shoplifting. Maybe even worse."

Before Mom has a chance to recycle those old chestnuts, my dad finally decides to chime in. "Let me try, Katherine." Then to me he says: "Dry yourself off, kid. We need to talk."

I've changed to a different pair of jeans and put on a fresh T-shirt. I sit on the bed, and Dad sits wrong-ways in my desk chair, his legs straddling the back.

"First, it's good to see you. I've missed you, kid."

"Why'd you come? I mean, I wanted you to visit..."

"I needed to figure out what's really going on."

"I *told* you."

He nods. He's my dad, the same guy I've known my whole life, but now it's weird to see him in person. He should look older, even sadder—the toll of living without my mom, without me. He looks exactly the same. Which makes me feel like it's not really him, but some imposter, modeled exactly on an old photograph but missing the *soul.*

"That's why your mom has to ask so many questions," he says. "We'll need to approach this differently, depending on what's wrong."

"What's wrong is that you don't believe me. And Mom's always gonna ask questions."

He smiles for the first time during the visit. A small moment of connection: I see the real Dad, finally. "I can't argue with you there. But I have the same questions, Brendan."

He wants the conversation to be about me—my delusions, my adolescent "acting out," whatever spin he and my mom want to put on things. I wish he could be the one on trial instead.

"You called Mom, just to cause trouble for me. Thanks a lot."

"Brendan, I talk to your mother all the time. Whatever happened between us, we always share *you.*"

This doesn't make any sense, and I tell him so. I've never heard Mom talking to him on the phone.

"I call her at work," he explains. "It's easy to catch her at her desk, and there's less chance we'll get into a shouting match." He leans forward and two of the chair legs lift off the rug. "I had to tell her about those things you've been sending me in the mail. We're both worried about you."

"What's the worry? That something interesting happens to me?"

"Oh Brendan, you've created such an elaborate story. A fantasy to try to get me to visit—which tells me something's wrong. Maybe you're still upset your mom and I separated. Or there's a crisis at school: with your grades, with friends. Tell me the truth. You need me here, that's the easy part, but I still don't know why."

I'm surprised he didn't mention drugs. Instead of trusting me, he'd rather think that I'm crazy. On Thursdays, this might be a time when I'd slam down the phone—because I'm angry and frustrated, but also because I wouldn't want him to know what came next, when I started crying.

I don't have that luxury now.

And I find myself sobbing, talking about how close we were when I was younger, how we bonded over those horror movies. Blubbering about the special connection we shared, and how sad I was to lose it. "We're the only ones who understood those movies." The bed shook underneath me as I tried to control the sobs. "Mom never liked them, but *we* did. Just us. And you don't seem to *get* it anymore."

My eyes are blurry, and Dad disappears from the chair. He sits next to me on the bed, puts an arm around my shoulder to comfort me, but I only feel worse.

"I was afraid of this," Dad says. "Your mother and I couldn't work things out. It's nothing to do with you."

He still doesn't understand. He's come all this way to see me, and I'm crying, and he won't make himself understand.

"Son, you have to move on. We can't go back to the way things were," Dad says. Then he corrects himself: "Your mom and me, I mean." Too late. He pretends he talking about his marriage, but he's also talking about the two of us. We don't mean the same thing to each other anymore.

Son, you have to move on. *He might as well have said,* I've got a new life now. I barely think about you, let alone those silly movies we used to watch together. That's all in the past.

I'm angry enough now that the sobbing subsides. Dad pats my back, then stands. "Give yourself a few minutes, then come talk with us in the kitchen."

Pulling the sheets off the bed, I use craft scissors to cut and tear them into strips that I knot together into an escape rope. The rain continues in full force outside, with a harsh and howling wind, but it's a second floor window so I won't have far to drop. I tie the makeshift rope to the foot of my bed, then lower the loose end out the open window.

I dump my school books from my backpack and gather some essentials—change of clothes, toiletries, wallet, my sketchpad and script pages—then sling the pack over my shoulder.

One last look at the room before I grab the knotted sheet and climb through the window and into the waiting storm.

I will go to Budget House, find my way inside and into the studio—and I'll survive there as long as I can, moving from room to room, inhabiting better worlds. When authorities find me, I'll have grown feral—more a case for animal control than for the police. I'll snarl and growl and leap at the uniformed men, and they'll have to shoot me dead.

If that's the path I choose—and believe me, even with the tragic end, this scenario right now seems more attractive than further conversation with my mom and dad—here is what happens in my immediate absence:

Dad knocks on the door. "Brendan, we're waiting."

"Don't you think it's time you stopped sulking?" Mom knocks too. Harder. Then she opens the door and walks into the bedroom.

It doesn't take long for them to register what's happened. The room's empty.

Dad crosses to the desk. "He didn't leave a note."

"Never was much of a writer." Mom goes to the open window and reels the wet sheet inside. She shuts the window with a bang.

"Should we call the police?"

Mom shakes her head. "I imagine they're pretty busy."

"Probably for the best," Dad agrees.

Mom wrings some water out of the ruined sheets, and absently begins untying the knots. "It's a kindness, really. Our lives will be easier without him."

And maybe I didn't make it to Budget House. Maybe storm winds blew stronger than I expected, and the wet rope was too slippery. I fell, and cracked my head on the sidewalk.

Upstairs, my parents laugh as they get reacquainted.

"Quite an imagination," my mom says. She laughs, but it's the kind of laugh she might make in the principal's office—when she's cornered, making excuses for me.

A pause. I'm halfway down the hallway from my room, and strain to listen. My dad doesn't say anything, and I'm worried he's left already. Gone to stay in a hotel, or even hopped the next flight to Cleveland.

"I understand," Mom says, in response to nothing.

As I turn from the hallway to enter the kitchen, I nearly slip on the rainwater that dripped off me earlier. I catch myself by grabbing the door frame.

"Oh, here he is now." Mom offers me the receiver to our wall-mounted telephone. Dad's back in his lean-spot against the counter. "Someone wants to speak with you, Brendan."

I cross the room and take the receiver. Mom has a know-it-all expression, and Dad looks a little confused. They don't grant me any privacy by leaving the room.

I offer a tentative greeting, then pull the cord as far as it will reach, standing near the door frame with my back to my parents.

"Is this Brendan?"

The voice sounds like the spirit in my dreams, a raspy whisper from a pile of bones.

"I almost ran you off the road the other day. My daughter told me about you."

"She did?" I notice an open phone directory on the kitchen table, next to Mom's legal pad.

"Not as much as I've heard just now from your mother, but yes."

I wonder how long they've been talking. While Dad was with me, Mom must have dialed every Preston in the small-town phone book. *Hello. Do you have a daughter named Melissa? There's something I need you to know.*

"I'm not the person you think I am," Mrs. Preston says. "My daughter either, for that matter." Not a spirit. It is more like the voice of a witch. With a matter-of-fact statement, she hopes to dispel every significant memory from my recent life.

Then I hear a hand muffle over the connected receiver, and she shouts an abbreviated version of her daughter's name. "Mel! Mel! Phone!"

My parents watch as I wait for Melissa to pick up on her end. Mom, at least, does me the courtesy of not taking notes—but I know she's considering how she might present my issues to the school psychiatrist.

In Melissa's home, I expect she's similarly under a parent's watchful eye. Either that, or her mother stays on the extension in a different room. Neither of us can speak freely.

"I didn't know my mom would call your house," I say.

"A surprise to me, too." Perhaps "surprise" is a code word. It stands for *We're busted,* or *I warned you this would happen.*

"Is there something I'm supposed to do? I'll apologize to your mother, if that will help."

"Too late for that."

Silence. I feel my parents' gaze on my back, and I want to slink out of the kitchen where they can't hear me.

"I'm not sure what my mom thinks," I tell her. "But my dad..." I slip to a paranoid's whisper, certain I'm overheard. "My dad thinks I'm crazy. He thinks I invented you, and the house you live in."

"Didn't you?"

My mom and dad are finally in the same room again and they have no thoughts for each other. They're too busy watching for any sign that my mind is breaking down. I wish I really had climbed out my window when I had the chance. I wish they'd been relieved that I was gone.

I think of them laughing, of Melissa laughing now and her mother also, and I can't help but join them.

"What's so funny, Brendan?"

"You," I say, then adopt a more serious tone. "The whole situation. It's unbelievable. I can see that now."

I sense a collective sigh of relief from my parents. *He's coming back to his senses,* they are thinking. Dad is proud that he's here: his visit cured me of my delusions.

Melissa doesn't respond. I hear a crackle on the line, which is perhaps her witch-mother on the other extension, exhaling the final breath of her world-altering incantation.

If I sleep at all that night, I won't dream.

The dreams are over. I'm the victim of a *Twilight Zone* ending—the character who realizes he's been trapped in his own imagination, and he's not happy to have the veil lifted from his eyes.

In this ending, I've never actually visited Melissa's perfectly ordinary house. I took some blurry photographs of nothing, convinced myself they framed elements from a long-ago movie. I made my own crude storybook page, stained it and burned the edges to make it look old. Oddly, this is the ending my parents seem to prefer.

The artifacts, sent to my dad, are tucked in the back of my mom's legal pad. For her, they're evidence of my unstable mind. Temporary insanity, your honor—oh God, let's *hope* it's only temporary—brought on my separation from his father and, I'll take some blame here, from the frequent moves from town to town brought on by changes in my job. We haven't had a steady home. No anchor for my boy to grab onto, and he's gone adrift.

Those items were my only physical proof. I'm afraid if I'm permitted to examine them again, I'll notice flaws in my own handiwork.

My only other proof is in my experiences. But memories are meaningless, if I can be persuaded to doubt them.

Earlier, I'd felt guilty about stealing that single, incomplete storyboard page. Now, I wish I had stolen more souvenirs from Budget

House. I want to rise from my bed and search my room, where I should have hidden a plastic heart in the back of a dresser drawer; a silver-painted translator gun behind my clothes hamper; the Lake Monster's eye staring from the top shelf of my closet.

All smuggled from the movie studio on different days. Why not? My friendships never lasted very long, so I shouldn't have expected things with Melissa to be any different. Besides that, she was a fickle gatekeeper to her father's treasures.

If I'd stolen them, at least I'd now have proof I could put my hands on.

Instead I try to sleep, grasping at empty air.

The next day at school, Melissa does not walk at lunch, and I cannot find her.

In Art class, she ignores me, buried in a drawing exercise: mindless shading of cubes and cones and spheres. The abstract shapes add up to nothing.

"Trouble with the weird girl, huh?"

Geoff's snide remark in English brings me back to reality. High school is not about movies and fantasy worlds. It's about teenagers being cruel to each other.

I've participated in that cruelty. I'm as bad as the rest of them.

"None of your business." I stare at my blank page of notes, and imagine a fresh infection eating away at his healthy eye. If people still remember what they wrote on his Get-Well cards a few years back, there'd be no need to put much effort into new ones. Just add a word: "Sorry about the loss of your ^other eye!"

After writing a particularly spiteful phrase, I cross it out. Then I write the titles of some of my favorite movies, and cross them out also.

In the seat beside me, Geoff probably imagines that I repeatedly write and deface Melissa Preston's name.

"Wait!"

Melissa moves so quickly along the road to her house. I'll never catch her if she doesn't stop.

I'd hesitated after she left the bus, not quite sure I was going to follow. Geoff and his buddies watched, anxious to add a new chapter to the school's gossip epic.

Finally, just before the bus pulled away, I had jumped from my seat and hustled to the front exit.

"Wait!"

I pause to catch my breath, leaning over with my hands resting on my knees. Far ahead, Melissa stops but does not turn around.

I straighten up, then jog to close the distance between us.

"You can't come to my house." She still doesn't turn around, even though I'm right behind her.

"Fine," I say. "But can we talk for a minute?"

"About what?"

We stand on this nearly deserted road. She looks like the vanishing hitchhiker of urban legend—the strange girl picked up by a good Samaritan, and delivered "home" to an address that turns out to be a cemetery. When Melissa turns around, her face will be a living skull.

"I'm really sorry."

"About what?" she repeats.

Melissa turns. No skull, but no emotions either. She hasn't been crying, doesn't seem to be angry. I can't read her.

Maybe I never could.

"I got yelled at last night," she says. "It's why I tried to warn you."

"I never thought my mom would call like that."

"Well, she did."

"When I talked to *your* mom, she was nice to me."

Silence.

I was hoping Melissa would say something about her father, about the movie studio behind her home. She needed to contradict my weird waking nightmare, where such wonders existed solely in my imagination.

"She told me she wasn't the person I thought she was," I say. "Do you know what your mother meant by that?"

"Think about it."

Not really an answer. The only interpretation I can come up with is that she's not really the widow of Bud Preston. *My daughter's not who you think she is, either.* Meaning, Melissa's not the director's daughter? I try to recall the precise wordings of our conversations—had Melissa *volunteered* that she and Bud Preston were related, or was it something she let me assume as fact? Perhaps this was all an absurd case of wish fulfillment.

Except my memories were too real. I'd visited Budget House on multiple occasions, uncovering new areas of the studio wherever Melissa permitted me to explore. The sets matched the movies I could recite from memory; their appearance matched the rare behind-the-scenes pictures in my magazines. But my experiences with Budget House weren't simply summoned by a desperate imagination. I'd lived there, for a time. I'd spent part of my life in a haunted house.

If Melissa lets me follow her down the road to the DEAD END sign then along the car-worn path leading off to the right, Budget House will not have disappeared in last evening's fog. The studio will be attached behind, a strange warehouse of memorabilia with special significance to me.

To me.

Always such an absurd coincidence that the *exact* films I loved would somehow originate from a town I moved to. Since I wanted to believe in the idea so badly, I never questioned it.

My memories are real, but they might not be authentic. I imagine an even more elaborate hoax: A facsimile studio built onto the back of a house in an extended *Candid Camera* gimmick. They've been filming me all this time.

Melissa, who's always been so hard to read—she's been in on the joke, always on the verge of busting out with laughter.

The well-groomed host can come out from between two trees where he's been hiding. His camera crew will follow. We gave you your wish, for a little while. As payment, sign this release form and we'll feature you in the next episode. Look this way and smile. Show everyone what an idiot you are!

It's The Ambush of Humiliation I always feared from my peers—writ large, broadcast to the nation.

"None of it was real." I intend my words to sound like an accusation, but they fall flat.

"Sure it's real," Melissa says, "but not as simple as you think. There are a lot of *feelings* you haven't considered."

She still avoids Bud Preston's name, and any mention of the studio behind her house. I can't tolerate the ambiguity any longer. "Your father..."

"I'm glad you like my father's movies, Brendan. It's sweet how you've brought me closer to him. But for my mother, those films bring back a lot of memories. We had fun digging around in the studio—but we were also digging through my mother's past. She said we invaded her privacy."

Her mention of the studio puts me back on solid ground, which is a huge relief. But she's right that I hadn't considered her mother's feelings. The movies brought me such joy: I couldn't imagine any negative associations they might have for someone (as I saw it) *lucky* enough to be married to my favorite director.

"He wasn't a nice person," Melissa says. "You can enjoy his movies as much as you want, but that's the truth."

I don't understand. Melissa had talked about these movies with me, let me go on and on about how wonderful they are, never contradicting me. Sure, she'd previously hinted at some conflicts between her parents, but she'd been too young when her father passed away. All she knew about him had been filtered through her mother, who would be telling a biased version of events. "How can you be so sure?"

"You idolize him. Maybe I can explain it best with reference to his movies. The script you saw in his office, for *The Withered Hag?* Well, my mother starred in school plays, and she was really beautiful when they got married. She always had dreams of becoming an actress, and never understood why my father never cast her in one of his films.

"This script, he said he had a part for her, a starring role. My mother's beauty had apparently faded too quickly over the years, and the script was my father's mean-spirited way of pointing it out. The title says it all. The witch in the script has my mother's name. The male lead keeps seeing a hideous withered hag on their property; in the end, he realizes it's his wife's true form. 'Your beauty,' he says to her as she withers into old age before his eyes. 'Bring it back. Oh God, bring it back!'"

Melissa waits for the significance to sink in. "Can you imagine what my mother thought when she read that script? And there's another unfilmed script, too, called *The Wailing Infant*. It's about a disappointing child that ruins the lives of her parents, and becomes a horrible crawling monster. Obviously, that's *me*. He wrote a spiteful movie about me, when I was just a baby."

The usual arguments come to mind. They're scripts. They're fiction. Writers often base characters and events on real life, changing them to suit the type of story. In horror fiction, that means making everything unpleasant. "That's not how he thought of you," I say. "Not really."

"Maybe not. But that script is all I have. My feelings about him aren't the same as yours."

If she'd loan me the two scripts, I could help her locate a more charitable interpretation of the wife and infant characters. But I don't dare ask: she'd think I was only interested in reading the rare scripts, rather than trying to help a friend.

I couldn't blame her if that's what she thought.

"Brendan, what happened to those pictures you took of me?"

"Oh, they're at my apartment." Partly true, since I thought I'd seen their corners sticking out of my mom's legal pad.

"I'd like them back," she says. "Along with that paper you took from my father's office. That's *all* you took, isn't it?"

"One page, and I only borrowed it." Even to my ears, the excuse sounds weak. I figure my mom's not the only one who can decode the word *borrowed*.

"If you'd asked, I'd have given it to you." She corrects herself: "If you'd asked *then*, I would have."

Another apology would be meaningless. I try to convince her I had a good reason, at least: "I wanted something to send to my dad, to show him I was telling the truth about Budget House. He still doesn't believe me."

"Why does that matter? I shared these things with *you*. It was *our* connection."

She speaks in the past tense. We are in the last reel. The final parting.

"I don't know," I say. "He's my dad. He's been so far away. I wanted to bring him closer."

"Yes, bring *him* closer."

As Melissa said earlier, there were a lot of feelings I hadn't considered.

The Return to Budget House

This weekend, I'm compelled to star in a sequel: *The Return to Budget House.* It won't be like the sequels that movies offer, but more like the ones we get in life—instead of a bigger budget, more action and special effects, we get illness, decay, and disappointment.

My dad is still in town. While I'm at school during the day, he works from his hotel room. He uses the hotel phone to consult about his latest marketing project for dishwasher soap or sugar cereal or some useless kitchen gadget.

Evenings are reserved for me.

It seemed important to spend time with my son, *is his euphemistic way of putting it.*

He's been watching me. Hoping for signs of typical teenage angst, rather than drug use, severe depression or other mental illness.

It's horrible to have him and Mom "worried about me" again.

Still, I can't summon the cheerfulness his visit should have inspired.

"How about a movie?" Dad suggests. "I can drive us to the Anniston 6. Or we can watch one of those old tapes on the VCR. The low budget ones you like."

We like, he used to say. "They're the wrong format," I tell him. "They don't play in our machine."

"Oh."

"Besides, they remind me too much of my friend Melissa."

"You broke up with your girlfriend."

"She was never my girlfriend," I say, and the corrective is so loud I've probably convinced him she *was*.

It's a catch-all explanation for why I'd be so moody, I guess. Since he won't believe anything else.

Now that the weekend is here, I've decided to take him up on his offer to entertain me. We get in his rental car—a white Ford Escort—and go for a drive.

He asks me where we're heading, and I say I know a shortcut to the mall in Gadsden. He lets me navigate.

Maybe he knows all along where I'm directing us.

"This road's not in very good shape," Dad says. The path has shifted from pavement to packed dirt, and it's still wet from the heavy rain a few days ago. Bits of mud and gravel splash up as we drive through, so my dad will probably have to visit a carwash before he returns to the rental agency. "It's a dead end."

"Ignore that sign. Trust me." I point to the right, and Dad steers us onto the side road that opens up into a clearing.

Budget House looms in the distance. I tell Dad to stop the car, and he does—mostly because he thinks we're lost. He turns in his seat, intending to question me, but I've already unbuckled my seatbelt. I jump out of the car, and without bothering to shut the door, I begin a quick walk to the house.

Part way there, I run backwards for a short stretch. My dad is out of the muddied car, and he follows at his own pace.

I slow down, but not enough for him to catch up. He's angry, watching and readying his words, and I'm waiting for him to see the house ahead: the ordinary two-story house with the strange mansion-style entryway.

He doesn't realize it yet, but I'm vindicated. I've brought him to the most dramatic proof available.

I've been telling the truth all along, Dad. Look!

As I draw closer to the porch, I decide to experience it through my dad's eyes. A squint of surprise, a slow realization, and an apology catching in his throat.

My dad's eyes aren't as generous as mine. An adult's eyes, rational rather than imaginative.

The porch is not part of a movie set. It is simply a badly painted addition to the front of an otherwise unremarkable home.

Blink.

Through my own eyes now, the porch appears altered. It's the same overhanging shape as the entryway that newlyweds Mr. and Mrs. Goodwin huddled under in *The Stone Stairway,* or the entry to a mad scientist's hilltop mansion in *Spider House*. But it's been painted over.

The faux marble pillars are now painted a solid beige, revealed as simple wooden supports. A coat of drab brown paint obscures the bas relief of Theseus and the Minotaur that used to decorate the mantle.

My dad walks up behind me. "What kind of stunt are you trying to pull, Brendan?"

"This is the house," I tell him, although my evidence suffocates under thick coats of paint. "This is Budget House."

If he really tried. If he reached back into his memory of the films, his affection for his son as we watched them together, he'd know that I'm right. *Look at it the way I do, Dad.*

He won't make the effort.

"It's just a house," Dad says. "Nothing like what you described to me."

"She changed it." I walk up the three step on the bland, covered porch. "Look at these empty screw holes," I tell my dad when he meets me at the front doors. "There used to be brass lion's-head knockers attached here. These same doors, in three different movies. Remember?"

"I thought we were done with this nonsense." Dad puts a hand on my shoulder, intending to guide me away. Instead, I break free and pound the side of my fist against one of the doors.

"Brendan, do you even know who lives here?"

I pound at the door again, then wait.

No footsteps approach, but I hear the click of a latch.

In the movie, the door opens by itself. If that happens now, I'm going inside. I know the way into the studio, and I can lead my dad there.

Melissa stands in the open doorway. She wears a blank expression, as if she doesn't recognize me.

She had refused to talk with me earlier when I'd tried to reach her by phone. I expected she'd be more reasonable in person.

"My mother's in a weird mood," Melissa says. "You can't come inside." She blocks the way, and for a brief instant I consider knocking her over.

"I came here to introduce you to my father. Dad, this is my friend, Melissa Preston."

Dad seems a bit startled, but he offers a polite greeting.

"You're trespassing," Melissa says. "I'm not gonna call the police or anything, but you need to leave."

And she steps back and shuts the door.

"That was her," I insist to my dad. "The daughter of Bud Preston, the movie director."

Dad doesn't deny it, but he seems worn down. "Well, we have to go."

We step down off the porch. The passenger-side door is still open on the rental car. His arm comes around my shoulder, and the gesture seems unfamiliar. I'm taller than I was the last time he did it.

I shrug away from him and bolt for the side of the house.

In person, rather than on a blurry Polaroid, the tree will better resemble the title object from *The Haunted Oak*.

After this week's storm, more of the leaves have blown off the branches. They form a wet, colorful skirt around the base.

It's still the same tree. I run toward it.

Dad's calling after me, warning me that we've got to leave.

Still the same tree, with the creepy face staring from the knots and burls of the trunk.

The same tree—

—but the face is gone.

Someone has been at work with a saw. The face has been sliced messily away, the wound covered with black tar to help it heal.

"They've butchered it," I say to my dad as he approaches. "Melissa or her mother." I grab his hand and put it against the wound. "Must have done it yesterday, since the tar's still wet."

"It's a tree." Dad motions to the woods surrounding the property. "There are hundreds of trees here. None of them really have faces in them."

"What about the house? Look at the back of the house!"

Dad casts a cursory glance that way, then directs all his attention to me.

"That huge warehouse attached to the back of the house," I tell him. "It's the movie studio!"

He won't look back at it. Only at me.

I'm the lunatic escaped from the asylum. Dad's my psychiatrist, and he's disappointed that I haven't responded to treatment. Whatever I say won't matter. He'll only attribute it to the madness.

My dad drags me away from Budget House.

One more attempt.

I don't want to go home yet, Dad. Let's just go to Gadsden like we said.

I've calmed down a bit. I don't want you and Mom to worry about me. I'll be fine.

Can we do one more thing? If this doesn't convince you, I promise I'll drop it.

I swear.

I'll never mention Budget House or those films again.

Deal?

I know you think I've been acting strange, and this is probably going to seem like the strangest request so far. You'll have to really trust me.

Please, Dad. It will make things good between us again.

That's what you want, right?

Since I'd been paying attention when I rode the bus with Melissa, it's easy for me to give my dad directions to Evergreen.

He hasn't lived in Alabama, so he's never heard rumors about the more notorious wing of the facility. I explain we're visiting a resident in a nursing home. "I've been here before, with my Social Studies class." I figure the cover story I'd used with Mom could smooth things along.

We turn onto the cobbled road, and Dad takes a parking pass from the guy in the guard booth. We find a spot in the Visitors' lot, then walk to the sliding glass doors at the main entrance.

"My friend Geoff did some rehab here, when he had some trouble with his eyes." I'm talking mainly to keep Dad from asking questions. If I stay casual and act like I know what I'm doing, he'll play along.

Of course, I'm practically jumping out of my skin the whole time.

As I take my dad toward the residential area, we pass the cafeteria and small lounge area. A gray-haired man in a wheelchair waits outside the door to an administrative office. The chair nearly blocks the hallway, and I'm guessing a staff member has abandoned him there and he can't manage to wheel himself out of the general path. The old man's head leans down, as if he's sedated or has fallen asleep.

I say a gentle Excuse Me, and touch the back of his chair as I squeeze past.

His hand grabs at my jacket. "Can I help you?" The old man's grip is surprisingly strong, and he twists the fabric to tighten his hold.

"We're here to see Tommy." I use the actor's nickname to reinforce that I know him. "Tommy Hendricks. He's—"

"I remember you." The man's large glasses make his alert eyes seem impossibly wide. "You're not here for Tommy."

Another twist to my jacket, and I hear the pop of a knuckle. If he twists too hard, his fingers will become trapped in the fabric. If I try to pull away, his frail bones might snap.

"This is my dad," I say, trying some misdirection. The old man's grip doesn't loosen.

My dad, already skeptical of this visit, is ready to leave. He indicates the path behind us: "This way, Brendan."

"What's your hurry?" the old man says. Giant distorted eyes blink at me as a glimmer of understanding washes over him. "What have you taken from my room?"

"We just got here." It's a simultaneous alibi to the resident and plea to my dad. *We just got here. We* can't *leave now.*

The man tugs down on my jacket, forcing me to stoop closer to his level. "There's one thing I can't stand…" He hasn't any teeth, so he puckers and spits as he struggles to form his words. "And that's a liar and a thief."

My last chance is slipping away. If I can't fix this situation quickly, Dad will step in and put a stop to the whole thing.

It's possible this man's from the rumored "wrong side of Evergreen," briefly unsupervised during a rare visit to the calmer wing of the facility. I've no idea what item he's talking about, but I can guess how his paranoid mind might operate. Since I'm already close to his face, I whisper into his ear. "Your nurse took it. I saw her put it in her pocket."

His eyes widen, and his grip loosens on my jacket.

I scoot past and move quickly down the hall toward Tommy Hendricks' room. My dad negotiates around the wheelchair without interference—the old man's head has drooped back down into calm slumber—and Dad hurries to catch up with me.

Hendricks' undecorated door is easy to locate among his neighbors'. It's shut, but I knock and turn the knob.

I remember how startling it was to confront, in person, the distortions and discolorations of acromegaly. Part of me wishes Melissa had warned me before the introduction—but at the same time, there was something wondrous about the surprise as his identity dawned on me.

My dad heard me mention the actor's name, but I'm fairly certain he hasn't connected it to the actor in Bud Preston's film. I decide the introduction should be a surprise for him, too.

He'll slowly realize who Tommy Hendricks is. And in that same moment, he'll realize his son has been telling the truth all along.

I step into the bright bare room, and my dad follows. As before, a floor curtain obscures most of the bed at the back of the room, but I see the lump of Tommy's feet beneath the blankets.

Good. I was worried he might not be here.

I stride past the curtain, keeping confident. Dad walks gently, practically on tiptoe. Afraid he'll wake a sick patient. Afraid he's doing something wrong.

The best thing I can think to do now is recite another line from a movie. It will cast a spell, helping Tommy get into his character.

I stand at the foot of his bed, raise a pointed finger to him and smile in greeting. "It's the twisted face!"

Tommy's sitting up in bed, reading a newspaper. He stares at me through his strangely contorted wire-frame glasses. "That's not very nice," he says. "I have a medical condition. I can't help the way I look."

I'm once again struck by incongruities: eggplant hands holding a newspaper; a swollen-smashed head purpled over with port-wine bruises; the eyes and nose and mouth melted out of symmetry, as if painted by a child who hasn't yet learned facial anatomy. Apparently inhuman features, yet he wears pajamas and glasses, and speaks with the voice of a frail, refined gentleman.

"It's me. Brendan. I visited here about a week ago with Melissa Preston."

"Who?"

He's joking around, because we had such an easy, instant rapport when we first met. "Come on, Tommy. I was just quoting a line from the movie you starred in."

"Why would anybody put *me* in a movie, looking the way I do?" There's a catch of remorse in his voice, and I almost think he's serious.

"A horror movie," I tell him—to jog his memory, not to compound the insult. "*The Twisted Face*. And later a small part as the Antique Store Owner in *The Crooked Frame*."

"Young man, I don't know you. I don't understand what you're talking about."

My dad seems ready to slink out of the room. He's totally humiliated on my behalf.

Thomas Hendricks lifts one of his eggplant hands to wipe away a single tear that travels down the rough terrain of his face. I'm sorry if I've upset him, but I almost feel like I have more reason to cry. He was my last chance.

"You told me the hard work was worth it." My voice grows shrill and accusing. "You knew you were part of something important."

I understand a bit about dementia: older people can forget where they are, even *who* they are, as their past slips into a fog of mystery. It's a tragic condition, and I feel terrible if my visit has prompted any mental anguish.

But the explanation I find more likely is that Melissa's mother works in this facility. She's gotten to Tommy, told him how to behave if her daughter's friend ever tries to visit.

Tommy was an actor, after all.

He acts scared now, his hands punching at the bed like he's wearing boxing gloves, searching for a call button to signal the Duty Nurse.

Dad pulls me out of there.

It's a 45 minute drive from Gadsden to my current home in Graysonville, and neither of us says a word.

At one point, "Crazy" by Willie Nelson comes over the car radio. Aside from the title's unfortunate commentary on my recent behavior, there's another sad context. Dad likes Willie Nelson, and I've never been fond of the guy's old-man quavery voice. In the past, if a radio station played one of his songs, one of two things would usually happen: I would switch the dial to a pop station, or Dad would turn up the volume as if to annoy me further.

Neither happens this time. Willie continues at low volume, and his mournful tone expresses an authentic sadness I'd never noticed before.

When we arrive outside the apartment building, Dad parks the car by the curb and turns off the ignition. Neither of us makes a motion to get out.

I dread returning home, because I know what he'll say to Mom. I also know Dad is leaving tonight to return to his job in Cleveland, and some woman named Alicia that he cooks dinner with.

He'll leave Graysonville thinking he's a failure as a father. I don't have the words to reassure him otherwise.

"I'm sorry, Brendan."

He looks at the steering wheel instead of me. I wish he wouldn't confirm the rest of his thoughts by speaking them aloud. There's no need: during the silent drive, I've already imagined the worst of what he'll say:

This has been too much. You've put such pressure on me, to be the kind of father I can't be anymore. The distance between us isn't just miles. We've both changed a great deal. We've literally grown apart.

It's like those movies and that director you've built such ridiculous fantasies around. I can't manage to recall the films with the same affection you've stubbornly persisted in. Any affection I felt for those movies is long gone. The past sometimes needs to stay in the past.

Can you imagine how it feels for me to travel all this way, hopeful I can get through to you? That I can break past all those childish stories and have a meaningful, rational conversation with the son I love?

The son I *used* to love?

God, I feel so sorry for your mother. After all our differences, I still wish the best for her. A good life. But how can she have that if you keep dragging her down with worry?

At first I thought those tall tales of yours hoped to draw me back into your life, maybe even back with your mother. Turns out, the situation is even worse. You've actually convinced yourself these stories are true.

I should have left you there at Evergreen. Apparently they have a special area for people like you who've lost touch with reality.

Why don't you do us all a favor and have yourself committed?

Instead, he says: "I believe you."

"It was him. It was really the guy from the movie."

Such a strange experience, to have Dad defending me to my mom.

"I was wrong about Brendan. He's just as sane as he ever was." Dad's intentional sarcasm in that last statement doesn't undermine the first. Actually, it's comforting because it represents the kind of joking around we used to do. We're back on track, finally—which makes me sad that he's leaving for the airport in about an hour.

All three of us sit at the kitchen table and wait for our Chinese delivery order to arrive. The atmosphere's significantly different from the previous time we were together in this room. For one thing, Mom's without her legal pad.

She's smiling, too—though she's quick to point out she's not happy that I've kept so many secrets from her.

"Nothing good ever comes from lies," she says, but she stops there instead of pulling out the full lecture / training module.

I get a bit of leeway, now that they realize I'm not crazy.

"You should have seen the wild chase he led me on—to that girl's house, then to an old folk's home the next town over." Dad grabs my shirt then does a wicked impersonation of the wheelchair guy: "*What have you taken from my room?*"

He says "I'll explain later" to Mom, but I'm guessing this will be a long-running joke, just for me and Dad.

"I felt like such a sucker for letting Brendan sneak me into Evergreen," Dad continues. "I'm planning to drag us out as soon as possible, but the kid's been so...*agitated*...and I'm kind of stuck playing along. Then we go into that room, and man, it's *him*. It's the Twisted Face."

Now I understand that frozen expression my dad had in Hendricks' room. I thought it was skepticism about me, unease about the whole barge-into-a-nursing-home scenario. I see it on his face now: at least initially, he'd been as starstruck as I'd been. My dad definitely had *not* forgotten his affection for those old Budget Studios movies.

"There couldn't be two people in the world who look like that. He's an older guy, but the shape of his head—that hadn't changed at all. It's unforgettable." Dad worked up a bit of excitement now, waving his hands as if sculpting Hendricks' head in the air above the kitchen table. "I'd never had to read *that* kind of face before. You have to look closely to figure out if someone's being honest, and probably not a lot of people have the nerve to stare down the Twisted Face. I did, though, and I knew he was lying to Brendan."

Dad presses his hands to his own face to shift his eyes out of alignment, to mash his lips to one side. "Not sure what the giveaway was—a rapid blink or a twitch of the jaw, or a tremor in his voice. He tried to make himself cry, too. An actor's cry, since he could barely manage a single tear."

I'm so grateful Dad's story vindicates me, but ask why he didn't stick up for me at the time.

"We had to race out of there," Dad explains to me and Mom. "The guy went all out, slapping the bed and ready to scream for a nurse. We weren't supposed to be in his room to begin with, so could have really gotten into trouble. And in the car on the way home, the whole time, I kept remembering how wrong I'd been to doubt our son. I was totally speechless."

"*That* part's hard to believe," Mom says.

For a moment, I feel like she's connecting with Dad, too. She was attentive and smiling as he spoke, and managed a good-natured joke at the end. I entertain the notion that my parents actually could reunite. We could go back to the old days, be a family again.

Just as quickly, I dismiss the thought. Dad's leaving in an hour. We should enjoy this moment while it lasts.

"I wish..."

"What is it, honey?" Mom says to me.

"I wish I could smooth things out with Melissa."

Maybe that's also too much to ask for.

"Give her some time," Mom says. "Now that you're being honest with *me*—"

—and I sense this will be another long-standing family joke: I failed at telling Dad the truth, yet succeeded so well with lying to Mom—

"—you could invite Melissa here for dinner. Things will be different if your friendship is out in the open, once the pressure of secrecy is gone."

"You might be right, Mom. I don't know why I didn't confide in you sooner."

The Director

Tonight I am a director. At my command the monsters take over Graysonville.

The door bursts open, interrupting the tedium of Camen's English class. The Lake Monster stands in the doorframe, brackish water dripping off its scale-covered body and onto the floor. All the students scream.

This Lake Monster is especially terrifying. Instead of a simple mask and hands, with the rest of the actor covered by everyday clothes, the makeup department has spared no expense. Thick tentacles undulate in place of arms, with lamprey mouths hungry at the center of each awful suction pad. The Monster's eyes blink realistically at the ends of animated stalks as they search the room for potential food.

The mouth on the Monster's face opens like the jaws of a shark, revealing several rows of large teeth. Mr. Camen tries unsuccessfully to push first-row Denny toward the creature, but it rejects the offer in favor of a larger meal. Tentacles python-wrap around the teacher's waist, jaws widen, and a dreadful amber ichor drips over Camen's head, paralyzing him. And with a loud crunch of bones, the Lake Monster begins to feed.

Panicked students race outside the classroom, pushing into each other, nearly slipping on a wet trail of slime in the doorway.

The closest exit leads to the playground, and the perimeter Melissa and I used to walk at lunch. As students rush outdoors, their screams rise in the open air.

A strange hum drowns them out. The sound is like a tremendous airplane engine, mixed with the hint of wailing, torturous music. Almost as one, the students glance upward.

A shadow arcs over the sun, and the schoolyard drops into darkness. Above them hovers, not a tin-foil flying saucer, but an uprooted alien city—buildings of impossible geometric shapes, connected with long transparent tubes.

As the city-ship moves closer, figures become visible within the transparent tubes. These living beings are not friendly humanoid visitors. Their thorn-covered bodies undulate in a sickening ambulation. Above the engine's thrum, the voice of an alien crowd transmits through a monstrous amplifier. Nothing could translate the clicks from these creatures' sharp mouths, but the general sense conveys a universally recognizable emotion: cruelty.

The city-ship descends, and the schoolyard is not large enough to contain it. Groups of students flee in different directions. Many of them are crushed, but the school building itself slows the craft's descent along one edge, allowing a select few to escape harm. For the moment.

Red-hot blasts of rocket exhaust shoot from the craft's underside, baking the school building's brick and glass and cinderblock, cooking crushed mounds of flesh and bone and clothing.

We follow the dozen students who escaped the alien attack, as they emerge at the front of the crumbling, burning school. A lone orange bus awaits, and they pile inside and beg the driver to transport them to safety.

- Where's that?

- Anywhere but here. Please hurry!

The bus speeds away. In the retreating horizon, several more city-ships appear in the sky.

One student wonders aloud if her family is safe. A senior boy suggests that the driver take them to the city square.

- It's where everyone will meet. We can figure out how to fight back against this deadly alien threat.

As the bus heads down a flat stretch of road with guard rails on either side, a heavy dead tree suddenly falls across the path and blocks their passage forward. The driver shifts into reverse, and the wheels grind loudly, but the bus stays still.

- Why aren't we moving?

- We're caught on something. Branches tangled in the front axle, maybe?

A thick dead limb flails across the front windows, animated by the fruitless spinning of the vehicle's tires. The branches wriggle like grasping fingers.

- Oh God, look! Look! There's a face in the tree!

- I don't see it...

- Right there, halfway up the trunk. See the nose and mouth? The closed eyes? Like a sleeping giant.

The eyes open.

Branches scratch at windows all around the bus...

Meanwhile, in the next town over, the Twisted Face strains against the straps of a custom-designed straightjacket. Local officials have charged him with multiple homicides, and they've placed him in a mental institution. His unconventional body is more flexible than his captors realize. The fabric of his restraints begin to loosen, just enough.

He plans revenge against the nurse, first, then the supervising doctor. Into town, he will find the arresting officer, the incompetent public defender, then the corrupt judge. They have called him a monster, and he will live up to their label.

The straps strain and release, strain and release, and with a pop, a misshapen shoulder dislocates from its socket. The straightjacket falls to the padded floor, and the Twisted Face smiles a grim smile.

This first exhilarating dream was not, as I think on it now, an example of vengeful wish fulfillment. Certainly my schoolmates were almost all killed, but there was nothing malicious in each imagined act. In monster movies, the mayhem is part of the fun. The traffic cop who gets chomped between the jaws of a rampaging Rhedosaurus is far more memorable in 20 seconds of screen time than the bland scientist heroes in every scene who eventually save humanity.

The threat makes life interesting. Monster movies exist to allow teenagers to surrender to the cathartic glee of campground dismemberments, alien invasions, or demonic transformations.

I wrote, produced, and directed the best film my subconscious mind could conjure. The entire town became my movie studio, with each location hosting a spectacular, full-color scene—backed by an orchestral music score, with complex makeup for the various monsters, intricate model work for the spacecraft, amazing pyrotechnic effects as the school exploded and burned.

It is the kind of movie I wish Melissa and I could have made together: a big-budget tribute to her father.

Due to its horror and science fiction elements, this film would easily attract a cult following. But it would also achieve the elusive popular and critical success Bud Preston was never able to accomplish.

Because the monsters would seem so real.

The Warlock

Later that night, I become a warlock.

Sleep studies reveal that we experience an average of three to five dreams each night, as we slip into different phases of REM sleep. Dreams can vary in duration, from the span of a movie trailer to that of a full-length feature. The dreamer's perception of time might be so distorted that one of those 2-minute dreams can seem endless, covering a wide range of locations and time frames.

We dream many dreams, but only recall a select few upon waking. It's especially rare that our waking selves recall two distinct dreams from the same night.

That night my mind is incredibly active, agitated by my visit with my dad to Budget House, the property's key features buried beneath paint or mutilated; anxious throughout a risky and apparently fruitless encounter with a duplicitous Thomas Hendricks; later surprised and overwhelmed with relief at my dad's restored faith in me; followed by a bittersweet ending to our too-brief family reunion.

The flurry of mixed emotions heighten my subconscious imagination to a fever pitch. Add to this concoction all the excitement over several weeks of discoveries at Budget House; and my sometimes happy, but often tense relationship with Melissa—who I'd grown to resent as a miserly gatekeeper, allowing only limited, monitored access to the memorabilia of her father's films. Evidence suggests she helped her mother to vandalize those treasures; now she planned to keep the doors of Budget House closed to me forever.

These intense emotions swirl through my dreams, first like a mind-enhancing drug that inspired a good-natured Technicolor violence. Later the emotions become the ingredients of a magical poison, dragging my subconscious down into a malicious phase.

Although I'm able to convince myself the Technicolor dream wasn't wish-fulfillment, I don't have the same certainty about the second one:

It's dark. I wake in a room with no windows.

My delicate fingers touch the wall beside my bed. I feel for a curled corner of paper, affixed there with Scotch tape.

Although I cannot see the poster, I know it depicts a field of flowers.

A cone of jelly wafts a sickly artificial fragrance from the end table. Instead of freshening the room, it stifles me. I taste its chemicals at the back of my throat; it feels like the cone has been jammed there while I slept. The jelly slithers, resisting my attempts to swallow it.

I'm suffocating. I need fresh air.

I sit up in bed and tear at the poster, ripping it from the bottom as if lifting a sash. There's got to be a window behind it.

Nothing. I scratch at the wall with my fingernails, beat it with the heels of my palms, with no success.

I gag and cough, and feel a ripple at the back of my throat. A thick phlegm lurches up then sits heavy atop my tongue, and a sour chemical ichor wriggles centipede legs over my taste buds. I spit it out, and it lands somewhere on the bed. Although I can't bear the thought of my fingers pressing into that vile jelly, I brush blindly at the bedspread hoping to knock the substance onto the floor.

My airway's clear, but I still feel sick in this dark, stale room.

The other poster depicts a mountain. As my eyes adjust, I can almost make out a familiar snow-capped peak, white wisps of clouds above.

Like a child tearing into a Christmas present, I grab the edge of the poster and rip straight across.

Again, nothing but bare wall beneath. Then a gust of mountain air blasts through, refreshingly cool. I breathe deep, grateful for the reprieve, until the air continues cold. My teeth chatter, and I hug my exposed arms close to my chest as I shiver uncontrollably.

I'm near the top of the mountain, exhausted from my climb and numb from the cold, and the air at this altitude becomes thinner and thinner. My head grows light, and I feel ready to pass out.

My fists bash out again, hitting a snow-covered rock face, pounding against painted drywall, creating a bigger opening for the swirl of arctic-temperature air, flecks of paint and snow and plaster falling, a cold burn stinging my face, and I've swallowed a handful of needles.

And it opens. The wall finally opens like a window.

I climb through it.

I am thinking of a boy from my school named Brendan. I thought we were friends, but he wanted the wrong things from me. He was interested only in a father I never knew, and in digging through souvenirs of movies better left forgotten.

I know everyone thinks of me as "the weird girl." I never expected a romantic relationship with him.

But I shared some of my family's secrets, brought him closer to those movies that he, for some inexplicable reason, seemed to value so much. I simply wanted him to see me as a friend.

I don't think he saw me at all.

Now that I've rejected him, his anger and disappointment—all his unrealistic, dashed hopes—grow so strong that they exert a supernatural influence.

Brendan tried to suffocate me in my own bed, then turned my room into an icy wasteland.

He dreams, and he sees through my eyes.

He enjoys my suffering.

And now, as I fall through the wall of my bedroom, keep falling until I land smack against hard concrete, he does something even worse.

I'm curled in the fetal position on a landing near the top of the Stone Stairway. Pain radiates from my left leg. When I reach to touch it, I feel a jagged piece of exposed bone, ripped through the blood-soaked fabric of my pajamas.

I'm certain that I broke even more bones in the fall, and that some of them have pierced internal organs.

That is not the most awful thing.

The awful thing is that...

...Brendan is making me see the world as he does.

The Stone Stairway is beautiful. It shimmers with the magical chiaroscuro of classic black-and-white films. Velvet shadows are both ominous and inviting. Gray tones pulse with an inner light, suggesting a wide spectrum of elusive fogged-over colors.

Here, a spiderweb in the corner is beautiful. The texture of a concrete rock flickers in torchlight like a living thing. And the shadow-dark shine of my own blood pools away from my leg and stomach then drips down a cement stair in lovely languid motion.

Beside me and below stretches the vast expanse of my father's movie studio—like him, unjustly neglected. I feel, now, the importance of those artificial, partitioned rooms, each containing a wealth of treasured artifacts from his brief, glorious days as a writer and director. I long to see these wondrous sets and props again, to offer the appreciation that's due to them. But the studio is dark and distant, and my leg is broken.

The real pain comes not from my shattered leg, a punctured lung or kidney. It comes from the realization that I've dishonored my father's legacy for so long.

My God, *this* is what Brendan tried to show me.

And I drove him away.

The fallen girl tugs at her wounded leg, then gives up. It is too painful for her to move.

A low moan echoes in the cavernous stairway. We might think it is the girl, bewailing her plight.

No. She turns her head and looks to the top of the staircase, indicating the source of that anguished cry.

A dozen steps above her, a white translucent figure holds a flickering kerosene lantern. The spirit has the shape of a beautiful woman, but a gust of wind ripples through her thin flowing robe. Her facial features ripple, too, as if her skin is made of cobwebs.

Another low moan, then a question. "Where," the spirit asks. "Where is the one I love the most?"

The prostrate girl waves an arm at the airy spirit. "I'm here, Mother. Save me!"

In response, the spirit descends the staircase. Her gossamer feet barely disturb the ground with each step. Closer to the girl. Closer.

"Help me up." The girl is still unable to stand, but she stretches both arms toward her mother's ghostly shape. The spirit's shining form steps onto the landing and glides toward her.

As she hugs the spirit's legs, her arms pass through. A sticky coating covers her arms, and soft cobwebs transform into long strands of thick gray hair, oily and unwashed.

"Where," the spirit repeats as it continues down the staircase. "Where is the one I love the most?"

The girl's head drops in disappointment. "I'm here," she says weakly. "Why didn't you help me?"

As the ghost reaches the bottom of the stairway, a wide spotlight follows the small raised lantern, illuminating different sections of the studio.

The scenes roll forward in sequence, like a movie montage that conveys various events in rapid succession. In each scene, a teenage boy pulls open curtains or shifts aside piles of clothing or stacks of paper; he uses a stethoscope to open a safe, or taps against walls to locate a secret panel.

Whatever item he finds, he places in a large rusty wheelbarrow.

The dream unfolds like an out-of-body experience. No longer seeing through Melissa's eyes, I watch myself as if I'm the star of a movie.

In the Antique Shop, my character reaches to the top shelf and pulls down the plastic model of a human heart. I grip the model with both hands and twist in opposite directions until it opens. A withered human heart sits inside the hollow plastic shell. I remove the heart, and place it in the wheelbarrow.

I lift the crystal ball from the medium's circular table, then pull off the gold-fringed purple tablecloth. A deep depression creates a hiding place in the central support post. I reach in, grabbing a hank of hair. The item's stuck, like cork in a bottle, and I brace my other hand against the table and lean back to tug harder.

The spirit's lantern flickers and wavers. "Where," she says, and I tug harder, shaking and twisting the hank of hair until I hear a wet pop like the sound of meat sliding off a bone.

The decayed, severed head finally breaks loose from its compartment. I hold it up, the same way the ghostly woman holds up her lantern. Even given the head's advanced state of decomposition, I've seen enough behind-the-scenes photographs to easily recognize my favorite director.

"Bring him back," the ghost says.

"I'll try." I reach into the compartment to retrieve the ear that had sloughed off when I tugged the head free. Then I put head and ear into the wheelbarrow, with the rest of the body parts I've uncovered.

The front wheel tilts awkwardly as I push the wheelbarrow over the unfinished studio floor. My cargo looks somewhat like a sleeping man, except the ingredients are scrambled. A severed leg, crooked at the knee, hangs over the side and kicks distractedly as I push.

The ghost isn't much help either. Her lantern sways as she follows, and the swirl of shadow and light makes me dizzy. A wind like an aging woman's eager breath brushes the back of my neck, and she begs for me to hurry.

I'm going as fast as I dare. It's not wise to rush dark magic. The slightest mistake could be disastrous.

I roll the wheelbarrow onto the simulated stone floor of the dungeon set. I've already prepared a raised coffin at the center, strange chalk symbols radiating from it and black candles waiting to be lit around the circumference.

As if from a distant mountaintop, a girl cries for help. I can't let her bother me right now.

I've lined the coffin with unspooled strips of celluloid—precious seconds of film spliced and sacrificed to cushion the bed of their creator. I lay the different pieces of Bud Preston's corpse into the coffin, inventing chants in a long-forgotten language as I try to place limbs in their proper order.

Binding chants, to assist the curled strips of film that crackle under the weight of bones and desiccated flesh.

The ghostly woman leans forward and attempts to mimic my magical phrasings. I do not understand the language that passes through me, but worry that her imperfect pronunciation will undermine the effect of the spell.

I light a match, and visit the thirteen candles at the circumference of the chalk circle.

A dim light rises from the floor of the dungeon. Since I no longer need the illumination from the spectre's lantern, I knock it aside.

I grab her, my fingers tangled in air, then cobwebs, then coarse hair—then muscles and sinew and flesh and bone. I twist and pull, and the ghost-woman screams while I tear her apart as if ripping a damp rag into strips. I pull her arms from her torso, rip off the fabric-flesh of her neck until her head falls off ghostly shoulders. I open an awful seam in her bosom, splitting her torso down the middle.

One leg comes off whole, while the other breaks above the ankle and above the knee.

As I pull the rag woman apart, the arranged pieces of Bud Preston's body magically stitch together inside the coffin.

And still the spirit screams, her unattached head face up on the dungeon floor, her eyes accusing me.

I raise my foot over her head, press the heel of my shoe into her open mouth. Beneath me, the head feels hollow and airy, like an abandoned wasps' nest. I lean into my foot, crushing the nest. The spirit's lantern extinguishes, and finally her screaming stops.

Then I hear a sharp intake of breath from inside the coffin. The corpse's eyelids flutter and struggle to open. Its stomach begins a slow pattern of rise and fall, rise and fall.

Success!

The eyelids open completely.

I realize with horror that I've made a dreadful mistake. I'd moved too quickly; the language of my chants was incorrect.

Because the eye sockets are empty.

The body in the coffin begins to convulse. Freshly attached limbs discover an agony of contorted motions.

He thrashes and writhes. My hero. I've brought him back to life, to suffer the torments of hell.

In a panic, I reach to the ground and grab one of the black candles. I throw it into the coffin.

Celluloid is highly flammable. The contents flash bright in a burst of magician's smoke. A hiss of escaped steam rises shrill in the air as the body parts writhe and burn.

He's still in agony. I don't know how long he will suffer, but I can't look away.

For a moment, I consider staying with him as the dungeon burns.

The stone of an actual dungeon would be resistant to flame. A wooden floor, painted to resemble marble, catches easily. The scent of cooked flesh rises from the coffin-cauldron, unnaturally bound limbs separating into a wriggling stew, and the area grows increasingly warm.

My eyebrows begin to singe.
And I turn tail and run.

No. What am I doing?

There's too much here worth saving.

I grab the soothsayer's purple tablecloth, spread it on the floor and toss items onto it: a native statue, the hideous mask of the deformed shopkeeper, the bound pages of an unfilmed script. I gather the four corners of the cloth and pull it into a makeshift sack that I can drag onto the next partitioned set, to rescue more treasures.

Flames light the areas I've left behind. The trees of the simulated forest set mimic an actual outdoor fire.

I have to hurry. With a cry of joy, I locate the spider model on the edge of the reporter's desk, and I bundle it with the other plundered items.

As I walk past the Victorian storefront, hot smoke thickens like drifts of English fog. I'm having trouble breathing, but can't cover my mouth—I need both hands to drag the heavy sack.

I'll feel better when I climb higher. I cross to the stone stairway and take my first steps.

The makeshift bag drags heavy behind me. What else had I taken—more books, the reporter's typewriter, the giant limb of the Haunted Oak? I grabbed whatever I could lay hands on. There wasn't time to sort and judge each item's value.

The sack gets heavier the higher I go. I'm not sure I can make it to the top without jettisoning some of my precious cargo.

But I persist, even though my arms almost feel ready to pop out of their sockets. The bag thumps up each step. Every dozen or so steps, I get a brief respite as I drag the sack across the landing.

Still, it feels almost as if I'm dragging the weight of a dead body.

Almost at the top. I strain and pull.

The bag pulls back.

It's stuck on something. I tug harder to twist and rip it free.

And it says, "Brendan, you have to help me."

Melissa holds onto the cloth. She lies on the ground, her legs at an odd angle. A snapped bone sticks out the side of a bloody tear in one leg of her pajamas.

I pull again at the bag. It's too heavy with Melissa attached.

Her eyes glow bright as flames rise from below. "I thought we were friends," she says. "What have you stolen this time?" Melissa scratches at the cloth, trying to pull the corners apart and reveal the contents.

I won't let her. "You don't know what it's worth," I say. "You never appreciated your father the way I do."

She's a girl, and she's wounded. I have to be stronger.

But I feel like she's winning. She has the desperate strength of someone in a crazed panic.

She's fighting for her life, but so am I.

Keeping one fist firm around the gathered corners of the cloth, I reach my other hand down to her wounded leg. I grab the snapped protrusion of bone and twist it.

Melissa screams, and I'm thinking about how she made my parents mistrust me. How she manipulated me, taunting me with a tiny fraction of the secrets in her home, then closing the curtain over the rest.

"I'm taking what I can." I twist my hand, agitating the wound in her leg. "It belongs to me."

Melissa's screaming in pain, and a glow from the rising fire illuminates the tears that stream down her face. But she won't let go of the tablecloth. One of the gathered corners slips from my grasp, and all the items spill out.

"Look at it, Brendan. It's all junk!"

What if she's right? Stolen pages covered with meaningless scratchings, plastic bottles wrapped with tinfoil, wooden boards coated with flecked and fading paint. Taken from the studio, far removed from the movies that brought them purpose, these items lose all their significance. My friendship with Melissa should be more important.

"They're treasures," I insist. "They're rightfully mine."

Melissa summons all her remaining strength and pushes at the cloth and the pile of spilled items. They sail over the edge of the stairway and into the inferno below.

A distant crash, and I'm left with nothing.

I grab Melissa's arm to help her up from the ground. Perhaps she thinks I'm apologizing.

She's much lighter than the bag of items I'd attempted to rescue from Budget House.

I lift then toss her over the side of the stairway. She screams all the way down.

In my dream, I push into the hidden hallway, where accusing eyes watch from patterns in the wallpaper. I open the thin latched door and step into Melissa's home.

The ordinary home. Sterile and windowless.

My nostrils burn from the odor of smoke mixed with artificial fragrance. I head to the end of the hall, to the bland carpeted stairs that lead down to the foyer exit.

Melissa's mother waits for me at the top of the stairs. Unlike the airy spirit I'd encountered in the studio, her hair is gray and disheveled, and her face is lined with wrinkles. She is the Withered Hag.

"I'm not who you think I am." She crosses her arms and blocks my way down the stairs.

"You're such a disappointment," I tell her. "Your beauty. Where did it go?"

She winces from the force of my words. As I watch, strange cracks appear at her neck and where her arms join her shoulders. A leg snaps at the hip, and another falls into three separate pieces. Her torso splits down the middle, divided along the same line I'd torn through the fabric-spirit of her younger self.

The segments tumble down the soft carpet of an ordinary staircase. I step over the pieces as I descend to the exit.

Hurrying onto the porch, I don't bother to shut the front doors behind me. I run across the field, and before I turn down the access road, I pause to take one last look at the shell of Budget House.

It looks like a scale model on a miniature set. I wish the bristled legs of a giant spider would skitter over the roof, an animated monster crushing the building in spectacular fashion. Or the forbidden chemicals in the mystic scientist's laboratory could combust in a huge fireball, prompting the audience to erupt in spontaneous applause as the end credits roll.

I am the only audience. A puff of smoke curls from the open doors of the building, accompanied by the sound of a sickly cough.

The Axe Maniac

As usual, Melissa moves quickly down the road from her bus stop. I never could keep up with her.

She's way ahead, the size of a fluttering moth in the distance. I don't yell ahead to ask her to wait. My voice would only make her run faster.

It's almost like she knows I am behind her, and she's afraid to slow down.

As usual, the road is essentially abandoned. There's no one nearby she could call for help.

In a movie she would stumble, giving her pursuer a chance to trod closer. She would almost make it to the door of her house, but would fumble and drop the key. As she curses and bends to pick it up, a shadow will loom over her. The shadow holds an axe. The girl screams and puts her hands over her face—as if that weak gesture could shield her from the sharp edge of descending steel...

At some point, Melissa must hear the rush of approaching footsteps, my exhausted breathing getting closer and closer. She won't stop, won't glance over her shoulder.

I'm frustrated that she ignores me. She's been this way at school, too. She will hug close to the opposite side of the hallway as she passes; in class, she deliberately places students or teachers between us to avoid a private conversation. She's begun to talk with other kids at lunch—a group of girls she's complained about in the past, so I know she doesn't really like them.

It's time to put an end to this foolishness.

I'm stronger than she realizes, and my legs are longer. I kick up gravel and dirt as I run.

Melissa was the size of a moth, but now she seems as large as a human infant. The illusory perspective changes as I approach: she ages into a child, then a pre-adolescent.

As she nears normal size, I raise the axe over my head.

If she turns around, I will hide the axe behind my back. Pretend to be normal. Her friend again.

We've reached the "Dead End" sign.

Melissa stops. Her shoulders slump, and she lets her backpack slide off and to the ground.

There's a weariness to her posture, and I notice the same attitude in her face, particularly around her eyes.

Perhaps, like me, she hasn't been getting too much sleep lately.

"Why did you do it?" I ask her. I could be referring to any number of things, but she catches what's uppermost in my mind.

"My mother did it, mostly, but she made me help." She looks to her left, and I know she can see Budget House at the end of the access road, its front porch drably painted over. Melissa must have held the ladder steady as her mother climbed to deface the bas relief in the overhanging mantle. "I'm most saddened about the tree. It's been there since even before our house was built. Cutting into a healthy living thing is wrong. I painted black tar over the wound, because I read that's supposed to help a tree heal—but who knows what long-term damage we did..."

"It's *all* like a living thing to me." I have to force myself to stay calm. She should know this already—how much the items from her father's movies mean to me.

I ask if she'd heard about my disastrous visit with Thomas Hendricks.

Melissa shrugs. "My mother works at Evergreen."

I wonder what Mrs. Preston offered as payment for Hendricks' performance: more pillows or blankets? an extra serving of Jell-O at dinner?

Melissa seems shy in front of me, like I'm a stranger. Maybe I am. Maybe I've always been. Her eyes look down, or off in the distance. There's an elusive emotion that she's trying to suppress, and I can't decide if it's lingering affection for me, or regret over what's happened to our friendship.

"The studio," I say. "Please tell me the rest of it's still there. Even if I can't see it again, I want to know the studio still exists."

Melissa still can't look me in the eye. "After our parents talked on the phone, my mother went a little crazy. It was the middle of that terrible storm when she sawed off part of the tree. Rain poured all around us as she splashed paint over the front porch. 'All this junk,' she said. 'Never brought me anything but grief.' She went inside and found a folder with scraps of paper inside. Phone numbers of people who'd inquired over the years. Collectors."

My heart sinks.

"When you visited with your dad, I told you she was in a strange mood. Mother bought empty boxes from K-Mart, and several rolls of shipping tape. And huge garbage bags, too. She was in a frenzy, packing some things up to sell, stuffing other things in bags to take to the dump. Brendan, I don't think she cared which items were worth selling or which she should toss away. I couldn't stop her."

Horrified at what she tells me, I raise my arms in frustration. Melissa takes a step back.

As if she could see the axe I'd imagined holding earlier.

In that instant, I can pinpoint the elusive emotion in her expression.

It's fear.

She's afraid of me. She's backing away from a threat.

"I don't have what you want anymore," Melissa says.

She reminds me of a kidnap victim in a movie. Her captors torture her to reveal the lock's combination, the stash of stolen money or drugs, the hiding place of a dead scientist's secret formula. But they've kidnapped the wrong person. *I don't have the information you need. Hurt me all you want: I can't tell you what you want to hear.*

I lower my arms gently, and try to show her that I'm puzzled. I try to assume a calm, reassuring expression, hoping it looks natural instead of making me seem even more like a crazed murderer.

Why would she think of me in this way? We'd become close friends, shared some really good times these past weeks. Even if our friendship's over now, I'll always be grateful for my brief times in Budget House.

I'm upset with Melissa, sure, but I'd never seriously consider harming her.

Then it hits me.

We *have* grown close. She became my anchor after my mom's job uprooted me, once again, and dropped me into an unfamiliar town. Melissa was my escape from the tedium of my uninteresting peers at school. And instead of simply reading behind-the-scenes articles in movie magazines, I actually got to *visit* the marvelous place where my favorite films were made. Melissa Preston shared that experience with me.

I'd been focusing too much on my own bond with the movies, and the bond they'd formed between me and my dad. The bond with Melissa was important, too.

A shared connection. A mental link.

When I dreamed that I was a warlock, what if I'd actually cast a spell?

There was no other way to make sense of how she reacted right now. Melissa *saw* what I dreamed last night.

That dream that began as if through her eyes, but was entirely controlled by the worst part of my subconscious: I woke her in a darkened bedroom, filled her with a suffocating panic until she broke through the wall and into a nightmare. I smashed her body onto a cement staircase, then conjured a spectre of her mother's youthful self to glide past, ignoring her. In the studio I became a grave robber, digging up pieces of her father. As a dark sorcerer, I tore her mother's spectre into shreds. Then, after causing her father's unnatural resurrection, I burned his reanimated corpse.

After I plundered Budget Studios for petty souvenirs, Melissa begged me for help. My subconscious had conjured a weighty dilemma: choose to save the movie souvenirs, or my injured friend. In a clear parallel to real life, I lost them both.

I dreamt I killed my best friend out of spite. Then I ran away as Budget House burned to the ground.

"I didn't mean anything by it," I tell her now. "I was upset and frustrated. Please believe that I didn't mean it."

Melissa doesn't ask me to clarify what I'm apologizing for. She knows. She has to know.

I want her to yell at me now. To say only a sick mind could imagine the awful things I'd dreamed about.

Melissa doesn't say anything. She still can't look me in the eyes, but I hope, at least, that she's not afraid of me anymore.

She's standing there at the intersection and the access road to her house, and she turns her head to the left, ear tilted slightly as if straining to hear something. Maybe her home calls to her, as Budget House sometimes called to me.

I don't hear anything now, and I'm far enough back in the road that I can't see the house in the distance.

Budget House didn't actually burn down, as it had at the end of my dream, but it might as well have. I know I'll never visit it again.

The Lost Reel

Can two people live in a small town and barely see each other? Well, our high school was pretty big, with more than 300 students. Even though Melissa and I had some classes together, it was easy enough to keep our distance. We stayed apart the same way the school's couples did after they broke up—though we were never really a couple. Not in any honest sense, at least.

Our policy of mutual avoidance became even easier after Mom's job predictably transferred her to work with a new company. I spent a few months of my Junior year in Altoona, Pennsylvania. I graduated from Webster Groves High in St. Louis.

Then off to college—my entry point to other lives in other cities and states.

Adult life fell into a typical pattern for someone frequently uprooted as a teenager. I was in a series of short-term relationships, but never settled down. My longest stint was a rented house shared with a guy named Charles and two orange tabby cats. Charles liked reading and going to restaurants, but he never cared much for movies, which was a sore spot with me.

To make money, I collect and sell film memorabilia, travelling to horror and sci-fi conventions with one-sheets and rare magazines and autographed actor photos for fans to purchase, and offering big-ticket items through a catalog I print semi-monthly and mail to a carefully targeted list. These days I do the catalog mostly out of nostalgia—90% of my sales happen via the Internet. I've actually made a decent living this way. Much more than I might have expected.

I've always remembered those magical weeks in Budget House. My collector contacts knew about my interest in Budget Studios, and I kept my ear to the ground about any sales of props or other memorabilia from Bud Preston's films. I followed a few promising leads over the years, but they never amounted to anything authentic.

I assumed the items Mrs. Preston boxed up found their way to a specialized collector who hid them away for some reason. The same impulse, I guess, that makes a rich snob buy a famous painting simply to hang it over his fireplace.

Then one day an online friend wrote to tell me Bud Preston's widow had died. Melissa's mother. I sent flowers to the funeral.

A few days later, I wrote a long letter to Melissa. I asked her forgiveness, taking all the blame for what went wrong between us. I told her about my life now, mostly alone, moving from town to town. My own parents had passed away within two years of each other—too soon, but it always seems that way, doesn't it? I wished her much strength in her time of grief, and expressed a sincere hope that her life was full and happy.

On one level, it might have seemed like I had an angle—that I was attempting to soften her up to allow the deal that eventually happened. That's not the case. I was just trying to fix something awful from my past.

A past I could never really let go of.

I heard a rumor that an opportunistic collector travelled to Graysonville to purchase any memorabilia from the surviving heir. Melissa shut the door in his face, but not before saying, "Of course I still have those things. They all stay with the house—and the house isn't on the market."

Then one night the phone rang, and Melissa Preston's name showed up in the Caller ID screen. I was almost afraid to answer it.

What was it—thirty years? Her voice hadn't changed a bit. She thanked me for the flowers, and the note. Then she said, "You didn't need to apologize, Brendan. We weren't good people then, either of us. Parents mess us up, or we do it ourselves. Who knows?"

"I think you're letting me off too easy." I almost laughed then, from relief—a weight of guilt suddenly lifted.

"What I *do* know," she said, "is that you love this house. Budget House belongs to you."

She'd decided to sell it to me.

Melissa opens the front doors and invites me inside. I'm walking into a film. It's a Hollywood ending that glosses over the emotional tensions sustained throughout the film.

Even though I spent very little physical time here, I thought of it as the house where I grew up.

The haunted house, with the movie studio attached to the back.

I know I don't deserve it. I shouldn't be rewarded for my callous behavior as a teen. But sometimes life gives you a break you don't deserve.

"Oh, and I found something interesting," Melissa says. She's aged better than I have, with a slight bit of gray in long hair that hangs loose to her shoulders. Her clothing is similar to what she wore when I knew her—out of place on a high school student, but well-suited to the mature woman in front of me.

We step into the living room, where I notice a large vase of flowers on the coffee table, surrounded by sympathy cards. I ask if Melissa returned home to care for her mother, or if she's remained here in Graysonville all along, but she offers only a vague answer. Next I attempt some small talk, and again she's evasive.

I get the sense that, in her view, I don't have the right to ask if there's "someone special" in her life right now.

She's invited me here for a business transaction, nothing more.

Melissa reaches beneath the TV stand and retrieves a flat metal canister. She hands it to me. Along the edge, a piece of masking tape with black magic marker identifies the contents as "THE INVISIBLE THREAT." I pry off the cover to find a 16mm reel inside.

"It's the film my father was working on before he died. Incomplete, of course."

The reel's only half full, so I judge it's about 15-20 minutes running time. I'm speechless. Such an incredible, priceless find: a Lost Reel from a Budget Studios Production.

"That would come with the house, too," Melissa says. "Though you're free to screen it now, if you like."

She still knows me well enough that I don't need to voice my eager answer.

Melissa takes me upstairs to the strange hallway entrance to her father's movie studio. At the top of the stairs, she flips a switch and instead of the faint emergency lights along the stone stairway, the arc lights flash on in rapid sequence. For the first time, I see the whole studio in full illumination. This is how it would have looked back in the day, when Bud Preston made movies here.

We walk together down the stairs and into the studio. I pass the different sets, last seen so long ago they now seem like images from almost-forgotten dreams.

Our destination is the Living Room set, where the giant limb smashed through the window frame in *The Haunted Oak*. Melissa has prepared the projector as she had for me once before, aimed at the broad side of the stone stairway.

"I'll dim the lights for you on my way out," Melissa says. "We'll talk more about the sale when you're done here."

"Don't you want to watch it with—?"

"I already tested it, to make sure the projector works." Again, evasive. Maybe it would be too much of a reminder of the previous time at this strange indoor drive-in. Our "date" that wasn't a date.

"Oh, there's also this." Melissa reaches into the pocket of her sweater, and pulls out a single key. "It unlocks my father's office, with the other equipment, and the archives: scripts and sketches and business records."

She hands it to me. I say "Thank you," but there's no way I can fully express my gratitude. Maybe I don't have to. Melissa knows. More than any person possibly could, she knows how much this means to me.

As she walks away, I place the reel onto the projector and carefully thread the film through the machine. Across the expanse of the studio, Melissa flips switches on the light panel at the bottom of the stairs. The arc lights slowly dim, but the emergency lights along the stone stairway remain on.

Melissa walks up these stairs to return to the ordinary portion of the house. Soon to be *my* house, though I can hardly believe it. I watch her ascend, and she pauses at the top to turn and wave down at me. I wave back, though she can't really see me in the theater-darkened studio.

With almost unbearable anticipation, I turn on the projector and start the reel.

It's a very rough cut, out-of-sequence and with missing segments, but I at least get the idea of what Bud Preston was trying to accomplish. His final film idea was a stroke of low-budget genius. *The Invisible Threat* was the ultimate way to save money: with an invisible monster, there's no need to spend a single dime on the costume.

To be honest, it's the kind of film, had Bud Preston finished and released it, that would have been extremely unpopular with reviewers. They'd probably label it his worst movie.

It is wonderful.

Today I am a Caretaker.

I live in the haunted house of my adolescence, among the movie sets that haunted my childhood and have always stayed with me.

I don't want to be one of those rich guys who buys a Picasso or Rembrandt, then hides it away from the general public. I love Bud Preston's films too much to keep all of this to myself.

At the same time, I don't want just anybody coming into this home. Every visitor needs to be someone who truly appreciates these films as much as I do.

Well, *almost* as much.

People from my mailing list write with requests, or I see postings on blogs or message boards. I usually get a good idea of who seems a good candidate to visit.

And I send them the whole story to read. If they're willing to come to Graysonville after that, I'm happy for a while to shift roles from Caretaker to Tour Guide.

As I am for you now. We'll head upstairs. I think you'll be very pleased with what I've done to the studio. It's still a work in process, but I've restored several of the sets to their original glory. I've also rearranged the archives, selecting key pieces to display outside the relevant location—the original script for *The Dungeon of Count Verlock*, for example, open to a page with Bud Preston's extensive notes, set on a pedestal outside the actual set the script refers to.

And yes, I'll screen for you that reel of *The Invisible Threat*. Like all Bud Preston's films, I never get tired of seeing it.

Here's the entrance to the studio. Go ahead and lift the latch. Let's go inside.

Bonus Features

Text adaptations of 4 Bud "Budget" Preston films originally intended for inclusion in *Monster Project* magazine Issues 101 – 104

About the text: *The following "novelizations," based on movies written and directed by Bud "Budget" Preston, were scheduled to appear in issues of* Monster Project *magazine. The original text has been retained, including some of the strange grammatical quirks of the anonymous author (in particular, the fondness for and overuse of ellipses).*

For more information about the history of these stories, consult the **Editor's Note** *included at the end of this book.*

A
HAUNTED
MAGAZINE
MONSTER
PROJECT
#101
JUL
MONSTER
PROJECT
ARE YOU
BRAVE
ENOUGH
TO ENTER...
Bud Preston's
THE DUNGEON OF
COUNT VERLOCK
THE
DUNGEON OF
COUNT VERLOCK

The Dungeon of Count Verlock

(A Budget Studios Production)

"Come back to the couch." Reece patted the cushion beside him. "Sit with me."

"Maybe later." Julia Dougherty stood at the windows, her fingers absently touching the tassel that held back one of the green curtains on one side.

"I bet you like what you see." The two adjoining windows overlooked the back yard, but in nighttime darkness the glass became more of a mirror. Reece winked at her. "I sure do."

"Stop." She half-smiled, but managed to resist his predictable charm. Would she even be here if she didn't feel like she needed him?

Her reflected stare provided no answer, her skin translucent in the sheen of glass…her eyes bright and blank…hair wisping like a torchfire atop her head. She wore a dark blue shirt that absorbed the interior room's light, making her neck appear severed at the collar. Her head floated in the dark of Reece Farraday's back yard.

"I think about that line of trees at the edge of your property," she said. "Those woods…You never know what's behind them."

"More trees."

"Yes, of course. And the path to the abandoned house further back…the mansion you told me about. We *know* what's supposed to be there. But when we can't actually see it…"

"I guess the dark is always kind of scary." Reece stood and moved beside her. In the reflection, his arm disappeared behind her missing torso...he hugged empty air beneath a severed head.

"I'm not just talking about the dark," Julia said. "During the day, too...that line of trunks...limbs and leaves intertwining. It's like a wall. The world behind that wall could change, and we'd never know."

"What you don't know, won't hurt you."

Julia shrugged away from him. "How could you say that? Especially now..."

"I'm sorry." His arm was no longer around her waist, and it was as if he didn't know what to do with it. Reece started to reach out to her...embarrassed, he changed his mind and lifted his hand to run fingers through his slicked-back hair. "I'm sorry."

"Tell me why I'm safer here," Julia said.

He summoned up easy, rehearsed arguments. She'd heard them before, but he guessed it would comfort her to hear them repeated. "I've got solid locks on the front and back doors. I'll keep you in eyeshot or earshot at all times...while you're sleeping, I'll be right down the hall. Just shout and I'll come running." Then the clincher: "They were alone. The girls who disappeared were all alone when they were taken."

"God, yes, I'll set it to music for you." She slipped into a mocking sing-song voice, a quick twirling dance move as accompaniment. " 'A Woman Alone at Night Was Abducted.' " Julia lowered her arms from the ballerina pose. "That'd be a great tune for the radio, wouldn't it? They'd play it every hour."

"It's a warning. They're just repeating the truth."

"And repeating, and repeating, and repeating, and repeating. Oh, I'm not mad at you. But sometimes we girls *want* to be alone...or at least, when we're with a guy we want it to be our *choice*. Not because we're scared."

"Oh, I get it," he pouted. "You'd rather not be here with me."

"That's *not* what I said." Julia crossed back to the windows, closer to him. She might have guessed he was playing at being wounded... but she could play along. "It's a kind gesture. And I took you up on it, so I must be okay with it on some level."

"On *some* level."

"I'm just being honest. Look, Reece...We haven't been dating that long. Certainly not long enough for me to be spending the night at your place. Maybe we'd get there eventually...I don't know. But this... this awful *situation* in our town...it's kind of moved things too fast between us." She took his hands between hers: a gesture of friendship or gratitude, rather than a lover's clasp. "Some maniac kidnaps women, and hey, *I'm* a woman, so suddenly I'm not safe in my own home anymore. I've gotta be locked up with you."

He broke away from her platonic gesture. "You make it sound like a prison."

"Maybe it is."

"Some prison's aren't so bad. Think of those 'country club' prisons, where they send crooked politicians or corrupt businessmen. You get fine meals, a soft bed, all the comforts of home." He tried another wink, the mock lechery actually working on her a bit this time. "And you've got an 'in' with the warden. Special privileges, you know."

"Yeah, that prison talk doesn't quite get me in the mood." But she smiled. In the window her flame top head floated closer. His arm again disappeared behind her dark-clothed torso.

Their faces pressed closer. He tilted his neck in position to kiss her...

But she turned away... Again, staring out the window, squinting at darkness and her own reflection.

"What? You can't see anything." Reece reached for the closest tassel and unhooked it, letting the curtain drop into place on this side. He went to the adjoining window and repeated the process. "There. Now you won't be tempted."

"I wasn't," she said dryly.

"Very funny." They were joking at the moment, like they were on the same wavelength. Maybe she would let him kiss her now. In her words: let it be her *choice*, rather than because she was scared.

He tried again, an arm around her waist, a tilt of his neck, closing his eyes...

She didn't struggle out of his grasp. They kissed.

He felt her lips slide away from his…closed tight…turning toward the curtained windows.

Reece opened his eyes. She slipped away from him.

He'd never seen anyone who was hypnotized, but that's how Julia looked to him now. Her expression was glazed over, facial muscles loose as if she was asleep…but her eyes stayed wide open, drawn to the obscured windows.

Never wake a sleepwalker…But she wasn't asleep, not really. He considered grabbing her as she walked past. Shaking her.

Instead he said her name, the gentle way you'd rouse someone in the morning: *Your alarm has gone off. You'll be late for work.*

She continued to the window, reaching for the closed curtain.

"Julia? There's nothing to see out there."

She pulled the dark green fabric aside…slowly…slowly.

The black back yard appeared, and the reflected room superimposed.

Julia moved closer to the glass…close enough to fog the image.

"It's your face," he told her. "Your pretty face."

She ignored him, staring into her own eyes.

Then a slam like a gunshot, a sudden shake of the glass that distorted her face with the warp of a funhouse mirror. Her own frightened reaction intensified the effect, and she jumped back, almost knocking into Reece.

"I got you," he said.

He steadied her, and she let him. She touched her face, as if to ensure her features hadn't been rearranged. "What happened?"

"You were in a kind of daze," he said.

"No, the window. Something hit the window from outside."

"Stay here. I'll check."

"I'm not supposed to be alone," she reminded him with a hint of sarcasm.

So the two of them went outside.

Neither of them carried a flashlight, but they could see well enough in the glow from the house. They looked inside now…a framed view of the room, and where they'd just been standing.

"Whoever was out here," Julia said. "This is how easily they could watch us."

"Now, don't jump to conclusions." Reece looked at the window and shivered...from the chill night air, or not wanting to admit the possible truth of Julia's statement. "It was probably a bird. They're stupid about glass. They see the light, and think they can fly right into the house, then, *bang!*" He shifted his angle to get a slant view of the window, and a smear of blood seemed to appear at the level of Julia's face...right where her face had been, that is, when she peered out into the yard. "It's your fault for opening the curtain again."

"Where is it, then?" Julia waved her arm at the tufts of grass around their feet, at the shrub bushes that pressed against the side of the house. "Where is this bird I supposedly lured to its death?"

Reece pointed at the blood on the window, then drew a line with his finger to the bush beneath. A glisten of red painted a section of leafage. He moved a branch, peering down.

Julia stood next to him, following his gaze. A round gray-white shape appeared deep in the clutter of branches and leaves.

"Feathers," she said, confirming his guess about a bird. A dead bird, curled up like a ball.

Reece pulled the branch wider, and something like a banded tail appeared behind the curled shape. "Or fur," she said, because she realized her eyes might have played tricks on her, with wet, matted fur simulating the grain of feathers.

Some awful rodent. But that didn't make sense. Without wings, how could the creature have flown at the window?

Reece pulled again at branches from both sides, spreading them wider. More of the shape revealed itself. The tail was larger than she realized, with a calico pattern rather than the stiff banded coils she'd attribute to a rodent.

A kitten or a small cat. A child's missing pet, no doubt, white with gray stripes, and a red collar about its neck. It had hit the window with such terrible force. Someone must have thrown it at the house...

Reece opened the gap even wider, revealing more to the shape than she expected. The calico tail had been some trick of the dim light, shadows cast by the branches and leaves…not a tail at all, but a small pale leg overcast with bands of shadow.

No fur, no feathers.

Skin.

"C'mere, little guy," Reece said, reaching in with both hands to lift the fallen infant.

Careful to avoid scratching the skin with the branches…careful also not to snag the cloth diaper (the original rounded shape she'd seen).

Reece held the infant. He *cradled* it in one arm, a cupped hand beneath the neck to support its head. The idea crossed her mind, then, that he might make a good father, if they ever reached that point.

But why did he cradle the head so gently? It was clear the infant's neck was broken. Its head was smashed in on one side, the tender still-forming skull flattened and the brain bashed beneath.

And there was the strange red collar circling the infant's neck. A line of varying thickness…a sticky, liquid ribbon.

Two violent circles at the widest point in the ribbon. Bite marks… Punctures.

"C'mon now. You're okay." Reece shifted his grip on the infant, his fingers working the arms from beneath, a puppet master bringing life. The arms flapped like wings.

He was moving the arms. The baby couldn't possibly still be alive…with that much blood loss, with that much damage to its head.

She remembered the awful, echoing thump as the baby was thrown against the window glass.

Suddenly, a screech in the night, from the forest behind her, from the strange abomination cradled in Reece's arms. The child's mouth opened, but the mouth looked like a ridged beak, then it opened wider to reveal the tiny animal teeth of a rat…a kitten…a bat.

Another shriek, a human infant in pain, starving to death. Tiny arms continued to flap…with the leathern flutter of bat wings.

"Go on," Reece said. "Go on." He bounced the cradled shape up and down, offering it to the night sky.

He tossed the child into the air.
It flew away.
Julia screamed.

"Drink this." Reece handed her a mug. "It'll make you feel better."

"I'm afraid it will keep me up. I already know I'll have trouble sleeping." Julia accepted the mug with both hands and brought it slowly to her lips. "Too hot." She set the mug on the end table, and adjusted a blanket over her legs. She hadn't bothered to change into the pajamas she'd brought in a small overnight bag, but had simply loosened the collar of her canary-yellow blouse to make the day's outfit easier to sleep in.

"My bed would be more comfortable," he said. "I don't mind the couch."

"I'll be fine here. Warm blankets. Lots of pillows. Did you save some for yourself?"

"I'm good." His expression showed such concern for her. A side of Reece she hadn't really seen before…a genuine tenderness, without that ulterior motive guys usually followed… "You gave me quite a scare out there," he said.

"Oh, *you* got the scare."

"Well, I was scared *for* you, okay?"

"Was it…" she said. "Was it really a bird, the whole time?"

He nodded. "A dirty white pigeon. A divebomber, I guess. Musta had a pretty hard noggin, since it was able to fly away."

She tried again with the too-hot coffee, taking a small sip. Reece had made it strong…probably hoping to clear her head. "I saw more than that. I could have sworn."

"Well, it was dark." Reece sat next to her on the couch…at a respectful, rather than amorous distance. Too far away to try that old chestnut, where he'd fake a broad yawn and then "accidently" put his arm around his date's shoulders. "I think I'm starting to understand what you were saying earlier," he said. "You know, how the radio and TV get you gals so excited about danger."

"Us *gals?*"

"It's like a hypnotic suggestion or something. Preconditioning. No wonder you expect to see something awful in the dark. They're making you jump at every sound and shadow, you know?"

"But you're immune."

He shrugged. "It explains what I saw: just a dirty ol' divebombing pigeon. Which one of us do you think is right?"

Julia took another sobering sip of coffee. Inside a bright house, wrapped in a blanket, surrounded by pillows, it was easy to dismiss what she'd seen...*thought* she'd seen. "You're right," she said. "I know you're right." She passed him the mug. "That's enough for now. This *gal* needs to get some rest."

Reece smiled as he stood from the couch. "I can take a hint. If you need anything, call me. I'll come running."

"Thank you," she said, and meant it. Thank you for being a gentleman...for taking care of me...for not saying you think I'm crazy.

"Leave the light on," Julia said as he paused near the wall switch. She hated to feel so vulnerable around him.

Reece's next remarks seemed to sense her insecurity...covering it for her: "It's an unfamiliar room. You don't want to stumble around if you get up in the middle of the night."

"Exactly," she said.

And he left her alone.

A phrase she'd earlier set to music began to run through her head: "A Woman Alone at Night Was Abducted."

Julia tried to sleep. She tossed and turned, punching pillows and rearranging blankets. She undid another button on her blouse to loosen its fit. Her rump sank into a gap between sofa cushions, and she switched to lying on her side...then her hips fell even farther into the gap.

The overhead light was too bright.

Why not turn it off? No need to act like an immature child. She was inside, locked up tight. The things that frightened her might as well be miles away...years away...it all seemed so long ago, like a dream.

Nothing really happened, anyway. There wasn't any screeching, bloody baby with leather wings.

The curtains remained closed over the windows beside the sofa. Maybe she could look into the back yard one last time, to reassure herself.

If she turned off the light, she could see outside better.

And nobody else would be able to see in.

Julia pushed the blankets below her waist then kicked them to the end of the couch. She swung her legs around and sat up.

She walked to the light switch at the other side of the room... clicked it off.

She stood, waiting for her eyes to adjust to the darkness.

She crossed to the adjoining windows. A small line formed where the curtains didn't quite overlap.

The curtains were thick fabric...she remembered how heavy they felt in her hand. Even so, the panel on the right fluttered slightly, as if stirred by a faint breeze.

She reached for the dark gap between curtain panels. Another phantom gust of wind anticipated her fingers, and the gap widened... then closed.

It moved like the gills on a gasping fish.

The fabric rustled. The cloth curtain was a stiff polyester, with a rough burlap backing to help block the light.

Why, then, did it rustle like leather wings?

Julia drew back her hand. A faint squeak sounded from outside... the mewl of a kitten or screech of a bat...a sweaty fingertip rubbing against glass.

At a strange height, a bulge began to form beneath the closed curtain. Julia watched it from where she stood, the same distance she'd stand when inspecting herself in a full length mirror.

She put a hand over her belly.

At the corresponding height, a pregnant bulge swelled beneath the curtain, nearly the size of a basketball.

Julia' reached beneath the bottom of her loosened blouse. Her fingers tensed, gathering the flesh of her stomach. She squeezed.

The swelling in the curtain flattened on one side...air deflated from the basketball.

She heard the cry again...too much like the wail of an infant, now. Julia squeezed tighter at her stomach, felt an awful crackle inside, heard the snap of tiny bones.

The curtain fell flat.

Julia released the gathered flesh of her belly. The snap of tiny bones continued to echo in the dark room.

Not bones.

Tapping. Tapping on the other side of the window.

A bird's beak against glass...rodent teeth...feline claws...the tiny fingernails of a human infant.

Leather wings flapping in a steady, wounded beat.

A summons of some kind.

Which animal was it? She pulled back the curtain...peered into the dark of the back yard.

Julia saw nothing. She leaned closer to the glass, and her own eyes stared back. Her eyes were bloodshot from the evening's earlier fright...from lack of sleep.

She blinked, and the bloodshot eyes in the window blinked, too, in exact time.

Maybe a split-second behind.

Julia saw nothing, but the tap and rustle and crack of bones continued. She put her palm flat against the window, and felt rhythmic vibrations through the glass.

She followed the sound outside.

"Did you call me?"

Reece knew she hadn't called, but he still thought he should check on her periodically during the night. He bumped against a chair as he walked into his living room. "Hey, I thought we decided to keep a light on."

The sight of blankets gathered at the end of an empty couch gave him immediate cause for concern.

The open curtain worried him even more. He ran across the room, cupped his hand on either side of his face and pressed against the window.

He stared into the yard, squinting for the line of trees behind his house.

In the distance, he just managed to spot a flash of yellow...a clothed figure as it disappeared into the trees.

It had to be Julia.

She found herself in the middle of the dark woods that stretched behind Reece's home.

Julia was staying with him, so she wouldn't be alone. Reece was protecting her, and she resented that protection, a little...she was strong enough to take care of herself...and then she'd had some kind of scare. A loud noise, an investigation, then a strange animal that changed its horrible, wounded shape as she watched.

No...that had been a trick of the dark...a distortion brought on by fright.

She'd pulled herself together...back to reality. Safe, indoors, sleeping on Reece's couch so he'd be close if she needed him.

So why was she here, now, alone in the woods?

Alone.

She wore her same clothes from earlier today...yellow blouse and tan slacks...but she didn't have shoes. Her stocking feet felt damp against cold, packed earth.

Had she been sleepwalking?

There were no clear signposts. Darkness frustrated her ability to read her surroundings...walls of trees pressed close, confining her to a thin path worn in the dirt. The path curved ahead and behind, making it impossible for her to get her bearings.

One or the other direction might lead her back to Reece's house... but which one?

Julia glanced up at the sky, hoping for a hint...some constellation shaped like an arrow, pointing toward safety. There were no obvious patterns in the dim stars…not that she could read them, anyway. She wasn't a sailor or astronomer.

A scythe moon offered minimal light. A cloud partially covered the crescent shape.

The cloud moved in midnight wind. It seemed heavy…sharper than expected.

It *flapped.*

The shadowy cloud broke away from the moon with a leathern rustle. The sky rippled like a black tarp snapped in the gusts of an approaching storm.

There was a shape in the sky after all…not a constellation, but a hovering breathing thing that passed over stars, winking them out as it moved closer.

Wind through trees, the violent rustle of air, the rhythmic flap of wings bearing closer.

She heard the shriek of an animal, then a thud on the ground… so near that she could feel the earth shake beneath her stocking feet.

Julia tried to pinpoint the location of the sound…on the path, slightly past a curve that disappeared into the trees. Before, she hadn't known which direction she should face to return to Reece's home… now, that goal no longer mattered…

That sound needed to stay behind her. She needed to run the other way.

Because there were footsteps echoing beyond that curve in the path. They sounded a steady scuff of leather-soled shoes in the dirt… but she could hear a muffled brush as well, like the rough pads of an animal's feet…and a staccato click, the curl of claws flexing with each step.

Julia ran, almost blind, following the path that led away from the pursuing threat. Her shoeless feet hit the ground hard, sharp rock edges occasionally scraping her arch or heel, but she ran…all the time fearing she'd run into a dead end.

The footsteps grew closer. Julia reached a straight stretch of the path, followed it long enough to know, if she turned her head, she'd see what kind of menace drew closer…closer.

She was too afraid to look. But she imagined it...a creature with muscled legs and arms, its leonine body covered with dark fur...a wide span of wings stretching behind, their tips clipping against tree limbs on either side of the path...animal eyes that shone with a bright red fire...a cold, black snout...a long jaw, open wide with a drool of anticipation, sharp teeth glinting in the dark...

Sometimes, they say, a monster you imagine is much worse than one you can actually see.

A gust of warm wind shook the surrounding trees. It misted the back of her neck, like the hot breath of her hungry pursuer.

She was still too afraid to turn her head...but she felt it...felt a dark shape growing closer...heard the rapid click and fleshy pad of animal feet...felt another hot, wet gust against the back of her neck.

She ran...

Until something caught her.

Reece probably lost some time retrieving a flashlight from the back of a kitchen drawer, but he'd need it to search for Julia. He'd hurry, before she had a chance to get too far...the light would help him discover clues along the trail.

And he could signal with it, too. He'd wave the light, and she'd be drawn to him.

He entered the woods at the location where he thought he'd last seen her. The trees were like anonymous faces in a crowd, impossible to distinguish from each other...but he hoped some tracking instinct would kick in to guide him.

There were paths once you got deeper. He remembered them from when he owned a dog, and used to take short walks...

He also remembered how easy it was to get turned around unawares...how easy it was to get lost.

One path, which he'd told Julia about, led to a large abandoned mansion. He'd asked around town, but could never find out how long ago it had been occupied...or who might have lived there.

For some reason, Boxer had never wanted to follow that path.

Reece moved his flashlight across the ground in front, hoping to locate fresh disturbances in the earth. Failing that, he searched for odd rocks or overgrowth or shapes in tree trunks, hoping to trigger some half-buried sense of direction.

Because he felt certain Julia would be headed toward that abandoned house. She'd made that strange comment about the woods, earlier…some weird fascination…

A shriek echoed in the night air. Julia, he thought, but sounding so scared that her voice lost some of its human quality…

The direction of the echo was hard to locate, but he felt like he'd stumbled into the mansion path. Something about the way it curved behind a gathering of leaning trees…clicking an uneasy memory into place.

He ran toward the sound…

And tripped. He hit the ground with a heavy thud that knocked the wind out of him. His flashlight tumbled ahead of him, its back compartment snapping off and the batteries rolling away… Reece stood, quickly dusted himself off, then rushed forward…leaving the useless flashlight behind.

A clue, perhaps, if people later tried to locate him…

He hurried, as fast as he could safely travel in dark and unfamiliar territory, hoping he was on the right path.

Reece grew more optimistic as he distinguished footsteps in the hidden distance ahead.

Still winded from the fall, he pushed himself forward. He panted from exertion as his footsteps scuffed along the winding dirt path. He opened his mouth to call out to Julia, to beg her to slow down, but he couldn't quite catch his breath.

A few times, he saw the subtle glow of a yellow shirt, glimpsed at a gap between trees, or at some tantalizing bend in the path.

Once, a large shadowy shape passed over the shirt, then retreated.

He reached a long straight stretch in the path, and he could see Julia at the far end of it. The yellow shirt, moving with a trance-like sway.

As Reece hurried closer, he expected her figure to get larger… Instead, the closer he got, the smaller she seemed.

An optical illusion...a trick of perspective. She seemed farther away, because he'd judged the shirt would be the size of her full torso. Instead, the patch of yellow was a smaller piece of cloth...part of a sleeve that had torn off, tangled in the fingered overhanging branch of a nearby tree.

Reece stopped, breathing heavy. He picked up the yellow patch of cloth, tilted it in the faint moonlight.

Were those drops of blood on the fabric?

Julia broke through a clearing at the edge of the woods.

She hadn't doubled back to Reece's house. Instead, she faced the ominous front of a large mansion.

An *abandoned* mansion, Reece had told her. But this one looked lived in.

Her feet were damp and sore and scraped from the unforgiving ground. Her arm hurt, too...four parallel scratches along her forearm. She'd gotten tangled in a tree limb, back when she thought some creature had chased her. The branch had seemed to grab at her...hold her back...and she'd fought it, pulling away, her shirt sleeve ripping as she escaped and continued to run.

Run from *what?* Nothing followed her...and she realized she'd been having another fright-induced hallucination...there was no real danger in these woods.

All the same, she had wanted out. She wanted to escape from the maze of forest paths...the smothering mass of tall trees all around, closing in, blocking the night sky. She wanted a cool grass lawn under her feet, or the predictable smooth surface of a sidewalk or asphalt road. She wanted the comfort of a suburban neighborhood filled with familiar, interchangeable houses.

Instead, she got a strange mansion. It might provide some shelter, though...if she could manage to get inside.

The large structure sat at the edge of the clearing, another bank of trees stretching behind it. She crossed an unkempt yard, dry grass cracking against her sore feet as she headed toward the mansion's ornamented entryway. The structure was three stories high, with several sets of tall windows on either side of a columned porch. A bas-relief frieze spanned atop massive double doors, a brass lion's-head knocker at the center of each.

She climbed the stairs onto the porch. She reached toward the ring beneath one of the lion heads, then thought better of it.

"Is anyone here?" she whispered...then paused as if she'd spoken loud enough to prompt an answer.

Why was she certain the mansion was inhabited? The house was quiet...shades closed...lights out.

"I feel like someone's been watching me," she said. A whisper, again...a dare. "Show yourself."

She reached again for the door knocker. "It's the middle of the night. If there *are* people here, they should be asleep."

Julia grasped the ring, tapped it gently. She stepped back and waited.

Louder now, explaining her situation to a paneled slab of wood. "I'm sorry to bother you. I got lost in the woods. My feet and arm are injured. May I use your phone? May I stay here and wait for help?"

No answer.

Julia recalled her musings from earlier in the evening, about the mysteries beyond the woods' edge. You can't see past the line of trees. Even if you know what paths stretch behind them, you can't be certain.

Doors are the same way. You knock on them, expecting someone to answer. It's often a familiar home, and your parent or best friend would answer and invite you inside. But a stranger could always open the door. Disturbing variations passed through her mind:

- A beautiful young woman bars the entrance, saying... "Your boyfriend doesn't want to see you anymore. He's with me, now."

- A doctor... "Your mother's inside, but too sick to have visitors. She's dying."

- A police officer... "Miss, can you tell us why you're here? What is your relationship to the victim?"

Julia shook her head, concentrating again on the door in front of her...stubbornly opaque...unmoving.

She again reached for the brass ring. Lifted it, then let it drop.

A sudden chill came over her. She hugged her arms close to her chest. She stamped her feet, which had begun to feel numb.

"Please answer." She barely spoke aloud. She was too strong to ask for help, so instead she asked: "What do you want? I'll do—"

A loud snap, like the breaking of a bone. The slide of a latch...the door creaking inward.

Candlelight flickered from a three-pronged candelabra. The man who held it looked like he was dressed for a formal dinner...a black tuxedo with a frilled white shirt at the open collar. A red broach hung about his neck...a cluster of jewels like small berries, full of juice.

"Ah, come in," he said. "I am Count Verlock." As the man smiled his greeting, his teeth shone bright and large. He was about the same age as Reece, but with a maturity her boyfriend lacked. Perhaps it was an illusion brought forth by the formal clothing, making him seem part of a long gone, more serious era.

"A count...?" Julia felt self-conscious now, in casual dress, hair disheveled from sleep, shoeless, a sleeve torn from her blouse and the arm bleeding. She wondered if there was some etiquette she should follow...eyes lowered, bowing before majesty...or if she should stand straight, a soldier at attention, awaiting some command.

"Come in," he told her, stepping back and waving an arm toward the interior of his home.

She stepped forward cautiously, but paused at the line of the doorway.

Wasn't there something about counts and invitations, about crossing thresholds? A vague memory about books or movies struggled to the surface...a supernatural threat, requesting entrance...the victim foolishly unlocking the door...a gracious hostess to her own doom.

Yes, that's right. She'd gotten it backwards. The danger was inviting a monster into your *own* home. This situation was perfectly safe.

She lifted her gaze...stared directly into Count Verlock's eyes. His expression was so welcoming. She didn't want to offend him.

Julia stepped into the antechamber. The marble floor was cold against her wounded feet. She glanced down...saw a smear of blood she'd dragged across the elegant tile. "Oh, I'm so sorry. I've ruined..."

"You're hurt." Count Verlock waved the candelabra closer to inspect her. She felt the heat of flickering candles as it passed over her face, over her chest, along the scratched, exposed arm.

And a heat of shame, too. "I don't quite remember how I got here," she said. "I should be better dressed."

The candles were almost close enough to singe the fine soft hairs of her forearm. With his free hand, the Count touched her elbow. He positioned his fingertips at the top of the four long scratches...then he traced the length of the bloody grooves all the way to the underside of her wrist.

"I'll need to clean this...and bandage it." As he removed his hand, the pads of his fingertips wore small circles of Julia's blood.

"Your feet," he said. The Count dropped to his knees setting the candelabra on the ground next to him. His position reminded her of a man proposing marriage...coupled with his elegant clothing, perhaps he was more like the fairy-tale prince, ready to test the fit of Cinderella's glass slippers.

At the same time, he reminded her of an awful predator lying in wait...a crouching animal, ready to pounce.

He supported her calf as he lifted one foot for inspection, then the other. His fingertips prodded gently at the soles of her feet, and the sensation was at once pleasant and worrisome.

Julia's stockings had been torn as she raced over the rough forest path. The Count's probing fingers moved bits of torn cloth aside...and she wondered if some of those shreds were actually strips of torn flesh.

She tried not to think about it...turned her head away, as she often might during a doctor's examination.

"Clean and bandage," he said. The candle flames flickered, and shadows danced across his face, distorting his handsome features. She looked down, and the Count's fingertips were no longer bloody. Instead, they seemed...wet.

Still kneeling at her feet, he smiled up at her. If he intended the gesture to be comforting, he failed miserably. Flickering shadows cast an illusion of gristle over his wide mouth of white teeth…flames illuminated the brooch of ruby jewels about his neck, aiming a reflection of bright red flecks onto his moistened lips.

"I will take care of you." He stood, then passed behind her to close the latch on the front door. It snapped into place with an echoing clang. "You will be safe here."

The Count stood next to her, pointing the candelabra forward to direct her into the next room. He touched her elbow, lightly prodding her forward.

Julia threw one last glance behind, at the solid oak door she'd previously stood on the other side of. As before, she couldn't see through it. The outside world might have disappeared, for all she could tell.

Or, Reece might be coming to find her. She imagined him running to the door, banging on it, slamming down the ring of each brass knocker, calling out her name, crying *Let me in, I want to help you…* and getting no answer.

She had made her choice, she realized. Her choice.

Julia allowed Count Verlock to lead her deeper into his mansion.

Reece stumbled out of the woods and raced across the dry lawn.

He recalled visiting this place a few years earlier, his dog struggling on its leash, alternating between angry barks and fearful whimpering.

"Calm down, boy," he'd said, placing a firm hand on Boxer's collar to hold him in place. "Nobody's home. Nothing here to worry about."

And the dog barked and whimpered at an abandoned house.

Now, Reece bounded up the steps to the front porch. One of the boards creaked beneath him, and his foot fell part-way through the rotted wood.

"Careful," he told himself. He tested the firmness of each new step as he crossed to the double doors.

One of the age- and weather-worn doors listed crooked in its frame. A rusted brass knocker hung in the center of the other.

He rattled the knob of each door…pushed his shoulder against them in turn, throwing his weight into it. When they didn't budge,

Reece put his fingers in the gap caused by the ill-fitting door, trying to separate them further.

No success. He searched the junk and debris that had gathered on the porch over the years, and found a tree limb. He fit one end between the doors, and pushed and pulled.

The doors wouldn't budge. The limb snapped when he renewed his attempts.

Enraged, he banged at one of the doors.

He wasn't sure why he felt so desperate. If he couldn't get inside, then Julia wouldn't have been able to, either.

Why was he so certain she'd come here?

He reached in his back pocket and removed the scrap of clothing he'd found in the woods.

The blood-stained scrap of clothing.

And then one of the doors creaked open.

Count Verlock had been gone a long time.

He had been leading Julia down a long staircase...so deep that she couldn't see the bottom from her current position. The Count had used his candelabra to light wall torches along the way, but the ones beneath remained dark.

A sound had caught the Count's attention, and he'd cautioned her to remain still. "Don't attempt to go forward on your own. There's no railing."

How long did he expect her to wait?

Julia moved next to the wall, taking comfort from the heat and light offered by the nearest torch.

She wondered again why he was taking her towards a basement. The house was three stories tall...surely there were more comfortable rooms above. And in her condition, with injured feet, these hard stone stairs seemed to make matters worse.

But she'd trusted him. The Count's deep voice had soothed her... "Clean, then bandage. A few more steps." He was a gentleman, and she felt safe with him. The idea that he might be connected with the town's recent disappearances had never crossed her mind.

Had it?

Now, Julia ran her hand along the wall. The stone felt cold, even the area around the torch. She lifted her hand and held it near the flame.

On the wall, the shadow of her hand repeated her movements. She flexed her fingers, curled and uncurled.

She brought her hand closer to the flame, and the shadow on the wall grew larger. Julia wriggled the digits again, then counted them.

"Too many," she said, then dropped her arm.

The shadow remained on the stone. Its eight digits wriggled.

A large spider scurried down the wall.

Julia jumped back. She stumbled, accidently kicking a rock over the edge of the railless staircase.

After a brief pause, she heard the rock hit bottom.

Where was the spider? She shivered at the thought of stepping on its plump, bristled body…its venomed mandibles clicking at her bare feet, drooling thick poison into open wounds.

Julia wondered what sound the spider's legs would make against hard stone…the fingers of a silk glove sweeping crumbs off a marble tabletop.

She moved back toward the torch again, grabbed it…rocked it back and forth…snapped it from its place in the wall.

As she waved the torch, all the shadows seemed to move like silken fingers…the plump legs of spiders.

Julia spun in a circle with the flaming weapon. She lowered it to the ground to warn away any venomous threat.

"I can't stay here," she said, giving voice to her anxiety. The way back…the way the Count had headed when he abandoned her…was already lit by other torches. But now that she held her own torch, Julia was free to illuminate her descent. "Which way?"

She listened, hoping to hear whatever had drawn the Count's attention. Far above her, she thought she could distinguish two male voices, arguing. One of them was Count Verlock. The other one sounded like Reece.

Then a woman's voice. "Verlock." A weakened voice…a whisper that seemed to echo all around. "You animal."

From nowhere…from everywhere: the sounds of a struggle…an angry splintering of wood…a frustrated clatter of metal.

"Release me." The same voice…so weak, like a hundred-year-old woman on her deathbed.

All around her, the woman's whisper…the quarreling men…the rattle of chains.

Julia hesitated. She thought of the women in her town who had disappeared. She considered her own plight, the weakness in her scratched arm, her tattered feet. A rush of empathy for the faint, whispering woman flooded over her. That could be her *own* voice, crying out for help.

Despite the confusion of echoes, Julia knew the whisper had to be coming from the bottom of the stairs.

An old man stood on the other side of the door.

Reece immediately assumed the man was a vagrant. A decrepit bum squatting on the abandoned property. He was dressed in an ill-fitting tuxedo that looked like it had been fished out of a dumpster.

A white shirt beneath had faded to filthy tatters, and a dark gravy or ketchup stain marred the patch above his chest. An awful smell rose up from the man, and Reece had to wave his hand in front of his face.

"Step aside, Pops," Reece said, attempting to muscle his way in.

The vagrant didn't budge. "I am Count Verlock," he said. "You are trespassing."

"Listen, Bub, nobody's owned this place for a hundred years." Reece pulled a strip of yellow cloth from his pocket…waved it like a flag. "My girlfriend ran this way."

A haughty expression crossed the vagrant's face. He reminded Reece of an ignorant low-life who tried to adopt the snooty posture and voice of an aristocrat. "Your girlfriend is not here." The man dismissed the torn cloth with a wave of his hand…a spoiled patriarch sending an ill-cooked meal back to the kitchen. "Perhaps she was running away from you. You seem rude." The self-appointed "Count" looked him up and down. "Unimpressive."

If Reece had time for games, he might have slapped the old man's face and challenged him to a duel. Instead, he decided to return to his original plan...pushing the man aside and searching the dilapidated building.

Reece looked at the frail man, judging how hard to shove him. He'd easily fold at a punch to the stomach. Or he could kick his legs, knock his feet out from beneath him.

His feet...

Discarded dress shoes, rescued from a dumpster. Laceless...the sole flapping on one...on the other, a large toe with a filthy unclipped nail, protruding from the tip.

But around these feet...

Rotting wood on the floor, and glistening streaks of red.

Fresh blood.

Julia stepped onto the landing at the bottom of the stone staircase. A wooden door reinforced with metal bars waited at the end of a short hallway. A small slot was carved into the door at eye level... and an inset door at the bottom, similar to ones she'd seen in houses that allowed separate exit or entry for small pets.

The woman on the other side whispered again...a harsh sound that emerged through the door slot and echoed through the steep chamber. "You abomination. Release me."

Julia raised her torch to the eye-level slot, but the interior of the room was too dark. She cleared her throat, as preparation to offering soothing words to the prisoner. Before she could speak, the other woman began to panic. The rattling of shackles...a sickly thump of flesh against unyielding stone.

"Verlock," the prisoner shrieked. "You're killing me!"

More rattling...the woman on the other side apparently thrashing about like a beached fish.

"Verlock...I know you're there!"

Julia looked over her shoulder.

She thinks I'm someone else, Julia thought. It was an awful feeling she never thought she'd experience. *The woman's terrified. She's terrified of* me.

And the prisoner shrieked now...a song of pained, incoherent syllables.

Again Julia attempted soothing words...a scratch still in her throat caused by her own discomfort throughout this night of horrors. She planned to say, "I'm here to help."

Instead, the words tumbled together in a gurgling hiss.

Behind the door, a horrible gasp...a frightened silence...a pleading moment of calm. "Oh god, not the *beast,*" she whimpered. "Anything but that...I beg you..."

Julia finally gained control of her voice. "No. You don't understand—"

Suddenly...the inset door flipped open...a skeletal hand reached through...it grabbed Julia by the ankle.

"Let go," Julia shouted and, nearly dropping the torch, she kicked with her other foot...knowing it was wrong...that she'd bring the tortured prisoner more pain...this woman's brittle fingers scraped and streaked with blood, a dark bruise encircling her wrist...and Julia's foot coming down, a horrible snap as she pulled her ankle free from the surprisingly resilient grip.

Julia tried reason again. "I want to..."

"I know what you want," the prisoner whispered. Instead of drawing back her arm, the woman slowly began to rotate it...palm upward...the underside of the wrist exposed.

Seeing the dark bruise around the woman's wrist, Julia had earlier attributed the injury to metal handcuffs or shackles...they cut off her circulation, and she'd fought against them, breaking free to reach under the door to her prison cell.

She held the torch closer. The underside of the woman's wrist was different. The skin here was cleaner than the surrounding area... white and pale.

Except for two crusted scabs at the center. Their raised shape, like the domes of two identical moles…the way they were positioned…

They looked like bite marks.

"Go ahead, Verlock." A hopeless resignation was evident in the woman's weak voice. "Feed."

She badly wanted to rescue this unfortunate woman.

At the same time, she wanted to be elsewhere.

In her mind's eye, she ran away.

She imagined escaping the dungeon of Count Verlock. She ran up the long staircase, the steps seeming to stretch endlessly above her.

Finally she reached the main floor of the building. She remembered a high-ceilinged dining room, the walls decorated with elegant tapestries.

She imagined herself reaching the front of the house…pausing outside the vestibule, looking in…

She saw:

Reece stands there, holding Count Verlock by the collar…that beautiful frill shirt bunched in Reece's angry fists. "What have you done to her?" Reece yells. "You better start talking."

Julia is so proud of him, the way he's come to her rescue…so rough and strong…

"I mean it." Reece shakes the Count again…almost seems ready to throw him against the wall. "Where is she?"

The Count is undeniably handsome, but how could she ever have been fooled by this well-dressed weakling? He's a milquetoast…especially in comparison to Reece. "I'm right here," Julia tells him.

And Reece is a statue frozen in place…the Count on tiptoes, nearly lifted off the ground from Reece's rough treatment.

Julia blinks her eyes.

The room…looks different.

The elegant chandelier so glamorous overhead…now many of its crystal hangings missing, cobwebs stretching from one broken candle to the next.

The gold trimmed tapestry on the wall…gone now, and the wall beneath chipped, stained, water-damaged.

The beautiful hand-woven carpet…rolled away years ago, to reveal a rotted, wooden floor.

"Reece," she says. "I'm right here."

Finally the statue moves. He turns his head.

His head lolls. His eyes are empty.

A large gash appears in Reece's neck…a chunk of flesh ripped out…bitten out.

The two men have changed position. Reece is the one nearly held in the air…

The Count's arm lifts…Reece's body rises.

Count Verlock holds Reece over his head with both hands. The fiend closes one hand about her boyfriend's throat…tightens his fist as if squeezing the last drops of water out of a sponge.

Verlock's vile fanged mouth catches these drops.

He tosses her boyfriend's emptied body aside.

Before her eyes, Count Verlock's elegant clothing begins to shred into wrinkled rags. His skin wrinkles, too, as if he's suddenly aged into the oldest person she had ever seen.

"Let's tend to your wounds," Verlock says.

Julia felt gentle pressure along the scratches in her arm. Later, an antiseptic ointment washed over the abrasions in the soles of her feet.

She'd been sleeping. She kept her eyes closed.

"Let's tend to your wounds," someone said. She heard the clatter of sterile instruments on a metal tray.

Next, she felt bandages rolled and tightened over her cleansed wounds.

The bandages clicked into place…over her wrists, over her ankles.

She opened her eyes to find herself in a dungeon, shackled to the wall.

Count Verlock stood close, inspecting her. He wasn't the handsome gentleman who'd first greeted her. This was an old man...a hundred years old...hundreds or thousands.

The old man who killed Reece...who'd been kidnapping women in their neighborhood.

Julia looked to one side, and saw another woman shackled to the wall. Her face had grown worn and thin, her eyes sunken into shadow, but Julia recognized the woman from a missing-persons report on the news.

She turned her head in the other direction...saw another of the missing women, bound as Count Verlock's prisoner...

His food...

The Count scratched at Julia's arm, making the wounds bleed anew. He picked bits of flesh off the bottoms of her feet.

Daylight.

Two police officers paused at a forked path in the woods.

Outside a dog barked, straining at the end of its leash.

"Hey Sheriff, give him a chance to refresh the scent," said the younger officer...the one holding the leash.

The older man removed a yellow scrap from a sealed bag...held the cloth under the dog's nose. "Here you go, Boxer."

The dog barked again, more certain this time, leading the officers down the right-most path.

Eventually, they emerged into a clearing. The abandoned mansion awaited them.

"What's the matter, boy?" The junior officer kneeled next to the animal. It whimpered now, its back legs shaking. "You brought us here. Why so skittish now?"

"I'm checking the ruins," the Sheriff said. "Bring Boxer along, will you Fremont?"

They crunched across dry grass to the front of the decayed house. Fremont practically had to drag the reluctant dog along with them.

When they reached the porch, the dog began barking again. The officers climbed up the unsteady wooden stairs, then paused at the landing.

A section of the porch in front of the double doors had collapsed.

"Hold back a second." The Sheriff knew his own weight was risky enough...the splinters suggested that the porch boards had snapped recently.

He leaned over, carefully peering into the freshly made pit. "Poor guy." A short distance below, a crumpled body was impaled on gory bits of rotted wood. "It's the boyfriend."

The dog started barking uncontrollably, the smell of Reece's blood driving the animal towards frenzy.

"Not him," the Sheriff said. "Found him. Now we need to focus on the girl." He pulled out the strip of cloth...rubbed it under the dog's nose.

Boxer strained at the leash again, as if ready to jump over the pit and attack the double doors.

The Sheriff reached across the gap and tested one of the doors. It opened easily. "Let's go, Fremont."

"Do you think we'll find her?"

"I don't know *what* we'll find." He turned on a flashlight, then stepped over the gap and inside the abandoned property.

Julia heard steps approaching.

"Verlock," she said, hating to hear the name aloud. Hating the weak rasp of her fearful voice. "You abomination." She shook at the manacles on her wrists...kicked her feet and the chains rattled.

The footsteps grew closer. "Release me," she hissed in a pained whisper. "You're killing me." The footsteps paused outside her dungeon, and she stared at the reinforced door. A shadow moved over the eye-level slot, and she thought she caught a gleam of white...a horrible fanged mouth, smiling in anticipation of the next meal.

Why was he taking so long to enter. Was this terrifying delay part of her torment? "I know you're there," she whispered.

Julia waited, her own teeth chattering from fear...from some unholy chill. She listened.

From the other side of the door, she heard...*panting*.

Then a weight fell against the door...the pad of an animal's feet... the frantic scratching of claws.

"Oh god," Julia screamed, finding her full voice. "Not the *beast!*"

She could never bear the Count's ghastly feedings. Each sucked drop of blood stole more than her life's energy...it stole her sense of self...her belief in humanity...in rightness. It buried any dim hope that she could ever escape.

And whenever he appeared to her in animal form, that experience was always the most horrible.

The door finally opened. Julia screamed as the beast came bounding into her cell.

A dog stopped short at the end of its leash. Two police officers entered.

The younger of them ran toward her...covered her with a blanket.

The shoulder belt of the police car pressed secure across her chest. Julia looked out the window as the scenery rushed by. The cemetery passed on the left, then a church.

A siren wailed...a strobe light flashed as the car raced forward.

"We'll get you to the hospital as quick as we can."

The driver was the older of the two men. She recognized him from newspaper photos as Sheriff Hazelbury.

Julia had a foggy memory of this man helping her...using some combination of pliers or bolt cutter or wire-picks to snap or unlock her shackles. And the younger man, so strong...carrying her up that long flight of steps and out of the mansion. Through the woods, past the back yard of Reece's house to a waiting squad car parked out front.

The world moved past her as she was carried…just as it moved past her now from the car. She'd worried that the officer would get tired from carrying her, but he never complained.

Maybe she wasn't that heavy of a burden. She'd lost so much blood, after all.

Julia looked toward the backseat of the car, but it was empty. "Where's your partner? Is he helping the others?"

The Sheriff half-turned to respond, keeping one eye on the road ahead. "Others?"

"Those other kidnapped women. In the dungeon with me."

He didn't respond. The scenery scrolled past…the cemetery on the left, then the church.

Julia almost wanted to unbuckle her seatbelt and jump from the moving car. "We have to go back for them," she said. "And Count Verlock. Did you find him? Did you arrest him? Kill him?"

"Calm down, now, miss." The Sheriff…kept one eye on the road, but looked more worried.

Julia strained against her seatbelt and shoulder strap. They felt heavy, reminding her of the persistent weight of metal chains, the confining cuff of shackles over her wrists and ankles.

The cemetery passed on the left, then the church. She knew she'd seen them before. The scenery was looping past like images projected onto a screen.

The screen of memory.

Julia started to wail. She pulled at the latch of her seatbelt…grabbed at the handle of the passenger-side door. Neither would budge.

The Sheriff pulled the car over, bringing it to a stop. Julia was shaking, thrashing in her seat like she was in the middle of an epileptic seizure. Sheriff Hazelbury put his arms on her to comfort her…to steady her…to keep her from hurting herself. He leaned his body over hers, to restrict her movements.

More weight. The Sheriff smothered her like the chains, like the shackles…like the press of Count Verlock's body looming over her, taking an unoffered gift of her life's blood.

"I'm still there!" Julia screamed. "The Dungeon of Count Verlock! Oh God, someone save me. I'm still trapped there!"

THE END

A
HAUNTED
MAGAZINE
MONSTER
PROJECT
MONSTER
PROJECT
#102
AUG
DARE YOU
ENTER THE
LAIR OF THE...
THE LAKE
MONSTER
NOT AN ACTUAL
LAKE MONSTER

The Lake Monster

(A Budget Studios Production)

"It's only water."

Holly stared into the stoppered kitchen sink, filled almost to the brim. She knew Sam was trying to be supportive.

But she'd never liked water.

"Take a deep breath first. Pinch your nose with your fingers. That sometimes helps."

"No, I need to hold back my hair."

"I'll do that." His hands ran through her hair, gathering the strands behind. Sam's touch comforted her…the same gentle way he'd touch her head and neck when they sat in the back row of the Bijou Cinema. "You ready?"

"As I'll ever be." Holly pinched thumb and forefinger over her nose.

Her face grew larger as she bent closer to the water's smooth surface. Her hand over her nose and mouth looked ridiculous…like some strange rippling growth that distorted the lower half of her face.

Holly's reflection stared back, a vague expression of terror in her eyes…a warning.

Don't do this.

Closer…nearly breaking the surface…

For an instant, the reflected hand over her mouth looked wrong. Dark scales crusted over her skin…her fingers wriggled like tentacles…

She closed her eyes. An icy chill tingled against her skin.

The surface of calm water is as smooth as glass. Holly imagined her face pressed against glass…tight…tighter…the glass resisting, and the weight of her face pushing harder…until the glass finally shattered, ripping into razor sharp crystals that forced cold needles beneath her skin, all along her face, and especially into her eyes, popping and tearing the jelly…so her world would grow dark with agonizing pain.

The cold water…the tingle like needles…

She opened her eyes, not out of bravery…simply to confirm she could still see.

And it wasn't so bad. She'd scrubbed the sink clean earlier, and the metal basin glimmered beneath. Lines of light wavered with the motion of the cool liquid, and her eyes didn't sting as much as she'd expected they would.

Twenty seconds already, by her estimate. She'd count to ten then come up for air.

The stopper-plug made a dark spot at the center of her vision. The water softened the smooth rubber, giving it the texture of an eel's skin.

The slimy round shape began to uncoil. Two bubble-white eyes opened at one end, and a lamprey mouth spread its tooth-suckered lips as the shape undulated upward.

It disappeared outside Holly's field of vision. She felt a rough tap against her fingers, where they covered her nose and mouth.

Holly pulled back, struggling to lift her head out of the water…

But she couldn't move. Sam held her head in place.

Testing her…? Encouraging her to stay underwater for a longer time…?

Trying to drown her?

Thirty seconds.

She pinched her nose tighter…squeezed her fingers together…pursed her mouth into a thin line.

With her other arm, she reached behind and above, swinging at Sam in an attempt to batter him away.

The dark eel shape pushed at the space between her fingers, widening the gap. Holly shook her head, trying to break Sam's grip.

It felt like another eel was oozing beneath her cupped hand, forcing its way into the corner of her mouth.

Forty seconds.

A gag reflex caused her to exhale a sputter of thin bubbles. The water grew cloudy now...spots formed in her vision, a sign she was losing consciousness.

A terrible ooze slithered between her fingers, and she felt a thick, slimy tube force its way into her left nostril. She tried to blow it out with a hard snort, but a nervous twitch made her inhale instead, drawing the eel deeper into her nasal cavity.

It filled her...through her nose, then dangling down the back of her throat...and the other one slithering past her gums and through her gnashed teeth, a hideous warm slime dragged over her tongue.

Fifty seconds.

Sam was killing her. She shook her head side to side, thinking, *No...No...*

As she thought those words, her mouth opened as if to speak them. Water rushed in...along with more dark, slimy shapes...like a wet rag stuffed further into her mouth, pushing small rocks and nails and dry twigs deep into the back of her throat.

Sixty seconds.

She'd breathed in too much water. She didn't doubt that she would drown.

The easiest thing would be to let go.

Her vision grew darker. She closed her eyes, welcoming...

Air. She needed air, and she would fight for it. With renewed strength, she flung her head back, lifting it from the water with a desperate gasp.

Sam held back the strands of her hair with a loose, gentle grip. "There you go. That wasn't so bad, was it?"

Holly twisted away from him, overwhelmed with a wrenching cough...that dreadful dry nausea when nothing comes up. She wiped at her mouth, pinched again at her nose...sputtered and spit as if to expel some rancid ichor from her body.

"Hey," Sam said. "What's wrong?"

And he genuinely seemed surprised.

Sam unplugged the stopper. A thin waterspout formed, twisting in a strange dance as the liquid circled the drain.

The last bit of water gurgled as it went down.

Holly called out to him from the den. "You're certain I was only under for twenty seconds?"

"Twenty, tops. I really think it was more like fifteen." He opened the refrigerator and grabbed two cans of cola, taking them into the next room.

He didn't dare offer her a glass of water.

She sat with a damp towel wrapped around her neck. If somebody just dropped by the house, they might have thought Holly had just dried off after a shower. She sat perfectly composed, and her breaths were calm and steady.

Nothing like she'd been a few minutes before…eyes wide, gasping, body shaking. Shouting at him…accusing him of trying to kill her.

He handed her a can of soda pop. She flinched slightly when he pulled the tab on his own. Sam wasn't sure if he should join her at the sofa, so he took the armchair across from her.

"Tell me again what happened," Holly said. "Don't leave anything out."

"You were doing great," he told her. "You held your nose then put your face completely underwater. I was really proud of you. It was something…you told me…you were always afraid to do."

"And then I just started shaking…? Thrashing my head around…?"

"No, not at all." He took a sip of his cola, noticing Holly hadn't touched hers…she'd set the unopened can on the top of her knee. "You were perfectly still the full fifteen seconds." He noticed she wanted to contradict his estimate, so he explained: "I'm used to keeping track of time like this. It's part of our training on the swim team."

"It seemed to last so much longer."

"Fifteen seconds. Right at the end…you pulled your head straight up all of a sudden. I'd been holding your hair to keep it from getting too wet...barely touching you, really...and you spun around like I'd been trying to strangle you."

"I'm sorry," Holly said. "I thought something horrible was happening to me. It's not your fault."

But maybe it *was*. "I shouldn't have put pressure on you. I just thought, you know, me being on the swim team and all... It just seemed weird that you'd be afraid of water. I was hoping it might be something we could do together. I could teach you."

Holly attempted a weak smile, partly to banish her recent panic. "It already *is* something we do together. I go to your swim meets and cheer you on from the bleachers. That's as close as I want to get to a swimming pool, okay? At least for now."

"Sure." Sam noticed how she'd left an opening...a suggestion that she might like to try again someday. But things had gone so badly this time. "It comes so easily to me, you know? Even when I was a little kid, my parents said I took to water like a fish. I hadn't realized how difficult this would be for you."

"A phobia is like that," Holly said. She lifted the soda can, staring into the label like it was some kind of crystal ball. "It defies logic. It's almost impossible to explain to other people."

Sam nodded, doing his best to appear like he understood...but some skepticism must have remained in his expression.

Holly stood up decisively. "You want to know why I'm so scared of water? I'll tell you. Better yet, I'll show you."

A dragonfly hovered over the calm surface of a wide, deep lake. A frog sat on a large rock at the edge of the water...its throat expanding into a warty balloon...then contracting. As if startled, the frog jumped and dove into the water, sending out concentric ripples.

For a brief moment, the rhythmic strum of cicadas halted...crickets ceased to chirp.

Because the snap of twigs and steady, heavy footsteps signaled the approach of intruders.

The worst kind of intruders: humans.

A female led the way. Her legs and arms were pink and bare, and long brown hair fell over and slightly past her shoulders. She carried a large rag.

A male companion followed. His body was tall and lean, and his hair was cropped close.

The female moved her mouth and strange squeaking sounds came out of it. She unfolded her rag, waving the cloth in the air before draping it over the large overhanging rock. She sat down on the cloth, then hugged her knees close to her chest.

The male sat beside her, half on the cloth, half off. He picked up a small stone and skimmed it at the lake. It bounced several times over the water's surface, then sank to the bottom.

"When I was younger," Holly said, "I came here sometimes with my brother." A long, leafy strand of grass had grown through a cracked section of rock at the edge of her towel. She uprooted the strand and absently picked at it as she spoke…wrapping it around her finger…tearing off a small strip…digging a fingernail into the green leaf.

"He was two years younger than me, almost. But he was always more confident, and liked to act like he was the older one."

"Guys can be like that," Sam offered. "We like to be protective of our sisters."

"Oh, he wasn't protective." She hugged her legs even closer to her chest…a kind of upright fetal position. She sat sideways to the water, as if wanting to keep the lake behind her, but needing to keep one eye on it as well. "He was sadistic."

And as Holly spoke to her boyfriend, the memory of that terrible day came rushing back.

The day when she was only twelve years old, and her brother told the story of a creature dressed like a man, with the head of a monstrous fish.

Russell walked along the edge of the large rock, arms out, teetering as he put one foot directly in front of the other.

"Careful," young Holly said. "If you fall in the lake, I won't be able to rescue you."

"That so?" Russell waved his arms in wide circles, pretending to lose his balance. "I bet if I fell in, I'd just learn to swim, to save myself. That's how it works for a lot of people."

"Nobody would ever drown if that was true."

"There's also those stories of mothers who get extra strength during a crisis...They're able to lift a car if that's the only way to protect their baby." He grunted and mimed the action...a scrawny ten-year-old in dungarees and a T-shirt, assuming a Charles Atlas muscle-man pose. "If you want to save me, you will."

"What if I don't want to?"

"That would be your choice, sister dear." He dropped the car he was lifting, imagining that it rolled off the rock and into the lake. "I guess you'll be an only child."

"That's a legend, anyway," Holly said. "About the woman lifting the car. Either that, or they exaggerated. It was probably a bicycle or a go-cart."

"You're wrong," Russell said. "It was actually a tank, I think. Or a school bus."

"Why not make it an airplane?"

"It happened with an airplane once. But that time was two moms, saving two babies."

"I'm sure." Holly moved closer to the large rock that her brother had treated as an obstacle course. She claimed a flat section farthest from the water and sat down.

She got annoyed with Russell's stories...the way he'd add new ridiculous details, not admitting they were untrue...partly out of fun, but partly out of spite. He'd never let his sister have the final word. Never let her be right.

He sat down next to her, a mischievous gleam in his eyes. "You're wrong about why people drown," Russell said. "It's not because they can't swim. Everybody learns to swim by instinct, if they need to. No, it's because there's something in the water...something alive."

Russell was headed into one of his more elaborate creations, she knew. As his sister, she was often a captive audience...especially on these long summer days when there was nothing good on TV, and she didn't have plans with friends. Russell would spin out some tall tale, usually borrowed from a comic book or movie...insisting he'd heard the "true" story at school.

"My friend Dwayne told me about a family that lived on the other side of the woods here. The mom and dad both drowned in the lake. They were both expert swimmers, and their son couldn't figure out what happened.

"The police wouldn't give him any information. His dead dad's sister moved in to help raise the poor kid, and she warned him not to go anywhere near the lake.

"Of course, the warning wasn't necessary. Why would he want to visit a place that had such awful associations for him? He sure didn't want to stand and stare at the water that swallowed up both his parents."

As if to punctuate his story, Russell picked up two stray stones... one for each of the parents...and tossed them toward the water. They hit with two distinct splashes.

"But the aunt's expression was so odd whenever she mentioned the lake...like she knew more than she was telling.

"So the boy kept his ears open. Sometimes he'd bring up the lake himself, and his friends would change the subject. Sure, they'd feel awkward talking about the place where the kid's parents died...but it was the same as with the aunt, too. They knew more than they were telling.

"One day, after he mentioned the lake...and his friends changed the subject...the boy got mad and yelled at them...and stormed out of the room.

"But he didn't go far. He only pretended to get really mad, to make his friends keep talking. The boy hid in the next room and listened.

"That's when he heard about the Lake Monster."

Young Holly rolled her eyes. She waved her hands in front of her as if pushing the story away…dismissing it.

"You don't believe in monsters," Russell said. "Of course you don't. And that boy didn't either.

"But something had killed his parents. His parents, who were *expert swimmers*. So he kept an open mind. He kept listening.

"And he found out a lot of other people have drowned in this lake. Not recently, or you would hear more about it. But if you go way back, look in old newspapers…a lot of strange stuff happened.

"We all know Loch Ness in Scotland has a dinosaur in it. Our town's lake has its own monster…quite a bit smaller…the size of a man.

"But with the head of a giant fish. It's lived in this lake for many, many years.

"And as the boy eavesdropped on his friends, he learned what his mom and dad must have done. He learned how to summon this monster from the deep."

Russell slid off the rock and scavenged in surrounding dirt and gravel. "You take stones like these. Flat. Skimming stones.

"You have to fling them at the lake, side-armed, so they skim the surface. Not like those two rocks I tossed in earlier. They have to bounce *at least* five times. You need to do it that way, five times in a row…which can be a pretty tough trick…but that's how you summon the Lake Monster.

"That boy wasn't so good at skimming. He could get to five or even six a couple times, but never enough times in a row.

"He worked at it all day, then late into the evening.

"It got dark. And he got better with practice.

"The stones bounced across the surface of the lake. One…two… three…four…five.

"After many attempts, he finally reached four times in a row, almost at the goal.

"He leaned over the water. The closer he stood to the lake's edge, the better angle he had for his side-arm throw.

"The boy flung the flat stone.

"It had grown so dark outside, that his eyes couldn't follow the stone's journey to its end. He had to listen and count each blip as it bounced off the water"

"Blip…blip…blip…blip."

Russell paused for dramatic effect. Waited. Waited.

"Blip," he said.

"Then nothing. The woods were completely silent.

"The boy leaned over the dark lake. He listened as hard as he could…tried to see any fresh ripple in the lake's surface.

"Two white stones appeared at the center of the lake." Russell lifted index fingers on either side of his face. "A head's distance apart. They began to rise from the water.

"The stones *blinked.* Because they were eyes. Bubble eyes on stalks, like you'd find on some exotic fish.

"As the stalk-eyes danced up from the water, a fish head emerged from beneath…a green scaled face with a wide red-rimmed mouth that opened and closed in a hungry rhythm.

"The creature's head was about the size of a human's…which made sense after what followed. The Lake Monster moved closer as it rose from the water, and it didn't glide or swim gracefully.

"It seemed like it *walked.* And this is the weird part…"

"Oh, *this* is the weird part," Holly said, unable to contain her skepticism.

"Yes, because there were small fins on each side of the creature's neck, but below that was…a shirt collar. Buttoned tight and soaking wet, but a regular dress shirt, and a suitcoat overtop that.

"The Lake Monster was part fish and part man.

"The boy watched…frozen with fear…as the strange creature emerged from the water, closer and closer with malicious steps.

"He knew this Lake Monster had killed his parents.

"And he would be next."

"Human arms lifted from the water. At the end of each sleeve were green hands covered with scales…webbing between the fingers and sharp claws at the tips.

"Those claws had torn his parents apart. I forgot to mention that the autopsy report showed the boy's parents had been mauled...much worse damage than any drowning would have caused.

"Partly eaten, too.

"The Lake Monster's mouth opened and closed...opened and closed.

"The boy stood at the edge of the lake, almost within reach of those arms...those flexing fingers with sharp claws at the tips."

Russell took one of the flat stones and side-armed it at the lake. It skimmed expertly along, bouncing five times.

"Well?"

Her brother didn't respond, so Holly clarified her question. "What happened to the boy? Did the monster get him?"

"Of course not, you silly. He got away, or how else would we have heard his story?"

"The *true* story," young Holly said. "And I'm the silly one."

"Maybe the boy went back later, after he'd spread the story around," Russell improvised. "I heard he armed himself with a spear-gun...to try and kill it. But the Lake Monster outsmarted him, and the boy ended up just as dead and shredded as his parents."

"The *boy*," Holly said. "What was his name? ...so I can check old newspapers at the library."

"Oh, you won't find this story in the papers. The aunt moved out of town, and the Sheriff kept things quiet. Didn't want to cause a panic."

"Hmm." Holly turned her head away, feigning that she'd lost interest.

"You believe me," Russell said. "I know you do."

"Hmm," she said again.

"Well, why'd you ask me if the boy escaped? Because you believed the story, that's why."

His smug confidence was enough to draw Holly back in. How dare he tell her what she was thinking...again insisting on the truth of a ridiculous story. She couldn't resist destroying him with logic.

"You should tell that one to little kids, and they won't believe you either. You don't make any sense. Why would five skimming stones be what summoned the monster? Why would people just *stand* there and let this slow moving creature get close enough to kill them? And why would it wear a dress suit?" Holly started to laugh…a mocking laugh that she hoped would get under her brother's skin. "I'm wondering if the creature has his suit dry cleaned when it gets dirty."

Russell's face turned a faint shade of pink. She was getting to him.

"And why stop at the suit? Let's add a necktie. Hey, I heard fishman wore gold-plated cuff links, too. Monogrammed with the initials 'LM,' for 'Lake Monster'."

Her brother's face was headed into beet red territory as Holly continued to scoff. Then Russell's mouth straightened into a tight line, his eyes cold. "I can prove it."

Prove what? That she believed him? …or that there actually was a monster in their town's lake?

Russell shook his closed fist. The stones he clenched rattled against each other. "I already did the first toss. Four more, and you'll see who's right."

He stretched his legs out in front then dropped off the rock, moving quickly to the lake's edge. Before he'd even stopped, one arm out, he flung another flat stone at the water. It bounced five or six times then out of sight.

Russell turned around, expecting she'd be impressed with his "smooth move." She didn't give him the satisfaction.

Her brother shrugged, then skimmed another. "That makes three."

Holly roused herself off the rock and walked part-way to the water…still keeping some distance.

Russell looked behind…faintly registered her movement. He blew on his closed fist, the way he must have seen TV gamblers blow on dice before the big-money throw.

The fourth stone skipped easily across the surface, again meeting the required number of bounces.

His throws were pretty good. Holly wondered if he'd visited the lake by himself on previous summer afternoons, to practice.

Russell turned around holding out his closed fist. "Why don't you try the next one?"

"No thanks." But she moved closer, curious.

"I get it. You're a girl. You couldn't skim five times. Even with my best stone."

"I'm sure I could."

Russell shook his fist. "Oh, well then…you've proved my point. You won't do it, because you're scared. You're scared you'll summon the Lake Monster."

"Don't be ridiculous." With that, she crossed the distance between them. She held out an impatient, open palm, and her brother dropped the stone into it.

He stepped aside, giving her clear access to the lake.

"Don't throw it *into* the water," he said, coaching her. "Aim parallel to the surface. Fling it really hard."

"I know," she said. "I watched you."

She stood right at the water's edge, one foot on dry gravel, the other sinking in mud. Her right arm hung over the lake. She cocked it back…flung the stone.

Blip…blip…blip…

She was surprised at the beauty of the motion…how satisfying it was the way the stone skipped the surface…like magic. It was a dumb thing, she'd thought, a boy's dumb thing…and yet it turned out to be so much fun.

And she was actually good at it.

Blip…

She'd made it to four, and she knew she would hit the magic number…in one instant proving she was as good as Russell was, proving his story was a lie, proving she wasn't scared.

But maybe, at the back of her mind, thinking "What if…? What if she actually summoned a monster?"

Time slowed to a standstill. She watched for the distant fifth bounce of the pebble.

She never saw it.

Her brother pushed her into the water.

How long was young Holly under? She couldn't swim.
But that wasn't why she almost drowned.
She almost drowned because something grabbed her.

She was a stone...but not a skimming stone...more like a heavy round ball that dropped...down, down a lake deeper than it seemed from above, down a cloudy mix of water and brown sludge...and she opened her mouth to scream and she tasted muck and filth... gagged and coughed...bubbles and frothy spray spreading from her mouth and nostrils, trailing up to a surface that seemed farther and farther above her...a low seashell hum in her ears...a pressure building there, and also in her eyes...her eyes stinging, too, so she closed them...hoping to shut out her awareness...block the idea that she couldn't breathe...that the waving of her arms didn't slow her descent...that the swivel of her legs didn't work either, that she couldn't find a lake bed to kick against, propel her upward... and then her legs slammed together...a strange current wrenching them closed, like the hug of arms...and the arms squeezed tighter, pulling her down as her breath began to fail...these tight arms, like an adult's arms...rough like sandpaper against her skin, or rough like the scratch of a tweed sportscoat...and Holly thought of a stupid story her brother once told, unbelievable, about some monster beneath the lake, dressed as if for a business interview... too implausible to scare anyone...but the arms slid higher, encircling her torso, climbing her...until a gritty pressure washed over her face in a warm wave...and a slug trail ran along one cheek, then the other...so that, on reflex, Holly opened her eyes, saw they weren't sea slugs, but were bubble-eyes on stalks...and she saw a monstrous fish head so large, so close to her own, its massive maw opening wide as if to swallow her whole...

Older now, Holly sat on a towel next to that same lake, finishing her story.

She held her hands in front of her face, indicating the size of the fish creature she saw.

Or thought she saw.

"What happened?" her boyfriend asked...Sam, captain of the college swim team.

"That's when I died," Holly said.

And she was gone. The towel lay empty on the rock next to where he sat. Sam put his hand on the towel, felt for heat where her warm body had been sitting moments before. The fabric was cool to the touch. He stared at the lake and the woods around him, seeming so much emptier now...and completely silent.

"Not really," Holly said, sitting where she'd been before. "I mean, I died like you might die in a dream. With absolute certainty that it happened...that my life had completely slipped away."

Sam was overwhelmed with confusion. "But how did you get out? You said you couldn't swim..."

"And my brother couldn't, either. So nobody to save me...which I'm sure contributed to my frantic state of mind." She paused as if needing to catch her breath.

Russell worried for a moment that she'd disappear again...if she couldn't provide a plausible explanation for how she survived.

"As far as I *knew*, my brother couldn't swim," Holly said. "I'd wondered if he'd been to the lake by himself, practicing how to skim stones. Which he had, I'm sure. But he'd also been teaching himself how to swim."

Russell nodded. "So...so he could save you."

"Yep. Like I told you, my little brother was sadistic. But he wasn't a killer."

"Wow." Russell didn't know what else to say. He reached out to her...touched her hair and the back of her neck as a gesture of comfort.

"I've never told anybody," Holly said. "Russell made me promise not to. Which always felt like a threat...though it was supposed to be out of gratitude, since he saved my life."

"After endangering your life to begin with."

"Oh, I know. I figured he'd been planning the whole thing for weeks...the made-up story, the stones, daring me to stand close to the water. Russell hadn't planned on the Lake Monster actually showing up, though."

"In your head, you mean."

"Uh-huh. All in my head. It was so awful and traumatic, so real...I had scratches on my legs, too, from the monster's claws." She ran her hands over the legs of her pants suit, as if smoothing over scars. "I'm sure I got caught in some driftwood or something."

Sam had always wondered why she never wore a bathing suit, or a short skirt.

"From that moment on," she continued, "I've been afraid of water. Of drowning, I guess. And that fear was what kept me quiet about my brother's cruelty...because I couldn't explain it. Not to my parents, not to anyone. I was so proud of my common sense, my logic. There was no way I'd admit to believing I'd seen a monster."

Holly opened her palm. She held the leafy strand of grass she'd plucked earlier, now twisted and crumpled...torn into nervous shreds.

"I'd like to have a talk with your brother." Sam imagined taking him behind the gymnasium, punching him repeatedly in the face. Giving *him* something to be scared about.

"It was a long time ago. Russell actually got better after that. He would help make excuses for me...so our family wouldn't visit Ocean City or rent a sailboat for the weekend. We became allies."

"It's his fault," Sam insisted. "Your phobia. I know siblings don't always get along... but for a kid to plan something that awful...that elaborate..."

"Apparently he wasn't as creative as I'd always thought. Years later, I'd gone to a bonfire party with friends from my high school. There was a group of guys from across town...older guys, so definitely not in the social circle my brother would ever have run across."

Holly pulled her legs close again, her body turned away from the lake, but her head tilted to keep one wary eye on the water's calm surface.

"People were drinking and singing songs, and eventually they started telling stories. I overheard someone repeat the same legend I thought my brother invented. The exact same monster story." She pointed over her shoulder. "About *this* lake."

Holly rubbed at her pants leg again, smoothing the fabric.

"I almost fainted. I insisted my friends needed to drive me home."

Sam moved closer, trying to position his body so it blocked her view of the water.

"The Lake Monster is real, I thought to myself at the time."

He hugged her close. Her last words were muffled as she spoke them into his shoulder.

"I've seen it. It grabbed me."

As Sam walked her home, the evening twilight was fading towards dark.

"You sure you'll be alright?" He held the screen door as Holly fished the house keys from the front pocket of her slacks.

"I'll be fine." She held the wadded up towel beneath one arm as she unlocked the door. A passerby might have assumed she'd come home after a refreshing day at the beach. "I just need some rest. My brother gets off the evening shift in about an hour...he'll keep an eye on me."

"Russell." Sam didn't hide the scorn in his voice.

"He's better now. Trust me." She leaned closer, kissed Sam on the cheek.

He smiled, acknowledging the kiss. "I'm glad you told me about the lake. It explains a lot."

"Good to hear I didn't scare you off."

In that moment, admiring her generous smile, her sweet kiss still damp on his cheek, Sam could almost believe she was the same old Holly...the girl he'd fallen in love with...fun, a bit quirky, but always rational...certainly not the type to believe schoolboy legends about monsters.

" 'Night, Sam." She stepped inside, taking a quick glace back at him while she closed the door.

Sam waited a minute, then stepped off the porch. He followed the windows of the house, watching for lights to go on as Holly walked through.

"The kitchen," he said aloud as that light flicked on. Faintly, a refrigerator door rattled as it opened, then closed.

"Her bedroom," as that light flicked on at the corner of the house. Was she taking a nap right away? ...or simply turning on as many lights as possible, to chase off the coming dark?

Sam checked the time on his watch, then ducked behind a tree at the side of the house.

He kneeled down, retrieved a cigarette from the pack in his front pocket. He lit a match, then blew out a few rings of smoke.

While he waited, he sifted through dirt at the base of the tree... and uncovered a few flat stones. He weighed them in his hand, rolled them over each other...imagined which was the best for skimming across the surface of a lake.

At night, the undisturbed lake is dark...its surface seems as solid as a highway road.

The woods around are also dark, but night air fills with the buzz of insects...an occasional rustle as a tiny mammal skitters through a pile of fallen leaves.

A human arm waves over the dark lake. In a smooth motion, it flings a small stone over the surface. Blips and ripples glow with uncanny light as they punctuate the glassy calm.

Another stone...then another.

Two more...

The arm drops. The human steps back from the lake, remaining in shadow.

A larger disturbance appears at the center of the lake.

The bubbles of two eyes...two summoned eyes...rise from the depths on two wavering stalks.

A tan station wagon pulled into the driveway. The man who stepped out of the car wore gray-blue trousers and a smeared white shirt with his name, Russell, embroidered over the front pocket. His slicked-back hair was still mussed from the paper cap he'd removed seconds earlier, now crumpled in his hand.

Russell's shoulders slumped as he dragged himself toward the front door. He was hoping for a quiet evening.

Then footsteps thudded the ground behind him…racing forward…

A human shape loped through the woods.

Part human, at least.

The torso was covered with a button-down shirt and jacket… woolen trousers covered long, awkward legs.

Water dripped off the soaked clothing, plashing onto the dry forest path.

Stalk eyes jostled and waved as the creature stumbled over unfamiliar ground. Its oversized head perched heavy above squared shoulders, bobbing from side to side as the jutting fish-mouth gasped open.

The Lake Monster's arms swung at each side, webbed fingers flexing at the ends of tailored sleeves…claws shredding at empty air.

Holly's brother turned around just in time.

Sam was planning to tackle him from behind, but he stopped short. Football wasn't exactly his sport, anyway. He should give Russell a chance to explain himself.

"She told me what you did," Sam said. "When you were younger."

"That so?" Russell stood straight, pushing his legs slightly apart… assuming a defensive posture. He was a bigger guy than Sam had expected…muscled from unloading furniture in the stock room, or hauling junk, or whatever it was the guy did.

"Don't play dumb," Sam said. "You really messed with her head. The poor kid."

"It isn't any of your business." Such a smug dismissal. Sam wished he had tackled him after all. Maybe even clocked him one before he turned around.

"It is definitely my business. I'm..."

"I know who you are." Again that dismissive tone...like he was deliberately trying to get under Sam's skin.

"Listen, I've been giving you the benefit of the doubt," Sam said, making one last attempt to reason with the guy. "Holly told me you've gotten better."

"I don't need you to parrot my sister. I know what she thinks of me." The corner of his mouth lifted in a smirk. "And of you."

That did it. Not only the guy's current rudeness, but his lack of remorse for the cruel trick he'd once played on Holly.

Sam lunged forward, fist cocked, aiming a punch at Russell's smirking mouth.

A noise woke her.

Footsteps in slow rhythm, like the drip of a faucet...distant splashes in the hallway outside the closed door of her bedroom.

Holly sat up in bed. "What time...?" The overhead light was on, so she'd gone to sleep early. She still wore her clothes from earlier in the day, including her shoes, and she hadn't even bothered to pull down the covers. Her fogged memories started to return. She'd been to the lake with Sam. She'd told him that nightmare story from her childhood.

Each wet footstep made a heavier splash as it moved closer to her room. Holly stared at the bedroom door...afraid it would burst open.

Because she knew what would be on the other side...what hideous webbed feet would slap and squelch against the wooden floorboards.

You could estimate a man's weight by the sound of his tread... and those steps were loud, even through the closed door. The creature was too heavy. It would overpower her.

Another wet plash as a webbed foot hit...followed by an oozy suction as it lifted from the floor.

Holly considered the window...would she be able to open it in time, pull up the screen, squeeze through it and escape?

Or the dresser...should she push that over the door first, to buy herself more time?

She realized she no longer heard the footsteps. Perhaps the creature had gone away....

Perhaps it stood just outside her room.

As she considered what to do, a pool of water began to form underneath the door.

The pool spread into the room...reaching out in a thin sheen, almost to where her feet hung off the side of the bed.

The musty odor of the lake assaulted her. Holly put her hand over her nose and mouth.

She stood up, and water parted around her shoes.

In the hallway, a new sound commenced...a fluttering...a burbling patter, like an infant trying to speak.

The sound seemed less threatening than the earlier footsteps... softer, yet insistent.

So insistent that she felt compelled to act. Against any sensible caution, Holly stood and crossed to the door, her shoes squelching through the thin pool of water...she reached for the doorknob.

More fluttering from the other side...a desperate, wet sputter.

She opened the door.

An extra surge of cloudy water lapped over the threshold...a few tiny shapes wriggled in the foul liquid.

More of these shapes wriggled on the hallway floor. Tiny shapes, gasping and flopping in insufficient water. Suicidal fish that had leapt to their deaths from some nightmare aquarium.

They were the size of pet-shop goldfish...but were not the lovely storefront attractions whose scales would glow as if from some internal light, a shimmer of remarkable colors.

No...these were fish that lived in shadows...coarse, gray-black monstrosities that lurked beneath rocks. The most obvious features were their cold, searching eyes...hideous whiskers over a lamprey mouth...dark, tattered fins with an awful fuzz of bluish mold.

The fish were dying slowly. The squirm of their death throes must have made the footstep sound she'd misinterpreted earlier.

One of them flopped out of the water and landed over the laced top of her left tennis shoe. Fish fins flailed, and a tiny mouth gasped beneath stiff whiskers.

Holly leaned over to inspect the strange creature. Its face looked more human than she'd initially thought…like a frightened old man.

The tattered fins looked more like arms. The tail seemed to split into two legs.

The creature rolled and flailed. Repulsed, Holly raised her other shoe and held it in position, preparing to crush the tiny fish.

She hesitated for a moment, then brought one foot down atop the other.

In that moment of hesitation, the fish scurried out of harm's way…

It rolled up the length of her shoe…and up the open cuff of her pant leg.

She screamed, slapping at her shin, shaking the leg and hoping to force out the awful slug-slime that seemed to crawl higher and higher.

A lump beneath the fabric of her pants…a warm wet sensation… spreading.

In a panic, Holly unfastened her pants and pulled them down… she struggled to slide them over her shoes, nearly falling over.

She flung the article of clothing away from her. It landed half inside the room, half out.

Most of the fluttering sounds were muffled…the dying fish now covered by a layer of clothing.

Holly noticed wriggling bumps beneath the dampening cloth. She straddled the threshold to her bedroom, and stepped on each bump, one by one, until the wriggling stopped.

In darkness, the Lake Monster continued its unsteady steps along the earth.

The ground beneath changed from the rocky mud of the forest... to the unkempt weeds of a wide field...to the manicured lawns, warm asphalt, and hard sidewalks of a suburban neighborhood.

It passed tiny spots of captured fire, enclosed in smooth bubbles atop long poles...or attached like barnacles to boxy, cave-like structures.

The humans had retreated to their dwellings. All was quiet.

Except for a nearby struggle. Sound carried strangely in air...a loose shimmer without an accompanying pressure against the ear... but the Lake Monster knew these were expressions of rage.

Rage was a familiar emotion.

In the sloping lawn that fronted the nearest structure, two human males ran at each other with raised, stiff-jointed tentacles. The Lake Monster did not know why they were fighting. Human customs were a mystery.

Perhaps, when they were done, the victor would consume the defeated enemy. Such was the way of the lake.

A scavenger could lie in wait, judging the battle's progress... deciding whether or not to enter the fray.

Holly jumped up in bed, gasping for air.

She must have had a bad dream. She remembered...that horrible, choking experiment with Sam...the walk she'd taken with him to the lake...to the source of her worst nightmares.

The overhead light was still on. Worn out, she'd come home and gone straight to bed, lying atop the covers. She'd been so tired, she only had strength to take off her pants. She fell asleep in her shirt top, which hung below her waist and modestly covered her undergarments.

Her bare legs stretched out beneath the shirt. She ran her fingers along the skin, tracing the faint, familiar pattern of scars that cross-hatched her legs.

Scars from her childhood, when she'd been caught in a tangle of undersea driftwood...or held by the groping claws of the Lake Monster.

She noticed the door to her bedroom was open.

Her pants lay across the doorway. The fabric looked dark...and the wood of her bedroom floor seemed too shiny.

Water!

Just a thin layer, but where was it coming from? Had it rained while she slept, water leaking through the roof?

Holly jumped out of bed, grabbed a dry pair of pants from her closet and shimmied into it. She pushed her bare feet into slip-ons flats, then rushed into the hallway.

The layer of water was thin, so wouldn't likely cause much damage. She was lucky she caught it in time...who knows what would have happened if she'd continued sleeping?

She tried to guess the source. The bathroom? No...a hissing sound from the kitchen...

Holly rushed to the kitchen sink. The faucet was turned to full strength. The stoppered basin continued to overflow, sending a slow, steady stream down the kitchen floor, down the hallway and into her bedroom.

Had she turned it on before she'd gone to sleep? Then forgot to turn it off?

She twisted the faucet to "off"...reached into the deep basin and pulled out the rubber stopper.

Water swirled, then gurgled down the drain. She felt it in the back of her throat.

A loud thump smacked against the side of the house.

One of the humans had fallen against the boxy structure. It shook a round head, waved both upper limbs in up a stiff gesture, hoping to ward off the next attack. The other male approached.

The Lake Monster, watching, tensed its webbed fingers...extended its claws...prepared to strike.

Voices shouted in contention outside Holly's front door. She thought she recognized each of the men, but she didn't want to take any chances.

She opened her silverware drawer and searched for a weapon… any weapon.

Her fingers closed around the wooden handle of a long, serrated knife.

Holly moved cautiously to the front door. She flipped the switch for the porch light.

The light seemed to agitate the combatants. She heard a masculine grunt…followed by a dull thump and another crash.

She opened the door.

Her first shock was her brother, home from his evening shift but his work clothes more scuffed than usual. A trickle of blood ran from his nose, and from one corner of his mouth.

And then her boyfriend, looking even worse…his polo shirt torn, hair in a crazed mess, even more blood on his face…the swell of bruises beginning to rise beneath each eye.

Sam had left her home hours earlier. Why had he come back? And why was he fighting with Randall?

In the back of her mind, an answer struggled to take form. Something about the lake…her brother's cruel story…how Sam reacted when she'd told him.

Caught up in their fight, neither of them seemed to notice her.

They were really going at it. Holly knew she needed to get them to stop, before one of them got seriously hurt.

She wondered how she could best interfere…whose side should she take in the argument.

Where did her loyalties lie?

And that was when the next shock hit…far more severe than the others.

Because she saw it at the edge of the lawn…shambling closer…

A creature dressed like a man, with the head of a monstrous fish.

"The Lake Monster!"

Sam had been lost in the daze of the fight, but his girlfriend's voice brought him back to his senses.

Holly stood on the porch. She was no doubt horrified to see him fighting with her brother, so a rush of shame washed over him…but she wasn't looking at him or Russell.

She was pointing *behind* them, her eyes wide with terror.

And the story was still so fresh in his mind…her brother's malicious prank, which Holly described so vividly…

So vividly that he could almost see it…

Which made him afraid to turn his head now…afraid to follow the path of her outstretched arm.

"Right there," Holly urged. "Behind you!"

Sam imagined the picture Holly had painted of that terrible incongruous monster…a large fish head, with eyes on stalks…the bizarre human clothing…the webbed hands, fingers tipped with sharp claws.

He turned his head.

With the slow pivot of his neck, he realized he'd let himself be distracted from the fight. Russell's fist cannonballed forward, a clear shot at his face…

And behind that…closing the distance and growing larger…the approaching face of an impossible monstrosity.

Then blackness.

She screamed in warning, pointed out the danger and stamped her feet, but neither of them would listen.

The Lake Monster lumbered closer. Desperate, Holly repeated the warning.

Her brother ignored her, but she finally broke through to Sam. Her boyfriend turned his head to acknowledge her.

Don't look at *me*, she thought. Look at the *Monster…*

It was so close, lifting powerful arms…flexed claws ready to slash at flesh.

Sam disengaged from the fight, his eyes widening as he saw…he saw…

Too late. Russell punched her boyfriend, knocking him to the ground.

"You fool." She slumped to the floor of the porch, all energy draining from her. Russell smiled in absurd triumph, so proud of himself...oblivious to the stalk-eyed terror that approached. "Oh, you stupid fool."

The Lake Monster grabbed her brother, twisting his body around as if it were a toy...its arms lashed at Russell's neck on both sides, claws tearing bloody gashes into his throat.

Holly fainted.

She imagined the Lake Monster carrying her inert body through the neighborhood...into the woods.

Wading into the lake, walking slowly to the deep middle...and the water rising over them until they disappeared beneath...

She drifted...drifted...subtle currents in the water shaking her.

Shaking her...

Her boyfriend was shaking her.

"Holly, wake up. Oh God, Holly, your brother...what happened?"

Her eyelids fluttered. The concrete porch felt stiff against her back. Sam kneeled beside her...large bruises beneath his eyes, bloody lip and nose, a torn shirt. He helped her struggle into a sitting position.

Russell lay face up on the front lawn. His eyes were wide open... and so was his neck. A large pool of blood stained the surrounding grass.

"I tried to warn you both," Holly said. "What were you fighting about?"

"Never mind that," Sam said. "Tell me what happened to Russell."

"You know what happened."

He sat next to her on the top step of the porch. "I was unconscious. You had called out...I looked at you...and your brother threw a punch."

"But before that," Holly said. "You saw it, didn't you?"

Sam looked at the ground, at the unmoving body, at the shredded flesh of Russell's neck. He stared beyond...at the section of lawn where Holly had pointed. Now, there was nothing there. But before...?

An unspeakable memory flashed over his face.

"You saw it," Holly said. "Just as I described."

Sam nodded. "Just as you described."

She breathed out a sigh of relief at the confirmation.

"But only for a split second," he added quickly. "It attacked your brother?"

Holly rubbed absently at her pants leg, remembering her own long-ago experience with those sharp claws. "His neck…It tore his neck to pieces." She looked down, registering the stains on her shirt-front…realizing what caused them. "The blood sprayed in the air. An awful spray."

He put his arm around her…held her a while in silence.

"Nobody will believe us," he said, his brow furrowed in concentration. "Unless…" Suddenly, he snapped his fingers. "Hey, you were asleep the whole time, okay? I'll handle things with the police."

"You can't…"

"Sure I can. It's obvious your brother and I were fighting. I'll tell them a third person snuck up on us in the dark…knocked me out…then went after Russell."

"You really think they'll believe that?"

"More than the Lake Monster, yeah. It's the best story we've got. Trust me."

He helped her stand, and then followed her into the house.

Russell headed into the kitchen to rinse off some of the dirt and blood from the fight. The tile was slick from a thin sheen of water in front of the sink, and he almost slipped and fell.

He'd have to ask Holly about that. Later, though. They had more important things to worry about now.

Russell took some ice cubes from the refrigerator…wrapped them in a wash cloth…then held it against his puffy eyes.

He rehearsed a few lines outloud before he picked up the receiver of the wall-mounted phone. "There's been an accident…No, no…I was attacked…*we* were attacked. That sounds better. Send an ambulance."

He dialed the emergency number. The line rang a few times before it connected.

A silent ambulance drove off into the night.

No need for the siren…the passenger was beyond medical help.

Sheriff Hazelbury stood beside the bloody section of grass where paramedics had earlier lifted the body onto a stretcher. "We'll have more questions for you tomorrow." His tone was comforting, without a hint of accusation. "I'll probably need to talk with Holly too. Poor girl. She's sure been through a lot."

"Yes," Sam agreed. "Losing her brother like this. Quite a shock."

"After what happened to her parents," the Sheriff added. "Oh, you didn't know? Holly and Russell's parents disappeared when they were younger. Such a tragedy. We found their clothing by the lake, but never discovered the bodies."

Sam crossed his arms over his chest as if to ward off a chill. "She never mentioned that."

"One of my first years on the force. Unsolved case…but at least their Aunt was able to step in…raise the kids, until they were old enough to take care of themselves."

"Their Aunt…" Sam had been trying so hard to concoct his story of a mysterious attacker…anything to avoid mentioning some absurd local legend. He'd almost talked himself into believing his own account…as if he'd never seen that flash of horror before his world went dark.

The Lake Monster…

"You say you didn't get a look at the assailant?" And maybe police officers used this trick all the time…repeating a casual question while your guard was down…when you think the interrogation is over.

"No. It was dark. The guy hit me from behind."

"Funny thing." Sheriff Hazelbury pointed at his own neck, made a slow parallel motion with his forefinger. "You saw how he was wounded?"

"I didn't look too closely."

"Don't imagine you did. Pretty disturbing." Again, the slow parallel motion with his forefinger. "Three cuts in each side of the neck. Strange way for a man to kill somebody."

Another flash of memory...webbed fingers raised in the night air...the sharp claws Holly's had described...

"Maybe I was wrong," Sam admitted. "Maybe it was a wild animal."

"We might have a clearer picture in the morning. Meantime, don't tamper with the crime scene. Lock yourself up tonight...in case the assailant comes back." Hazelbury put ironic emphasis on "assailant" this time.

"I will," Sam promised. "I'll keep an eye on Holly, too."

"You do that."

Holly called to him from her bedroom. "Are they gone?"

Sam stood over the kitchen sink, splashing cold water onto his face. He turned off the faucet. "Yes. But they'll be back."

Her bedroom door creaked open, and gentle footsteps trod down the dark hallway.

"The Sheriff's asking questions...but if we stick to our story, we'll be fine."

"Our story?"

Cool water dripped down his face...trickled over his neck and down his chest. "You were asleep the whole time," he reminded her.

Light footsteps, closer to the arch of the kitchen entryway. He could almost see her figure emerge from the unlit hallway.

"Thank you, Sam. For everything."

He smiled. "I'd do anything for you."

"I'll never be afraid of water again." She stepped slowly into the light. She stood with her arms at her sides, hands slightly behind her back. He noticed she'd changed her shirt, as he'd asked...removed the white button-down one that had caught the spray of her brother's blood...replaced it with a dark blue pullover with an open collar.

A towel was draped around her neck…just like the one she'd worn when they walked to the lake.

"I did it to help him breathe," Holly said.

She'd changed her shirt…but this one seemed to have blood on it, too.

"Oh, Holly…"

The towel about her neck was wet. A white towel…with red stripes.

"To help him breathe," she repeated. One of her hands opened behind her back…a large knife with a heavy wooden handle clattered to the floor. "I gave my brother gills…just like mine!"

The towel fell away from her neck.

THE END

A
HAUNTED
MAGAZINE
MONSTER
PROJECT
#103
SEP
MONSTER
PROJECT
WHO
IS...
THE
SPACE
VISITOR
Bud "Budget" Preston's
THE SPACE VISITOR

The Space Visitor

(A Budget Studios Production)

Cory read through the latest issue of *Future Space* as if it were a complicated instruction manual...studying each word balloon to decode a secret message...examining each illustration to uncover geometrical truths about the unexplored galaxy.

The stories themselves were the main attraction, depicting journeys into space...arriving at two-mooned worlds with plants that breathed and screamed, or an ocean of purple water filled with strange mind-reading fish, or the ruins of a once-majestic city whose buildings crumbled at an Earthling astronaut's touch.

Even the advertisements within the comic book fascinated him. Not the silly ads for pellet guns or sea monkeys or 100 plastic soldiers...but the list of overpriced back issues that tantalized with further space stories.

And a mail-order pamphlet titled "How to Contact Other Worlds."

Cory imagined what was in the pamphlet...wondered if it could possibly deliver on its promises.

- LEARN how today's scientists reach for the stars!

- SEND your own messages into deep space!

- BE THE FIRST to communicate with ALIEN LIFE!

They wanted five dollars, plus postage, for the pamphlet, which was more money than any full-sized book he'd ever heard of. The high cost convinced him the information must be good…they wouldn't dare ask so much otherwise. But it also put the booklet out of his price range.

He'd decided the makers of the comic book had read this pamphlet…why else would they have put the advertisement between their covers?…so maybe they revealed some of the secrets within their stories.

The position of the spaceship dials in page three of the "Jaunt to Jupiter" story…might be a clue about how to tune a radio signal.

The distress signal in "Marooned in the Asteroid Belt," where the Captain identifies himself and his crew as *Residents of the Third Planet Seeking Assistance*…might clarify the proper phrasing when communicating with other lifeforms.

The gesture of Major Williams in "Ice World," a raised thumb beside his forehead as he meets the ambassador from the Icicle Creatures…might be the universal replacement for a hand shake, considering how other beings wouldn't always have hands.

Cory referred to his comic book again, added a few notations to his log book, then created a new entry with this afternoon's date and time.

He set the comic aside, placing the log book atop his father's work table. He slid the metal stool closer to the table, flipped the switch on the HAM radio that occupied most of the back wall, and watched as the dials lit up. The speakers slowly crackled to life. He slid the large metal microphone closer, and blew into its grill to test the volume.

The garage to their house was big enough for one car, but not big enough for a car *and* Dad's tools and half-finished projects…bookcases without shelves, a table with three uneven legs, four broken lawn mowers parked along one wall.

And the huge radio transceiver Dad brought back from last year's Electronics Expo: a HAM VHF 50 watt tabletop. Dad had secured an amateur radio license, used the set non-stop for about a month… then, as with a lot of his hobbies, practically abandoned the equipment and let it gather dust.

Radio signals spread different ways…followed the curve of the Earth or bounced off clouds, twisted around or through solid objects.

Cory didn't understand all the logistics, but he managed to combine strategies from his comic magazines with tips from his father's barely-opened manuals. One thing he learned was that 15-27 MHz were the best daylight bands to reach long distances; for nighttime communication, 1.6-15 MHz was best for long distances.

Good to know, since he was planning to reach the longest distance of all, into the farthest reaches of space.

Cory made a quick sketch of the dials, so he could indicate the positions he chose for each attempt. As he twisted a knob, the speakers alternated between static and high pitched wave-sounds.

He wasn't sure which was better...electronic squeals or silence... but he was determined to try every relevant combination.

This time, flipping back at earlier log notes to check, he reproduced the "Jaunt to Jupiter" sequence.

Static...wave-squeal...static.

He positioned a cassette recorder beneath the speaker, and pressed the RECORD button.

"Resident of the Third Planet." He spoke each syllable carefully, and knew the importance of repeating each word in case part of the signal got cut off. "Resident of the Third Planet seeking contact."

Wave-squeal...static...static.

"This is not an emergency. I repeat, this is not an emergency. Resident of the Third Planet seeking contact."

Silence...wave-squeal...silence...

He leaned close to the microphone again, preparing to repeat his script.

Faintly, over the speakers..."Fif...net."

A surge of static, then a wave of the needle as if one dial shifted position on its own. Cory reached up to hold it in place...wondering if he should tamper with the knob in one direction, then another, to force a clearer signal.

"Third Planet," Cory said. "Please repeat."

Nothing.

"Fifth Planet." The robotic voice twitched with the wave-squeal from the radio, creating a definite other-worldly quality.

Mary's Violet Eyes Make John Sit Up Nights, Cory thought. *Eyes is Earth…Four…Five…John is…Jupiter? Just like in the story?*

"Jupiter." Cory could barely contain his excitement, but reminded himself to speak each syllable carefully. "We call your world, Ju…pi…ter."

He waited through another flutter of static. He thought maybe he'd lost the connection.

A robotic voice finally asked, "Who…are…you?"

"I am called Cor…ey." He enunciated slowly, modifying hand-lettered dialogue from his comic's word bubbles. "Our planet is inhabited by a race of intelligent beings. We've created transport using steam and combustion engines. Our scientists have split the atom."

A long pause, a muffled crackle, then a monotone request. "Take us to your Leader."

"That would be the President of our United States." It was actually happening…Cory had somehow stumbled on the right combination of dials, and was communicating with members of an alien race! A historic moment…he'd succeeded where so many other had failed. Now, he worried he wouldn't rise to the occasion, that he'd say the wrong words and disappoint his unearthly listeners. "His name is Ken…ned…dy. I don't really know him."

"'Course you don't, cause you're just a dumb kid!" The connection was perfectly clear…the robotic voice was now identifiably human.

Other sounds came over the radio speaker…several background listeners, finally giving way to suppressed laughter…a series of sputters and guffaws.

"This wouldn't be Grady's brother, by any chance? Or maybe I should say Gra…dy." Another burst of laughter followed. Cory could imagine a group of twelfth graders…smoking, drinking beer, gathered around another wireless transceiver…so pleased at how easily they'd humiliated their friend's little brother.

Mom set the oval tray on the kitchen table, the soft brick of meatloaf already sliced into even portions. Cory took a slice with the serving tongs...placed it next to the small grouping of green beans he'd reluctantly accepted onto his plate...then waited for his brother to pass the bowl of mashed potatoes.

"I heard you've been using Dad's ham radio," Grady said.

Cory scowled at him. Across the table, his father said, "That's not a toy."

"I know!" The words came out stronger than he'd planned. His brother was the one he was mad at, after all.

"He was playing spaceman with it." Grady passed the bowl of potatoes with exaggerated politeness, as if to disguise the fact that he was finking on his kid brother.

"I wasn't playing. I was being a scientist. An astronomer." Cory scooped some potatoes for himself, then gently put a portion on his mother's plate as she joined them at the table. "Ask him how he knows," Cory said, before quickly supplying the answer. "His friends were spying on me."

"Were not," Grady said. "They just happened to be at Ralph's listening to tunes, when some dumb kid cut into the radio broadcast. 'I'm from the fourth planet' or something stupid. So they turned on their mike and messed with him a bit."

The corner of Dad's mouth turned up in a half smirk. "And you had nothing to do with that?" he asked Grady.

"Nothing. I swear."

Dad nodded, taking a bite of his dinner and pretending to mull over Grady's weak denial. Cory knew better. Dad had already decided...as usual, taking his brother's side.

Just a bit of mischief. No harm done. Maybe toughen Cory up a little...jolt him out of that silly fantasy world.

So he turned to his mom for help, asked her why older kids would be so cruel. "They should know what a significant discovery that would be for me," he said. "Contact with alien life. They shouldn't joke about something so important. Why would they do it? Why?"

With her fork paused in mid air, Mom looked at his father for a moment. Cory always wondered if they had a kind of telepathy...or some series of secret signals that helped them decide what to say.

Would she agree with Dad? Or had he, with a blink or eyebrow twitch, given her permission to contradict him?

"Well, dear," Mom said, "I guess they knew it wasn't likely to happen. There's no aliens out there anyway. Even if there were, you wouldn't be able to reach them on your father's amateur radio, for goodness sake."

After dinner, Cory stepped onto the porch and stared up into the gray twilight sky.

An airplane crossed overhead, a faint blinking light at the end of the entrail.

Beyond the wisps of clouds, the heavens spread far above and around. As evening grew into night, their planet's atmosphere would disappear under a dark blanket...tiny pinpricks of stars shining through.

More airplanes would cross the sky...red or white lights blinking. And then the flash of a falling star...a comet or meteor. Bits of motion among fixed, predictable constellations.

Many of these lights could be explained. But any one of them might also be an alien ship...passing their Earth without a second thought, continuing into the vastness of space.

Cory lay restless in the room he shared with his brother. Grady slept with heavy, regular breaths, his face toward the opposite wall.

The glow-in-the-dark hands of Cory's bedside clock indicated quarter past two.

Cory moved blankets noiselessly aside...pushed his feet into slippers...grabbed his windbreaker from the back of his desk chair and pulled it over his pajama top.

He walked out of the bedroom, nearly on tip toes the whole time... careful to avoid a creak on the stairs...a slow slide of the front deadbolt, then through the door and outside...

There was no door from the garage to the interior of their house, so heading outside was the only way to access the radio. The rolling garage door was his biggest worry...a noisy, unoiled contraption. He slipped in the key he'd borrowed from the kitchen hook, then strained to lift the door.

He only needed to lift it a short bit...enough to roll himself beneath the bottom lip.

It rumbled like thunder. Cory lifted slowly, hoping to lessen the noise...but it only seemed to prolong the storm.

Finally, he held it steady...a good three feet above the ground. Cory waited a moment, listening for any disturbance within the house...his Mom or Dad alert for a burglar's entry...Grady waking with a snort, noticing that his brother's bed was empty.

The night remained calm and quiet.

Cory rolled beneath the opening, and let the garage door rumble shut after him.

He pulled the light chain over his father's work bench, and the bare bulb clicked on.

His comic book lay on the floor beside the metal stool...his log book was open on the desk where he'd left it.

Cory rewound the cassette tape, so his new recording would erase the embarrassment from earlier that day.

Perhaps Grady's friends had actually done him a favor. As Cory considered their cruel prank, he'd thought about trying at a different time...when nobody else would be likely to interfere.

That's when it hit him...His *method* might be correct, but his *timing* could be off.

Aliens didn't work on a 9 to 5 schedule...they didn't plan their space travel to avoid Earth's rush hour traffic.

The middle of the night could actually be the best time to attempt contact. The sky was clear and quiet...and with fewer radio or other broadcast transmissions to interfere with Cory's own signal.

At night, 1.6-15 MHz was best for long distances...

He sat on the metal stool, then leaned forward and flipped the switch to his father's radio. With a ballpoint pen, he made a new log entry for 2:25am, then adjusted the dials to match. He moved the microphone in place, and leaned closer.

"Testing." He blew into the microphone grill. "Testing...one... two..."

His signal...he was sure of it...his signal would travel farther this time. Not simply a few streets over, to the party house of his brother's cruel friends.

The signal went into the air, bounced off clouds, around space rocks and stars...went deeper into space.

Cory pressed the RECORD button. He swallowed, his mouth dry and scratchy. He wished he'd thought to bring a glass of water.

Wave-squeal...static...silence.

His speech was ready...all the practiced phrases he'd borrowed or adapted from the pages of *Future Space*.

But Cory didn't get the chance to speak.

A crackle sounded from the radio. Then a strange rhythmic pulse. Not quite a human voice, but it sounded like a language.

Syllables. Repeating syllables.

"T'hais...shygh..." Then a pause. "H'uan...Pt'hou..."

The same pattern repeated again. Cory felt a chill of excitement. The quality of the voice...not a human, not a machine, not a human pretending to be a machine.

There was definitely something...alien about it.

"T'hais...shygh..." A measured pause. "T'hais shygh...H'uan... Pt'hou..."

But Cory hadn't begun the proper sequence of phrases...hadn't identified himself or his planet.

He leaned to the microphone, said, "Let's start over. I hadn't done it right."

He took a breath, readied his prepared announcement.

The alien voice switched to a new phrase. "H'lea...T'hyrg... Yu'vrg." Pause, then repeat. "H'lea...T'hyrg...Yu'vrg."

Cory wished he could understand. He wished he'd paid more attention during the foreign language unit, when his teacher over-pronounced French or Spanish phrases, expecting her students to repeat them accurately in unison.

There had to be some secret to language…some connection, some key…even when the words were different.

But school language lessons never worked. The teacher spoke clearly, and the class responded in a mangled mumble. "Bonjour!" from Miss Mangraviti, and students would say "Bun Jay Or!"

The alien voice continued its mantra. "H'lea…Thyrg…Yu'vrg."

He'd once learned a trick from an astronomy book, about looking through a telescope at stars…or at Mars or Venus or the moon. You weren't supposed to look directly. The better view came from the corner of your eye.

Was there an equivalent approach to listening? Instead of straining his ears to comprehend the voice, he should relax…a kind of inattentive, passive listening…capturing sounds at the fringes of his attention.

"H'lea…Thyrg…Yu'vrg."

It sounded like…almost like…*Let's Start Over.*

And the earlier syllables, following his own warm-up of the microphone. "T'hais shygh…H'uan…Pt'hou…"

Testing…One, Two.

The alien voice was repeating Cory's syllables. Parroting him… except a parrot doesn't really understand the phrases it pronounces.

He pressed his mouth close to the microphone and spoke slow and clear…"You want me to keep talking? So you can learn words from my language?"

Pause. Then: "K'le…th'ulk…y'guh." *Keep talking.*

Contact.

This was the real thing, Cory was certain. The alien listener hadn't repeated all his words, but had *interpreted* them…selecting two as a specific answer. He was communicating with a being from an advanced civilization…with advanced cognition…accelerated ability to process and decipher an unknown language.

Keep talking. So, he obliged with further speech…his full script about Third Planet and Earth and Combustion Engines and Splitting Atoms…adding details about himself and his home life, favorite foods and music, sports teams, TV programs, comic books…all tumbling out in a dry over-enunciated babble…and Cory worried, *I'm not interesting…this alien will die of boredom…will click off the connection…fly away as far and fast as possible.*

As if in response to his insecurities…the rumble of a rocket engine vibrated through the speakers. The sound was low and deep and shook the whole garage…a spacecraft breaking the sound barrier to escape Earth's tedious orbit.

"What in the world are you doing up so late? Out here in the cold!"

His mother stood framed in the wide-open doorway. The sliding garage door had made that deep rumble as she'd lifted it, simulating rocket noise.

"Get back inside, young man." Her arms crossed the front of her terrycloth robe…her slippered feet tapped impatiently.

He tried to protest…to explain his wonderful, historical accomplishment…

"Enough of that nonsense." Mom flipped the OFF switch on the radio, and gave a light swat to his shoulder. "This instant. Inside."

Just before she turned off the device…had his Mother's scolding words gotten picked up in the transmission?

His actual night's accomplishment, perhaps: he was the first human ever to be humiliated while a space alien listened.

Cory gathered his tape recorder and logbook. In his rush to obey his mother, his foot scuffed against his issue of *Future Space*, tearing the cover.

He pulled at the garage door, and it clattered to the ground. As he followed his mother back to the house, he cast a quick longing glance at the sky, hoping for a flash of light overhead.

The light was on when he got to their bedroom. His older brother was sitting up in bed, his pillow propped against the headboard. "Playing spaceman again, I bet."

It crossed his mind that Grady had been the snitch…waking in the middle of the night and noticing Cory's bed was empty…then telling Mom and Dad.

"It's not a game," Cory said.

"You're gonna be in such trouble tomorrow."

"I don't think so." He raised his tape recorder. "I have proof."

"Proof that you're a dork."

"Something really happened, Grady. I'm serious."

It shouldn't have mattered what his brother thought. Grady spent more time partying with friends than learning anything at school, and Cory didn't need his brother's approval.

But Cory was still bursting with excitement after his contact, he was *sure*, with a being from outer space. It was news he wanted desperately to share...and Grady was his only audience.

And if he could convince his brother to take notice...well, that might really be something.

"Just listen." He pressed the REWIND button...the player whirred and the wheels spun beneath the clear plastic window.

"I'm going back to sleep."

"It will only take a minute." Cory noticed a distinct whine in his voice, and immediately regretted it.

"Such a baby," his brother said.

Probably as close to *go ahead* as he was going to get. He pressed PLAY.

Cory wasn't sure how far the tape had gone back. He adjusted the volume dial on the side of the player, which created a rustle of static.

"Doesn't sound like anything."

"Just wait. There's a voice. Like a foreign language."

Grady squinted, as if contemplating voices from the recording. Cory's voice came through clear, but the sounds from the radio's speaker were distant and muffled.

"Did you hear that?"

Grady nodded. "Yeah. It's like blooba click gluck. And listen to yourself. You sound so goofy."

"I'm pronouncing." Indignant, as if Grady could never hope to understand the sophistication of his little brother's grand experiment.

He adjusted the volume higher...but unfortunately, at this portion in the tape the alien voice had dropped out. Cory heard his own enthusiastic "teaching," and the tumble of words seemed even more foolish now that his brother was listening.

"Oh my god," Grady sighed. "More *pronouncing...*"

Then a huge rumble on the tape, followed by their mother's voice. "What in the world are you doing up so late!" The recorder also picked up Cory's weak protests...the humiliation as he scrambled to collect himself, to excuse his breaking the rules...

"Busted!" Grady said, laughing.

"That part's not important." Cory pressed different buttons on the recorder to cue up an earlier portion of the tape. "Listen to the alien voice again."

He turned the volume higher.

"What in the world are you doing up so late!"

"Wait," Cory said. "I didn't rewind far enough." On tape their mother continued to yell at him, and his brother kept laughing.

Cory might have nodded off a couple times, but the night's events quickly overwhelmed his dreams and shook him awake. He couldn't help reliving the exhilaration of authentic contact with an alien being...undermined by his mother's intrusion, and his brother's mockery.

His brother slept soundlessly across the room...facing the wall, his covers pulled high.

The house was quiet. He heard the engine of a car along the road outside...turning the corner...its headlights weaving through half-open curtains... throwing shadows across the room, rippling across the wall above his bed.

It was unusual that someone would be driving this time of night. And was this the same pattern that passing headlights typically followed?

As the car drove closer to the front of their house, a strange pulse vibrated with the rumble of the engine. It sounded less like an automobile...more like...

...an imperfect *imitation* of a car's engine. As distorted and otherworldly as the alien had sounded, when it repeated Cory's syllables.

A pulsing sound beneath…some strange combination of a breath and wave-squeal, a heartbeat and radio static…

At this point, the soft glow of headlights should have disappeared at the edge of the window frame, while the car continued down the road.

Instead the lights froze in place. Next, shadows shifted and stretched in another direction. The driver had decided to make a U-turn.

The headlights rose higher in the window frame, as if the car had lifted off the ground.

The engine clicked off, but the lights continued to hover.

Cory called out to his brother, trying to wake him. A whisper at first, then more frantic.

The lights hung suspended outside the window…more lights than a single car would have…They blinked and flashed in a strange Morse code that was both frightening and hypnotic.

Cory felt a sudden wave of exhaustion, his eyes heavy. Perhaps he was already dreaming. He could pinch himself. Close his eyes, reopen them…and the lights would be gone.

The horizontal row of lights bent and tilted like a carnival ride… they paused in a vertical line.

"Grady!" The tape recording hadn't convinced his brother, but *this* was proof…right outside their window. "Grady wake up! Look!"

Large white lights blinked into a purple glow…then red…then the orange of a blazing fire.

Cory closed his eyes tight. Behind his lids, more flashes of color… the blink and pulse of a muted light show.

He put his hands over his face. The bedroom felt warm…

Those lights were not intended to illuminate the path ahead, he realized…they were part of some alien weapon…warming up through pulses and a sequence of colors…then burning a laser beam through the window glass and into his bedroom.

"Grady, I'm scared. We've got to get out of here…"

He removed his hands from his face, opened his cowering eyes. The outside lights had disappeared…

If they were ever there to begin with.

The room seemed warm, yes...but that was a flush of shame. He had called out in his sleep, desperately trying to wake his brother to warn him about...nothing. And now he felt like a fool.

Luckily, Grady hadn't stirred.

The window framed darkness. No engine rumbles or other-worldly pulsations thrummed outside the house.

Breathe. Calm down. Try to get back to sleep.

Cory closed his eyes again, let his head press into his pillow.

He attempted counting sheep. *Testing...one...two...* The sheep were covered with golden scales, and had tentacles instead of legs. Instead of jumping, they hovered over the fence...

This night would never end...

The bed creaked beneath him as he tossed and turned.

Not the bed...the door to the room, slowly creaking open.

Mom or Dad had heard him cry out, and they were coming to check on him. He turned his head to the doorway, rehearsing a drowsy apology. *Must have had a bad dream. I didn't realize I'd been so loud.*

A shadowy figure stood in the hallway. It wasn't Mom or Dad.

The vaguely humanoid shape stepped into the room. Its arms and legs wiggled as if they had extra joints in them. The head had strange crags and protrusions...like the surface of a rock, and yet...shiny.

"K'er Gl'uck."

Shadowy arms waved limber on strange joints...reaching forward as the shape lumbered closer to Cory. The room was almost completely dark, but small peaks of light flashed off the otherworldly face...like shimmers of sunlight on an agitated lake.

The sunken eyes had a large almond shape...dark and soulless.

In a burst of strength, the alien leapt across the room, arms raised. It crashed against the side of Cory's bed, then scrambled up and over him.

Shadowy knees hemmed him in on either side. The alien face sparkled. Stiff padded hands gripped his shoulders, pinning him down.

It was too dark. Cory wasn't able to count the number of fingers on the alien's hand. In his mind, if the visitor had four fingers and a thumb, it would be closer to human...as if that would make it more likely to be friendly...or able to respond to reason. Cory tried to catch his breath...tried to speak...

One of the alien's hands immediately clamped over his mouth. The skin had a coarse, rubbery texture...like the dry scales of a dead fish. The alien's face moved closer to his own...a hiss, then a voice like a mouth muffled behind cloth. "K'er gl'uck. Sc'hnick toe."

The almond eyes flashed wide...blinking beneath a thready webbing.

They looked familiar...

"Grady, you jerk! Get off me!"

And that laugh, familiar too...even beneath the nylon stocking pulled over his head, a layer of tin foil beneath to give that mechanical shine to his face.

"Had you going."

"Did not. Now get *off!*"

His brother's head moved closer again. The improvised mask looked so fake now, even in darkness...Cory couldn't believe he'd fallen for the gag.

Grady whispered into his ear. "What are you gonna do? Run to Mom and Dad?"

His brother's knees still pinned him down.

"Or maybe your space visitor will come to your rescue." The idea set Grady off into another fit of laughter, while Cory struggled and seethed.

Their father's angry voice sounded from distant darkness. "Quiet down, boys."

"I know you're out there." The cassette whirred in the recorder as Cory spoke slowly into the microphone. "I'm attempting communication at the same time as last night's successful contact."

He put a check mark next to the date and time in his log book, then spoke the details aloud for the sake of his recording. "I'll keep talking, both to offer information about human culture, and to provide further syllables for your language banks. This planet is named Earth. I'm calling from the United States of America, in the state of Alabama. My name is Cory, and I've lived on this planet for eleven full rotations around our Sun."

No response. He shifted his weight on the uncomfortable metal stool, prepared for a long night.

"I'll keep talking," he said.

In the back of his mind, Cory recalled a common scene from a police show. *Keep him talking. Keep the kidnapper on the line. We need 30 more seconds to trace the call.*

Crackle. A mechanical buzzing...a rhythmic tone that seemed to approximate language. Not the silly way his brother paraphrased it, monotoned through a stocking mask and tinfoil...but the way a machine would talk...vocal cords of fluttering metal...

If he listened the right way, Cory was certain he'd distinguish intelligible syllables.

"Reugh...Z'ligh...Kee...Ayua.."

Cory relaxed his attention...stared at the radio as if the dials could reveal meaning...then let the numbers blur...

"Reugh Z'ligh." Something like *Visit.*

"Kee-Ayua." Something like *Here.*

A slow rumble began to build...but it wasn't the sound of the garage door being lifted.

A few tools rattled as the shelf above the radio began to shake... the table itself trembled, and Cory felt vibrations through his metal stool...through the ground.

The whole garage was shaking.

And he knew they didn't have earthquakes in Alabama.

Cory stood, accidently knocking the stool to the ground with a clatter.

Last night he'd been frightened by fanciful dreams...by his brother's silly prank. Tonight he would be brave.

He stumbled to the garage door and pulled it up, the wheels resisting in their grooves as the earth shook from side to side.

Cory stepped into open air.

A light passed over his face, nearly blinding him. It moved away and resolved into a glowing circle in the sky. It flattened to a line, a shape turning as it rode a wind current, spinning for a fresh approach.

The boy waved his arms. "I'm here! Visit here!"

The spacecraft moved closer, heading straight for him. Cory stood in the driveway, exposed between the garage entrance and the car parked outside.

The ship divebombed…an immense craft, travelling at incredible speed. Cory stood his ground.

The earth trembled anew. A flash of light and metal and fire filled his vision…then stopped.

The spacecraft made a sudden fresh movement…a tumble up and back and over the roof of the house…

Soaring in a startled zigzag, then a dramatic drop past their backyard.

A heavy thump sent a jolt into Cory's legs, knocking him to the ground.

Maybe it wasn't a crash, exactly…but it hadn't been a smooth landing, either.

The front door opened, and his mom came running. "I thought I'd find you out here." As Cory stood up, she inspected him front and back. "Are you okay? You could have been hurt."

"I'm fine." Cory stared over the roof of the house, attempting to calculate the angle of the ship's descent.

"Get inside. Back to your room." There were other words she didn't convey directly, but they would come tomorrow… *Your foolish behavior has go to stop. We're taking away your comic books…they've given you these ideas…You're not to use your father's radio ever again, you understand? I'll take a sledgehammer to it myself, if I have to.*

All because of a small earthquake, as far as Mom understood it. An unusual, but natural occurrence…

Cory was the only one who knew the real cause. The first chance he got, he was going to find out where it landed.

He stared out the bedroom window. Their backyard ended at a field…beyond that, a wooded area.

Cory expected to see scorched earth. Broken trees or fences.

The yard and beyond appeared undisturbed. Where was the crash site?

Mom and Dad scolded him that morning over breakfast, citing the dangers of a small earthquake that, according to the newspaper and the local TV news, never actually happened. Meanwhile Grady offered suggestions between shoveled spoonfuls of Quisp cereal. *Are you sure grounding him for a month is long enough? You want to make sure he learns his lesson. I'll help you keep an eye on him.*

As keen as Grady was to extend his brother's punishment, he'd be an inattentive warden. In the afterschool time before his parents arrived home from work, Cory knew he could easily sneak outside to investigate.

True to form, Grady hadn't come home from school yet. He was probably smoking cigarettes behind the 7-11, or taking an aimless drive in his friend's used Firebird.

Cory grabbed his pen and spiral logbook. He opened the dresser on Grady's side of the room, and "borrowed" his brother's InstaMatic camera.

Outside, Cory flipped open his logbook and consulted a map he'd sketched earlier. The drawing depicted their house as a crude rectangle, with an approximate attempt to indicate property boundaries to scale. In the margin, he'd drawn a circle to represent the proportional size of the spacecraft, and a dotted line indicated the trajectory the craft had apparently followed as it glided over the house.

The circle on his diagram was approximately the size of a quarter. He took that item of change from his pocket and positioned it over his map, sliding it along the path he'd indicated.

"It has to be here." He looked up at the grassy stretch of field at the edge of the forest line. "There's nowhere else something that large could have landed."

Cory paced the indicated stretch of land. Puff dandelions sprouted amidst tall grass. He plucked one by the stem and blew on it, dispersing the wispy seeds.

The ship couldn't have landed or crashed here. The grass and weeds would have been crushed. He'd miscalculated...his diagram was incorrect.

He stepped back a few feet and aimed the InstaMatic at the field, taking a picture. The camera spit out a cardboard-stiff square where the image slowly developed. Cory shook the image to speed up the process.

Using a binder clip, he attached the photo on the page next to his scribbled map. The colors of the image were muted, but patches of green grass shone through. On the stretch of forest beyond the field, leafy green trees appeared on either side of the frame. Summer trees, with the middle group seeming bare...more like fall or early winter.

"That's odd..."

Most likely it was a problem with the imprecise InstaMatic image...or perhaps the film cartridge wasn't fresh...

Because the actual trees all looked roughly similar...green leaves without unseasonably bare branches.

And yet...

Cory wouldn't have noticed it without the photograph as comparison...but there was a faint discoloration in the air, localized around the top half of those middle trees. The leaves were still on the branches, but they weren't quite as green. And they looked a little... flat, as if a strong, constant wind pressed against them.

He gripped his quarter in a tight fist, cocked his arm back, then threw the coin as hard as he could.

The coin glimmered in sunlight as it spun, twirling towards the upper branches of the middle trees. Cory waited for the quarter to rustle and bounce through branches and leaves.

At its highest point, an even brighter flash of light burst off the coin. A metallic clink followed, and the quarter dropped straight down.

Cory ran to retrieve it.

The quarter had fallen just beside the grass, in a dirt and gravel path that marked the edge of the wooded area. The coin felt warm when he picked it up.

Washington's profile was distorted, as if a hot poker had been pressed into his eyes and ears and mouth.

Cory held the coin flat in his palm...looked again at the strange blurring and flattening of the middle trees. Then he pinched the top of the coin with his forefinger and thumb, lifting it so it balanced on its edge in his palm...

An approximation, he realized, of the hidden spacecraft.

From everything he'd read in comics...seen in movies and on television...he'd been led to expect a flying saucer. This actual spacecraft was shaped like a disc, confirming those typical drawings and the wire-hanging models from science fiction movies...but it didn't necessarily travel with its wide body parallel to the ground.

The saucer was hovering on its edge right now...invisible, save for a flattening of leaves where it pressed against a grouping of trees. Cory noticed a faint shimmering of the air above...a flickered muting of colors that corresponded to a dull circular shape on his InstaMatic photograph.

He waved his arms at the massive, barely perceptible shape that hovered above him. "Visit here!" he shouted...followed by identifying phrases from his radio signal. "Third planet from the sun. I'm Cory. I represent the planet Earth."

More waving of his hands. The muted colors flashed briefly, and the ship's camouflage device blinked off to confirm the scope and size of the saucer...an enormous silver plate hovering perpendicular to the ground, its surface textured with a prismatic circuit board of lights. It glowed like a strange moon dropped from the sky.

Another blink, and the moon disappeared. After that brief display of light and life, the muted trees behind seemed dead.

"Engines of combustion and steam," Cory continued, encouraged that the alien ship had revealed itself to him...however briefly. "We have split the atom. Like you, we have ventured into space. We have traveled by rocketship to the satellite that orbits our planet."

A whirring filled his ears, the sound of something…unwinding.

Another blink and flash of lights outlined a shape like a lever being pulled…or an elevator descending.

Beneath the lowest edge of the upright saucer, a flat metallic ledge appeared and continued to drop. It looked like a futuristic porch swing, but instead of chains, ropes of light suspended it from each side.

The empty seat stopped and hovered two feet above the ground… an invitation…with light-ropes stretching up into apparent nothingness…the muted, deadened circle that hovered above him.

Cory walked forward and sat on the metallic bench. The seat felt warm beneath him, like a living thing.

The contraption lifted him into the air, and he disappeared into the invisible unknown.

Grady once described a cruel trick to play on an unsuspecting pet. *You go outside and lay a mirror on the ground, reflecting the sky. Then you lift a dog and drop it on the mirror. The animal freaks out, I'm telling you. It thinks it's been dropped into the sky, and will fall forever and ever. CJ told me this one…can't wait to try it on Jen's toy poodle.*

Cory now felt like the victim of that same prank. He knew he was inside a spaceship…at the same time, he was walking on empty air.

The cylindrical corridor surrounded him. Out of the corners of his eyes, the curved walls appeared solid, like a window made of glass beads. When he touched them, the surface was smooth…

But when he looked at them directly, the glass beads turned to faint bubbles that evaporated and popped. He saw through them, to the line of trees outside…to the field that stretched behind his house…to his house in the far distance, and the rest of his neighborhood beyond.

If he stared straight ahead, he could walk forward on that carpet of glass beads…if he glanced down, his feet hovered perilously over a bursting membrane of air…the field a neck-snapping, back-breaking twenty feet below…

This alien race must have a different way of seeing...a more complex understanding of how molecules interact...how gravity and pressure and reflection of light create the comfort of solid walls, a sure footing beneath.

Cory closed his eyes for a moment, felt the walkway as a solid cushion, and took a silent step forward. It was a slow process, like learning how to walk all over again.

He opened his eyes and tried to blur his focus. His house appeared in the distance, as if he was looking out a window. A large metallic box floated beside his house...a shelf of lights and levers and dials attached to one side.

Cory took a few more unsteady steps. His house stayed the same size, but that metal box grew larger as he approached.

Turned out it wasn't a metal box at all. It was a room within the ship.

A control room, perhaps...and with apparently solid walls and floor.

Cory stepped inside and examined the bank of lights and levers and indicators. Part of the shelf might have controlled the communication devices, with a webbed grill over a speaking apparatus. At the center of another shelf of dials and levers, a transparent dome contained a small replica of the spacecraft...faint red lines along the dome's surface represented longitude and latitude coordinates.

Where was the pilot of the ship?

Cory turned all the way around, and saw no sign of an alien crew member.

Than a hand dropped onto his shoulder from behind.

A gloved hand, with four fingers and a thumb.

Cory twisted around, breaking away from the alien's grip. A humanoid figure dressed in a metallic spacesuit stood before him. A visored helmet covered the alien's entire head. Over the mouth portion...if this being *had* a mouth...appeared a screened filter reminiscent of a gas mask.

For a moment, each of them waited as statues. After everything he'd already experienced...the strange wonders of this invisible ship... Cory was struck dumb as he finally met an actual alien being.

And what might the alien be thinking…Just as excited to encounter a member of a strange new race? Hopeful and overwhelmed with joy?

Frightened, perhaps?

The boy decided to break the silence. "I'm Cory," he said. He extended his hand in greeting.

The alien stood still, regarding him with…curiosity? mistrust?

"Oh, I'm sorry," Cory said. "Handshakes. It's an Earth custom." As a corrective, he performed the gesture of Major Williams from the comic book story, "Ice World"…a raised thumb held beside his forehead.

The alien watched…then slowly lifted an arm…

Aiming a silver pistol at Cory's head.

He thought of his brother, and the awful trick he'd played last night. Maybe he should have heeded the implied warning…the possibility that a space visitor would be hostile.

"No," Cory said, hands out in a pleading gesture. Would the alien understand the fear in his voice? The universal expression of self defense?

The muzzle of the pistol sparked…a wave-beam flashed outward.

The boy felt a terrible burning in his head, as if his brain were being turned inside out.

He was nearly blind…a field of black with faint specks of light…a clarity of stars observed from space…

Cory brought both hands to the sides of his face as if to hold his head together. One by one, the stars began to flicker and die.

The beam continued to pulse, and his head throbbed with it. The wave gun was…*taking* something from him…draining his knowledge.

Then, abruptly, the pulsations stopped.

A voice sounded in his head. "I'm disappointed."

Clearly, it was the alien…communicating through some form of telepathy. The syllables were correct, but the phrasing was an unpracticed, robotic mimicry. All the same, there was something familiar about the *tone* of the alien's inexact speech.

All too familiar.

"You do not understand the concepts you have spoken about," the voice intoned in his mind. "You are a mere child...And thus are of no use to us."

The room began to drift into focus again. A blur of control lights flashed around on all sides, and before him stood a fuzzy humanoid shape. The alien figure could just as easily be the taunting shadow of his brother last night...the scolding pose of his mother or father...his teacher at the front of the classroom, asking an impossible question. *You are not good enough*, they all said. *You will never be good enough.*

Cory jumped at the space visitor. The element of surprise worked to the boy's advantage, and he easily knocked the alien to the floor of the control room. He knocked the wave pistol from the gloved hand, sending it skittering to the opposite side of the room. Remembering Grady's sneak attack the night before, Cory pressed his weight over the alien's chest, his knees hemming in the metallic torso from both sides. He put one hand beneath the space helmet to grab the alien's neck. He squeezed.

The neck felt frail. The alien body wriggled in protest beneath him...the metallic suit seemed to deflate.

Cory bent one arm and raised it...his elbow positioned over the visor of the alien's helmet. He brought his elbow down hard, several times...cracking the visor until it splintered into shards.

The space visitor began to gasp and choke as the gas-mask element fell away and rolled across the floor.

The gurgle was too much for Cory to listen to. He felt an otherworldly expression of pain in his own head.

The inside of the space helmet was a goopy, gray mess...like a bowl of unrecognizable food, spoiled and liquefied in its decay. Cory reached inside the bowl and grabbed a glass-like sliver of the crushed visor.

As the suited body struggled beneath him, Cory wondered how closely the alien matched human physiology. Was there a circulatory system, with a major artery at the neck?

Cory slashed at the alien's throat. The visor shard easily pierced the thin metallic fabric of the spacesuit and dragged slowly through the alien's frail neck. A gush of green liquid bubbled out of the opening.

The alien stopped moving.

Cory stood up. He looked around the room, wondering what to do next. He didn't know which of the controls would operate the light-bench, returning him to Earthly ground.

He dropped the shard of glass. The wave-pistol would be the better weapon, if he needed it.

Before he could get to it...another gloved hand landed on his shoulder.

Accompanied by a whirring sound, a strange silvery bench appeared out of thin air...slowly lowered to the ground on chains of light.

A boy sat calmly on the floating bench. He wore a dazed expression, as if he'd lived through an intense trauma, but had not yet come to terms with what he'd experienced.

Once the bench stopped and hovered over the ground, the boy stood up. He checked his surroundings to orient himself, noting the stretch of trees behind and the field of overgrown grass ahead.

The bench slowly whirred and reeled back into nothingness.

A camera and an open spiral notepad lay on the ground in front of him. He walked past them, not bothering to pick them up.

His movements were stiff and uncertain...as if the ground felt unsteady beneath his feet.

A thick green liquid stained the front of his shirt.

In his left hand, he carried a metallic pistol.

Grady dribbled a basketball, then stopped to aim a shot at the netless hoop over their garage door. The ball hit the rim, then bounced sideways into the front yard.

He rushed to retrieve it, then turned around...

His little brother stood in the driveway.

"You're not supposed to be out here," Grady said. "You're grounded."

His brother ignored him, walking directly to the closed garage door. Cory leaned down to grab the handle.

Grady threw the basketball…it bounced hard off the door, just missing the side of Cory's head. "Beat it, kid. You can't use Dad's radio anymore."

"Z'leag Kwarg." Cory straightened up and glowered at him.

Time to put the kid in his place.

"Oh, stop with the stupid space talk. You're done with that game for a *long* time."

"Attar'ab Ot'cin," Cory said.

"You better go inside, before I rough you up. And clean that paint off your shirt, while you're at it. You look disgusting."

The boy raised his arm, and he had some stupid toy raygun in his hand.

"Jerk." Grady stepped forward, his hand out. "I told you, no more space games. Gimme that."

"You look disgusting," Cory said. But it wasn't his little brother's voice…it was more like Grady's own, distorted through a garbled tape recording. "I'm going to rough you up."

Cory aimed the gun.

Grady knew it was only a kid's toy…but his brother wasn't really acting like a kid anymore. He felt a moment of fearful hesitation, then jumped forward to smack the toy out of his brother's hand.

The weapon fired…

"Did one of our kids leave the garage door open?"

A tan AMC Pacer approached the house from the road. As it turned into the driveway, the father said, "Look at my workbench. I thought we told Cory to stay away from my radio."

"It's not Cory." The mother unbuckled her seatbelt as her husband shifted the car into park and turned off the ignition. Both parents exited the Pacer and headed straight to their eldest son, who leaned over and spoke excitedly into the radio microphone.

"Grady," the father said, "I know we'd made this radio off limits for your brother…but I don't want you using it, either."

The teenager whispered something unintelligible into the microphone…a foreign phrase…hissed, like a command.

"Turn it off," the father said.

Grady pushed back the metal stool as he stood up. Something unusual appeared in his expression…a new awareness, perhaps.

"Attar'ab." The voice through the radio speaker was so loud that it startled both the parents. The mother raised one hand to cover her mouth…a recognition that there was something *wrong* with the transmitted voice. Something inhuman.

"It has begun." This new voice from Grady's mouth spoke in their son's tone and timbre…but it shared a fluttering otherworldly quality with the voice from the radio.

"I have borrowed each of your offspring," the voice continued from their eldest son's mouth. "The smaller one has committed a terrible misdeed."

"Listen, Grady, we don't have time for this foolishness." Her husband approached the situation the same way he'd treat a few low grades on a report card…a call from the liquor store where Grady had shown a fake ID…a warning from police about vandalism at the abandoned factory outside of town. He couldn't grasp the true horror as it unfolded…but the mother knew.

She knew.

"I contacted my superiors." That terrible voice…their son and not their son. Grady closed his mouth completely, but the next phrase continued at the same volume. "They agreed to take appropriate action."

"Okay, never mind how you did that trick…" The father blustered through…still not believing. "I don't care who you are. You're my own kid…or you're some strange force that's taken over Grady's body. Either way, I should spank you."

Grady's mouth curled into a terrible smile. It was an…*unpracticed* smile…the correct muscle movements, but no understanding of the emotions that should lie behind it. Mouth still closed, the voice spoke in their minds. "You need…a demonstration."

Grady's arm reached behind to the work table, lifting a harmless toy spacegun that must belong to his younger brother. The trigger might cause a small spark or explode a cap…flicker an LED light or buzz an annoying electronic sound. Nothing more serious than that…

A huge wave of pulsing light ripped the air in front of the gun…a lightning bolt force that flashed towards her husband's head and engulfed it.

The father's face instantly became numb under the barrage of pulsing light waves. A strange shaking battered at his skull, and he feared the bone matter was melting within his head.

His brain became a sponge, soaking up alien light rays…converting pulses into images…images into concepts, histories, collections of facts and feelings…the weight of an Earth's encyclopedia squeezing into his mind…as his planet's past flashed across synapses…the code of other languages and lifetimes and cultures…animal species existing alongside man and species long extinct…the kingly Tyrannosaurus and the massive blue whale…tiny insects and microscopic amoeba…phases of life in Arctic temperatures, in tropical heat…his mind expanding and soaring with birds above mountaintops…slithering on a reptile belly in caves…diving deep beneath the ocean's surface…and in cities ancient and new, participating in blasphemous ceremonies, his hand raising a sacrificial dagger over an innocent child…in a modern hospital, those same hands in sterilized gloves, guiding a new infant into the world…his world…a world he'd never before experienced with such sublime awareness…an overwhelming knowledge that made him hunger for more…and then a language of mathematics filled his head…calculations about the vastness of space…formulas that twisted time, joined distances to each other…and he was travelling…travelling…

"That's enough," the alien said through his son's mouth. The light pulse stopped.

The new-found knowledge, so intoxicating and affirming…began to fade.

The father felt incredible remorse and loss.

"I trust I've made my point," the alien said.

He lashed out at this being that inhabited his son's body, struck at not-Grady's face and, in that moment of surprise, wrested the laser pistol away.

"Stop," the alien warned. "You don't know..."

"But I *will* know," the father said. "I will."

He pointed the gun at his own head and depressed the trigger button.

The waves hit with an incredible blast...so strong he almost dropped the pistol. He held on as it vibrated in his hand...as pulsations battered his head at close range...a jackhammer tearing through his skull...drilling into his brain...

The knowledge came back to him in a rush...everything he'd comprehended before...ideas grasped as if through actual experience...as his mind expanded...

The mother had watched her husband get shot in the head...a joyous expression on his face as if he experienced religious rapture. She next saw a father reach out and strike the image of his son...stealing that glorious weapon from him, and then turning it on himself.

In the initial blast, his head almost seemed like it was on fire. Through the dying flames, she noticed a strange bald spot at the crown of her husband's head. His hair was falling out...

No...the scalp beneath was...stretching. Expanding like a balloon.

More skin showed beneath as the scalp spread...hair follicles seemed to dance away from each other.

The pulsations from the wave grew louder, the beat increasing with a staccato urgency.

His whole head expanded as more helium entered the balloon. Her husband's widening face wore a blissful smile as his head rose taller above his shoulders.

She jammed her fingers in her ears as the pulsations grew louder... the beats so close together they merged into a steady, shrill drone.

Fingers still tight in her ears…a wince in her eyes…tension in her shoulders…

The balloon popped.

A deafening silence fell as the pulsations ceased. Her husband released the raygun, and it fell to the ground.

His headless body followed…

"I am sorry."

For a moment, she could almost believe it was Grady's voice. There was human emotion…authentic regret.

But it wasn't Grady. She backed away in disbelief from her husband's mutilated body…sprays of his blood, of his brain matter, stained the front of her shirt. Grady would not have done this. A son couldn't watch his father's head explode and say, simply, "I am sorry."

She turned away from the horror…only to find another.

At the back of the garage, she noticed a pair of shoes sticking out from behind a stack of cardboard boxes. Cory's shoes…

"Oh God, what else have you done…" She hurried to the back of the room, pulling heavy boxes away.

As she feared, she uncovered her youngest son's body. A mess of green liquid soaked the front of his shirt…a pool of red ran beneath him. Above the neck…nothing.

"Your smaller offspring set things in motion, unfortunately." All emotion was gone as the voice transmitted from Grady's closed mouth. "This one on the ground signaled to our ship…made many ambitious promises…which, it turned out, he could not fulfill. We quickly learned his mind was too immature to accept knowledge from the transference pistol. He lashed out like a savage, destroying my physical form."

The mother shook her head back and forth. "Cory was a good boy. We are a good family…"

"My experience proves otherwise. Another crew member used the transference pistol to project my mind-essence into your smaller offspring's body. Following his memories, I came here to seek a more mature vessel. This older offspring was disappointing as well..." Grady's hands pointed at himself, then at her husband's body in the driveway. "Your male partner demonstrated arrogance, greed, and violence."

"We are a good family..." She kneeled down next to Cory's body, placing a mother's loving hand beside where his head should be, as if to caress his absent cheek.

"Unfortunate." For his parting words, the alien began moving Grady's lips again, as if to provide the mother more comfort. "A civilization should not perish simply on the basis of one or two momentary mistakes...though many have, in the course of my travels. I reported my findings back to my ship, using your primitive communications device. My crew consulted with our home world. Unfortunate..."

The mother looked into the space visitor's face, hoping to pierce the illusion of her son's eyes...to reach through the alien's cold words and find some sympathy. "What have you done?"

A shadow passed over the mother's kneeling form. She glanced up through the opening of the garage, and saw a glowing circle suspended low in the sky. Another circle appeared...then another... then another.

"I am sorry," the alien repeated.

The glowing shapes blocked out the sun...the sky...

THE END

A
HAUNTED
MAGAZINE
MONSTER
PROJECT
#104
OCT
MONSTER
PROJECT
YOU'LL
NEVER
FORGET...
THE
TWISTED
FACE
THOMAS HENDRICKS in
THE TWISTED FACE

The Twisted Face

(A Budget Studios Production)

The man's heavy boots scraped along the pavement, creating an echo that made it sound like he was being followed. He stopped and listened, pulled up the collar of his overcoat to hide his face. The night's silence reassured him, and he continued on his way.

He preferred not to be seen. To move quickly from shadow to shadow, undisturbed.

"Got a light?"

Where had this woman come from? The streetposts remained dark on this section of Main. She had emerged from the alley nearby, perhaps…or lay hidden in the recessed entrance to a closed antique store, jumped to the sidewalk as he passed.

Cheap perfume and cheap liquor wafted from her direction. He kept his head lowered as he reached in his overcoat pocket for a lighter. His fingers brushed against metal, and he was careful not to cut himself on the blade. It was not time for the blade…he didn't need it. But the metal was cool and comforting.

"C'mon, promise I won't bite," the woman said.

He risked a quick glance. She was dressed for a night out, but the festivities had apparently ended early. Her coat hung lopsided, as if someone had draped it over her shoulders while pushing her out the tavern door.

The tavern was three blocks over, and he wasn't sure why she'd wandered here. She might soon regret that decision.

His fingers closed around cold metal…the rectangle of his cigarette lighter. He flicked the lid, sparked the wheel, cupped the flame against late-night wind.

The woman leaned forward, a cigarette balanced awkwardly in her lipstick-smeared mouth. She inhaled deeply, catching the flame, and faint light flickered over her face. Shadows distorted her features. He couldn't make anything out.

That meant she couldn't see him either. He snapped the lighter closed, suffocating the small flame.

An exhale, a puff of smoke in the dark.

Above, a dormant lamppost flickered to life. The smoke glowed. The woman made another deep inhale, but the lit cigarette slipped from her gasping mouth, falling at his feet.

He looked down at his boots, a circle of light surrounding them. He crushed the cigarette beneath one heel.

"Oh God, the Twisted Face!" The woman inhaled again, ready to gasp a stronger scream into the empty night…but his fingers grabbed her throat, cutting her off.

The man's grip tightened. Her fists battered at his outstretched arms…the blows strong…then weak, weaker…her arms falling to the side…the body going limp beneath her crushed neck, her purpling expression…

He was right…he didn't need the blade. But he might use it anyway.

"I'll tell you what I saw: Nothing. But I heard her yell. Heard her say, 'The Twisted Face.'"

"That was probably the last thing she said." I set a grisly photo on the table top of our interrogation room. The witness, if you could call him that, was a squirmy low-life we'd brought in several times previous on misdemeanor charges…public intoxication, solicitation, an incident of "accidental" shoplifting.

"I don't need the picture." Eddie Morland averted his eyes, squirmed in the hot seat the way any guilty person would. "Saw it in real life. Up close."

Trouble was, Eddie always looked guilty. Following his usual pattern, he probably *was*...but of a lesser crime than murder.

Brutal murder.

"When was that?" My partner, Detective Newell, leaned over the table...basically getting in Eddie's face. "When you were killing her?"

I made a subtle hand signal, indicating my partner should ease back a bit. Newell was always chasing the idea of an instant confession...a nervous witness breaking down in front of his pointed questions, his intimidating physical presence. Things never quite turned out that way.

"You heard her cry out," I said. "Why didn't you help her?"

"I'm a little guy. I stay out of trouble."

"So you went for help," Newell prompted.

"Nah." The eyes averted again...another guilty squirm in the station's hard-back chair. "I was way across the street. Just kept walking, ya know? But something bothered me. I went back later."

"You gave the guy time to finish his work." Newell slammed both palms down on the table. "You say you didn't kill her, but you might as well have."

The loud noise rattled poor Eddie...and truthfully, it rattled me a bit, too...even though I expected it.

Looks like Newell had actually nailed it this time. My partner had prodded the true source of this guy's guilt...Eddie's suspicious twitchings in the interrogation room.

The witness broke down, just like in the TV shows. "When I went back, I didn't recognize who it was. Her face was so cut up. I didn't realize it was Louisa, until you guys told me a few minutes ago."

"I can guess *how* he knew her," Newell said, and I was glad my partner hadn't voiced the thought while the witness remained in the room. "Louisa Gerrold wouldn't 'a spent time with that skunk unless he paid her."

"Doesn't matter." I lifted the photo from the table, imagined what it would be like to find someone mutilated like that...an acquaintance...someone whose body you might have touched...whose face you might have caressed with a gentle hand. "He'll have a hard time living with himself, that's for sure." I returned the picture to the case folder...my notes from the interrogation would be typed up and added later.

"Guess we know the next step."

I nodded. It was typical that Newell would jump to the obvious conclusion...but for the life of me, I couldn't think of a sensible alternative.

Trengrove. We'd have to visit Trengrove.

The apartment building was the kind of place that was too hot in the summer, too cold in the winter...faded brickwork that likely wouldn't stand up to the huff-puff of Mother G.'s big bad wolf...paint peeling off interior walls...lobby light bulbs dead in their sockets.

The landlord's mostly given up. So have the tenants, apparently, but the guy still expects them to pay their rent.

I stepped over a pile of newspapers to check names on the lobby mailboxes. In the dim light, the faded labels were too hard to read. The metal compartments were supposed to be locked, but the hinged doors all lifted when I tried them. Second row, fourth from the left, I found a few junk fliers addressed to Arthur Trengrove...Apartment H.

I pointed up, to offer Newell a silent signal. We didn't want official-sounding voices to alert the occupant to our presence.

As we tried to ascend quietly, each step creaked louder than the one before. Newell was a heavy guy, anyway, which didn't help. We might as well have blared the siren, amplified the suspect's name through a bullhorn.

At one point, Newell grabbed a banister, and it wobbled beneath his grip. He let go, trusting his own unsteady sense of balance.

On the next landing, we creaked along a dim hallway until we located the door for Apartment H.

Newell readied to make an assertive knock, but I stayed my partner's hand. "Look at the door," I whispered.

"There's nothing wrong with—" Then it dawned on Newell, too.

Right. There was nothing wrong with the door. Nothing wrong, in this dump where *everything* was wrong and falling apart. Yet right here stood a door in perfect shape...unblemished paint, flawlessly aligned in its frame...like it had never been used.

"Gonna be a shame if we have to bash it down," Newell said in his closest approximation of a whisper. He thumped a meaty fist on the door, which didn't creak...but sent up a small cloud of dust with each thump.

"Police," I said. "Detectives Keegan and Newell. Open up."

No answer.

I let Newell do his thing.

Shame to ruin that perfectly good door.

Inside we found a mostly normal apartment. As clean as one could expect, in a place so run-down that cleanliness wasn't worth the bother.

In the main room a few stacks of books and newspapers rose from the floor...piled within reaching distance of a large cloth-covered armchair with unusual indentations on the seat- and back-cushions.

There was some disarray around the small bedroom closet... in the even smaller bathroom with an open medicine cabinet above a cracked porcelain sink. But the scattered clothes and toiletries didn't necessarily indicate habitual sloppiness.

Instead, the occupant had likely left in a hurry. Not the smartest move, if you want people to think you're innocent.

But our search of the apartment hadn't revealed any incriminating evidence.

At one point, Newell lifted a small yellow pill-tablet from among several that had apparently fallen beneath the sink. "You think these are worth taking in?"

“Doubt it. I’m sure he was on a lot of legitimate prescriptions… all things considered.”

My partner flipped the tablet off his thumbnail, and it plinked in the sink…rolled into the unstoppered drain.

“Funny thing,” I said. I was looking over the sink, thinking back to my survey of the bedroom and the entrance from the hallway. “There’s aren’t any mirrors here.”

“I wonder why,” Newell said. And we left it at that.

Basically, I’d known Trengrove for a brief while in my early school days.

I’ve known of him since, of course. Hard not to, considering the guy’s appearance. I figured that also explained how his front door stayed pristine…as a courtesy to his neighbors, or simply to avoid their frightened reactions, Trengrove likely made it his practice to come and go via the fire escape outside his kitchen window.

One thing he learned, pretty early on, was to stay out of people’s way…hide himself in the shadows.

When I was in second grade, I helped teach him that lesson.

People like to think children are basically good-hearted, but the Trengrove kid put that idea to the test.

We all pretty much failed.

The night-time intruder stretched the fingers of his gloved hands, and the leather made an ominous creak.

There had been no need to restrain the old man, as he’d done to the woman in the adjoining room. Cameron Wentworth III lay in his bed, unable to walk on his own…needing his daughter or the day nurse to guide him into a wheelchair and push him through the house.

This huge house that Wentworth didn’t deserve.

So many rooms. Three lavishly furnished bedrooms were located on the first floor, with several more upstairs…though in this old-fashioned building, the lack of an elevator made that top floor too impractical for Wentworth to visit.

Half the mansion remained inaccessible to its owner…rooms and hallways with elegant woodwork, textured wallpaper, polished brass and chrome fixtures…stocked with priceless paintings and sculptures and collectibles better suited to a museum, where everyone could enjoy them.

Wentworth's lifelong business took collectibles away from others…placed them out of the public's reach, and mostly out of his own.

"I know you can see me," the intruder said. "Stop pretending to be asleep."

There had been no need to drug the older man, as he'd done to the woman in the adjoining room. Wentworth's movements were slow… easy to anticipate. As the old man ceased playing possum and opened his eyes, reaching for the bedside table, the intruder quickly moved the telephone away…pulling a large knife from beneath his waistcoat, the intruder severed the cord leading to the wall outlet.

He waved the knife in front of the gentleman's face, watching a glint of light reflect from one cataract-clouded eye to the other.

"Beverly?" At the same time as he cried out for his daughter, Wentworth reached for a signal bell at the other table. His trembling hand knocked over a collection of pill bottles and a water glass… closed around the bell, shook it…but his hand surrounded the base and muffled the sound.

"Let me help you." The intruder pried the bell from Wentworth's frail fingers, held it up by the handle and shook out a clear, elegant sequence of rings. "That should wake her. Your daughter, right…or your nurse? It's hard to tell the difference."

Wentworth's head settled back into his pillow, exhausted from his fruitless efforts. His eyes, previously wary of the gleaming knife, of the threat posed by a midnight intruder, finally focused on his visitor's appearance and grew wide with fear. "Monster," he said.

"I'm glad you like my face," the intruder said. "It's the last you'll ever see."

He raised the knife.

"Yours won't look so pretty, either."

Wentworth screamed for a bit...then stopped. The intruder continued his knifework for several minutes, then headed to the adjoining room.

"Do you know why he let you live?"

Beverly Wentworth shrugged. She was still in shock, obviously, which was why I hadn't wanted to talk to her yet. I certainly wouldn't have ushered her into the interrogation room...or decided to fire questions at her as if she was the chief suspect.

But my partner had gotten to her first, and Newell liked to do things by the book. I didn't believe a rich guy's daughter should get special treatment, either...but she'd clearly been traumatized. Tied to a chair, gagged, drugged...her father killed in the next room...and the whole time thinking she'd be next.

"Had to be some reason," Newell said. "And why didn't he take anything? All that expensive stuff just lyin' around, and nothing stolen. How can you explain that?"

The woman shrugged again.

I gave Newell my "ease up" hand signal, and he finally let me take a turn. After introducing myself, I expressed my sympathy for her loss, my regret for the traumatic experience she'd endured. "We want to catch this guy, Miss Wentworth...So nobody else has to suffer the way you and your father did."

She nodded...lifted her eyes. Even though she was the same age as me, I got the unsettling notion that I was talking to a child. Shock will do that to people.

"Do you think you can give us a description of the killer?"

And just as quickly as it had begun, our connection broke. "Oh, no," she said, and she buried her face in her hands.

I reached for a box of tissues, in case she needed to dry her eyes.

Newell was quicker, sliding a thick 3-ring binder across the table. "Check in here, if that's easier."

All my years with Newell as a partner, and this was probably his most clueless move yet. That binder of mug shots...full of petty local criminals, some of the harder-faced creeps from the national registry...none of those faces would look anything like the chief suspect in this case:

The guy Beverly had reportedly muttered about when the morning staff arrived and found her father, dead and mutilated...found Miss Wentworth bound to a chair in the adjoining bedroom.

The name she apparently cried out several times in the squad car during the drive to the station...in a panic, as if she thought he were there in the backseat with her, sliding closer, his knife raised, hot breath washing over her bared throat, that face distorting even more as it loomed ever nearer.

Miss Wentworth accepted a tissue and wiped at her eyes. "It was dark, and I'd been drugged. My vision was cloudy."

Newell sighed audibly. He always hated when a witness was too afraid to testify.

She ignored him, speaking directly to me. "Even under those conditions, I knew who it was. It was Arthur, from our school days... don't you remember? Little Artie Trengrove. The Twisted Face."

We gave Miss Wentworth some time alone to collect herself, then sent her to our sketch artist. No picture of Trengrove on file, since he hadn't been arrested for anything...and he sure as heck hadn't posed for family photos at the Sears Portrait Studio...so we needed Miss Wentworth to supply a detailed description.

Miss Wentworth.

Beverly.

"You *know* her," my partner said when we returned to the main room of the station house.

"Yeah," I shot back. "Can't you tell? We travel in the same social circles."

I didn't want to go into all of it right there, in front of everybody... especially Chadwick at his nearby desk, the guy's pencil hovering over an Incident Report, so obviously pretending not to listen. I made the quick comment that mine and Beverly Wentworth's social circle, at that time, had been *Second Grade*...all part of her affluent father's attempt to toughen her up, expose her to lesser beings like myself in the public school system. He pulled her out of Pelham Elementary soon enough, though...sent her to a ritzy private school in the next county.

"I'm surprised she remembered me," I said. So young, so many years ago...in the same classroom for a scant month.

Maybe I wasn't surprised, after all. She remembered me because of Artie Trengrove...how we treated him...the shameful role her father and my own mother played in that poor kid's education.

"Now, students, let me introduce you to a new classmate. His name is Artie, and I want you all to make him feel welcome."

Us kids were already intrigued. When we arrived that morning, a new desk had appeared along the inside wall of the classroom. The empty desk was considerably larger than the chair-desk contraptions the rest of us used...with a larger surface, and a detached chair with sturdy arm grips. Some of us wondered what student would deserve such special treatment. Even Beverly Wentworth...whose father was impossibly rich...sat in the same kind of chair-desk as the rest of us.

The Assistant Principal entered and held open the door. As he glanced expectantly down the hall, a clanking sound echoed from outside the room...unsteady clicks like the approaching steps of a malfunctioning robot.

"Remember how it felt on your first day," our teacher prompted. "You probably felt very nervous, until you saw smiles from all your new friends."

All twenty of us turned our heads to the door, eager to greet the new kid. Once we saw Artie, we would imagine him sitting with us as lunch, joining our four-square team during afternoon break, sharing crayons and arithmetic answers, and other polite things we'd been taught to do...Maybe sharing some of our bad habits, too, leaning close to whisper a riddle in his ear while the teacher sing-songed about Christopher Columbus or planets in the solar system.

Click...*Click*

For some reason, the teacher and school administration had decided not to prepare us. Kids were supposed to be open-minded, more accepting...and especially *our* kids, here at Pelham Elementary, trained in proper schoolroom etiquette, taught the best possible manners.

The administrators must have decided, "Our students will greet little Arthur with open arms. All that's needed is a gentle reminder about friendship and mutual respect."

Click...*Click*

A metal brace came into view in the door frame. Some of the boys got excited, thinking perhaps it really was a robot...they'd have their very own robot pal! His eyes would light up when he spoke...he'd be great at math...could store popsicles in a freezer compartment in his stomach...might shoot laser beams from his fingertips.

Click...A leg came into view.

By this point, it became clear to some of the more worldly boys and girls that the new student was wearing leg braces, walking with metal canes over his arms. Not a robot...just a kid our age with some physical afflictions.

Click...*Click*...A distended stomach, next...a purple-sleeved arm, with a boxing glove at the end.

Click...And now the boy's head, covered in a hideous mask...

The smiles must have vanished from all our young faces. The teacher pretended nothing was amiss...in the same voice that prompted us to begin The Pledge of Allegiance each morning, she instructed us to "Give your new best friend a warm hello!"

The sound of children screaming filled the classroom. To this day, I'm not certain I was one of the screamers...would like to think I had more presence of mind, that I'd actually lived up to our school's lofty goals of social grace...

But I was seven years old. I was thinking...and probably my peers were, too...that I'd be partnered with this new kid during P.E.

or Music…have to sit close to him on the bus…across from him at lunch, each bite of food turning rotten in my mouth…

And at one point, little Artie would think of a joke he didn't want the teacher to overhear. He'd lean close, breathe warm over my ear… the mush of those strange lips as they formed words…the wet sputter of laughter over misaligned teeth…a gleam of mischief shining from eyes buried amid the puffed folds and purpled growths along the terrain of his mixed-up face.

Yeah, I was probably screaming along with the rest of them.

I was one of those worldly kids who'd seen metal leg braces and arm crutches. My aunt was a nurse, and once when I visited her at Birmingham Hospital, I saw a kid with polio or spina bifida. On young Arthur Trengrove, the contraptions were…different. The braces were obviously meant to straighten his leg bones, but they seemed intended to contain skin growth as well…the boy's pants legs strained against wire grids, the cloth puffing out in a quilted pattern. And the metal arm crutches were bent in odd configurations, to accommodate the strange twists and turns of the boy's figure. As he moved in that awkward robot clank, those crutches appeared alternately as straight lines, then as the letters *L* or *Z* or *K* in strange succession.

The purple shirt sleeve my young mind had noticed over young Artie's arm…was actually the arm itself, bruised and swollen and emerging from a summer-cut T-shirt. The boxing glove…was the hand itself, puffed fingers rolled into an unavoidable, rounded fist.

The mask…on top of it all…of course wasn't a mask at all. Artie's misshapen head wobbled over his shoulders, the skin bruised and covered with growths textured like dark, spoiled cauliflower. The features were all scrambled…the nose a puffy, bruised plum…the eyes out of alignment…a swelling beneath the jaw pushing the lips into a crooked frown…

Artie started crying, I think…though it was hard to see any wet tears rolling down the strange terrain of his face. He did lift those eggplant hands, though, to rub at his eyes.

As I found out sometime later, Arthur Trengrove suffered from acromegaly…a disease that caused large cysts to form on the skin, mutating the face, limbs and body. The growths could also press into the skeleton, twisting it into grotesque postures...though metal braces were sometimes prescribed to correct or slow the skeletal abnormalities.

There wasn't really a prescription to correct for other people's reactions...though our teacher sure tried. With Artie still in the room, she berated us for our rudeness, insisted we should behave like proper little ladies and gentlemen...show more hospitality.

I'll give the teacher credit. She did her best to appeal to our inner goodness. "Imagine how *you* would feel if you looked different from everybody else. And if those other people screamed when you walked into a room."

She paused to let her point sink in. Artie was sitting in the desk and special chair that had been prepared for him. His heavy, misshapen head was down, as if he was the one who should feel ashamed at the teacher's words.

"Put yourself in Artie's shoes, for a minute," she said, reinforcing her point. "Think about what it's like to be him."

I think some of us already did. I think that's part of the reason we had started screaming.

That was a pretty tough day at school...though much tougher on Artie than on the rest of us, obviously. At some point, things calmed down a bit. We didn't get used to his appearance, exactly, but it made us slightly less nervous.

The next day was a bit better...although some of us came up with a cruel nickname, "The Twisted Face," which we whispered behind Artie's back...or wrote on notes we passed in secret, a crude monster drawing scrawled above using the "Bruise" shade from our box of Crayolas.

More improvement the following day, and it almost seemed like we'd make it to the end of the week...if some of the parents hadn't gotten involved.

My mom led a small, vocal complaint at an impromptu parent-teacher meeting. At the same time, Beverly Wentworth's rich, influential father pulled his daughter from the school in protest.

When we showed up on Friday morning, the large, specially-designed desk had been removed from our second-grade classroom.

"So you never saw Miss Wentworth again?"

"Not until today."

I'd stepped outside with my partner to give him the rundown on that strange week, my second year of school. The condensed version...to fit within a two-cigarette break at the edge of our station parking lot.

Newell didn't need to hear those parts about my feelings...the guilt I tried to avoid when thinking back about Artie.

"How about Trengrove...any run-ins with him?"

I honestly couldn't think of any. The guy obviously had to buy food or toiletries like the rest of us, travelled to-and-fro to some backroom job away from the general public, maybe went to a barber shop or a library once in awhile during off-hours. But generally, he wasn't somebody you ran into on downtown sidewalks or while strolling in the park.

If I had run into him, if there'd been some opportunity for a brief discussion...I wonder if I'd have been able to look him in the face.

I wonder if I'd have been able to apologize.

"Our paths might have crossed here and there," I finally said. "No significant interactions, though."

"I seen him a couple times," Newell said, "and that was plenty... To be honest, the guy gives me the creeps. You know what I hear...?" At this, Newell blew a puff of smoke out the side of his mouth and leaned forward in a conspirator's whisper. "I hear, our regular handcuffs won't fit over that guy's big, lumpy wrists."

Our smoking break over, we were headed back to work when we ran into Linwood. The guy cracked the door open with his shoulder, and he held up a sketch pad to halt us from going inside.

"Figured you two would be out here gabbing," he said. "Always on break, while I'm busy working."

"Drawing," Newell corrected him.

"Be nice, partner. Drawing's a skill, ain't it? Takes practice."

Linwood nodded appreciation, then it dawned on him I was probably being sarcastic. He gave it back to me in turn. "Thanks a million, you two. Really appreciate the lovely assignment you tossed my way."

"Like a grenade, I'm guessing."

"Well, the thing is..." Linwood opened his sketch pad, his thumb seeking the most recent page. "I do *realistic* drawings, right? Not stuff for the funny pages...or the horror magazines."

He held up his latest piece of artwork, sketched in response to Beverly Wentworth's descriptions. Newell let out a shaky breath.

"Yep," I said. "That's Trengrove all right."

As if there were any doubt.

Linwood's drawing consisted of hard dark lines, shaded with textured smears of pencil lead...in all the wrong places. It was about as realistic an image as we could expect.

In that drawing, I saw the peer shunned from my second grade classroom, as he would have grown into an adult. The features hadn't changed much, but there was a depth in the expression that I couldn't attribute solely to artistic license...more a reflection of bitter struggles over the intervening years, anger at an isolated life that grew more challenging with each passing day, no relief in sight.

"Now all we have to do is find him," I said.

"Face like that," Newell commented, "Trengrove can't hide too easy."

Except, I thought, he's had a lifetime of practice.

I put out my hand, and Linwood carefully tore the picture from his sketchpad.

"We'll get this on the 6 o'clock news." I held the page by the corner, careful not to smear Linwood's meticulous shadings. "Fax it to the *Gazette* for their evening edition."

"And then we just wait around until somebody calls in a tip," Newell said.

"Not exactly." I pointed to the side of my head, tapped a few times. "Research."

“I appreciate that you both decided to consult me about this case. Not everyone in your line of duty understands the value of a trained specialist in the human mind.

“Some might say we’re in the same profession, you and I. The profession of deviance. Mental illness.

“We look for patterns in behavior…and these patterns allow us to make predictions.

“Two matters interest you the most…and please correct me if I’m wrong, gentlemen. First, you wonder where the killer could be hiding. Second, you wonder who might be the next target, so you can prevent that crime, and perhaps catch the killer in the act.

“Good…I will now offer my psychological observations…germane to each of these critical matters.

“I am familiar with the suspect. No…no…he was never one of my patients…I couldn’t discuss him if he was one of my patients, you understand. But I am familiar with the *type*…from case studies, in Europe and also here in these United States.

“From the details I’ve gleaned from press coverage, and from your preliminary remarks here in my office…there’s no clear connection between the two victims. One was a random woman killed in the street…the other was an elderly gentleman of considerable wealth, attacked in his own home.

“Both of these victims…their faces were mutilated, yes? Cut up with a knife, I should think?

“Please sit down, Detective Newell, don’t be alarmed. You wonder how I know, since you kept some details from reporters, correct? I realize my observations sometimes make me seem like a magician…a mind reader…but I assure you it’s pure science.

“I’ve seen the sketch of your suspect, of course…and that tells me a great deal. Looking like that…spending a lifetime looking like that…it shapes a person’s mind. Distorts it underneath, as if to match the unpleasant exterior.

“He kills a woman, because all women have rejected him. A

prostitute, also, which is surely significant…symbolizes the physical…ah…intimacy that's been denied him.

"He kills a rich man, an old man who has lived a full life…cuts up his face, too, destroying the normal features nature has denied him. There's your connection. And that old man, surrounded by beautiful things.

"You visited the suspect's apartment, no? Were there beautiful things there? I didn't think so. And the mirrors were broken. Or…I see you nodding, detective…there were no mirrors in his home at all.

"Oh, these pictures you show me now…Yes, you can trust to my discretion. One doesn't want to examine such things, but it's necessary, isn't it? In our professions, you and I…we must study unpleasant things.

"I see that I was right about their faces…quite right.

"Ah, yes, thank you Detective Keegan. I shall return to the original matters of concern. The suspect's likely hiding place…predictions about the next victim.

"Well, quite honestly, I have no idea about either. The city's a large place, and he could be anywhere. The next victim could be young or old, male or female. There's really no way to narrow it down.

"I said as much to the reporter who visited me earlier today. He seemed *very* interested in my theories. What? Of course I'll give you his name. He's not my patient, so I wouldn't be violating a professional confidence.

"Oh, before you leave…one request.

"If you catch Mr. Trengrove…*when* you catch him, I should say, to remain optimistic…I should very much like to be consulted further. He is not currently my patient, as I said…but I feel like he should be…like he could profit from my scientific guidance.

"A mutual benefit, I should think…supplying a chapter for my next book on human deviance. I have manuscript pages I'd be happy to share…my work in progress, awaiting your feedback.

"Oh, yes, I understand you're in a hurry. Crime waits for no man, as they say.

"You're very welcome. I expect I'll hear from you soon."

That evening, a young couple loitered in front of a sidewalk newsstand. Faces stared from the covers of assorted magazines: the President on the current issue of *Look*...a smiling celebrity on *Dentistry Today*...Lassie on the cover of *Dog Trainers*...a vintage Chaney in full makeup colorized on the latest *Monster Project*.

"God...imagine running into that freak in a dark alley." The young man wasn't referring to his president...to film stars with bright teeth or soft fur...not even to the gruesome silent-era Phantom...

He was referring to a black-and-white sketch printed on the evening edition of the local newspaper.

"I'd be afraid to meet him in broad daylight," his girlfriend said.

They walked past, without buying anything.

Once they'd crossed the intersection, a man in a gray trenchcoat emerged from the shadows. His boots fell heavy on the sidewalk as he clumped forward in awkward steps.

The newsagent did not look in his direction. Experience had trained him to recognize the intentional tread of a likely customer. The frivolous young couple had at least paused to browse, but this heavy walker would continue at a steady, lumbering pace.

The newsagent didn't glance at the sketch on the cover of the evening *Gazette*...didn't compare it to the asymmetrical shape atop the shoulders of this trenchcoated man...a head half-hidden by a precariously-balanced fedora.

The boots continued their steady pace. The walking man swayed slightly with each step, almost as if he was going to fall, but a strange familiarity with the motion...a long-applied corrective to an unusual twist of bones and sockets...kept the man from toppling.

When he reached a nearby building, the man didn't need to grab the handrails to ascend the half-dozen concrete steps. As twilight approached, timed dome lights flickered on either side of the building's metallic sign...POLICE STATION. The man's shadow, like any man's shadow would, distorted in zig-zag ripples as it traveled over the concrete steps...and yet, this shadow was even more distorted... an accordion of nightmares.

A strangely gloved hand pushed open the right-most door, and the trenchcoated man lumbered into the station. The clerk seated behind a tall reception desk did not initially glance up, pencil behind his ear as he studied mysterious, empty squares within the newspaper's crossword puzzle.

"Detectives Keegan or Newell, please." The voice attempted to mimic refined, upper-class speech, but a sputter and whistling lisp undermined the intended effect.

"Keegan's back there." Initially, the clerk didn't look up. He had reached for his ear-pencil, ready to fill in an L or Z or K in a crossword square...and now abstractedly tilted his head to indicate the open office of desks arranged behind him.

Finally, the anticipated reaction came...as the visitor zag-walked past the front reception, the clerk finally glanced out the corner of his eye...registered the odd locomotion, the unusual shapes prodding beneath unexpected sections of trenchcoat...the lopsided head, the bruised textures of skin, the misaligned eyes, bent nose and crooked mouth, a hat balanced improbably on top. And the clerk's jaw dropped, eyes wide, his head giving an involuntary shudder that shook the pencil from above his ear.

Similar reactions followed as the visitor made his way through to the back of the main room. A woman, complaining to an officer about her neighbor's incivility, turned her head and screamed...a father, reporting his daughter's stolen bicycle, covered the girl's eyes... an officer looked up from his paperwork, suddenly reached to open a desk drawer and accidently knocked over a full cup of coffee.

People were too shocked and flustered to stop the visitor. He walked past unchallenged, checking the nameplates on each officer's desk...finding Newell's empty...continuing to Detective Jonathon Keegan's desk at the back.

The detective looked up as the visitor approached. Straight on... unblinking.

"I understand you're looking for me," the visitor said.

I stayed late at the station, even though we didn't have any real leads. Sure, the shrink we visited had given up a reporter's name, but I considered that a wild goose chase...which is why I let Newell check out the guy on his own.

Last thing I expected was for our chief suspect to walk right into the police station. Right up to my desk.

Arthur Trengrove. The Twisted Face.

My chair scraped awkwardly on the floor tiles as I stood up. My right arm twitched a bit, because I'd typically bring it forward to shake the hand of any visitor. Newell's comment echoed in my mind...*our regular handcuffs won't fit over that guy's big, lumpy wrists*...and I couldn't bring myself to follow the usual social niceties.

Then I thought back to my second grade teacher, berating all us kids about how rude we'd been to a newly-arrived student. I couldn't bring myself to touch Arthur Trengrove's hand...wasn't even sure the guy would welcome that kind of contact...but I could show him respect in other ways.

I looked him right in the eyes. I owed him that much.

It wasn't easy. An adult face strikes you differently than a kid's would...larger, for one thing...but also the sense that life's disappointments had carved additional furrows into that rough terrain... resentment behind those cold, misaligned eyes...and the sense that I'd contributed to that awful assembly line of rejections...and my mother had, as well.

I'd studied Linwood's sketch, too, which I thought might have prepared me. But the drawing was black-and-white, flat scratching on the page, vague smears of shade and texture. It didn't have splotches of purple and dark red, a horrible hint of blood vessel tributaries beneath folds of swollen flesh. The drawing didn't...move.

"Good to see you again, Artie." My right arm twitched again, craving that automatic handshake.

"It's been a long time." A bit of spray came from his mouth as he struggled to talk, and I tried not to imagine warm droplets hitting my face. "I go by Arthur."

I looked right at him, tried so hard not to wince. My right arm twitched again...this time wanting to wipe at my brow. Nervous sweat, trickling from my thinning hairline...or spittle from my visitor's distorted mouth.

Handshakes aside, I tried to act the way I'd act with any other visitor...particularly a suspect. I let my instincts kick in...read the situation, Trengrove's manner...even, difficult as it was, every twitch and detail in his expression.

There was one clear fact I couldn't discount. He had come to the station of his own free will. He knew we were looking for him... would treat him as a suspect...and that his appearance, just like happened to the poor ol' Frankenstein monster, would likely cause the public and police officials alike to prejudge him as guilty.

He knew all this, but showed up anyway.

And I knew, as sure as I'd known anything in my twenty-plus years in law enforcement...that I was staring at the twisted face of an innocent man.

"Let's go someplace where we can talk privately," I said.

On the way to the interrogation room, we'd both gotten puzzled stares...from civilians, and from my fellow officers. They were looking mainly at Trengrove, but I was a curiosity, too. I felt those "what does he think he's doing" stares and thought...maybe I was getting some small dose of the rude glances Trengrove suffered every day of his life.

Probably not, though. Whole different order of magnitude, I suspected.

I closed the door, shutting all of those glances out.

Immediately I felt a measure of relief...even though I was now alone in a room with a man who looked like a monster. It struck me that Trengrove was a bulkier guy than me. If he was able to stand up straight, he'd probably be seven feet tall.

I was taking a big risk.

Newell, he would've gone by the book. He'd have found some way to handcuff a Trengrove wrist, with the other cuff hooked to the metal loop in the table. Assumption of guilt, every step of the way… questions aimed not so much to get at the truth, but to break the suspect into confessing. *Why did you kill those people? Are you some kind of sicko? As messed up on the inside as you are on the outside? We know you did it, so let's not waste any more time.*

I knew better than that. I just did.

"It couldn't have been easy for you to come here."

Trengrove nodded to acknowledge my point…the hat, absurdly balanced on his head, did not slip off.

I motioned for him to have a seat, and he kind of loomed over the chair, eased into it sideways like an animal sneaking up on its prey. My own sit-down, across from him at the table, was a little less noteworthy.

Trengrove reached beneath his trenchcoat, and I heard an odd rustling…the fabric thumped out as that strange hand struggled to grip something.

Nobody'd bothered to frisk him. He might be carrying some odd, modified pistol…with a bulkier hand grip, a bizarrely placed trigger.

My own gun was in the main station, locked in my desk drawer.

Trengrove pulled out a copy of the *Gazette's* evening edition, his face taking up a full quarter of the front page. He spread the newspaper on the table, turned it towards me and smoothed it out as much as he could.

His hand lay next to the police sketch, and I got the sense that he wanted to crumple the paper, destroy the offensive image he never needed to confront in his mirror-less home.

With some effort, Trengrove's forefinger uncurled from his rounded fist…a fat worm extending from a large, spoiled gourd. He traced the finger beneath an offensive headline, trailed it over the reporter's name. "The article asks for people to come forward. A witness, perhaps?"

Trengrove didn't mention the reporter's crude assumptions… phrases like "presumed dangerous" and "obviously deranged"…he didn't mention the article's use of "deformed" and "disfigured" adjacent to Trengrove's own name.

"I'm not a witness in the conventional sense," he said. "But I can see things through the killer's eyes. Up to a point, that is."

Here, Trengrove began to sound like those crackpot psychics I always refused to consult...or the useless psychiatrist Newell and I visited earlier today. Still, my instincts told me to be patient.

"I can't see the actual murders," Trengrove clarified, "but I can see the moments leading up to them. I can give you some insight into the killer's motives."

I'd been trying so hard to treat this guy with respect...or, at least, treat him the way I would any other visitor to the police station. If that were the case, I should have laughed now, said *That caps it*... thrown him out of the room with a sarcastic quip.

Trengrove leaned back in the chair. It was an awkward, creaking motion...rather than the casual gesture he'd likely hoped to convey. "I'm very close to solving your case for you," he said. "I might even tell you who will be the killer's next victim. By the way, Johnny..." He attempted a smile, but one side of his mouth stayed puffed and closed, the other curling at the edge, splitting to reveal the gray gleam of crooked teeth. "...how's your mother?"

The room's temperature must have dropped twenty degrees, judging from the fresh goosebumps along my arms...little hairs rising on the back of my neck.

I'd shut myself in the room with a monster.

I was unarmed. The other guy was larger, but I might have the advantage of mobility...or, perhaps Trengrove's slow, awkward motions were an act, practiced to put others off their guard. He could launch himself from the chair, use his weight and sprawling physiognomy to overpower me.

Those eggplant hands really were boxing gloves, ready to pummel me into unconsciousness. Then he'd lean over me, unfurl some of those wormy fingers and force them into my mouth, push them to the back of my throat, strangling me.

Or, was I too obsessed with Trengrove's horrifying appearance? Had I forgotten the knife that carved the faces off his victims?

More to the point, though, was the implied threat directed at my mother. What kind of detective was I, to miss the obvious clues of the previous murder scene? Cameron Wentworth III, brutally murdered and mutilated...who had, years ago, removed his daughter from Pelham Elementary to protest Artie Trengrove's enrollment there... supporting my own mother's PTA tantrum, gathering other families' support...until their combined, considerable influence pushed the Board to erase young Trengrove from the school rosters. The key parents, murdered in retribution...the children, who teased young Artie but lacked adult judgment, might be spared.

There was just one problem with this deduction.

My mother was already dead.

"Seven years ago." I held a blank expression, so Trengrove wouldn't think he'd rattled me. "Complications from diabetes."

"Oh, I'm sorry to hear that." Again, the guy's unusual features were so hard to read...the forced sputter of his voice didn't follow predictable inflections. It was like trying to judge somebody's age or nationality from only a whisper. I had no idea what emotions lay behind Trengrove's syllables, except...despite the threat I'd interpreted earlier...I got a strong impression that his expression of sympathy was genuine.

"I know how hard it is to lose a mother," Trengrove continued. "Mine was everything to me. My only caregiver, my closest friend. Mother was also my teacher...since, as you'd recall, the public school wasn't a very welcoming place for me."

And there it was. The subject I'd hoped to be able to address with him someday...but not in the middle of a murder investigation. "Look, Arthur, I realize I owe you an apology. The protest with the school board was my mom's idea...I was just a kid, and can barely remember what I felt about it then. I hope it's enough to tell you I don't agree with her now."

At first, Trengrove didn't react. Then an odd gurgle sounded from his chest...a bile rising...a deep breath before a low, animal growl... and Trengrove's head shook, and a phlegmy hacking commenced from the back of his throat, and I thought he was choking—

—so I hesitated, briefly, waiting for other signs to confirm my guess. Would he wave his hands beneath his neck to indicate his struggles to breathe? Would his face, if it was possible, become even more purple? Before I could act, I figured out the proper explanation for his distress.

Trengrove was laughing.

I would have been even more disturbed by that, if I hadn't known somehow...grasped by instinct...that it wasn't a bwah-ha villain's laugh, but was more like Trengrove's version of an astonished guffaw.

My awkward apology had surprised him. Delighted him.

"I was *rooting* for your mother," Trengrove said, after he'd taken a few deep breaths to get his laughter under control. "I didn't want to be in that school, any more than you kids wanted me there." He waved his hand to tamp down any polite, insincere objection. "Oh, I wasn't dumb. I knew what I looked like. The last thing I wanted was to spend every day in a full classroom, with every other kid pretending...and not doing a very good job of it, I assure you...pretending not to stare at me."

At those words, I felt an urge to look away. To *pretend*, perhaps a little better than I had in second grade.

"I was grateful to your mother. And to Cameron Wentworth, too. Anything that helped pull me out of public school...and back into my home where I'd be safe from constant, cruel scrutiny. And with a mother who loved and accepted me. Mother was an amazing, patient teacher...and I had a voracious appetite for learning. I'd rush through the normal curriculum, and would seek out other subjects... sociology, psychology, ancient civilizations, religions of the world... the more unusual, the better. You see, I was learning about people... of all sorts...without having to leave the house."

The corner of Trengrove's mouth rose on one side...and I realized I'd adjusted my expectations to recognize his genuine smile. I'd adjusted another expectation, too. Initially, I interpreted his voice as a forced, sputtering imitation of upper-class refinement. The more I heard him talk, I realized he was more refined and knowledgeable than just about anybody I'd ever met.

I recalled when Newell and I visited his apartment...how run down it was...no mirrors...nothing of value that I could see. There had been stacks of books everywhere, piles of newspapers, and I hadn't given them a second thought.

"My other youthful passion was mystery stories," Trengrove said, as if reacting to my thoughts. "I also made it a point to study modern methods of detection and forensics...and I applied those methods to crimes I read about in newspapers."

"Solve any of them?"

"My success rate has been impressive." Trengrove's features curled into what I guessed was a proud expression, with a hint of smugness. "However, I've let investigations run their natural course, without interfering. Until now."

He'd brought the conversation back to where we started, back to the recent killings. I thought about that quack psychiatrist we visited earlier...how that guy blathered on about patterns of deviance, confident in his assessments yet unable to offer a single piece of useful information. Trengrove was confident, too, but I had a feeling his input might be more helpful.

I decided to call his bluff...if it really was a bluff. "You said you know who the killer is."

"Almost," he said. "I need a piece or two more, to complete the puzzle."

As I led Trengrove around the office, granting him free access to gathered evidence, I didn't need to ask what my colleagues were thinking.

I could read it on their faces.

Edwards and Madison, with jaw-dropping skepticism: That's our chief suspect, and he's walking around like he owns the place!

Chadwick, with typical rudeness: What's up with the freak? He's putting me off my sandwich.

Winkle, with his snooty, pursed-up face: You shouldn't let him go through those files. That office is off-limits to civilians.

And Newell, if he was here, would be the first to actually speak up: I don't care if Trengrove came here of his own free will. Place him under arrest. I've got some tough questions for him.

My partner's predictable reaction actually spurred me along. Newell probably realized the reporter was a dead end, and would be headed back soon...especially if one of my fellow officers had radioed a heads-up that Trengrove was on the premises.

I needn't have worried. Despite Trengrove's physical challenges, he didn't waste any movements...always seemed to know exactly where he wanted to go.

I trailed him...close enough to look like I was still in charge...but also keeping out of his way.

After Trengrove had collected a few items, we walked back to my desk. The guy was still hunched over, but I could swear he'd pulled himself up a little straighter. His back was to the rest of the officers still on duty as we headed into the late shift. Trengrove knew they were watching, but he didn't care.

Because he was confident. Because he'd figured it out.

The first item was the evening *Gazette* Trengrove had brought with him into the station. He held it up in one hand, ran his fingers over his own picture with the other.

A finger crossed over the article's byline, as well, and I half-wondered if I hadn't been too hasty in dismissing the reporter as a suspect.

"Feel this." Trengrove handed the newspaper to me...expected me to repeat his motions over the page.

I did as instructed. "Newsprint," I observed. "Mostly smooth."

"Correct." Trengrove produced the next item. "Now this." He held it high, ran his fingers over the surface.

Winkle gasped in the background. "We're not supposed to touch those. He doesn't like it."

I glared at Winkle to get him to pipe down…took the offered page from Trengrove. The surface was rougher than I expected. More so than it should have been, considering the clear outlines, the hatched-in details, and the smeared pencil shadings that added texture.

Now Trengrove lifted the sketch pad, which Linwood stored in his office desk when he was off-duty. Winkle gasped again, and I gave him a cold stare.

Trengrove folded back the cover of the sketch pad, indicating the rough frills along the inside edge. "A lot of the pages have been removed."

"Makes sense," I said. "He tears out finished ones, so we can feed them through the copier or the FAX machine."

Trengrove fanned through the pages. A few on the top had scribbles or other half-hearted drawings, with blank pages in the back half. "He left some of the used pages in the book, but an important one was missing. I think we can recreate it."

Trengrove set the sketch pad on my desk, then reached beneath the fold of his coat. He produced a folded over sheet, frilled along one edge as if it had been torn hastily from the pad. He opened the page.

"It's blank!" Madison was the one who interjected this time…a wide-eyed audience member, blurting out reactions during a magic show.

"Not entirely." Trengrove held it up as he'd done with previous items, ran fingers across the surface using his other hand. "I'll need some assistance with this next part. My dexterity isn't up to the task, I'm afraid."

I could swear Madison almost jumped from his seat at that moment, almost shouted *Pick me!*

Considering that I was closer, and I'd figured what Trengrove wanted done, I took over.

Trengrove handed me the blank, unfolded sheet, along with a stick of artist's charcoal borrowed from Linwood's office. I cleared a space on my desk, lay the sheet out flat and, using the side of the charcoal piece, began a light shading over the page.

As I was working, the other squad members left their own posts and gathered around my desk. They grew so focused on my task, I could swear some of them even forgot Trengrove was standing there. Or, at least, they forgot to be bothered by his appearance.

With my light touch, the charcoal didn't color the scratched impressions that had pressed through from a previous page. A face began to form in white scratched lines beneath my charcoal shadings. For a brief moment, I enjoyed the illusion that I had become a talented artist...since the portrait I restored was quite beautiful.

"Hey, I know that lady." Chadwick this time...as involved as the rest of them.

I knew her, too.

A bit more information appeared along with the line drawing... letters that had been pressed into the previous page with hard, angry movements...traced and retraced as if they intended to scar the woman's portrait.

Terrible, terrible words.

"Come here, darling."

A ray of light from a bedside lamp fell across her face. She was even more beautiful in person, this woman whose image had magically appeared in negative...white lines on a shaded gray background...in the page discarded from Linwood's sketch pad.

The man she addressed did not respond to the sultry invitation in her voice. He stood silent in a shadowy corner beside the bedroom door.

"I've been waiting." She pulled the bedspread aside, patted the empty half of the mattress, but the man she addressed still did not move or speak. "I figured you were working late tonight...at your *extra* job. I knew you'd come back to me when you finished."

The man remained in the shadows...as if he felt more comfortable there.

"I don't smell any blood on you, darling." The woman stood from the bed, and the thin fabric of her nightgown whispered as she crossed to the dark section of the room. "I guess this time you didn't bring any knives to clean. No bloody clothes for me to put in the washing machine."

The man's hat hung low over his forehead, making the shadows even darker over his face. She lifted her hands as she moved close, reaching up, caressing the man's head from both sides...her fingertips trailing over the surface like a blind person attempting to read a face...a lover hoping to savor every detail.

"Oh," she exclaimed, "take that horrible mask off. I told you I don't like it."

Her fingers tightened now, grabbing at the bumps and growths... pinching the soft rubber, which was warmer than she expected...a sponginess that repulsed her...a strange stiffness, too...bones protruding in the wrong places...and she curled her fingers, tried to dig under the edges of the mask...the latex slipped beneath her fingers, like skin, and she couldn't find an opening.

I'd had enough. I stepped into the room and turned on the overhead light.

The woman...the girlfriend of our sketch artist, Jesse Linwood... saw what was in her hands, what her fingertips had caressed so lovingly.

It was a long time before she stopped screaming...before she calmed down enough that I could put the cuffs on her.

"Get that monster out of here."

"He helped us arrest you," I said to Maria Spenser. "This... 'monster'...also happened to save your life."

Trengrove leaned closer to where Maria sat, her arms handcuffed and linked to a ring in the center of the interrogation room table. "Your boyfriend was the monster." Trengrove might have spit a little bit as he spoke...on accident of course. Maria's cuffs rattled, as if she'd hoped to wipe her face with her hands.

Then she looked at her hands, remembered what she'd touched earlier at her apartment.

I wanted Trengrove here, knowing his presence would intimidate her. We had circumstantial evidence, an implied confession…but we needed something a bit more concrete to convict her as Linwood's accomplice.

Linwood. A trusted co-worker. I liked him as much as I liked the other guys in my squad…which maybe wasn't much, but it still hurt to think about it. The things he'd done to those bodies…

"Jesse's been doing good work. He…" Then Maria stopped… remembering where she was…the trouble she and her boyfriend were in.

"Yeah," I said, "cleaning up the streets. One prostitute at a time. And one greedy old man, too, killed because he'd hidden priceless museum pieces from the rest of the town…that was Wentworth's offense, wasn't it?"

"Jesse likes beautiful things." Maria twitched her head…a reflex intended to highlight the shine in her long, blonde hair. "That's all I'm sayin'."

I held up a morgue photo of the first victim. "That's why he cut up Louisa Gerrold's face? She wasn't a bad looker."

Maria avoided the gruesome image. She flashed an *I-want-my-lawyer* expression, and didn't say anything.

"Your beautiful face was going to be next." Trengrove's mouth sputtered on "beautiful," and I'd never heard the word pronounced with such scorn.

"You're as crazy as you are ugly." She stared at her hands and shivered like something was crawling on them.

Trengrove produced the rescued sketch, draping the page over her hands. "Recognize your boyfriend's handiwork?"

Now her eyes went where we wanted them to. I figured she was the kind of gal who couldn't pull herself away from her own image… even if that image was a ghostly, line-sketched drawing…with words like *bitch* and *whore* and worse scratched over it. Much worse.

"That's not…" Now she sounded like a little girl. She actually tested a pout, to see if it would work on us.

"It's his artwork," I said. "His handwriting. We lost the original, but the impression came through onto the page beneath."

She shook her head, that blonde hair flashing in the hot interrogation lights. "Jesse wouldn't write those things about me. He wouldn't."

But she knew. I could tell she knew. I pressed her. "Your boyfriend's in the next room with my partner, Newell. Probably spilled his guts already. Newell's kinda rough, which makes people wanna talk to him."

"It doesn't make sense." More flashing of the hair. Linwood's drawing didn't do justice to the hair...you had to see it in color, in motion. But to be honest, blonde didn't appeal to me at the moment. "I covered for him," she said. "I *helped* him fulfill his mission."

Bingo. A confession.

"In a strange kind of logic," Trengrove explained, "your boyfriend probably held that against you. He was a killer, and you helped him...in his eyes, that made you ugly. It made you his next target." The way Trengrove said "ugly," the way he threw her own insult back at her...it sounded worse than all the words on Linwood's page, combined.

Ugly wasn't scratched on a page. It was scratched on Maria Spenser's soul.

The door to the interrogation room swung open, and Newell barged into the room. I could tell from his expression that things had gone well.

"Did our buddy Linwood sing?" I asked.

"Like a canary." Clearly it was the kind of breakdown confession my partner always hoped for, but rarely got. That he'd had to wrench it out of a former colleague, must have only added to Newell's sense of accomplishment. "He gave her up, too." As he pointed an index finger at Maria, I noticed blood on the knuckles of his right hand... scrapes already starting to scab over.

Newell probably didn't feel a thing. But the other guy...

Once we'd ushered Maria Spencer to a holding cell apart from her boyfriend...who, ironically, we locked in his old office while we waited for transport...Newell and I faced the collective gaze of our squad room peers.

They wanted the whole story.

I let Trengrove give it to them.

Sure, Newell was anxious to mime his interrogation techniques, a "convincing" fist swinging in the air...and there would be time for that...

But Trengrove had pretty much worked it all out, well before Linwood confessed. Before we arrested him...before we'd gone to his girlfriend's apartment. Before Trengrove came to the station, and found the incriminating sketch.

He'd worked it out the minute he glanced at the front page of the evening *Gazette*.

"Even on the newsprint reproduction," Trengrove explained, "I could tell there was something wrong with the image. First, with the person who *drew* the image. Something psychologically 'off' about the artist."

Some mutterings in the crowd..."We worked alongside him and didn't see nothin' "...or, "Takes a real sicko to do what Linwood did."

"There was a tell tale nervous twitch that appeared in many of the lines," Trengrove continued. "And the shading effects introduced an uneven texture, inconsistent with the photo-realism a police artist hopes to achieve. Something was wrong with the artist...something was wrong with his materials. I put two and two together, and came to the station to report my findings."

Trengrove had already deduced some damage to Linwood's newspaper sketch ...a pressing through from earlier drawings, but with such an angry, obsessive, *psychotic* pressure that it distorted several pages at once. He knew a thorough search of Linwood's office would turn up evidence to confirm his theories.

Once Chadwick recognized the woman in the discarded sketch as Linwood's girlfriend, things fell into place. We sent a squad car to pick up Linwood for...aggressive questioning. And Trengrove had an idea about the girlfriend, and how we could test her level of involvement.

Because Linwood, who saw himself as a defender of beauty... of *proper* beauty, as his broken mind defined it...had chosen to disguise himself as the town's most infamous converse to beauty (and Trengrove bowed as he explained this part, a flourish that actually prompted a few officers into polite applause).

Linwood, as a professional artist and amateur sculptor, had skills to create a mask that approximated Trengrove's features. He wore it during his evening strolls, seeking to punish "traitors" to beauty... making sure a passerby heard Louisa Gerrold shout "The Twisted Face" before he strangled and mutilated her...letting a drugged, foggy-eyed Beverly Wentworth think she recognized a second-grade classmate as her father's murderer.

And the third crime, perhaps the one Linwood planned all along, with previous killings serving to offset his connection to the latest victim.

Maria's beauty didn't hold up. Linwood saw past it, decided she was evil...and maybe that's what broke his mind.

More likely, a mind like that was already broken. Funny that none of us could see it.

I gave Trengrove a lot of credit. He was actually as good a detective as he said he'd be. And I felt kind of proud that my fellow officers saw it too, respected Trengrove as he explained how he put the pieces together.

Even Newell, who waited patiently while Trengrove laid everything out, step by step...basically stealing my partner's thunder by anticipating all the details that fell out in Linwood's interrogation. At different moments during Trengrove's monologue, Newell nodded with enthusiasm, said "He's right!"...as surprised and pleased as the rest of us.

At the end, Newell still got to mime a few air punches, and mimic Linwood's insane, simpering confession to an appreciative audience... so he counted it a good day.

And we caught a serial killer, prevented further crimes...which I know pleased the whole department.

Myself, too, since I'd get most of the credit for the collar. For Trengrove's work, essentially.

Artie Trengrove. Arthur.

The side benefit for me...one I couldn't even begin to put a price on...was the lifting of an unconscious burden...my long-held guilt over a childhood wrong I'd forgotten, but that had still weighed on me over all these years.

And the idea that, since we'd discovered a kind of mutual respect... that maybe I hadn't seen the last of Arthur Trengrove.

I accompanied him outside the station, offered him a ride home since it had gotten dark. He declined, saying he was comfortable walking in the shadows. I waved good-bye as he continued ahead, his legs and arms cycling through a strange lumbering balance. He walked, I realized, like someone riding an invisible bicycle.

"Arthur," I called after him, testing the first name I'd never used aloud. "Do you mind if I ask you a personal question?"

I jogged a few steps to catch up, and he turned to meet me.

"You want to know what it's like to be me," Arthur Trengrove said. "What it's like to live...looking like this."

"Well, yeah. But that's not what I was gonna ask." I pointed to the top of his head. "When I used to go to the movies as a kid, in the crime serials they always had fight scenes. The guys on each side wore hats as they rolled around a warehouse throwing punches, jumping around...and we noticed that the hats never fell off." I looked at him in the dark now that we'd stepped past the front lights of the station. "How does your hat stay on?"

He looked at me, those eyes buried in bruised donuts of flesh, the misshapen head tilting slightly to indicate he was wondering whether to dignify my strange question with a response. He made that half-smile again, then lifted one hand to squeeze the top of his fedora.

Arthur lifted it off his head. Beneath, a jutting growth of deformed bone rose from the left side of his scalp, almost a horn...by coincidence, shaped to make a snug fit inside the indentation of his hat, holding it firmly in place.

He pushed the hat back in place. Before he walked away, he offered a parting bit of wisdom. "You think it must be awful to be me. Everywhere I look, I see people recoil in horror. You'd never want to trade places with me."

I'd been smiling before, but I held a straight expression now, out of respect.

"It's actually not so bad," said Arthur Trengrove. "My world has no illusions. When people react to me, I see their real faces."

THE END

Editor's Note:

As previously mentioned, these stories were scheduled to appear in issues of *Monster Project* magazine. Unfortunately, a proposed financial arrangement fell through between the publisher and filmmaker Bud "Budget" Preston and, in the fallout, the magazine ceased publication. Details are scarce, but most blame the filmmaker's notoriously tight wallet for the dissolved partnership—though Preston's quick temper may have also been a factor.

The announced issues featuring prose retellings of Preston's most (in)famous films never saw the light, though test printings of those issues have long been rumored to exist. The main supporting evidence was a blurry photograph of Preston in his crowded office with magazines spread across his desk. However, the resolution of the photo, and the haphazard arrangement of the covers, made it impossible to identify any unpublished issues of the magazine.

Still, the rumors would persist. Fans of Preston's quirky filmography—I count myself in that number—would jump at each teasing mention of discovered magazines, with the same energy special effects fans would jump at news of missing 1933 footage from *King Kong*'s spider pit sequence.

Most promising was a claim from a lesser horror author (I won't stoop to mention this fraud by name) that he was the one who transformed the film scripts into *Monster Project* articles. When pressed, however, this author could never produce the stories. Excuses varied: "I'm planning to publish them in my next collection" — "I lost them in an office fire" — "I have them, but won't release them because I never got paid for the job." Eventually he gave a two-word interview answer that ended further inquiry: "I lied."

Much hope lay with Bud Preston's estate, but his reclusive widow had been uncooperative with fans and film researchers alike. I'd sent her an advance copy of my own fictionalized tribute to Preston's legacy, *Life in a Haunted House*, but that gesture failed to gain her trust.

In online interviews here and there, I dropped mention of my forthcoming book on Bud Preston, which brought a few unsolicited and unlikely claims to my Inbox. One of the emails contained an attachment that purported to be a scanned cover of issue 101.

Everyone knows you're not supposed to open attachments from an unknown source, but I couldn't resist clicking on it.

The cover looked real.

My source—a book collector and film buff who wishes to remain anonymous—told me he had more items to show me, if I was interested.

If I was interested? After viewing another scanned piece of evidence, I arranged the earliest possible meeting.

I brought my checkbook with me.

The actual magazines remain with the collector, but I purchased scanned pages of each. Instead of working with Preston's estate, I was able to secure publication rights from the owners of *Monster Project*'s back catalog—thanks to some ambiguous language in the initial signed agreement between Preston and the magazine.

I'd rather not specify how much I spent. Let's just say that, in current U.S. dollars, Bud "Budget" Preston could have funded at least four new movies with the amount.

The actual authorship of each of the stories remains a mystery, though I have a few theories. If any readers have their own ideas, I'd love to hear them. Seek me out at www.normanprentiss.com

Made in the USA
Middletown, DE
08 September 2024

59967024R10203